What They're Saying About Craig Parshall's Legal Suspense Novels

The Resurrection File

"Powerful...one of the most fascinating books I have read in years."

> TIM LAHAYE,
> *coauthor of the bestselling*
> *LEFT BEHIND® series*

"Craig Parshall has written a gripping book that is a must-read."

> JAY ALAN SEKULOW,
> *Chief Counsel, The American*
> *Center for Law and Justice*

"A compelling, realistic story...Incorporates...spiritual awakening without ever being preachy."

> FAITHFUL READER.COM

Custody of the State

"I simply couldn't put *Custody of the State* down!"

> DIANE S. PASSNO,
> *Executive VP, Focus on the Family*

"This is not only a great mystery, but also a deeply moving, redemptive book...Deserves translation to the big screen. Bravo!"

> TED BAEHR,
> *Chairman of the Christian Film & Television Commission*

"Authentic characters and a believable story line make *Custody of the State* gripping and even unnerving reading."

> CHRISTIAN LIBRARY JOURNAL

The Accused

"An author not to be missed!"

> ROUND TABLE REVIEWS

"Grisham and Clancy…move over! Craig Parshall has truly arrived…*The Accused* [is] a super thriller—a masterful tale of suspense as well as romance…it could be a superb motion picture!"

—KEN WALES,
Executive producer of the CBS television series
Christy *and veteran Hollywood filmmaker*

"I was riveted from the first page. Not only an excellent novel, it is also a highly accurate account of military justice and the covert world of special operations."

LT. COL. ROBERT "BUZZ" PATTERSON, USAF RETD.,
Author of the bestselling book Dereliction of Duty

Missing Witness

"A legal thriller wrapped inside a very poignant love story with a twist…Fresh, compelling storytelling…with enough grit to appeal to a mass secular audience."

CHRIS CARPENTER,
producer, CBN.com

"The author has a true gift for storytelling."

TEENS4JESUS LIBRARY

The Last Judgment

"A fitting finale for [Parshall's] Chambers of Justice series. *The Last Judgment* incorporates all of the elements that made us wish the series would continue indefinitely."

FAITHFUL READER.COM

"Craig Parshall is a master at weaving morality into the narrow, litigious [confines] of the courtroom."

CBN.COM

TRIAL BY ORDEAL

CRAIG PARSHALL

HARVEST HOUSE PUBLISHERS

EUGENE, OREGON

Cover by Left Coast Design, Portland, Oregon

Cover photos © Brand X Pictures / Alamy; AbleStock / Photos To Go

TRIAL BY ORDEAL
Copyright © 2006 by Craig Parshall
Published by Harvest House Publishers
Eugene, Oregon 97402
www.harvesthousepublishers.com

Library of Congress Cataloging-in-Publication Data
Parshall, Craig, 1950–
   Trial by ordeal / Craig Parshall.
      p. cm.
   ISBN-13: 978-0-7369-1513-7 (pbk.)
   ISBN-10: 0-7369-1513-3 (pbk.)
1. Commercial real estate—Fiction. 2. Homeless persons—Fiction. 3. History teachers—Fiction. 4. Church buildings—Fiction. 5. Organized crime—Fiction. 6. Chicago (Ill.)—Fiction. I. Title.
   PS3616.A77T75 2006
813'.54—dc22
                                                            2005019199

Printed in the United States of America

06   07   08   09   10   11   / LB-CF /   10   9   8   7   6   5   4   3   2   1

To the memory of my brother-in-law and friend,
Charles DiFrancesca—
to me, you were the real story of Chicago

Acknowledgments

This is a novel about the law—the good, the bad, and the (occasionally) ugly. Though every bit of it is fiction, the story probably gained some momentum from the general impressions I have gained over my thirty-four years of trial practice as a lawyer. For those reasons, my appreciation goes out to two lawyers who helped transform a fledging law student into a litigator: my first trial-law mentors, William (Bill) Reilly and Richard (Dick) Hippenmeyer. Bill had a sage and powerful knack of breathing decency and common sense into even the most bitter and emotionally laden lawsuits; and Dick's skills as a trial lawyer (in particular, his brilliant refinement of the art of cross-examination) were legendary.

Thanks also to Chicago lawyer Tom Bretcha, who, for many years labored with me (and dozens of other defense lawyers) in *N.O.W. v. Schiedler et al.,* a lawsuit whose duration and breadth has now exceeded epic proportions. Though that case has nothing in particular to do with this novel, it did give me the opportunity to spend large amounts of time in Chicago, fraternizing with the lawyers of that area; as a result, Chicago was an easy choice of locale for this story. My sister-in-law Ruth Parshall, an Austin, Texas, architect, was kind enough to edit some of the architectural trivia in this novel, for which I am tremendously grateful. Any inaccuracies on that score are mine, not hers.

Bob Neff, beloved friend of Christian broadcasting formerly of Moody Bible Institute, and his family and friends, will hopefully find a fitting tribute to him in the person of one special character in this novel. To simply say this character was "inspired" by Bob's triumph of faith amid incredible physical challenges would demean the real fact; for it was I who was profoundly inspired by Bob. The writing of that part of the novel simply followed.

Editor Paul Gossard put up nobly with my experimentation and my rewrites, and his suggestions were genuinely helpful. Lastly, thanks to my wife, Janet, and all of my (now grown) children, who always help to remind me of those important things that are worth fighting for and writing about.

ONE

~

I WAS STANDING IN FRONT OF A DOOR. It belonged to the little office of some lawyer I had never met before, at least professionally. I hesitated before going in. After everything I had endured, and in light of the nonstop avalanche of misery brought down on me by certain men—men whose indifference toward my plight made me think they had hearts that pumped embalming fluid rather than blood—I knew how high the stakes were. And I understood exactly how close I was to disaster.

I remember thinking to myself—quite literally—*This is it. Do or die. If this doesn't work, I'm a dead man. I'll get a cute little obituary in the* Sun-Times *and then only because of the grisly way I met my fate. End of story. Another unsolved murder.*

Sure, going through an attorney's doorway is not that big a deal for most people. The bad thing has already happened. A car accident. A dead relative who left a messed-up estate. A son picked up on drug charges. A daughter wrongly fired from some job. So they pack up their brown-paper bag full of complaints and drag it over to their local lawyer. Otherwise, why would they be there?

But I had concluded that my situation—my case—was different.

You have to know I'm a young, untenured college professor… well, I used to be. So I'm real familiar with the age-old philosophical question about the existence of evil. It goes something like this: How can a good God permit terrible catastrophes to occur? I used to think I had an answer to that because, frankly, I didn't do too much thinking about the God part. I simply took God out of the equation and concluded that bad things happen because the universe is ungoverned and chaotic.

But after everything that had been happening to me, I had come to a different answer. I'd concluded that the devil must be the real cause of the world's miseries.

To me, the logic of it was irrefutable. The devil obviously caused catastrophes just so he could keep lawyers employed.

So there I was, getting ready to meet with this lawyer. I tried to give myself a pep talk that this guy would sort of be the last, best hope for me. But down deep I had a hard time believing that. The paint on his office door was peeling. On one side was a Chinese dry-cleaning store—on the other, a pawnshop. In that neighborhood English was a third language. Not an auspicious part of downtown Chicago—definitely not the Gold Coast...and not the Magnificent Mile.

I put my hand on the rusty doorknob, knowing if this didn't work, things would get even worse. Mind you, life had already become pretty dismal. Think of those pictures of bombed-out sections of London from World War II. Blackened parts of buildings still standing upright, but with no roofs, with walls missing, surrounded by piles of smoldering rubble. Basically, that was my life.

And at that point, if this lawyer couldn't perform a miracle, guys with thick necks and guns in their coats were coming after me.

So I opened the door and walked in.

But...I may be getting ahead of myself. Before we go into what happened next, you need to know the whole, sordid, nerve-numbing story. From the beginning.

PART 1

~

Two

~

My name is Kevin Hastings. I mentioned I was a professor. I taught history at Essex College, a small liberal arts institution in Chicago. It was one of those cloistered little schools tucked into one of the few wooded green spaces in the city. You know, red-brick buildings covered with vines. I was one of the younger instructors, and I considered myself somewhat hip, fairly well-liked by the student body and, for the most part, decently treated by the faculty.

After working on my dissertation for several years, I finally completed it. The head of my department, Dr. Harvey Albright, had been there for twenty-odd years and was a fixture at Essex. He was also chair of the college's tenure committee. Of course I wanted tenure, but he had been slow to recommend it. The college had a five-year waiting rule before granting tenure, and I was already into my fifth year. The problem was—as Dr. Albright saw it—my prior four years shouldn't count because I had taken longer than I had promised to complete my PhD work. If he had his way, I would have to put in another five years.

Ordinarily I might have grinned and borne it…all except for Charlotte. Charlotte Krenshaw was the beautiful strawberry blonde who was the love of my life. She worked as an assistant at a big brokerage house downtown on West Jackson. She also had an intense devotion to abstract art. We had been together for almost two years. And like most females, she wanted financial security. Well, that is the nice way of putting it. Anyway, I had no problem wanting to deliver that to her…that was the least I could do.

So for me it was a simple matter of convincing Albright to change his mind and put me on the fast track for tenure approval. When that happened, a bounce in pay and solid-gold job security would be coming my way. You can see that my two priorities, lovely Charlotte and career advancement at Essex College, were inextricably interwoven.

Now, as a nontenured teacher I was given the most-despised classes to teach. Naturally. Like Early Medieval English History 308. Happily, though, I still had my notes from my grad-school days at the University of Chicago. My instructor and mentor—Professor Aubrey Sumner Tuttle—had specialized in that period. And there was one section of his lectures I had found particularly amusing, in a perverse—and now, looking back, very ironic—kind of way.

Tuttle would lecture on ancient medieval legal systems. I'm sure that sounds deadly boring. But it wasn't. He was an elderly man by then—tall, with pale skin and thinning hair. Thick glasses. Though he was beginning to show signs of Parkinson's disease, he would slowly cross the front of the hall in a shuffling gait and, with halting speech, deliver lectures full of acerbic wit and punctuated by his genius for the comic pause.

The section of medieval law that I found so entertaining was Tuttle's explanation of the barbaric way in which the ancients would resolve their legal disputes. Exquisitely designed tortures and excruciating rituals were supposed to create a just disposition of a disputed claim. And in between his descriptions of those arcane legal techniques that rivaled the Inquisition in their absurdity and cruelty, the professor would interject his own amusing asides.

I found the whole thing so fascinating that I took extra detailed notes on those lectures. Maybe that was because I had seriously entertained going to law school at one time. I even took the entrance exam and did fairly well on it. But in the end I decided to go the route of graduate studies in history.

Charlotte would encourage me from time to time to think again about law school. She heard a lot about the beginning salaries of lawyers in the big downtown firms. But after my dreary journey through dissertation writing and doctoratedom, I simply didn't have the stomach for a three-year stint in law school. Besides, I had a friend who'd gone—and he described the first year as "the valley of the shadow of death."

Looking back, I can only wince and try to smile. If you really want to experience the valley of doom and death, just walk through the recent history of the life of Kevin Hastings.

As I muse on that painful subject, I have found myself thinking back again and again to the lectures of Professor Tuttle. I'm willing to bet that when you hear the whole story, you'll begin to see why.

It's strange, though—it all began pretty simply. The dark beginnings of my ordeal can be traced to the day I happened to stroll through a hotel lobby in downtown Chicago.

Three

~

EARLY THAT MORNING, I HAD CALLED Charlotte on her cell phone during our commutes. She was stuck in traffic on the Kennedy Expressway.

"Sorry I missed you last night," I said. "I just got your voice mail…"

"Yeah, I turned in early. I must not have heard the phone ring."

"How's the commute?"

"Oh, just miserable," she moaned. "It's a parking lot. How about you?"

"Not that bad. At least I'm moving. So, how about dinner tonight—"

"You know what?" she broke in. "I'm looking at my watch, and I don't think I'm going to make it to work on time. I'd better call in—let them know I'll be a few minutes late. Do you mind, Kevin dear?"

"Naw, go ahead. But—"

"What?"

"Well, like Dick Dineras is going to care if you're ten minutes late."

"I know…but he had something he needed me to do first thing in the morning…I'm just trying to be the good little secretary."

"Hey, give me a break! The guy's given you raises every six months like clockwork. You really think he's going to care?"

Silence on the other end. Maybe I had been a little too sharp with her. But I didn't care for Dineras.

He was part of the up-and-coming financial glitterati of the

Chicago Loop. From what Charlotte had said, within the year he would be making full partner at Upshaw & Bolt, the brokerage firm. I figured him to have already amassed a small fortune. The Christmas before he had invited Charlotte and me to his Christmas party. It was a glitzy catered affair at his red-brick Georgian mansion on Sheridan Drive. (I figured he'd kept the house in his divorce settlement.) Charlotte oohed and aahed at the mahogany paneling, custom-designed furniture, and the collection of original art on the walls. Dineras was affable but just a tad condescending toward me. Since that was our first meeting, I chalked it up to a false start.

But I'd have another contact of sorts with Dick Dineras. I would see him a second time. And it would be later that day.

"Sure, go ahead and call in to work," I finally said to Charlotte, as I finished the commute. "We'll talk later about dinner. I'm just pulling into campus. Love you, honey."

She blew a kiss into the phone and added, "Hugs and kisses."

At my office, I found an envelope Scotch-taped to my door. There was a note from Fred Hatch, the associate dean. Gladys Woolrick, the noted author, was in town and would be giving the convocation speech that afternoon on campus…and would I mind picking her up at her hotel and escorting her over to Essex?

Like I explained earlier, I was not yet tenured. So of course I dutifully ran right down to my VW Jetta and headed over to the Ambassador East Hotel. I figured I could get Woolrick back to campus and still have enough time to look over my notes and make my 11 AM lecture.

The Omni Ambassador East is one of the legendary hotels of Chicago. Some famous Hitchcock movie was shot there, but I forget which. Gladys Woolrick was waiting in the lobby. She was a short woman, thin, in her sixties—with hair piled up real high on her head in a kind of wild tangle. I suppose that comes with the territory for an avant-garde novelist and poet.

Dean Hatch had thoughtfully included Woolrick's bio with the note. As we exited the lobby I was all ready to talk to her about her new novel *The Strangled Rose*. (Which I had not read—but the bio said it dealt with a woman on death row convicted of the murder of her husband by driving him to suicide through psychological manipulation. Not exactly light reading.)

But then something happened.

I caught a glance of someone in a window of the Pump Room, the pricey restaurant in the swank hotel. I stared a few seconds. It looked for all the world like Charlotte sitting at a table. I stared more closely and noticed she was laughing. Her hands were motioning in front of her face as she talked, and I could see her smiling and nodding her head up and down. Something, or someone, really had her attention. I couldn't see who she was talking to. But in the pit of my stomach I had a feeling. Let's call it a wild guess.

"Excuse me," I said to Woolrick as we reached the sidewalk. "I have to do something...I'll be right back."

So I left the famous novelist and convocation speaker standing out by the curb while I dashed back into the lobby and over to the host desk of the Pump Room.

"Excuse me," I said to the maître d', "I am trying to locate someone...having breakfast here...over in that booth there," and I pointed over to where I could see the back of Charlotte's head, which was blocking the view of person she was talking to.

"You mean over in the Frank Sinatra booth?" he asked with a wry smile. "I guess you've already located whoever you are looking for..."

"Who is that table reserved to?"

"We have a policy of not giving out names of our guests—are they expecting you?"

"You know what..." I said vaguely, searching for some discreet way to get to the bottom of the whole deal, "I believe I need to visit the restroom. Where is it?"

"Are you a guest of the hotel?"

"Well, I just met with one of your guests—how about that?" My voice was getting agitated.

"Over there in the back," the maître d' said.

I walked slowly toward the restroom, taking in a view of Charlotte. She was smiling—her hands were wrapped around a cup of coffee. Across from her sat Dick Dineras. He was smiling too.

I slowed down to a crawl, my eyes glued on them. Then Dineras gestured a little with a hand and—slyly placed it down, right on top of Charlotte's hand.

"Shake it off," I muttered to myself. "The guy's a snake…Charlotte, for crying out loud, move your hand."

I had come to a complete stop. Then—Charlotte bent forward and said something, and she took her other hand and put it on top of Dineras's.

I glanced over at the desk. The maître d' was getting nervous watching me standing in the middle of the restaurant, staring with a kicked-in-the-gut kind of shock at the two lovebirds in the Frank Sinatra booth. He looked like he was ready to come over. I had to make a decision. Did I want to confront the two of them right there—then promptly get escorted out?

Maybe there was a logical explanation, I tried to tell myself.

But no. There couldn't be.

Then I realized I'd left Gladys Woolrick out on the sidewalk.

I walked past the maître d'. He gave me a look as if he really would liked to have said something like "Has she been cheating on you long, or is this the first time?"

Instead, he gave me a simple, "Good day, sir."

"Yeah," I said sarcastically as I scurried past. "I'm sure it will be."

Woolrick was still standing at the curbside, one arm across her chest and the elbow of the other perched on it with her chin resting in her hand, as if she were doing a Jack Benny impersonation. She was not happy.

I apologized quickly and cleared papers, books, and fast-food wrappers off the front seat and helped her in.

On the ride to the college I was so preoccupied by the revelation in the Pump Room that I found it hard to respond to her questions, and when I did, what I said was semi-incoherent. Here's a sample:

Woolrick: "What did you think about my theme in *The Strangled Rose*—that history is ultimately all about the perceptions of those who count the least—the news reporters, the writers, the professional historians, and in the case of crime cases, the judges—but always those on the outside looking in? And they are forever trying to make connections between cause A and event B. (Pause.) But, of course, I felt that Maude Constance, the so-called murderess—she had the only history worth telling. And no one cared. Well, what do you think?"

Kevin: "About what?"

Woolrick: "About the connection. History. You teach history, don't you?"

Kevin: "Oh. Yes. I teach that."

Woolrick: "Well, what about my thesis? In *The Rose*? Do you think I 'grew it' sufficiently?"

(Pause.)

Kevin: "I was never very good with plants."

I slammed my car into its parking spot and walked Woolrick over to the dean. Just outside his door she stopped and stared me in the eye.

"Mr. Hastings—you are a rather odd person, I must say."

Then she disappeared into Hatch's office.

I ran over to my office. I had five minutes to gather my papers and walk over to my medieval-history class, glancing at my notes as I went. I was still in a fog over Charlotte. I decided to simply read at length from my notes of the lectures of Dr. Aubrey Sumner Tuttle. The subject was "Trial by Hot Iron." I gave credit (as I always did) to my old professor.

With what I am sure was a look of sullen despair, I read to my students about the machinations of the ancient ecclesiastical courts. Leaning against the table, my posture demonstrating that my heart was not where my mouth was, I droned on. It was ironic that on the day Charlotte's betrayal was unveiled, at the very point my life was about to unravel, I would be lecturing on medieval tortures designed to settle legal issues.

According to ancient custom, a person on trial could voluntarily choose to submit to "ordeal by hot iron." He would be taken to a cathedral, and in front of witnesses and judges, he would lay hold of a hot iron. Not just hot—but red-hot, having lain in a blacksmith's cauldron for hours. The smoking pot with coals glowing would have been set up by the altar just for the occasion. The accused was required to walk (not run) for a full nine yards with the glowing bar grasped firmly in his hand. His hand would then be wrapped in bandages. The witnesses and judges would return three days later to inspect the wounds. If the hand was completely healed (a near miracle) he would be declared innocent.

Professor Tuttle, who obviously had had his own tussles with the local court system, observed,

> Mind you, the "trial by hot irons" was entirely voluntary on the part of the accused. Imagine—choosing to hold molten-hot irons in your hand while you walk nine yards. Then a few days later a "jury not of your peers" rips the bandages off of your pus-ridden, scalded hand, and bases their decision—the ultimate verdict—on the state of the blisters on your palm. Which strikes me as somewhat familiar—pretty much like a typical day in Cook County Circuit Court.

The handful of students still paying attention chuckled a bit. I didn't. I finished the class and trudged back to my office, oblivious to the fact I was about to commence my own legal ordeal, and that it would resemble that of a man choosing to carry molten irons…for the viewing pleasure of his sadistic opponents.

FOUR

ON THE SAME DAY, at almost the exact time I was lecturing my Essex College class, a meeting was taking place at a Chicago restaurant and nightclub just south of the Loop. "High Rollers" had finished their lunch crowd and would not open for dinner until five-thirty. The staff had been told to "take a hike" while two men remained. One, dressed in flashy imported sports clothes, was Buddy Mangiorno, a man in his late thirties, who ran the establishment. The older one was Vito Mangiorno, Buddy's father.

I knew nothing about these Chicago characters. At least not at the time.

Vito had receding silver hair and saggy bags under dark piercing eyes. He was only a little overweight, with broad shoulders. When he talked, Vito didn't usually raise his voice. He didn't need to. To the outer ring of his "outfit"—and always in his dealings with outsiders—his orders were delivered in a quiet, smooth, businessman's voice, even with some friendly banter. In the inner circle, though, things got a little more blunt sometimes.

"New chef?" he asked, pausing in between bites of his angel-hair pasta in clam sauce.

"Yeah. You like it?" Buddy replied.

"Sure. It's good."

After a few more bites of pasta and a couple of gulps of red wine, Vito got to the point.

"So what's the deal about the dry cleaning?"

Buddy drew a blank on that.

20

"You know," Vito repeated, lowering his voice a little and bobbing his head this way and that. "The *dry cleaning...*"

"Oh, yeah!" Buddy was getting the message. "Like laundry, like that kind of dry cleaning."

Vito raised his index finger and pointed it straight at Buddy's face. Then he put it to his lips. Certain words were not to be used. Words like *laundry*—as in *money-laundering*.

As the head of the three Chicago "outfits," Vito had practically cornered the market for illegal gambling in the greater Chicago area, for control of the highest-priced prostitution services, and for interstate delivery of "crystal meth," the fasting growing illegal drug in the Midwest.

So the real problem was how to hide the money, how to mix it with otherwise legal profits of seemingly legal business operations. The days of being able to launder it through labor-union pension funds were coming to an end. The goal now was to locate a legitimate high-cash business into which large amounts of illegal gains could be funneled with little or no chance of being traced.

"So, what have you done about our dry-cleaning situation?" Vito asked again.

"I'm working on it..."

"That's the same thing you said the first time I asked you— the other day. Second time, that's no answer. Talk to me, without talking, *capisce?*"

"Look, Pop," Buddy retorted, "you don't have to worry about using code words here. The place is safe. I have it swept for bugs every week."

"You know they have this military-type stuff now, listening devices—they point it here, they point it there, and they can listen to you right through brick walls. I saw it on a TV show about the FBI. So don't sit there and lecture me about this stuff. And don't disrespect me."

"Hey, I'm not disrespecting you—"

"Then answer my question and don't act like a moron," Vito answered in a voice edged with irritation.

"Okay. I'm looking into pool halls—"

"Not enough income. Too difficult to hide Mr. Franklin and all of those other great American presidents."

"Franklin wasn't ever President."

"Whatever...go on."

"Car washes, car-detailing places?"

"Naw, same problem," Vito groaned.

"Well, what ideas do you have?" Buddy responded.

"Why do I always have to do all the thinking all the time?" his father snapped. "You ever want to take over this operation? Or do you want to spend the rest of your life shaking hands with customers and listening to complaints about the spaghetti being served cold or your singer singing off key? Get with it!"

After a pause, Buddy's face lit up.

"How about a parking lot?"

Vito thought for a few seconds. "I like the idea. Gotta be a high-rise parking tower, though," he added. "The other kind don't have enough cash turnover."

"Which means being close to the city. Maybe *in* the city," Buddy added.

"Yeah, where all the rich yuppies want to park their Benzes."

"I think most of those parking structures are owned by big corporations, though. It's harder to lean on them."

"Then get a vacant lot or something," barked Vito. "Make sure it's zoned for business. Talk to Tony DeVoe. I pay him enough in legal fees. Have him look it up. Then I'll have one of our construction outfits build the thing. How long could that take? Just pouring cement. I did lots of that when I was younger. Cement work. Bricklaying. Stuff you kids today wouldn't know anything about. So get right on it."

"So if I find the right piece of real estate somewhere..." Buddy's voice trailed off.

"So? You buy it up," Vito snapped.

"How much are we talking?"

"I'll pay some pretty good dollars."

"If they won't sell?"

"Then use...you know, persuasion."

"I thought we were trying to stay low-profile. Staying away from that kind of thing."

"Listen careful to me on this." Vito motioned with his hands, open-palmed, toward Buddy. "Once in a while something has to happen to someone so everybody else will remember it for a long, long while into the future. So the next time I say I want this or that, or whatever, people are going to think back to the consequences—what's going to happen to them if they say no. It only takes one or two of those—every five, ten years or so. People talk, and they remember when somebody's daddy doesn't come home to the wife and kids at the end of the day. And a few years later they find his bones in the woods or a landfill or something. It's like teaching. Like a learning lesson for everybody. That's all I'm sayin'."

Buddy had gotten the lesson. The next day, he sent a few guys out to scout out high-rise parking lots and potential sites.

~

Of course at the time, I didn't know much about organized crime in Chicago. Or about Vito Mangiorno or his heading the three criminal "outfits."

And I most certainly did not know, back then, that I was about to be swept right into their path.

FIVE

THAT NIGHT, BACK AT MY APARTMENT in the suburbs, I knew I had to call Charlotte. Things had to come to a head. When she answered, I dove right in, explaining how I'd seen her with her boss at the Pump Room.

"Exactly what were you doing with Dick Dineras?"

"Eating an early lunch."

"You lied to me."

"I did not."

"You said you were going to work."

"I did, just like I said." Charlotte had an unnerving sense of calm in her voice. "When I got there, Dick said he had some confidential things to discuss—and he had to do it outside of the office."

"Things—like what?"

"Like a lucrative promotion his brokerage firm is offering him, and a merger opportunity as well."

"What does that have to do with you?"

"He wanted my advice."

"I don't believe that."

"You can believe it or not, but it's true. You see, Kevin, Dick really values me—as a business associate, and also as a person."

"That guy is playing you like a rented trombone," I sputtered back, trying to find some benign phrase for what I really wanted to say.

"What are you insinuating?" Charlotte asked sharply.

"That Dineras is trying to get you to move into his mansion with him, that's what I'm saying."

There was an excruciating silence at the other end of the line. Finally Charlotte spoke into existence what had been hanging in the air between us like a specter for a while.

"You know," she began slowly, "for a long time I have been getting the feeling...I don't know how to put this..."

"Don't bother," I replied. "Let me put it out there for you. Your heart has not been in our relationship. I've become a convenience while you've been looking for something better."

"Not better," she said with a manufactured sense of injury, "just different, Kevin."

"And Dick Dineras is different—his mansion, his Ferrari, his vacation condo in Key Largo—that's what's different?"

"Why do you despise what he's accomplished? I find him to be a remarkable, caring man."

"Do you love him?"

After a pause, she laughed quickly. "I don't know that yet."

"Well," I retorted, "I can't wait around for you to find out."

"No," Charlotte said in the very last comment she would ever make to me, "I really didn't think you would. Be well, Kevin dear."

~

It took me a few days to sort it all out. But after a while, the fog lifted and my head started clearing. I was back to near-normal in my routine. The pain from the break with Charlotte was still there, but I was managing. And I was simply going to push on. But something had happened to me. A snap. A lightbulb had popped on. Not quite an epiphany, but something significant nevertheless. I was really wondering what I was doing with my life. What was I building? Where was I heading?

Partly it was Charlotte, but also I have to give credit to Dr. Harvey Albright, who sat me down that week and explained his final decision. He would *not* be recommending me for tenure now—such a privilege would be at least two years away for reasons the two of us had previously discussed. So, all of the groveling, all of the chauffeuring of outside speakers and visiting scholars, all of the additional tasks foisted on me—which I patiently accepted— had not been enough.

And so I smiled at Albright and thanked him warmly. He gave me a puzzled look.

I am sure he had no way of knowing why I was glad. In a strange way the tenure disappointment had emboldened me. It had freed me up to take risks. To search for adventure and self-definition. I felt like the hero of an old story who was about to "make his way in the world"—or better yet, "go out to seek his fortune."

History tells us the ancients mark their significance in life by leaving massive physical monuments. Great lion-faced sphinxes, for instance. The Egyptian pharaohs of Memphis were best known for this. But the Assyrians left similar figures—fantastic winged beasts that guarded their palaces and temples. The ancient Mayan chiefs left the huge stepped-stone temples that rose up from the jungle floor. The Mesopotamian kings had their towering ziggurats.

I had no such pretensions. I had simply decided I needed to get rich.

That would be my goal. And not just because I had lost Charlotte to a man with well-padded pockets. As I thought on it, whatever I wanted to do with my life, wherever I would be heading, having a lot of money would certainly make the road easier.

So the beginning of my journey toward what I hoped would be wealth, but which ended at quite a different place, was not marked with any kind of monument.

Unless, perhaps, it was a simple real-estate flyer for a piece of property in Chicago—a flyer I still have, by the way.

I knew I had to stick to my teaching position. I did like it, and I needed the regular income. My parents had passed away a few years ago, and the inheritance together with what I had managed to save made up a fairly sizable savings and retirement nest egg. It was enough for investment, but I wasn't skilled in the markets. I did some studying—considered taking on some shares in the stock market, or investing in gold, oil exploration, or mineral rights, or starting a business on eBay. I started subscribing to the *Wall Street Journal*. I read every financial magazine I could get my hands on. But nothing clicked.

Eventually I called up my Uncle Mort. He'd retired in Rockville, but he used to sell real estate in the greater Chicago area. Mom and Dad had stopped talking much to him after he divorced my Aunt Alice and then got remarried, but he'd gotten back into contact with me after their deaths. He was always glad to hear from me and give me advice.

"Real estate. Take my word for it," he said. "Booming market. Buy cheap, sell high. Quick turnover, that's the key."

"What kind of real estate—homes? Condos? What?"

"You know, the average schmo says, 'Look, if I'm going to start, I'll start small. Buy a little house. Sell it. Buy a bigger house, and so on.' I say no."

"No?"

"No. I say—think big. Commercial real estate. The bigger the better. That's where the big money is."

"Yeah, but I don't know anything about commercial real estate."

"No matter," Mort reassured me. "Read the papers. See what's selling. And drive around the city. Spend a lot of time doing that. You never know, sometimes you just fall into one. You get lucky. That happened to me. One big piece of prime commercial real estate. That's how I paid for my retirement."

I took his advice, and during every free hour I had, I drove unrelentingly through the streets of Chicago. Around the Loop and into the financial districts, along the Magnificent Mile, along the Gold Coast and the lakeshore. All through the South Side, and the West and North Sides too—all the way up to Oak Park.

I didn't really know what I was looking for, but I figured I would recognize it when I saw it. All I knew is that it had to be for sale and had to have lucrative prospects. And I had to be able to swing the down payment.

Then one day, I saw it. It was an old, strange-looking church just a few blocks from the Loop—an ideal location. The building was a little like a Buddhist pagoda, but with a stainless-steel steeple rising from its center. However, the cross at the top had been removed. The windows were boarded up, and the place was clearly in need of a lot of fix-up. The for-sale sign was on the front door.

I stood there gazing at it. Something seemed so very right. Then a man walked out the front, escorted by a woman in a brightly colored jacket who was on a cell phone. With her free hand she locked the door, shook the man's hand, and dashed off to her car. The man slowly walked toward me.

"Hi," he said with a warm smile. His medium-length hair was combed somewhat awry, and his sport coat must have come from some discount place. I noticed one of his shoes was scuffed badly.

"Interesting place, isn't it?" he asked.

"Yes," I answered politely. "Are you connected with the owners?"

"No," he answered. "Actually, I was trying to buy it. Had an offer in, but it expired today. We couldn't get the financing. So they put the sign back out."

I nodded, intrigued by what seemed to be a miraculous bit of timing.

"Say, let me introduce myself." The man gave me a grin and a firm handshake. "I'm Jim Loveland, pastor of the Windy City Mission."

I shook his hand and returned the smile dutifully.

"Interested in buying it?" he asked.

I hedged a little—said I was "just looking it over."

"Well, I came over today to get an extension for the financing. But no deal. You know, I always figure the Lord knows better than I do where His work ought to take place. You know what the Bible says…"

The pastor guy paused for a moment and sort of went into sermon overdrive:

The God who made the world and everything in it
is the Lord of heaven and earth and does not live in
temples built by hands.

I nodded politely again, not really understanding the point he
was making. Furthermore, I didn't care. And it struck me as weird
how he was bent on finding a silver lining behind his black cloud.
I had always found that kind of religious certainty in the face of
bad circumstances curious and downright incomprehensible. All I
knew was, his bad luck might prove to be my good fortune.

"You have a church?" he asked.

"I'm really not a churchgoing fellow," I replied.

"Our mission is just a few blocks from here. Big sign outside,
you may have seen it. We are actually running out of space where
we are. You ought to come by some time. I think you would be
surprised at what we have going on."

"Sure," I said, with not the least intention of ever dropping
by.

The man left, and I walked up to the locked front door of the
church. Inside a little metal box was a pile of flyers that described
the property, gave the asking price, and had the agent's name and
number.

I grabbed one of the flyers, folded it up, and dashed to my car
opposite on the street. I pulled out my cell phone to call Uncle
Mort.

Hoping I had just stumbled onto my golden ticket, I put my
car into gear and sped off.

As I drove, I was still clutching the real-estate flyer tightly in
my hand.

Six

Mᴏʀᴛ ᴡᴀs ᴇɴᴛʜᴜsɪᴀsᴛɪᴄ. He even drove down from Rockville in his Cadillac Seville to look at the property himself.

"Prime location. Really sweet," he said.

"What's the down side?" I asked.

"First, can you come up with about ten percent as a down payment?"

"Yes, I think so. It will strap me, but I can do it. I'll have to cash out my 401(k) and my money market and use all of my savings."

"Okay. Now listen up. I've done a little calling around on this property. The owner is a group called the Nuveau Art Foundation. They've fallen on some bad times. The director had to scram because of financial misdealings. The place used to be their headquarters and an art museum. It was some kind of church before that. Anyway, to avoid foreclosure and more scandal, the art foundation has to get it sold. There's been a little vandalism, but nothing significant. There's been one other offer—"

"Yeah, I know about that," I replied. "A mission just down the street. Their offer expired when they couldn't come up with the financing."

"Okay. That puts you in the driver's seat."

"But how do I know this is a solid investment?"

Mort smiled.

"In my opinion," he said, "they've got this baby priced to sell—way under market. They want to unload, and unload fast."

I had to ask him one more time.

"So, you really think I can sell this off at a profit?"

"Look," Mort said, "if I were in your shoes, I'd grab this. This is very lucrative from the location standpoint. Right down near the commercial centers. Now of course, if you have a fast turnaround on the sale, there's always short-term capital-gains tax to worry about."

"So what do I do?"

"That can be handled. Just talk to a tax accountant or lawyer. I think you can still do installment sales so the title doesn't actually transfer to your buyer until after one year—so I think you can get the benefit of long-term capital-gains treatment."

It was all sounding pretty convincing. And then Mort said the thing that sealed the deal for me.

"Besides," he said nonchalantly, "you're not married—no kids, no one depending on you. You can afford to take a risk. Of course, you have to feel good about this yourself. I don't want to talk you into anything."

"Can you help me out on the details?"

"Sure, no problem. You can save the broker's commission by handling the paperwork yourself. I'll walk you through it. But before the closing, you need a good property lawyer to make sure you're covered."

"Can you recommend someone?"

"Absolutely—a La Salle Street law firm. Top shelf. Gentry, Dorset, and Blumenthal. Lloyd Gentry's sort of the gold standard. You wouldn't get *him*. But any of his associates would serve you well, I'm sure."

It all seemed to make a lot of sense.

So I called the agent for the art foundation and told her I would be putting in an offer immediately. She was very pleased, gave me her fax and then her address so I could drop the offer off in person the next day at her office. I drove up to Rockville, and in his living room Mort walked me through the process of filling out the offer. I faxed it to the agent's office at an all-night copy store. The following day, I left extra early, braving the worst of the morning rush hour, to get to the real-estate office by 8:30 AM and hand in the original, signed offer to purchase.

One day later I received a call from the agent, who excitedly announced my offer had been accepted. I drove down that night to pick up the signed acceptance.

By its terms I had twenty days to get a commitment for financing or else waive the financing clause altogether—which meant that in that event I would pay cash for the whole property at closing.

The only way I could pay cash would be to get a buyer for the property before closing, a slim possibility at best. But I'd already talked to my bank, and they were willing to finance ninety percent. I was prepared to tough it out, figuring I'd have to make payments for only about six months or so—by that time I hoped to have a solid buyer. After that point, with my savings depleted and having to make payments on my own apartment and on the property, I would start feeling the squeeze. The point is, though, I never believed the squeeze would come. I felt I was too smart to let that happen.

You may think I was being too optimistic. But here was my logic: Mort told me the night we filled out the papers, "Your offer will be the second one this property has generated in just a few weeks—why wouldn't it continue to crank up offers after you buy it?"

In a few days I contacted the law offices of Gentry, Dorset, and Blumenthal. When I walked in for my meeting, I was impressed. Everything was opulent but not overdone. Marble floors. Wood-paneled walls. I sat down in a green crushed-velvet settee next to a Spanish-leather couch and listened to the receptionist answer muted telephone rings with honey-voiced efficiency. After a while, a twenty-something paralegal appeared and took me into the inner sanctum. As we sat at a long conference table he went through a series of questions, then took my copy of the offer to purchase. After glancing at it, he asked me if I'd done it myself.

"Yes, with the help of my uncle—he's a retired real-estate agent."

"Not bad," he said, studying it. "Not bad at all."

He showed me the standard fee agreement and let me know that one of the associate attorneys would be in touch with me before closing.

As the paralegal walked me to the lobby, I couldn't help overhearing some office chat about the day's developments in some kind of high-priced property deal Lloyd Gentry himself was handling.

Heading down the elevator and out of the massive lobby of the skyscraper where Gentry, Dorset, and Blumenthal occupied two entire floors, I felt secure.

I had an acceptance of my offer on a prime commercial piece of Chicago. And now I had a Gold Coast law firm guiding me safely to the promised land.

~

That afternoon I was continuing my lectures on medieval legal procedures and their impact on cultural, religious, and social structures. In twelfth-century Europe, an aggrieved party could chose to settle a legal claim against his offender through "trial by combat"—challenging him in combat. More usually, though, a plaintiff would hire a champion, who would do battle for him.

Then I made the connection to the development several hundred years later of retained legal advocates. As I spoke I couldn't help thinking of my own recent retainer of the gold-plated, highly recommended firm of Gentry, Dorset, and Blumenthal—who would "champion" my purchase of an investment that was going to bring me a slice of the good life.

A student raised his hand.

"What if the 'champion' blows it—doesn't adequately defend the honor or claim of the aggrieved party?"

"Then perhaps," I said wryly, bringing a few laughs, "he should have hired a different champion."

The irony of that comment still rings in my ears.

SEVEN

A FEW DAYS HAD GONE BY. I had been getting my classes ready for midterms, and for a little while I actually hadn't been consumed by my real estate deal. Then one day I walked to my office and found a note taped to the door from the department secretary. It simply read, "Call Troy Armstrong. ASAP. Urgent." And it had a phone number.

I didn't know any Troy Armstrong, but I called right away. A secretary answered, "Law office," and then connected me. Armstrong introduced himself as an "associate" of Tony DeVoe, Esq., of Tony DeVoe & Associates.

"What can I do for you?" I asked.

"Our client is interested in buying the church property you just signed off on."

I was dumbfounded. The closing was still ten days away and I was already getting a nibble on the line. A possible buyer so quick? Incredible.

I tried not to show my giddiness at the prospect of cashing in so quickly on my investment. "Well, I would be interested in talking with you about that," I countered. "Who's your client?" Frankly, I really didn't care—I was just trying to act casual.

But Armstrong went mildly ballistic.

"*What'd you ask me?*" It was the kind of tone you'd expect from a guy whose sister I'd just insulted.

"I was only saying, you know, who's your client—who wants to buy the prop—"

"Right now, Mr. Hastings," Armstrong growled sarcastically, "that's for our law office to know—and for you not to know."

"Look, I don't know how we are supposed to conduct business then…"

"What," he guffawed, "you never heard of an undisclosed principal?"

I was starting to get his drift.

"I think I see what you mean," I answered cautiously.

"That's good. Now, at the right time, and the right place, the client will be disclosed. Right now all you have to know is this—that our client is a certain business concern, and he—the business concern—wants to do business with you on this property. Okay?"

"Sure. So, where do we go—"

"You just leave the rest up to us," Armstrong interrupted. "The next contact will come from attorney-at-law Tony DeVoe. *Personally.*"

He punched that last word as if promising a visit from foreign royalty. Or maybe, on the other hand, from Blackbeard the Pirate.

"Okay. You know how to contact me if you have any further questions. Later we can do some talking about what price I will be—"

"Mr. DeVoe, on behalf of our client, will be offering you a fair and reasonable price. You can bet on that. You will be satisfied with the price he will be offering."

Though I was a novice in real-estate negotiations, I was pretty sure things were already going in a direction I had not anticipated. I thought that negotiations usually began with the *seller* setting the opening price.

But then, I still had a lot to learn about Tony DeVoe, Esq., and his undisclosed principal.

So I called Uncle Mort and got his take on all this.

"Some folks are funny like that," he said casually. "Don't want you to know who's bidding until the last minute. Sometimes it's some rich doctor in the middle of a divorce, and he doesn't want his soon-to-be ex to find out. Or maybe just a businessman who wants an edge on the competition and is paranoid about secrecy. Whatever it is, don't worry about it. Did you get ahold of Gentry's people?"

"Yes. Already had a meeting with a fellow over there. One of the associate lawyers will be getting in touch with me before closing."

"See, I figured they'd take good care of you."

Then Mort and I got into the dollars and cents of the proposed sale to the "undisclosed principal."

I was buying the property for $720,000. I considered this a huge amount of money, but Mort assured me that in the world of commercial real estate, it was "chump change." He thought, realistically, I might be able to double my money. "Ask 1.6 million," he suggested.

"You're kidding!" I exclaimed.

"Do I sound like I'm kidding?" he said with a chuckle.

It all seemed pretty extraordinary. In a matter of weeks I might be doubling my investment, and we were talking about figures close to two million dollars. I was no Donald Trump, but I was already getting a gut thrill from this whole world of wheeling and dealing.

Two days later I found another note taped to my office door. It read, "Call Tony DeVoe. ASAP. Urgent," followed by the number. When I called, the receptionist said Tony DeVoe wanted a *personal* meeting with me. "As soon as possible."

I suggested late that afternoon after my last class. By the time I could fight the traffic crosstown, however, I knew we would be running into suppertime. I was put on hold briefly.

"Mr. DeVoe wants to meet you for dinner," she said when she got back. "Six-forty-five PM. Here's the address and name of the restaurant. Mr. DeVoe says be sure and don't be late."

I jotted it down and dashed off to class.

By the time I was finished for the day and heading south of the Loop to the club, it was six. I thought I could make it. But traffic into the city was unexpectedly snarled. At six-thirty-five I grabbed my cell phone and, as I crawled along amid the mass of cars, tried to reach DeVoe's office. I got their voice mail.

At six-forty-five I was still several blocks from the restaurant. At six-forty-nine my cell phone rang. Its screen read "unknown caller." I answered it.

"This is Tony DeVoe. Where are you?"

I looked out the window. "I just passed the Greek Town area. A couple of blocks more and I'll be there."

"Hurry up." Then he hung up.

A few seconds later I started wondering, *How did he get my cell number?* I was sure I'd never given it to Troy Armstrong. And I hadn't given it to the real-estate agent either.

I didn't know—then—that this was all part of my opponent's mind-game warfare. Tony DeVoe was letting me know I was vulnerable. That they could find out anything about me they wanted. That I couldn't run fast enough, or far enough, to keep them from finding me.

It took a while for that to dawn on me. The cell phone call was the first hint.

The second was the nightclub Tony DeVoe had picked.

As I pulled up and left my keys with the valet, I glanced at the name on the marquee—High Rollers.

It didn't mean anything to me at the time. But DeVoe had picked it for a reason. He figured if I had street smarts about the Chicago underworld (which I didn't) I would walk in knowing a lot about who the "undisclosed principal" might be. And then I would be more than ready to deal on their terms.

On the other hand, if I walked in like a teenager on my first date, all starry-eyed and naïve, talking up the great food and wonderful atmosphere, that would let him know something too. That I was, as they might say, "a babe in the woods." Which I was.

"This lasagna is great," I said enthusiastically. "I usually don't like Neopolitan. But this is really excellent. Nice atmosphere too," I added as I tried to make conversation. We were at a table halfway between the long, horseshoe-shaped bar and the little stage, where a woman was singing to piano accompaniment.

DeVoe smiled at my remark. He was sitting across the black-and-white-checkered tablecloth, eating his manicotti. Fortyish, he had a blond dye job on his hair, tinted glasses, and big gold cufflinks with diamond studs. His suit was dark and shiny and looked expensive—maybe imported silk.

"You come here a lot?" I asked.

"Pretty regular," he said, studying me while he was chewing.

"Tell me about the owner."

"He's a guy I know," DeVoe said—and laughed a little to himself .

"So, you know him—the owner, I mean?" I was struggling to make small talk.

"You ask a lot of questions, Mr. Hastings."

"Call me Kevin," I replied, still trying to break the ice.

"You can call me Mr. DeVoe," he said, deadpan. I half expected a smile from him indicating a joke. But none came.

A waiter came over with a dessert menu, but the lawyer quickly waved him off.

"Down to business," he announced abruptly. He pushed his plate to the side to keep his sleeves out of the marinara sauce. For a few seconds he stroked his thumbs over his fingertips, back and forth, as if silently caressing bills of large denominations. Then the finger rolling stopped.

"I represent a business concern that wants to buy out all of your rights and title to the church property your offer was just accepted on. We know you're near closing on it. So you go ahead and close. But we want a complete assignment of your interest now, and a title transfer immediately after the closing."

Then DeVoe reached inside the monogrammed pocket of his white shirt and pulled out a piece of paper. He unfolded it, looked at it, looked at me, placed it on the table—and slowly slid it over for me to read.

On the note was written "$1 million."

As incredible as it seems, I experienced a rush of disappointment. I had my heart set on Mort's figure of 1.6 million. I had pictured myself being interviewed by the financial-page reporter from the *Tribune* sometime in the future, saying, "You know, it all started when I doubled my money on a piece of prime commercial property in less than sixty days."

Doubling my money—that was the bell I really wanted to ring. If I jumped at DeVoe's figure, I would net only $280,000. And after deducting my down payment and paying the Gentry firm, together with closing costs, I would actually see a profit of around $200,000. Great money, of course—but not the kind of jackpot I had somehow talked myself into believing I deserved.

So I pushed the paper back to him.

"I think the property ought to go for at least—1.6 million," I countered. Now I was starting to feel like Donald Trump. But it didn't last long.

DeVoe took his napkin, wiped his mouth, and tossed it down on the table. "That is the only offer you are going to get. Ever," he replied. "I know how much you are paying for the property. I know how much you make as an associate history professor at that dinky college of yours. With this kind of offer you ought to be kissing my feet. But I am going to do you two favors, Mr. Hastings. Not one—but two. You want to know what they are?"

I nodded, feeling a little like a fifth-grader in the principal's office.

"Okay. First, I'm giving you twenty-four hours to reconsider the very disrespectful manner in which you have treated my client's offer. End of business tomorrow—accept the offer by that time."

I stopped nodding. Now things were getting out of hand.

"And the second favor—I am going to show you the identity of my client."

With that, he took his pen out, wrote something on the paper, and tossed it closer to me to read.

Under the offering price were the words "VM Contractors."

When I reached for the note, though, DeVoe snatched it up, stuck it back into his shirt pocket, and wagged an index finger at me.

"I keep the note," he said. Rising, he put a wad of money in the waiter's hand. Then, without any formalities, he walked through the front door. I saw him climb into the back of a large automobile and get driven off.

Just then a couple at a nearby table smiled and applauded as a waiter, with expert aplomb, touched off a tableside display of cherries jubilee into a burst of flame.

But…it should have reminded me of something else. If I had been paying attention, I should have gotten at least the vague feeling that the coals of the blacksmith's fire were being lit for my inquisition, and the hot irons were being prepared.

EIGHT

WHEN I GOT BACK HOME THAT NIGHT, I logged onto the Internet. By now I was having really bad feelings about my meeting with DeVoe. But, as humans are wont to do, I avoided the catastrophic explanation in favor of a less honest but more comfortable theory. I figured that the rough tone of our meeting and the lawyer's aggressiveness were simply hardball negotiating tactics.

There was nothing on the Internet about VM Contractors. Nor could I find them listed in the telephone directory for Chicago and surrounding areas. So I called Mort. He said he'd never heard of them but promised he would make some calls. He asked how the rest of the meeting went, and I gave him the short side.

"And where'd you meet?" he asked.

"Place called High Rollers," I answered.

"Hmmm."

Mort and I spent a lot of time talking about the price. He was getting squishy on the 1.6 million figure.

"What do you mean, I should seriously consider the 1 million offer?" I demanded. "What about the *1.6* million?"

"Look, everything's a gamble. There's nothing precise about any of this," he said. "Just sit on it until noon tomorrow. Let me do some checking."

"Checking on what?" I asked.

"Into things, that's all."

"DeVoe gave me until end of business tomorrow to accept or reject their offer."

"Just let me get back to you by noon, that's all," he said with a note of concern in his voice.

The next day I had two classes in the morning. Then I dashed back to my office, clicking on my cell phone as I ran. But there were no messages, and nothing waiting for me at my office. I called Mort but only got his voice mail. I left an urgent message for him to call me.

I waited at my desk the rest of the afternoon, grading exams and checking the clock. Then about four o'clock Mort called.

"Sorry, Kevin. Look, the person I was going to ask about your deal wasn't available. So I have no answers for you."

"How about some advice then—should I take the offer, or make a counteroffer?"

"Definitely not counteroffer," he said quickly.

"What kind of negotiating is that?"

"It's not. It's what you might call extraordinary circumstances."

"Extraordinary...like what?" I said, baffled—though I wasn't sure I wanted to hear the truth. "Something about the property?"

"No, nothing like that."

"Something about the deal itself?"

"No."

"Then *what?*"

"Well," he said, pausing for a moment, "it's about the other party."

"VM Contractors?"

"I don't want to make unfounded accusations. I put a call into an old friend of mine who's still down at the *Tribune*—he's a reporter. Knows everybody and everything in Chicago practically. But he wasn't around. So I don't know anything for sure. Just that—"

"Look, Mort, you're my uncle. My confidant," I said. "Give me some guidance here. What are you saying?"

"That maybe...just maybe...and I'm not saying this for certain. But the people making this offer...just might not be very nice people, if you get my drift."

"What? You're saying—"

"Not on the telephone, Kevin," Mort said loudly. "Just let it sit where it lies. Be safe. To be careful, and still make a really sweet profit on this deal, I would call them up right now and say, 'Okay, 1 million. Got yourself a deal.'"

"I don't know what to say," I replied, finally willing to put the pieces together.

"To be honest, Kevin, 1 million is still a very good turnaround on this. I know a lot of folks who would cut a toe off for a return like that."

There was something in Uncle Mort's analogy that didn't sit right with me under the circumstances.

Alright, I told myself, *maybe there* is *something shady about the buyer. The point is, I'm still making nearly a quarter-million on the deal. So—why not? There's nothing illegal in any of this.*

I asked Mort to stand by his phone in case I needed more advice.

Then I called DeVoe.

"I will take your offer of $1 million," I said. "But no financing. Cash upon closing." That had been Mort's advice.

"Cashier's check," the lawyer replied.

"Fine."

"There's one special condition I am putting in," he added. "Page two, under 'special warranties and assurances.' Read it carefully. Make sure you can sign off on that."

I gave him the fax number for the all-night copy store. Then I drove over. The clerk handed me the envelope and took my money.

I got Mort on my cell as I opened the envelope. Then I started reading the document DeVoe had already signed as agent and attorney-in-fact for VM Contractors. Mort said it was all pretty standard stuff. Then I got to the second page with the "special warranties and assurances." I read the special condition:

> Seller warrants and represents that the property is fit
> and proper for commercial use and purposes, to wit:

the demolition of all existing buildings, and the construction of a multilevel parking structure.

"Okay," Mort chimed in. "That's a warranty. Means you are promising they can do what they intend for the lot—tear down that old church and build a parking garage."

"Well? How can I promise that?"

"Not that unusual. Tell you what. I think I've still got my copy of the Chicago zoning codes here somewhere. Let me check on it. I'll call you right back."

"Hurry—DeVoe is waiting at his office for me to fax my signature back on this."

Forty long minutes later Mort buzzed me. "Here's the deal. The property's clearly zoned for very broad commercial purposes now. There's a long definition of what that includes—but the point is, it does encompass 'commercial parking establishments *up to five stories in height*.' So let's counter with that exact language. Write that in over what they put, initial it, and fax it back. See if they'll bite..."

I followed Mort's instructions exactly. Then I waited. I half expected DeVoe to call me and question me on the change— though I didn't know how he could argue with that.

But he didn't. In less than an hour a countersigned version of my changes to the agreement came grinding slowly through the fax machine.

A moment later, I had the document in my hand.

As I waited for my change from the clerk, who was swallowing slugs from a two-liter bottle of Mellow Yellow and working the cash register with his free hand, I stared at the paper.

There in the copy store, with the bluish neon lights flickering and buzzing above, as I watched the passersby hunching against the chill as they trudged home in the dark—that's when I realized I was committed to selling the property to VM Contractors, come what may.

I might as well have been holding some medieval writ, commanding me to show myself to the torturers and then and there submit my body to a legal process by pain.

NINE

Two days before the closing, I still hadn't heard from anybody at the Gentry law firm. I was starting to get pretty nervous. So I called their office and asked to speak with the paralegal who had interviewed me. The receptionist put me on hold. After a few moments she came back and said he was not available, and would I like his voice mail? I was having trouble hearing her over the noise in the background—which seemed out of place for the quiet, finely honed operation I'd seen earlier, so I quickly agreed to go into voice mail.

After leaving my urgent message—"Would the attorney handling my closing this Friday please confirm with me that everything is on track?"—I assumed I would get a call back. But by the next afternoon, I still had not heard back. I telephoned again.

The closing with the art foundation was scheduled for the very next day at noon. Attorney Tony DeVoe had assumed I would take about an hour-and-a-half to two hours at the real estate agent's office. DeVoe had set my second closing—where I would be seller—at his office for three o'clock. Counting on me to keep things simple, by four he expected to be on his way to the Cook County public-records office to record the documents conveying the church property to VM Contractors before the weekend.

At the closing with DeVoe I was to get a cashier's check for $1 million. On the following Monday I planned to use about 650,000 of that money to pay off the bank mortgage on the property. The remaining 350,000 (less closing costs and lawyer fees) would be mine. I would put 72,000 back into my savings and retirement. That would leave 200,000 or so profit to invest.

~

What I have just described is how it was all *supposed* to work. That is, if everything went as planned. Of course, I'm telling you this whole story because it did *not* go that way. Not even close.

As a historian by profession, it has been my observation that most catastrophes have happened not because of one single failure—or one single cause—but because there have been a convergence of several seemingly isolated but nevertheless critical events.

Take the sinking of the *Titanic,* for instance. (An apt example, considering what was about to happen to me.) The ship's design was flawed. It was unusual to encounter an iceberg in that sea-lane. Then, at the Senate subcommittee that held an inquiry into the tragedy, one of the witnesses called was a sailor. He was on lookout that night for icebergs and testified he didn't have his binoculars with him. They had been left at the previous port of call.

The question was put to him whether, with the glasses, he could have seen the iceberg soon enough to direct the ship out of its path.

He reluctantly told the crushing truth. Yes, he said, we could have saved the entire ship—and the more than one thousand souls who perished.

With one set of binoculars.

~

When I called the Gentry firm that Thursday afternoon, now very anxious about the closing the next day, the background noise at the office was even louder than before. Banging—and the sounds of drills.

"What's going on over there?" I asked, annoyed and barely able to hear the receptionist.

"You'll have to excuse us," she said courteously. "This week we are doing a major renovation on both floors. Putting in satellite connections for video conferencing and updating our computer system. And some redecorating. I think it's going to be beautiful when they're finished on Monday—"

"Could I please talk to whoever my attorney is for the church-property closing tomorrow at noon?" I said, interrupting.

"Tomorrow?"

"Yes."

"At noon?"

"That's right."

"I'm sorry, that doesn't sound familiar. What did you say your name was?"

I told her—even spelled it out. I gave her the name of the para-legal who had met with me. She told me he—and most of the staff—were on vacation that week due to the construction work.

"Isn't there someone who knows what's going on?" I cried out in frustration.

"Yes—Mrs. Hammersted, the office manager."

"Great, let me talk to her."

"She's in the hospital, sir, I'm sorry."

"Look, I've got a closing scheduled for tomorrow," I pleaded. "This is very important. Someone should have had this on a cal-endar or in a file or something."

"We do have a computer calendar system, but unfortunately our computers are all down today."

Then the receptionist paused and muttered to herself some-thing about a printed master calendar. I heard her digging around in her desk.

"Here it is," she said. Then she started telling me more than I cared to know. "I hate this. They do the whole thing in six-point type, itty-bitty little print you can hardly read. And I broke my glasses...have to have my boyfriend bring me back and forth to work because I need them for driving..."

I was getting a desperate feeling.

"Okay. Here is today's date. I thought I'd looked at this thing at the beginning of the week and we had nothing assigned for any of the attorneys for any of these days...And tomorrow...let me see...my, that print is small."

There was a deadly silence.

"Well, yes. I can make it out, and it does have a closing for you, Mr. Hastings. At noon. But there are no initials of an attorney next to that entry. Which might mean it never got assigned to one of our associate attorneys. I am sorry. I wonder how I missed that."

"Sorry?" I yelled. "Are you kidding? Ma'am, I would advise you get ahold of one of the senior partners right away and clear this up. And get back to me immediately."

I gave her my number. I was supposed to attend a faculty meeting that afternoon, but I felt I had to babysit my project instead. So I huddled in my office with my cell phone cradled in my hand. Thinking about the *Titanic*. And the missing binoculars.

What I found out much later in the saga was that Lloyd Gentry, who had successfully won a huge real-estate-development lawsuit in circuit court and was taking the week off, happened to stop by later that afternoon. The desperate receptionist recounted my problem, explaining she had tried in vain to line up any other attorney for the closing.

Gentry dug around for a while amid the filing cabinets, stepping over workers punching holes in the walls for the new cable lines. Then he located the paralegal's file. After glancing at it for a moment, he chuckled.

"What the heck. How hard could this little closing be? After all—have to keep the clients happy. So I might as well hand-hold this one myself."

At the end of the day I got a call back from the obviously pleased receptionist, who gushed that "attorney Lloyd Gentry himself will be handling your matter tomorrow, Mr. Hastings."

I was more than a little surprised. An immense sense of relief, followed by well-being, washed over me. I was getting The Man himself. The fabled king of real-estate law. What looked like a disaster in the making had suddenly turned full circle—into a triumph. No more *Titanic*. The lifeboat drill was canceled. Back to the glittering ballroom for dinner and dancing.

I was so pleased by the news that I hardly heard the receptionist say that Gentry saw no need to speak with me beforehand—instead, he would simply meet me at the real-estate agent's office the next day.

When Lloyd Gentry arrived I could instantly see I was in good hands. He nonchalantly noted to the real-estate agent that he had "parked the Porsche in the back lot—that does belong to your office here, doesn't it? I'm okay parking there?"

Smooth.

He was wearing a well-tailored suit with a shimmering silk sport shirt underneath. He apologized for his "informality," but he said he had a "tennis match at two with some old friends at the club."

"A little cold for tennis," I remarked.

"The club has an extensive indoor facility," he commented with a smile. Then he introduced himself to me.

"You must be Mr. Hastings," he said with a warm, in-control voice that let me know everything would be just fine.

The agent and her young closing attorney shook hands with Gentry, effusively greeting him in a way that showed the humble admiration expressed by those of a lower caste.

We were all seated, and the paper-clipped packets of papers and documents were passed around and explained. No one from the art foundation was there. I asked if that was unusual. I was assured it was not. The representatives from the foundation had already presigned their documents. Everyone was smiling. The only sound in the room was the scratching of the tip of my ballpoint on reams of documents as I signed my name over and over.

When it was all done, the agent rose and shook my hand vigorously.

"Congratulations," she said enthusiastically.

"Thank you."

"Well, you are now the proud owner of the old Tornquist Universalist Church property," she added.

I wasn't sure what that meant. But I figured it was good. So I smiled. As I was escorted out I looked to Gentry for some info on the point.

"Tornquist?" I asked him.

As we made our way to the parking lot, he curtly explained.

"Yes. G. Dudley Tornquist. Architect. He's the one who designed the church."

There was something in Gentry's face—an expression I found somewhat baffling and a little disturbing. As if he had just heard information he wished he hadn't heard but was trying to maintain his composure.

I was about to leave for the closing at Tony DeVoe's, but I thought I would ask just one question.

"Mr. Gentry, I know I never talked to anyone at your office about this second deal…"

"What are you talking about?"

"I have a closing I'm going to, right now, on this same property."

He didn't say a word—just looked at me.

"You see, I'm selling off this same property, this…Tornquist church or whatever it is…to a construction company in a few minutes. I know this is short notice, but could you check over the papers for me? I have them right here."

I handed the papers to Gentry, who took them with reluctance. Gentry scanned them with little interest at first, but when he came to the page with the special condition I had agreed to with Tony DeVoe and VM Contractors, he let go of the paper, touching only the bottom edge of the packet with his fingertips—as if it had been laced with anthrax.

"This is your signature?" he asked.

"Sure. Is there a problem?"

"Page two of this agreement—bold letters—you saw that part before you signed?"

"You mean where it says that I warrant and guarantee they can tear the church down and construct a parking garage?"

The lawyer nodded the way a doctor does when the patient

finally understands he's getting a really bad prognosis and it's starting to sink in.

"Well, yeah, but my uncle—a real-estate agent—says it's zoned for business purposes, including parking structures. So what's the problem?"

As Gentry handed me back the papers he took a step away.

"I am not talking about zoning, Mr. Hastings," he said. "I'm talking about something called 'landmarking.' If a building has been landmarked, you can't tear it down—generally speaking. At least without permission of the Commission...have you bothered to check with City Hall on this property?"

Now I was the one shaking my head and finally getting the drift of the bad prognosis. Gentry kept on talking.

"This agreement you just showed me—*just showed to me for the very first time here where we're standing*—you never disclosed this to any of the staff of my law firm previously, did you, Mr. Hastings? You never told us you expected to be able to raze the Tornquist church building, isn't that correct?"

At that point in my life I was no expert in the law, but I certainly knew a cross-examination question when I heard one. And there was an ugly tone to the attorney's voice.

"Not exactly. But then," and with this I summoned some rebuttal gravitas of my own, "neither you *nor any of your staff* ever bothered to ask what I proposed to do with the property after I bought it. And furthermore, no lawyer even bothered to meet with me until you breezed in here a few seconds before the closing. And no one, certainly not you, told me anything about 'landmarking.' So, Mr. Gentry, tell me straight—is there something for me to be worrying about?"

By now Gentry was next to his sleek red Porsche, and he *bleep-bleeped* the door open with his key remote. He turned to face me one last time.

"Given the context of this conversation...and the new facts you have just revealed to me as your lawyer...I feel it would be inadvisable, indeed probably a direct conflict of interest, for me to represent you any further."

Then he crawled into his sports car and closed the door. He lowered the electric window just enough for him to shoot out one last admonition.

"But I'll give you one last piece of advice, Mr. Hastings—you go to that closing this afternoon and lead your buyer into believing they can demolish that church and build a parking garage there... without getting some additional independent legal advice...well, let's just say this—you could be in for a legal nightmare from which there is little chance of escape."

With that, Lloyd Gentry put his ferocious-sounding vehicle into gear and powered quickly out of the parking lot.

I stood there, utterly alone, with my closing papers in my hand. I glanced at my watch. Twenty-five minutes until the meeting with Tony DeVoe.

TEN

~

I FRANTICALLY TRIED TO GET AHOLD of Uncle Mort. I called his home, but all I got was a busy signal. I glanced at my watch again. Now I was fifteen minutes away from the closing with DeVoe.

I climbed into my Jetta, still redialing Mort's number as I wheeled out of the lot. Then Mort finally picked up.

In a burst of information overload, I yelled into my phone everything Lloyd Gentry had told me. About the property being connected with some semifamous architect named Tornquist. About the possibility of the church being landmarked. And if it was, the fact that no one had contacted City Hall to find out whether the proper agency would permit demolition of the building and construction of a parking garage in its place.

I could hear the concern in Mort's voice. He put the phone down and scrambled to another room looking for his copy of the Chicago zoning code.

He returned to the telephone a little breathless. "Okay. Like I told you from the beginning, the area where the church is located is zoned for business...including commercial parking..."

"But that's not the issue," I yelled. "Gentry says that land-marking regulation takes precedence. You have to get permission before you do anything. How do we find out if it's been designated a landmark?"

"You know," Mort muttered ruefully, "my copy of the code is a little bit dated...and I don't have anything in here about land-marking. I mean, I know generally what happens...but—"

"Is there any way I can find out?"

"Listen, let me call over to the zoning office, okay?" he suggested. "Then I'll call you back...just keep circling around the block until you hear from me."

I drove toward DeVoe's office. It was 2:45 PM. Fifteen minutes before the closing. Miraculously, a car swung out of a parking spot and I quickly pulled in.

I drummed my fingers on the steering wheel. "Come on, Mort—come on..." I was forcing the words through clenched teeth.

One ray of hope appeared. Maybe all of this would be moot after all. Perhaps Mort would find out that the church property had not been declared a landmark. I would be home clear. If it took a few extra minutes to verify that, it would be worth it. Even worth all the Neanderthal rage I would catch from DeVoe for being late.

My cell phone rang. I clicked it on with the speed of light.

"Kevin?"

"Yeah," I said breathlessly.

"Mort here."

"Yeah. Right. Okay," I sputtered at my uncle's apparent inability to appreciate my emergency. "So tell me quick. What'd you find out?"

"You won't believe it."

"At this point I bet I will," I shot back.

"I got connected to the Commission...that's what they call it over there at City Hall—"

"Mort!"

"Yeah?"

"Give me the bottom line. Please. I'm in a hurry."

"Well," he said with a sigh. "It was declared a landmark all right. Couple of years ago. Under the ownership of the art foundation. They probably figured it to be a perk to have the city landmark them."

"Where does that leave me?" I pleaded.

"Did the agent for the art foundation…the seller…did they ever disclose all of this to you?"

"Absolutely not!"

"And Lloyd Gentry—did he ever talk to you about the land-marking issue *before* the closing today?"

"Not at all. The first time I met him was today, five minutes before the appointment. And the landmarking stuff only came up as we talked in the parking lot *after* I had just bought the property."

"Wow—what a mess," Mort said candidly.

"What am I going to do?"

There was a pause.

"You have to get ahold of that DeVoe guy and tell him what you just found out."

"And what if he insists on our going through with the closing today with all the same terms—my guaranteeing they can demolish the building and build some huge parking structure?"

"Gentry's right on that score," Mort said reluctantly. "You can't afford to do that. You'd be signing yourself up for a one-way ticket to a legal catastrophe."

"So?" I said, straining for some closure.

"Look, buy some time. Tell DeVoe you'll apply to get the land-marking restriction lifted. That sort of thing. You'll petition the Commission for permission to tear down the church. Plead hardship. Tell him you'll need to put off the closing for a week or two… maybe even longer."

"Longer?" I shouted. "You're the guy who warned me that these are *not nice people*. That's what you told me, Mort. You think they'll just sit around twiddling their thumbs while I spend weeks pleading my case over at City Hall?"

"I'm sorry about all this," he said with sincere sadness. "Mean-while, I'll try to get you the name of another lawyer. Someone you can talk to about all of this…now that Gentry says he would have a conflict of interest helping you any further."

I knew my uncle was trying to be helpful. But I was sinking into a quagmire, deeper and deeper by the minute. Like someone up to his chest in quicksand, I had the distinct feeling that whichever way I turned, any movement, the least thrashing, would just send me down further. If I told DeVoe the truth, I had every reason to believe he and his sinister "undisclosed principal" would wreak immediate retribution—perhaps legally, or even worse, illegally. I had no love for the idea of being sued for breach of contract. But being stuffed into a car's trunk was something that offered even fewer appeal rights.

Nor could I simply waltz into the closing and sign away the property under the fraudulent misrepresentation that DeVoe's client could immediately convert the site into a massive parking garage. I knew too much by then to claim simple ignorance. I had eaten from the forbidden tree, and my eyes had been opened. Like the original pair in Eden, my knowledge had been bought at a bitter price, and it all might end up getting me a one-way ticket to a landfill.

I thanked Mort for everything and begged him to go ahead and find another lawyer I could consult about my desperate plight.

Then I fished around in my papers for Tony DeVoe's telephone number. From where I was parked, I could see the front window of his law office sandwiched in between retail stores and eateries. It seemed a lot better for me try to work my way out of this remotely, so I dialed the number.

"Law office," the receptionist said in a monotone.

After I asked for DeVoe, there was only a momentary silence. Then the attorney answered.

"Why are you calling me on the phone?" he said sharply. "We've got a closing in three minutes."

"I know. It's just that—there's somewhat of a…we've got a slight problem."

"Wrong," he shot back. "*You've* got a *big* problem. Problem number one—you call me on the telephone when you should be in my office right now with your ballpoint in your sweaty little hand, ready to sign. And problem number two—is you trying to say *we've* got a problem. 'Cause it's not *our* problem at all. Whatever you think the issue is, it's totally and absolutely *yours*. But the fact you're trying to weasel me at the last minute like this tells me you have a lack of respect. For me. And for my client. And that is not a good thing, Mr. Hastings."

"I'm just trying to be straight with you," I replied. Then I launched into the business about the church being an official landmark. That I couldn't convey the property now with the assurance a parking garage could be built there—at least not until I petitioned the City of Chicago to grant some kind of waiver. And that would take time for me to hire a lawyer and file the necessary papers.

Then I suddenly had a burst of imaginative problem-solving.

"On the other hand, if you and your client would be willing to take title to the property with the knowledge of this landmarking problem, and if you—being a lawyer—would like to then petition the city for the appropriate exemption…"

There was a pause at the other end. Then DeVoe started speaking.

"You know how old my mother is?"

"I would have no idea—"

"She's eighty-five."

If he was waiting for me to figure out the connection of his last comment to our discussion, he was going to wait a long time. But apparently he was not going to wait.

"And the fact is," he said, "on the day I throw my mother—who I love with all my heart—out of the window of a ten-story building…that's the day I will accept your chicken-neck, scum-sucking offer, you little punk."

DeVoe had just filled in the connection for me.

"So get in this office right now and sign that deed. And then you just better make sure the city lets us build our parking garage. Just like you promised already. In writing. And after what you told me, I'm holding your cashier's check until you actually get that approval from City Hall."

"Well, my agreement to convey was signed before I knew the property was a landmark," I shot back. "And just for the record," I continued, trying to flex some muscle of my own, "you're the lawyer. I'm not. Maybe you should have figured out that the church building might be landmarked, huh? Maybe *you're* the one who blew it..."

The words had come flying out before I could screen them. You know, to make sure they didn't get confused with something else, like "I have an immediate death wish."

DeVoe was self-detonating. "Where are you?" he snarled. "Right this minute, punk—where is your car?"

I was silent, not moving a muscle. My engine was off. I waited.

"You're right outside, aren't you?" he said in a kind of sick sneering tone.

Grabbing for the key in the ignition I tried to start the car. But no go. Then I saw I had the stick in gear. I fumbled it into neutral.

Out front I saw a squat, thick-shouldered man in a sport coat— that had to be Troy Armstrong—rushing onto the sidewalk and looking around. Then he pointed right at my car. DeVoe, tinted glasses, and wearing a dark suit, ran out right after him. The two of them started trotting toward me.

Turning the ignition again, this time I heard the engine kick in. I slammed it into gear and wheeled out into the street. Armstrong came barreling out at me from between two parked cars, grabbing at the passenger door handle.

I swung violently into the other lane to avoid him and then gunned my little Jetta straight ahead.

As I looked in the rearview mirror I could see both men standing there, unmoving, in the middle of the street—like two dark-granite obelisks. Staring after me.

Eleven

~

Tossing and turning that night, I repeatedly returned to my bizarre interaction with DeVoe earlier that day.

What kept rolling around in my brain was this—why did the whole thing end up like a bad TV cop show, with tough-guy threats and a car chase? I couldn't shake the feeling that before the credits ran on this episode there was going to be bloodletting...with some hard-boiled Chicago detective holding a notepad and gazing down at a chalk outline on the sidewalk.

But then, just as quick, I would tell myself I was letting my imagination get the best of me. Granted, this was a deal that was going sour...but that was a far cry from a dispute where someone was going to get hurt.

Get serious, I would reassure myself. *This isn't the range wars in the Old West. People don't get shot over land any more.*

Then, however, I would think back to Mort's vague but ominous characterization of the people I was dealing with. I knew little about organized crime in Chicago and had labored under the misconception it had somehow moved out of town. My uncle's comment had let me know how naïve I was.

My mind would start wandering to the landmarking issue. I had figured it might help if I knew something about this architect who designed the church. So before I'd gone to bed, I'd checked up on G. Dudley Tornquist on the Internet and printed off a couple of articles about him.

Finally, around three I think, I drifted off.

~

I jerked awake when the phone rang. It was Tom Taylor. He and I had been in high school and college together. Which should have made us permanently close friends. He was married, still living in the Chicago area, and worked at an advertising firm.

But over the last year I had been an absentee friend. My relationship with Charlotte had had me spending almost all of my nonworking hours with her. And the few times Tom and Liz, his wife, had gone out to dinner with Charlotte and me, Charlotte hadn't hesitated to tell me she didn't like Liz. I think Tom had caught on.

He'd sarcastically told me that even though he was married he still had "time for his friends." Anyway, the sole exception to my absence was our occasional Saturday morning at eleven, when he and I would meet some other not-young-not-old business types for pickup basketball at the suburban Y.

In the middle of the twists and turns of my life that week, I had completely forgotten about our game.

"Dude, what's the deal?" Tom yelled. "We're all down here, suited up and ready to sweat. When are you gonna get here?"

"Actually," I said groggily, "I'm still in bed."

"You sick or something?"

"Not sick. But maybe you're right about the 'or something.'"

"We're kinda stuck here, Kevin—one side's gonna have only four players if you don't hustle up."

"I think I'm going to pass on b-ball today," I said. "Things are just...sort of strange for me right now, that's all. I don't want to go into it."

Tom was silent for a few seconds. I could hear the dribbling of basketballs in the background.

"Is this about Charlotte?" he said. "A few weeks ago you said things were falling apart with her. All right. So life goes on. But I can't even get you to call me back during the week. And now you won't come down here to the temple of grunt and groan for some hoops with the gang. You just want to hole up in your cruddy little apartment."

"Hey—there's nothing cruddy about where I live."

"You know what? I think you're pulling a Howard Hughes with me," he said sarcastically. "Next thing you know you'll be barricading yourself in your room, growing a beard, and watching reruns of *Ice Station Zebra* while you obsess about germs—"

"Okay. Knock it off." I wasn't in the mood for Tom's too-clever humor. And I wasn't about to go into the ugly details of my now failing venture into real-estate speculation.

"Fine," he said, finally relenting. "We'll play anyway...down one player, that's all. When you want to come down from the mother ship and join the earthlings, let me know."

I thought about staying in bed, but Tom had riled me sufficiently so I couldn't. I dragged myself into the kitchen and went through the cupboards. They were empty except for one cereal box with some tasteless flakes still lingering at the bottom. I swung open the refrigerator and found I had no milk. In fact, it was completely empty, except for a jar of sweet gherkin pickles, a container of ketchup, and two bottles of beer. I seriously considered having an all-alcohol breakfast. But the beer had been Charlotte's brand, so I passed on that.

In the maelstrom of my life, I had forgotten a simple thing like grocery shopping. All I wanted was a quick breakfast. I threw on some jeans and a sweatshirt, and without bothering to shave, I trudged down to the parking garage. A place called Dan's Diner was just about five minutes from my apartment. I hadn't ever eaten there, but it looked like the kind of place that served breakfast all day long. I decided to bring with me the articles from the Internet I had printed off the night before.

Dan's was crowded, the tables and booths all taken, but I got a stool at the counter. I ordered some coffee, fried eggs over medium, and bacon. As I waited, I started diving into the research I'd dug up about Tornquist. Then my cell phone rang. It was Mort.

"How did things go yesterday with DeVoe?"

"I decided not to go through with it." I lowered my voice.

"Things got pretty ugly. I'll have to talk to you more about that later."

"Sorry—you are in a bind," he said sympathetically.

"So I'm sitting here at a restaurant getting some breakfast. And reading up about this G. Dudley Tornquist," I said in a normal tone again. "You know, the architect who designed the place. Trying to figure out what the big deal is about the guy."

"Well, call me later," Mort said.

As I turned back to my papers, I noticed that the person sitting next to me—a woman about my age—was staring at me.

She had brown hair tied into pigtails. Big brown eyes. Her black nylon team jacket had the white embroidered letters "SFLAP," and her pink T-shirt said "Beautify Your Space." Cute.

I was trying to think up something to say, but she beat me to the punch.

"The big deal about Tornquist," she said seriously, "was that he was opposed to expanding the Chicago School's skyscraper sky-line—the post-Sullivan steel-and-glass monoliths everybody has in mind when they talk about Chicago's Loop. He envisioned a different kind of architecture. But he never got the recognition. Everybody was taken up with either Frank Lloyd Wright or the skyscraper boys—you know, Bruce Graham, Mies van der Rohe, those guys…"

"Wow," I said. "That's really interesting. You sound like an architect."

"Not really," she said, finishing up her bowl of oatmeal and strawberries. "Urban-planning degree. And art school."

"Art school?" I said. Thinking back to Charlotte's love for the big-canvas chaos of Jackson Pollock, I asked, "So, you probably like modern, abstract style?"

"Why would you assume that?" she said, with some sharpness to her reply.

"Oh, just a guess," I said, struggling to keep the conversation alive.

It didn't work. She slapped some money down on the counter, waved warmly to the waitress, and started toward the door.

"Actually," she said, tossing a remark casually back to me, "Vermeer is my favorite. I love his work." Then she nodded at me and disappeared into the street.

Vermeer. Very interesting. Seventeenth-century Dutch master. A mysterious, luminous quality to his scenes of intimate, ordinary life. But with an element of loneliness in the figures. Much more to my taste as a history professor.

I wonder who she is.

"Two eggs over medium, bacon?"

I looked up at the waitress holding my plate of food over the counter, poised to set it down as soon as I cleared a space.

I resisted the temptation to ask the waitress about the architectural expert. Instead I dove into my breakfast and began reading up on G. Dudley Tornquist, happy for the brief little interaction and for human conversation—any at all—that took me, momentarily, away from my situation with Tony DeVoe.

TWELVE

~

IT'S REALLY AMAZING HOW HISTORIANS can write volumes upon volumes about disasters, wars, tortures, human atrocities, treachery of all kinds—and yet, at the same time, studiously avoid ever mentioning the word *evil*. I have a theory about that. Most historians pride themselves in not only discovering the factual contexts of great people and great events, but also in talking about the underlying meaning of the broad sweep of history. At the same time, though, they usually try to avoid the appearance of imposing their own personal, moral judgments.

That's not to say they wouldn't all agree that Hitler or Stalin— even serial killers like John Wayne Gacy—were all bad people. They would. It's just that there's this feeling that making absolute moral statements about things makes you less credible—less scholarly.

But this is what I say—I say those historians ought to experience what happened to me after I left Dan's Diner that day. And *then* let's talk about evil.

On the way back to my apartment I was stopped at a light, gazing off in the distance and not really thinking about anything in particular.

I hadn't noticed the van in back of me with three men in it. Nor did I notice when two of them got out and strode in my direction—big guys wearing gloves and dressed in dark, baggy workout suits, baseball caps, and, except for one, dark glasses.

Only when one of them swung my car door open did I realize they were there. The other one reached in swiftly, tapped my

64

seat-belt release, then yanked me out by my sweatshirt. It was clear they had the routine down.

"Hey, what are you doing?" I yelled and shoved him back a few inches.

The other guy pulled out a revolver and stuck the barrel in my mouth.

"One more word and I leave your brains on the street," he grunted, then pulled the gun out as one of the others jumped in my car and put it in gear.

While I still had the taste of cold steel in my mouth, the third guy swung hard into my stomach. As I doubled over he brought his knee up square under my chin so hard that my teeth chattered together like a marionette's. I blacked out and collapsed to the pavement.

When I came to, EMTs were bending over checking me out. They put me on a gurney and slid me into the ambulance. After several X-rays at the hospital, I was told there were no fractures—just a mild concussion and some neck strain. My gut was still aching, but they said there didn't seem to be any major damage.

The emergency doctor wanted me to stay overnight for observation, but I refused. Somehow, the idea of staying in the hospital made me feel more vulnerable—not more secure. I had to sign a paper saying I was being discharged "against medical advice."

I caught a cab to the nearest precinct station to make out a carjacking and criminal battery complaint.

But I stopped short at one question the desk sergeant asked me.

"Can you name anyone who would have reason to hurt or harass you, or to deprive you of your property?"

"Say again?" I asked, trying to collect my thoughts.

The officer repeated the same question verbatim.

I didn't answer.

"Mr. Hastings, it's a simple question. Do you understand it?"

"Of course," I replied.

"Is there some reason why you're hesitating?"

"Not…really…"

"Is there something you want to tell us? This is a criminal incident. You came in here to report a crime. You have to play ball with us if we're going to have a chance to catch the perpetrators."

"All I want is to get my car back."

"Your car?" the officer said with a look camouflaging a smile. "We get a huge number of auto-theft complaints every day. Only a small percentage of stolen cars are recovered. I'm just trying to play straight with you, Mr. Hastings."

"I just want my car…"

The officer nodded wearily, tossed the file to the side of the desk, and said they would be in touch if they got any leads.

I went home by taxi and limped into the garage to take the elevator. To add insult to injury, as I walked toward my parking space I saw someone else had parked their car there.

Then I stopped. My mouth dropped open.

It was my VW Jetta—but with the windows smashed and the doors bashed in. On the driver's side there was a spray-painted message in white:

DON'T BE STUPID

Not only did I understand who the message was from and what it meant…I also understood the hidden text.

That next time, I wouldn't be so lucky.

THIRTEEN

~

WITH A JAW THAT HAD SWOLLEN UP, and whiplash in my neck and back, I lay low on Sunday. I finally got around to calling my uncle and filling him in on everything—including yesterday's developments.

Then Mort gave me the rest of the picture. It wasn't pretty. When he'd finally been able to connect with his friend at the *Tribune* and had mentioned VM Contractors, the guy had gotten right to the point.

"Oh," he'd told Mort, "that's Vito Mangiorno's company. No doubt about it."

"Vito Mangiorno?" I asked.

"Yeah. A mob boss in the region. Sorry about the bad news."

Somehow "sorry" just didn't cut it. He just wasn't getting how bad this was becoming.

"I've been attacked, Mort," I yelled, setting off a spasm of pain in my jaw. "And my car's been kicked in like a tin can. And these guys expect me to make good on my guarantee on the demolition of that church and their parking-structure plan. And they expect it like right now. That was the message in their little welcome-wagon greeting yesterday. Now...don't these guys know all of that is impossible?"

"Not really impossible..."

"Oh?"

"No. It's not over till it's over..."

"Look," I replied. "They punched me in the guts and did a tap dance on my face. Seems to me I'm getting pretty close to the 'it's over' part."

"I've got the name of a lawyer," Mort said.

"No offense, but we didn't do too good with the last lawyer you recommended."

"This guy is different. Name is Jack Thomas. He used to handle practically all of my real-estate closings. He'll give you the straight scoop, I promise. He's no La Salle Street high roller like Gentry, but he's honest, and he knows what he's talking about."

The following day I called his office first thing. His assistant said he had an opening midweek. I said that wouldn't do, that I had an emergency. Then I told her who'd sent me. Upshot was, Jack Thomas could meet me that day, late afternoon.

I hesitated before deciding to take my beat-up car. But I had to get some help. I crouched low as I drove to the attorney's office, though I figured nobody would recognize the car in the condition it was in. Or me in the condition I was in. Funny thing about pain—it really gets your attention.

Jack Thomas was a no-frills, straightforward lawyer, like Mort had indicated. After he assured me of strict confidentiality I spilled my story, every jot and tittle.

Afterward, he glanced at his notes for a minute or two, looked me over, and then asked me what I wanted to accomplish. What I wanted, I explained, was some way out of this mess with the least damage possible. Either Mangiorno had to be convinced to back off on his right to purchase the property for his intended purposes—or else I needed some kind of fast track into City Hall to get quick approval for demolition of the church so I could conclude the sale.

"All that is going to cost you plenty in legal fees," Thomas said.

"Great," I muttered.

"Mr. Hastings, please understand. What I am going to propose to you has nothing to do with me. I'm not your man. I do property work and real-estate closings. Title searches. That kind of thing. What you need is a litigator. Somebody who is going to bare-knuckle box for you until things get turned around."

I asked him to explain. He replied that an immediate legal attack had to be mounted with the Commission on Chicago Landmarks to lift the restrictions on the church.

"You have to realize," he continued, "that few of these requests ever get granted now. Primarily due to political pressure from preservationist groups."

"Well, do you have anything to propose?" I asked almost hopelessly.

"Your only chance is to do as follows," he replied. First, he said, a petition had to be filed with the commission. It had to look rock-solid enough to satisfy DeVoe and his client that approval for demolition was practically a foregone conclusion...however doubtful the result might actually be.

Thomas also said I probably had a valid claim against the real-estate agent, and possibly the art foundation, for fraud in not disclosing to me that the property was restricted by a landmark designation. I might be able to rescind my purchase and get my money back. That was a backup plan if the commission turned my petition down.

"And how am I going to pay for all of this?" I said woefully. "I've already told you I drained my savings and retirement to finance the purchase."

The attorney paused a second. "You have a pretty good case, I'd say, for professional malpractice against Lloyd Gentry and his firm for failing to advise you in advance of your purchase."

I was starting to calculate the casualties of the legal war Thomas was proposing.

"You see," he continued, "I think Gentry knew he blew it when he advised you of the landmarking possibility only after the closing. And when he told you in the parking lot he could no longer represent you, because of a 'conflict of interest,' he knew that conflict arose from the valid legal claim for malpractice you now have against him for his negligence, and that of his firm."

Something still didn't add up for me, though.

"How would a lawsuit against Gentry help me finance everything else?" I asked.

"Ordinarily, it might not. Except for this one lawyer I have in mind. I've known him to take on multiple cases for the same client as long as he is guaranteed a really high fee percentage of one really good tort lawsuit. In other words, he gives you several licks at several cats as long as he comes away with all the cats, the stick, and the shirt you're wearing when you swing the stick. Does that make sense?"

"Okay—who is this guy?"

Thomas opened the center drawer of his desk slightly and pulled out an old-fashioned wooden business-card box, from which he carefully removed one of the cards. It was almost a ceremony—done with the same care you'd imagine the president would use when he handles the black box with the red nuclear button inside.

I reached for the card, but the attorney held up his hand.

"Now, Mr. Hastings—you'll have to copy this information down. I need to keep the card—it's the only card I have for this lawyer. He's not listed in any phone books I know of. He has a...special practice."

"Special?"

"Yes. Hard to describe."

He took a minute to mull it over.

"Let's put it this way," he concluded. "If this attorney were a country—"

"A country?"

"Right. A country. If he were a country, then he would be Iraq."

"And why do you say that?" I was getting a nauseated feeling.

"Because he is sort of like a weapon of mass destruction. From a legal standpoint, I mean."

I wrote down the information on the card, which read:

HORACE FIN
Attorney and Litigationist

Thomas carefully placed the card back in the box and closed his drawer. Then he folded his hands on the desktop.

"Good luck, Mr. Hastings."

There was something in the way he said that—the tone of voice, or perhaps it was the slightly sympathetic look he gave me.

It was as if he was trying to be cordial while sending me off on a reconnaissance mission from which I might not return—a mission to seek out nuclear devices that might well detonate on me...all the while thinking, *Poor guy, but I'm glad it's him and not me.*

FOURTEEN

~

DRIVING DOWN WEST DIVISION STREET past warehouses and truck bays, I wondered whether I had written down the wrong address for attorney Horace Fin. I checked my note again. No, I was heading in the right direction.

After turning down a narrow, grimy industrial lane I found the address and pulled in. Fin's office was located in a low brown-brick building with a loading dock to the side. The gold letters in which his name appeared made an odd contrast. The whole place looked like it had been a shipping and receiving warehouse at one time.

I had called first thing that morning for an appointment. The receptionist answered, "Good day, office of Horace Fin," in a thick Slavic accent. I had told her it was urgent I talk to Mr. Fin as soon as possible.

"What is your business—legal matter or shipping of goods?"

"Well...it's a legal matter."

"Very good. Mr. Fin will see you today. 2:00 PM. Thirty minutes for conference. First thirty minutes, $100. Cash or check. Payable in advance when you arrive at office. We don't take Visa or MasterCard or American Express."

That had struck me as a little unorthodox. But things were about to get even quirkier.

When I entered the building there was no lobby to speak of. Instead, there was a large open room with a tiled floor and several old metal desks in the middle. A woman was parked at each desk, and each was talking on the phone. Each had an electric typewriter on her desk. But there were no computers anywhere. And the entire room was ringed with rows of metal filing cabinets of various colors and shapes, none of them seeming to match.

Not finding anywhere to sit, I introduced myself to the woman at the desk closest to the front door.

"Hello," she replied in the thick accent I'd heard on the phone, "I am Karin Kzatkorinsky. You can call me Miss Kat. You have the one hundred dollars?"

I nodded and handed it to her. She put it in a metal filing box.

"Mr. Horace Fin will see you."

"Where is he?"

She motioned to the back corner, where I saw a large greenish bubble-glass window and an old-fashioned glass office door. I worked my way back to it, and knocked. I could see the shape of a person on the other side.

"It's unlocked."

I swung the door open. A large man with his back to me was hunched over a desk against the wall, with another massive wooden desk at his back. He swung around in his chair and scooted up to the other desk, which faced me.

Horace Fin looked to be in his late fifties. His head was bald at the top—his long wispy hair hung to his collar. He was wearing a crumpled white shirt, suspenders, and a wide brown tie with orange and yellow triangles.

The attorney snatched a cigar from the box on his desk, lit it, and in between putrid puffs, gave me a monologue.

"Kevin Hastings. History professor. Man in trouble. Real-estate deal goes south. Why? It would appear that Vito Mangiorno—through his corporate alter ego, VM Contractors—the man we may describe as the author of your present unpleasantness, now seeks to enforce the terms of your contract to sell him a certain property—the Tornquist church building to be precise—so that he can demolish it and raise up one of those concrete monuments to our modern mobile culture. That is to say, a multilevel parking garage. Why a parking garage? Well, let us just say I have my own theories on that...but, I digress.

"So, what is the problem? Well, it seems that the Landmark Commission has designated said church as protected and sacrosanct...The Mangiorno organization, in the person of their retained counsel, Tony DeVoe, has a core meltdown when you disclose this to them after you have purchased the property but before you transfer it to them for the agreed-upon price. Your closing with Mangiorno fizzles, DeVoe has an unhappy client, and you get mysteriously worked over and carjacked the next day by hoodlums who—oddly—return your vehicle to the proper parking spot. Badly in need of bodywork, of course, but the message is clear—they know where you live, and next time things will get much nastier. Is that about right?"

"How...how do you know all this already?" I stammered. Then a light went on. "Did you talk to Jack Thomas about me?"

A wide smile broke over Fin's face.

"I thought everything I told Thomas was to be in strict confidence."

"I guess you can't trust anybody these days," he quipped.

While I was struggling to figure out this lawyer in a wrinkled shirt with a necktie from the Truman era, he continued.

"Actually, no problem, really—when you called to make the appointment, you said Thomas referred you. When an attorney refers somebody to me, I always call him or her for the bottom line. You know, get the inside goods on the client...just in case he's squirrely or something...confidentiality doesn't exist between two attorneys who both have represented a client...well, at least most of the time...point is, I wanted to find out all the dirt on you before you came in here."

"Nice," I grumbled.

"Oh, don't be offended. If you think I'm hard on *my* clients, you ought to see what I do to my opponents and *their* clients." Fin folded his hands over his expansive midriff. "So, do you have any questions for me?"

"Well, all kinds, actually..." I fished through my papers. "Here's one for starters, though—your card says you are an attorney. I understand that...but it also calls you a 'litigationist.' Don't you mean you're a 'litigator'?—someone who litigates cases in court? Tries cases—like a trial lawyer?"

"No, not true," Fin said, blowing smoke rings. "Trial lawyers drag you through a trial. Bad for you, and bad for everybody. I consider it a badge of dishonor to have to go to trial…Mind you, I've gone to trial—plenty of times. Whooped the big boys downtown. The penthouse $700-per-hour guys who arrive at court in chauffeured limos—but see, I am an expert in making sure cases never get to trial. The other side gets to a point where they whimper and beg for me to settle with them before that."

"And exactly how do you do that?"

"You want me to spill all of my trade secrets?" he bellowed with a laugh, which made him begin coughing.

"At least you can tell me your overall strategy for my case."

"You want my strategy?"

"Sure."

"Okay. Here it is. I sue the Landmark Commission so they grant you—that is to say, Mangiorno, your buyer—the right to build that parking structure…that way you can get your money from Mongiorno. Meanwhile I sue the real-estate agent and the art foundation for fraudulently failing to disclose the landmarking to you in advance. I also sue Lloyd Gentry and his firm for malpractice for failing to give you decent advice prior to your closing, and because I think you've got a good case there, I'm willing to take on all of the legal matters for you as long as I get what's coming to me from the case against Gentry."

"What kind of fee would that be?" I asked hesitantly.

"Forty percent of whatever we recover or $450 per hour, whichever is greater—together with associated costs and expenses and incidental fees…"

"What kind of incidental fees?"

"It's all right here," he said as he tossed a massively thick document on the desk. It looked at least sixty or seventy pages long.

"Don't worry," he said with a smile, "it's written in big print. Won't take you that long to go through it."

"Can I take it home to study it?" I said.

"Nope," Fin said casually. "But you're free to read it out in the lobby."

"There's nowhere to sit," I protested.

"So you can stand. Good for the circulation anyway."

I stood up. "And what about DeVoe and Vito Mangiorno? What are we doing about them?"

"Not to worry," Fin said reassuringly. "Leave them to me. I'll have them purring like kitty cats. They'll be more than happy to wait while we get the landmark issue untangled. You'll see. I'll call DeVoe right away."

I took the document. Its cover read, "Contract for Attorney's Services: Caution—Read Carefully." It was as thick as a small book.

"So before you go out into the lobby to look it over—and be sure you sign it before you leave—I've got a question for you," Fin said.

"Sure, what is it?"

"How do you feel knowing that Lloyd Gentry, a guy who drives a Porsche and makes a couple of million a year easy, didn't even meet with you until the day of the closing—and then just stands by and watches as you get helplessly thrown to the man-eating lions—by that I mean DeVoe and company—how does that hit you?"

"Well, I have to say it does make me angry—you know, upset—"

"I bet," Fin said with a serious look on his broad face. "Now, you know what I think? I think *Lloyd Gentry is a selfish, incompetent human being whose favorite color is green…just walking around and not caring whether he is crushing the little guy or not.* Wouldn't you agree?"

I took a few seconds to consider Fin's unusual expressions before I responded.

"I suppose I would…"

"Hey, you don't sound very convincing. You want to win this case or not?"

"Yes, I do."

"Well?"

"Well, absolutely—yes, I agree with what you said about Lloyd Gentry."

"Everything I just said?"

"Sure," I answered.

"That's better," Fin said with a smile. "And what you think about what Gentry did to you, you're not afraid to testify to that, right?"

"Not a bit."

"In fact, you don't care if the whole world finds out what you think of Gentry, right?"

"No, I don't. I'm not afraid of telling the whole world if need be."

"Great." The lawyer smiled more broadly. "Now, you get along. I've got things to do. We're marching to war, Mr. Hastings. Nice last name, by the way. You know all about that battle, I suppose, being a history professor?"

"Sure," I replied. "October 14, 1066. Battle of Hastings. William the Conqueror leads the Norman invasion, defeating the Anglo-Saxons. He took over the English throne and—"

"And he rewarded his supporters," Fin interjected, "by giving them grants of land, Mr. Hastings. Land. Property rights, Mr. Hastings. You see? So, I say that you and I are engaged in an ancient and noble conflict."

As I walked out to the area where the women were working at their metal desks and began studying the agreement, I must confess I was mildly impressed by Fin's grasp of history.

Instead, I should have been thinking about the way my new lawyer would soon be resembling the warlords of medieval England...complete with the use of devices of torture as a substitute for law.

FIFTEEN

~

THE FOLLOWING DAY I ARRIVED at my office at Essex and found another note taped to the door. It said Dr. Harvey Albright wanted to see me "immediately" following my lecture.

After my class I walked over to Albright's office, the largest one in the Humanities building. It had an impressive (though non-functioning) fireplace, leather furniture, and built-in bookshelves lined with books, including some of his leather-bound first editions.

He greeted me in the middle of the room with his usual air of stiff, official courtesy.

"Have a seat, Kevin," he said. "May I get you anything? Tea? Coffee?"

"Nothing, thanks," I replied as I sat in a slick brown-leather armchair near his mahogany desk.

"So…how are things going for you, Kevin?"

I wanted to tell him the awful truth. *My savings have all been drained in a vain pursuit of get-rich-quick real-estate speculation scheme. In a matter of weeks I will have to start making mortgage payments on a property, but because I couldn't go through with the sale to my buyers (I am in breach of my agreement for sale with them, by the way), I have no cash with which to make those payments, thus rushing me toward the dismal prospect of foreclosure. My girlfriend has left me for a Gold Coast broker. My car resembles something that went through a demolition derby. My jaw feels like I went ten rounds with a kick boxer. I've got a lawyer who proposes to solve my legal crisis but whose office looks like a front for some kind of illegal tele-marketing racket. And—oh, yes, I almost forgot—the mob is after me.*

"Fine, sir," I said instead, with a carefully manufactured sense of confidence. "I am doing just fine."

"Well, that is good, Kevin. That's good to hear."

Then Albright cleared his throat a little and got to the point.

"Kevin, I asked you to chat with me because, well, frankly, I am a little concerned about your effort here at Essex."

"Oh?"

"Well, yes. Just…concerned."

"Exactly what is the issue?"

"As I indicated, it's about your effort."

"Yes, but if you could specify…"

"You have been missing a number of classes…some of the students have been complaining."

I knew he was right. Between the meetings leading up to my purchase of the Tornquist property and my meetings with lawyers, I had skipped a number of lectures.

"Some personal matters," I said quietly. "They just came up…a one-time situation. Not likely to be repeated…"

"I certainly hope not…for everybody's sake."

"Sir?"

"It's just that, ever since you and I had our little talk together and I told you that you would have to exert some additional effort for a few more years before you would be entitled to tenure here at Essex—"

"Yes?"

"Well, since that time it has appeared your effort has been declining. Your commitment to the institution—".

"I'm not sure I understand."

"For instance, when you escorted Gladys Woolrick, our very special convocation speaker, to campus—"

"I picked her up on time. I delivered her to the college as required," I snapped, my voice showing an increasing agitation.

"She said, as a matter of fact, that your interaction with her was…somewhat unusual. I had the distinct impression she felt quite emotionally uncomfortable with the whole experience."

"I was supposed to be her chauffeur," I shot back, "not her therapist."

"No need to get confrontational, Kevin," Albright said. "Just some food for thought. For you to do some…personal and professional…reflection."

Then he stood up abruptly and walked over to my chair and reached out his hand. That was the signal, I had guessed, that his warning had been delivered, and now he had more important things to do.

We shook hands.

"I am very glad we have had this little chat, Kevin," Albright said and motioned me toward the door.

On the ride home I was doing that "reflection" Harvey Albright had talked about. I now knew that my job was precarious. But not hopeless. Unlike the rest of my life, I figured I could stay the course at Essex. I had always managed to do that. I would turn things around with Albright. I was confident of that.

But there was still this sinking feeling. That my last tether to the "mother ship," as Tom Taylor might call it…the world I had created for myself…the sole, remaining safety line, which was my teaching position…was showing signs of fraying. The strands were slowly pulling apart.

It was starting to get dark. I decided to drive by the Tornquist church property. I had the keys with me. I realized I had not walked through the building since I had bought it. Maybe it was because it had become the source of all my misery.

I parked outside, walked up to the front door, and unlocked it. I switched on the lights in the vestibule. I looked up. The interior swept up into a raftered steeple tower that reached a dizzying height. The streetlights from the outside sent some shimmering illumination through the colored glass panels in the walls. As cars passed by, their headlights swept through the stained-glass windows and then vanished into the dark.

For some reason, at that very moment, I felt the crushing

tonnage of my complete loneliness and isolation. I walked through the doors to what must have been the sanctuary of the church. When the art foundation took it over, they'd yanked up the pews and altar and replaced them with a series of wall dividers and panels that must have been used for art displays. But now it was all empty.

For some reason the pink T-shirt the pretty girl at Dan's Diner was wearing came to mind. "Beautify Your Space," it said.

What did that mean?

Maybe it meant that whatever space in the world you are given, you are responsible for it. Whether it's good or bad. Beautiful or ugly. That is your responsibility.

But as I stood there in that vacant building, listening to the distant rush of cars passing by outside, to the sound of people heading back to their homes, I knew one thing.

That my "space"...my life...had turned desperate and ugly. Exactly how things had turned that way so quickly I was not sure. But I was certain it was so.

What happened next is a little strange, really. Because there was nothing very spiritual, I didn't think, about the Tornquist property that night. But it was probably the depth of my personal entanglements and problems that motivated me.

I hadn't prayed since I was in fifth grade in the Methodist church Sunday school. But I decided I needed to hedge my bets. Horace Fin, as unlikely a character as he was, seemed to be my last hope. And he needed all the help he could get.

So, while I kept my eyes opened, I spoke out loud to the silence around me. As I did, I distinctly remember a certain embarrassing awkwardness about it. As if entering an unfamiliar house, and calling out, not knowing whether anyone was home.

As far as I can recall, it went something like this: *God...if you are out there...I would appreciate it if you would help Mr. Fin to get things taken care of with this property. And that he would win the case in the commission to get permission for demolition...and maybe it would be nice too to win the case against Gentry's firm so I could recover some money there too…it's not that I want to be greedy…I'm just looking for some way out of this mess…*

Then I turned, went back to the vestibule, clicked off the lights, and locked the doors behind me.

It wasn't until later I considered the irony of that prayer. That I was asking God to enable me to rip down a church so I could honor my agreement with a leading figure in Chicago organized crime.

But for the time being, I felt a little better about things. Just a little.

Until the morning I opened up the newspaper.

Sixteen
~

Not wanting to give more cannon fodder to my professional nemesis, Dr. Albright, I decided to get onto campus early every day thereafter. Whatever problems I was having in the legal arena, I wanted to keep them entirely separate from my professional life.

Two days after my meeting with Fin, I hurried out of my condo in the morning, figuring I would stop by Dan's Diner on the way to the campus. I had slotted thirty minutes for breakfast. The way the waitresses shuffled customers in and out, that seemed like plenty of time.

And of course, there was also an added reason for my stopping by the diner. Unfortunately, though, the woman in the jacket with the strange monogram who loved paintings by Vermeer wasn't anywhere around.

I ordered the same thing I'd had last time and picked up the *Sun-Times* another customer had left at the counter. I was onto page five of the paper when something grabbed my attention. I stared at the article in horror. I checked it twice to make sure I wasn't hallucinating.

The headline read, "Prestigious Gentry Firm Sued for Malpractice."

As my eyes quickly scanned down the page, I was to be even more horrified.

At one point it read,

In a statement released by the attorney for the plaintiff,

Kevin Hastings, a professor at Essex College, strikingly criticized Lloyd Gentry's handling of his real-estate deal. According to Horace Fin, Hastings' lawyer, his client contends that the well-known La Salle Street real-estate lawyer is "a selfish, incompetent human being," and further notes that "his favorite color is green." Hastings states that Gentry and his law firm are known for "not caring whether he is crushing the little guy or not." The latter comment apparently refers to Hastings, who stands to lose much if his newly purchased property, the old Tornquist church building, cannot be torn down to make way for a planned parking garage. The lawsuit filed in circuit court blames Gentry for not "fully and timely investigating the property and using due care to advise his client of the landmarking status before he bought it."

The article concluded by noting, "Hastings' attorney has also filed a petition to the Commission on Chicago Landmarks asking that the landmarking designation for the property be rescinded. Hastings is seeking the demolition of the church, the first known architectural project of the late G. Dudley Tornquist, so it can be replaced by a five-level parking structure. Neither Lloyd Gentry nor any representative of his law firm was available to comment on the lawsuits."

The restaurant was starting to spin around me. I needed to find Fin's telephone number immediately. No sooner had I signed the lawyer up as my advocate, having executed his encyclopedia-length retainer agreement the day before, than he had me misquoted—atrociously—in the *Sun-Times*.

I opened my briefcase just as the waitress arrived with my breakfast. I located Fin's number and quickly started punching it into my cell phone. I rose to leave—and noticed the waitress's stunned look.

"Emergency," I whispered to her, and threw a ten-dollar bill on the counter.

As I turned, I almost ran face-first into the woman who had

worn the pink T-shirt and black team jacket. This time her hair was down, and she was all business, wearing a pin-striped pantsuit.

"So," she said with a bright smile, "I suppose this time you're going to ask me about Vermeer?"

"Actually, no," I shot out, then regretted it and started backtracking. "I mean, I'd love to, but..."

"Hey, it's okay. Whatever," she said flatly.

"See, I just found out I have, well, sort of a crisis."

"Sure. Don't we all?"

"But I'd love to talk sometime...I notice you come here regularly..."

"No, it's fine. Really. Have a nice day," she said, giving me a little wave and seating herself at the counter, then reaching for the *Sun-Times* I had left there.

At the door, listening to the line ring at Fin's office, I turned back to fetch the paper. But I saw the girl reading it, so I let it go. In the parking lot there was a newspaper box. I stuffed some coins in and got my own copy.

I was already in my car driving to campus when someone finally picked up. It was "Miss Kat."

"Good day, office of Horace Fin."

"This is Kevin Hastings again. I need to talk to Mr. Fin immediately."

"Mr. Fin can see you. Today. Three-thirty. Thirty minutes for conference. First thirty minutes, $100. Cash or—"

"No, you don't understand," I barked. "I'm Kevin Hastings. I'm already Mr. Fin's client. I came in the other day."

"Oh yes, Mr. Hastings. Good to talk. Mr. Fin is here. You hold, alright?"

I waited as I drove. Finally Fin picked up.

"News travels fast," he quipped.

"What's going on here?" I yelled. "Why did you make that preposterous statement to the *Sun-Times*? How could you do that without talking to me first?"

"Why, Kevin," he said with a confident chuckle, "we *did* talk. Just the other day. Remember?"

"Yeah, but I never gave you permission to release any statement…and certainly not anything like that…"

"Well, let's see." There was a rustling of papers. "Here it is. Let me look at the transcript."

"Transcript?" I shouted. "What are you talking about?"

"I recorded our conversation in my office," Fin said blandly. "I do it with all my clients."

"I didn't agree to that."

"Sure you did—"

"How? When?"

"It's in the retainer agreement you signed in my office. Page twenty-four. 'Client hereby consents to attorney recording all conversations that take place within the confines of attorney's office.' I mailed you a copy of the agreement after you signed it. Haven't you received your conformed copy yet?"

"No, not yet."

"Well, it's on the way," Fin said in an upbeat tone.

"But about that terrible statement you gave to the newspapers—"

"Hey, how can you say it was a 'terrible' statement, Kevin? Be careful about that, now. After all, that is exactly how you described Gentry."

"No, that's how *you* described Gentry," I shot back.

"But you adopted the statement as your own. I've got it right here on the transcript. And furthermore, you authorized me to publish that statement anywhere and everywhere."

"No, absolutely not!"

"Kevin," Fin said in a soothing voice. "Get ahold of yourself. I'm looking at the transcript. Here is what you say: 'I'm not afraid of telling the whole world, if need be'—"

"You baited me into saying that."

"Now, Kevin," he replied smoothly. "That's a very negative thing to say. We need to preserve, at all costs, the relationship of trust between the two of us. That's critical for the success I'm trying to achieve for you."

By that point in our telephone conversation I was drawing a

blank. My own lawyer had apparently sandbagged me into agreeing with statements that had tarred and feathered one of Chicago's most prestigious real-estate attorneys—and his firm to boot. And he had also managed to make it look like I had authorized the release of that statement to the press. Which, in a tortured and hypertechnical way of looking at it, I guess I had.

But as I considered that, I was also beginning to appreciate—in a perverse kind of way—the special talents of Horace Fin. After all, if he could do this to me, his client, then to what kind of legal death-march would he be capable of subjecting our lawsuit opponents?

That last thought gave me a glimmer of hope. Even if, at the same time, it was a rather grim one.

"So, anything else, Kevin?"

"I guess not," I muttered.

"Good. We'll be in touch. Not to worry. You're in good hands. Now is when things really get fun."

After he hung up, I began thinking over Fin's final, surprising statement.

As a student of history, it shouldn't have surprised me, though. In the ordeals of medieval legal procedure, there were bound to be those administrators of pain who enjoyed their work. The kind of torturer who kissed the wife and kids back at the thatched-roof cottage as he went off to work and had a smile on his face and a bounce in his step as he went.

Perhaps, I thought to myself as I neared the turnoff for Essex College, *my lawyer is one of those.*

In a morbid way, this fact might actually work to my benefit in my legal cases. But another realization also lingered. And it bothered me down to my soul.

That my fate was now tied to a man who apparently specialized in destruction, and whose stock in trade was a form of legal terror.

Seventeen

~

DURING THE REST OF THE WEEK, I crawled my way through my schedule of lectures at Essex. In addition to Early Medieval English History 308, I had been saddled with a full load of introductory-level history classes. Strangely, Dr. Albright made no attempt to corral me. I was certain he had read, or at least had been informed of, the *Sun-Times* article. Particularly because Essex was mentioned by name. That was the kind of publicity that usually drove Albright, and the administration, right up the wall.

But this time he was quiet. That worried me. I passed him twice on the commons between classes. He didn't wave, just gave me only the slightest nod of his head. But he did throw me a look—like I was being seriously considered for the position of human sacrifice to the volcano gods.

When Friday night finally came I hopped into my rental car and headed home. I had filed a damage claim with my auto-insurance company, and my Jetta was at the shop getting undented, repainted, and new glass installed. The insurance company assured me it would all be covered except for my deductible. I considered the fact that my car-damage claim was proceeding smoothly as a major turnaround...compared to the rest of my life.

Turning a street corner, I thought I caught a glimpse of Charlotte crossing the street at a crosswalk. I actually did a U-turn and drove back to the intersection. I drove past her and then slowed down—I figured Charlotte wouldn't recognize the rental car.

It wasn't her. But it did make me realize that I still wasn't over her, not by a far stretch. It was just that my recent tribulations had preoccupied me entirely and kept my mind off her. I wondered what she was doing. And whether things were getting more serious between her and Dick Dineras—or whether she had finally tapped down to his essence and realized that, underneath it all, the guy was a complete scoundrel.

On the other hand, with his flash and money, I calculated it would take quite a long time before Charlotte would ever bother to dig down to the bedrock of the man—if there was any. It could be months—even years—before she might come to that revelation.

And what I was ignoring, of course, was that she was the one who'd wandered off the reservation—who'd left me for Dineras. That certainly said something. What it said was that I needed to forget about her and move on.

Which was exactly what I had been trying to do when I got involved in the real-estate speculation venture that had become the bane of my existence.

So, I had come around in a full circle again. I was going nowhere.

Then my cell phone rang. It was Tom Taylor.

"Kevin?"

"Yeah."

"I can't believe you actually took my call."

"What's up?" I asked him wearily.

"You sound depressed. I suppose being hounded by the *paparazzi* will do that to you."

"Very funny."

"No, really," Tom continued. I could tell he was getting cranked up. "Next thing you know the guys from the tabloids will be climbing all over your condo complex. Cameras with those big telephoto lenses taking shots of you in your underwear or taking out the garbage—"

"Knock it off, Tom."

"Then they'll start interviewing the neighbors. You know, like they do with serial killers, or crooked politicians, or movie-star lovers who get into a drunken brawl and the cops have to come in with a domestic-abuse warrant—"

"Tom—I always appreciate hearing from you," I replied. "But is there a point to all of this?"

"Hey, I'm just playing with you about the *Sun-Times* thing. And also, I wanted to see if you're shooting hoops with us tomorrow."

"Actually, I think I will."

"Great. See you at the Y at the usual time. Oh, and one other question."

"Sure. What is it?"

"Who all's on your legal dream team? I was laying bets you had the OJ team...but one of the other guys at work was saying, no, you probably had the Michael Jackson team."

"Clever."

"Seriously. What's the deal with this lawyer you've got, the one quoted in the papers?"

"It's a long story. And I can't really go into the lawsuit at all—"

"Right," Tom snapped back. "Because if you did, then I could write one of those tell-all books after the case is over and do the talk-show circuit."

"See you tomorrow," I said, unamused.

The next day, I showed up on time. The rest of the group was already out on the court.

Tom was right. There was something good about working up a sweat. For an hour and a half I was able to forget about things. I made a bunch of layups—even got off one or two three-pointers that were picture-perfect. I was feeling good. Tom, as usual, was getting in everybody's face—even mine—and we were on the same team. But I didn't care. It was pure recreational therapy.

After we showered up and were dressing in the locker room, Tom was trying hard to get the lowdown on my lawsuit against Gentry.

"Seriously, dude," he said. "I've heard of his law firm. Our PR people have actually had some contact with his office. I think we did an advertising campaign for them a couple of years ago.

Gentry's firm is golden. Really high-powered. I hope you know what you're doing."

"Don't worry, I do," I quipped back.

"Lawyers like that, you libel them, you stain their 'rep'—they don't like that. They can make you hate life pretty quick. I bet this Lloyd Gentry is going to really play hardball with you. But then...I'm sure you already know all that."

I simply nodded. Tom probably thought I was just following orders from my lawyer not to discuss the case. Actually, I was sinking back into despair. Everything he was saying was something I had feared would happen. The risks in my battle plan with Horace Fin were starting to add up.

When I finally got back to my condo and got my mail, one letter grabbed my attention. It looked like some kind of urgent notice from the electric company. Which struck me as odd because I paid my utilities like clockwork.

Probably another rate hike, I thought to myself. As I took the elevator up I also discovered a letter from the water utility. Just beyond the window of the envelope, on the inside, I could see the words "SHUT OFF."

Inside my place, I ripped open the two envelopes. Both of the letters inside claimed I had failed to pay my bills and that service was going to be terminated. My mind started racing.

This is crazy. I am current with both of these. What's going on?

I went to my phone and dialed the water company first. I was going through the message menu when the lights suddenly went out. The phone went dead.

I fumbled around until I found my cell phone. Then I called the electric company. On hold and listening to a recorded voice telling me about the additional services I could receive through my electricity provider, I glanced over at the kitchen sink. I had this bad feeling.

Walking quickly over I turned the handle first for the cold water, and then the hot.

Nothing came out.

I raced into the bathroom and pushed the toilet handle. The water slowly gurgled down, disappearing permanently.

Still on hold with the electric company, I clicked off my cell phone. Then I walked into my living room and sat down on the couch.

Trying to get a grip on things and not get too paranoid, I tried to think it through logically. I pulled out my check register. Both utilities had been paid, and I had made a check mark next to the entries, indicating that the checks had cleared.

I called the electric company again. After fifteen minutes on hold, I finally got a human being. He checked his screen and said I was three months in arrears.

"That's impossible!" I yelled. "I have my check register right here. It shows I have paid every month, right on time."

"How about you fax me the last three months of cancelled checks, and I will get this turned around for you, Mr. Hastings."

"My bank doesn't send me the cancelled checks. I can order copies, but not until Monday."

The electric company account person apologized but said he could do nothing until proof of payment was provided.

That's when I decided to call attorney Fin. I really didn't expect him to be in the office on a Saturday, but I left an energetic message on his voice mail.

Surprisingly, about thirty minutes later he called.

I explained how two of my utilities had been shut off despite my excellent payment record.

"I know this sounds far-fetched," I said, "but is there any tie-in between my utilities and our lawsuits?"

"Never underestimate your opponent." Fin said he was going to grab his law registry.

"I'm sure Gentry's office is in here," he mumbled. "Usually the big firms give a list of their more impressive 'representative clients.' Here they are...let's see...interesting...they not only do real-estate and property work, they also do a lot of municipal collective bargaining. Clients...okay...well, hey, what do you know—"

"What is it?"

"Gentry's firm represents the employee unions of almost every municipal utility in the city of Chicago. Electric...water...public works...waste disposal...even animal control. Wow. There it is."

"You think Gentry's behind it?"

"Probably."

"So what am I supposed to do with my utilities cut off?" I exclaimed.

"Well," Fin said, ruminating on it for a few seconds, "I guess you're going to have to rough it."

"Is that your advice? Rough it?"

"Until I figure something out. But don't worry. I'm on it."

After hanging up I was now convinced I had given up control over my own life. I was at the mercy of others—and they were going to sit up nights figuring out how to cause me misery.

I trudged over to the refrigerator and opened the freezer top. It was into full defrost. Water was everywhere.

At least, I told myself as I strained to find the silver lining, it wasn't full of food.

EIGHTEEN

~

HAVING NO RUNNING WATER OR ELECTRICITY, I checked myself into the Night Light Motel for the weekend. It was a cheap one. That was intentional. There were still lingering thoughts in my mind about my job security at Essex. Of course I had no savings to fall back on. And in a matter of days I would be facing not only my apartment rent, but also the mortgage payment I had incurred to finance the purchase of the Tornquist property. It seemed my financial status was a house of cards constructed on the deck of a rolling ship. I needed to save pennies every chance I got.

In the past I had often driven past the motel and looked with mild amusement at the semi trucks and dumpy-looking cars parked there—the kind you hoped would never hit you because you could pretty well bet they didn't have any insurance.

Now I was one of the "residents" (as they called it). I got the feeling that most of the people were long-term "residents."

When I checked in, the tall, skinny man who was the motel clerk was leaning back, watching a girl trying to ingest something disgusting on a TV reality show.

"No way would I swallow that," he said, shaking his head earnestly. "No matter how much money they'd offer me. I mean… what if it don't die going down?"

Rather than engage him on the topic I just asked for a room. I also asked if they had papers available.

"Papers?" he asked blankly.

"Newspapers. Morning newspapers."

He shook his head. I dragged my things down to the room at the end of the motel, just off of the parking lot.

The guy in the room next to me wore a cowboy hat, listened to country tunes all day, and smoked cigarettes. I, on the other hand, had a "nonsmoking room." Which meant, I figured, I was free not to smoke. But the guy in the room next to me was also free to suck on Marlboros as often as he wanted, even to the point where the smell was seeping through the wafer-thin wall.

After a few hours of listening to him talk loudly and profanely on the telephone, and noting his frequent references to "alimony" and "child support," and "her rotten lawyer who's going to be road-kill if he crosses me one more time," I deduced he was living semi-permanently at the Night Light because of a divorce.

My room was on the first floor. So as cars and trucks drove in and out of the parking lot all night long, their headlights swept through the worn curtains on my window and washed over my walls like a searchlight in a gulag.

In retrospect, spending a weekend at the Night Light was humbling—which should have been something positive and edifying in an altruistic sense—but I didn't look at it that way. Instead I grumbled to myself that somebody was going to pay dearly for this inconvenience. I couldn't wait until I could sic my mad-dog lawyer on Lloyd Gentry for the dirty tricks he had pulled.

Sunday evening I made a point of calling the front desk and asking them to give me a wake-up call for 7:00 AM.

The last thought I had as I lay on my bed was one of revenge. Then I drifted off to sleep to the sound of George Strait singing "All My Ex's Live in Texas" on the radio next door.

~

I awoke to the sunlight streaming in through my semi-sheer curtains. As I tried to pry my eyes open all the way, I kept thinking there was something awry. Something missing.

I rolled over to look at the clock radio. It wasn't working. That's when I thought to myself, *I'm sure glad I asked for a wake-up call. Wake-up call?*

I bolted straight out of bed and scrambled over to the nightstand. I snatched up my wristwatch. It said 9:50 AM. The clerk at the desk had been so busy meditating on the digestibility of hard-shelled beetles by TV contestants that he had forgotten to give me the wake-up. I had just slept through my first lecture of the day in Introduction to History 106.

I screamed out loud and leaped out of bed. I looked again at my watch. I still had time, if I really hurried, to make my next class at 11:00. I threw my clothes into my overnight bag, grabbed my briefcase, and ran out to the front desk. After yelling at the clerk for my missed wake-up call—a different man from the one who checked me in—I dropped off my keys, dashed out to my rental car, and blazed my way out onto the freeway. Where I was promptly stuck in a barely creeping, sluglike traffic jam.

Even though driving was insanely slow, I still calculated I could squeak onto campus just under the wire. I was already thinking how I would explain the missed class to Albright. The problem was not the lack of exigent circumstances excusing my absence. The real dilemma was that I had too many excuses—all of them real—but the sum total of all of them was like one of those championship domino displays I've seen on the news, made up of impossibly intricate, law-of-physics-defying chain reactions, with dominoes cascading into one another in geometric patterns that are dazzling and evoke gasps and then applause from the onlookers.

Only the dominoes in my life would evoke no applause, no appreciation. Just despair.

After parking my car, I dashed across the quad toward the Humanities building. I looked at my watch: 10:51. I was going to make it.

As I followed the sidewalk that wound gracefully around to the front entrance, there was the sound of a crowd shouting. And someone on a bullhorn. There was chanting. And another bullhorn.

Coming around to the front steps, I ran right into a huge crowd that had gathered in front of Humanities. There had to be a hundred people or so. I also saw three Chicago Police squads parked nearby, one of them actually on the front lawn. On the grass.

Man, the administration is going to go ape over that, I mused to myself. *They just planted new grass there last spring.*

Then I caught sight of the signs. One of them, professionally lettered, read, "Society for Landscaping and Architectural Preservation."

Another, which looked hand-painted, read, "Your History Prof Is Wrecking History."

And another—"Save the Tornquist Building."

That's when I could hear the dominoes cascading down around me, clicking and tapping into each other with breathtaking speed.

Off in the distance, a television truck from a Chicago station, with a huge antenna tower, was just arriving.

A Chicago cop was announcing on his bullhorn that the group was on private property. That they were trespassing. He ordered them to "remove yourselves from the premises and move over to the public sidewalk."

There was a girl in the front, with her own bullhorn, and she was leading the chanting mob in a round of "Save the Tornquist, Dump the Prof! Save the Tornquist, Dump the Prof!"

As I squeezed through the crowd she was just a few feet away, and then suddenly our eyes met. And for just an instant she stopped the chant, and dropped her bullhorn from her face.

It was the girl who loved Vermeer.

She had this startled look as we stared at each other.

"That's him. That's Hastings!" Someone shouted.

I muscled my way through and dashed up the stone stairs of the Humanities building. As I did, I heard them resume the chant: "Save the Tornquist! Save the Tornquist!"

Inside, I sprinted up the stairs to the second floor. But as I looked up, I saw Alice, the history department secretary, standing at the very top with something in her hand. Next to her, with his arms crossed, was Dr. Harvey Albright. When he saw me, he put out both hands towards me like a traffic cop stopping traffic.

"Alice," Albright said to the secretary in an official-sounding tone.

She dutifully handed me a thick packet of papers.

"This is the notice of the special faculty meeting of the administration," Albright intoned. "Called to consider your immediate suspension—without pay—as a member of the faculty of this institution."

"What!" was all I could say.

"I suggest you read this. All of the charges against you are detailed here. The special meeting begins in fifteen minutes in the large conference room of Old Main. If you fail to be there, we will conduct the hearing in your absence."

Then, after turning to leave, Albright wheeled back around and delivered another order.

"And do not speak to the media about this as you make your way across the quad. I repeat—you are to give no statements to the press."

Surprisingly, despite the lightning bolt that had just hit me, I was able to muster one comeback.

"What about freedom of speech?" I shouted to Albright's back.

He half turned—ever the historian—and gave me his reply.

"If Lincoln could suspend the writ of habeas corpus during the Civil War," he said with cold finality, "then I can order you to keep your mouth shut."

Nineteen

I took a side entrance out of the Humanities building to avoid the chanting mob outside and hurried back across the quad toward Old Main, the administration building. The TV crews were still in front, and I had managed to slip out without notice.

As I jogged I was leafing through the thick sheaf of papers that contained the accusations against me. They were in the form of a typed chronology. Albright had apparently been "keeping book" on me for months. Every tardiness, every complaint from a student, every skipped lecture was there. It was clear to me as I huffed my way to the picturesque, columned building that none of these instances were out of line with the occasional practices of almost every other professor on campus.

But I kept reading as I walked down the Old Main hallway, and I felt myself arriving at a dreaded realization. And by the time I was nearing the conference room I was convinced that my job problems at Essex might be irresolvable. Taken as a whole, particularly in the hands of a department chair who seemed to harbor such malice against me, the allegations could make me look incompetent and insubordinate. The general heading of the grounds for my removal was described as "extreme lack of scholarly professionalism." That was a euphemism if I had ever heard one.

I tried to maintain my calm and construct some kind of instant defense to the charges as I approached the large double doors ahead. But all I could come up with was a limp comparison of my errors to those of other professors—and I knew that wouldn't wash. The associate dean and his personal secretary were standing like guards on either side of the door. As I entered I only had two thoughts on my mind. And they were both questions.

What's motivating Albright to destroy me? was one of them.

And the other was this—*How in the world did they pull this hearing together so quick?*

I should have been busy, mentally planning my defense as I walked in the conference room and was shown a chair at the end of the long, burnished walnut table where I took my seat.

Instead, I was plagued by those two questions which seemed to have no answers. Foolishly, I speculated that if I could just get to the bottom of those two issues, then perhaps I could unveil the sinister conspiracy that was building against me. Armed with that, I could rally some of the dissenting faculty members—there were sure to be a few, I reasoned—and with them, I could then sway the rest of the disciplinary assembly that had gathered.

Little did I know that the truth was far simpler—much more banal and ordinary than any of my wild ideas of conspiracy.

The room was usually used for the twice-a-year meetings of the Board of Directors of Essex College where they would discuss the dry realities of endowments, budgets, and building projects.

But that day it would be a hall of inquisition. A place of punishment.

Harvey Albright arrived fifteen minutes later and sat down at the other end of the long table. Next to him on one side, was Victor Bouring, the vice chancellor of the college. He was standing in for the president of Essex, who had diplomatically absented himself from the hearing. On the other side of Albright was Hubert Jankowski, the aging legal counsel for the college.

I had seen Jankowski at other official institution meetings before. He wore his usual lawyer's uniform—dark suit, striped shirt, and bow tie. He had silver-white hair and was slightly hard of hearing. An alumnus of Essex, he seemed to have been its attorney from time immemorial.

Albright turned to the lawyer and asked that he give a short explanation of the need for the emergency meeting.

Jankowski gave a bewildered look and then cocked his head.

"*The need for the emergency meeting—the business about due process—suspension without pay,*" Albright said loudly enough so the lawyer could hear.

Jankowski smiled and nodded. Then he gave an elaborate, plodding explanation. In short, he said that even though Essex was a private—and not a public—institution, it had always been the practice to afford the "same procedural due process rights" to faculty members that would normally only apply to a public university. That having been said, the elderly attorney pointed out that if Essex wanted to suspend me immediately pending a final hearing, but to do it *without pay*, then it had to hold a preliminary kind of hearing to make sure, as a precondition, that the allegations had some substance.

Without pay. Those words now struck me like a high-speed bullet train. Why didn't that fact register mentally when Albright spoke to me at the top of the stairs at Humanities? Where he said that the meeting was being "called to consider your immediate suspension—without pay…"

"So if I am suspended today—" I blurted out.

"Yes…exactly…then it will be without pay. You will be off payroll immediately. Pending the final hearing," Albright countered.

Bruce Eddington, a faculty member from the math department, raised his hand. Bruce had untamed hair and thick glasses. He went about campus with the look of an academic radical about him. Those who got to know him realized he was simply an eccentric. But he was a brilliant mathematician and was responsible for bringing several hefty grants to the college for esoteric math projects he was pursuing in conjunction with the computer-science department and that held promise in both the private and the public sectors. Thus, eccentric or not, he was not only tolerated at the college, he was actively befriended and fêted by the administration.

"Yes, Bruce?" Albright said with a smile.

"Just a point of order…actually…well…it should be clarified

that if Kevin is suspended here at this meeting—but then at the formal hearing later on he is not terminated—then he would be entitled to recoup his back pay that he lost in the interim…on a dollar-for-dollar basis—is that correct? Am I correct on that?"

"Yes, that is quite correct," Albright replied. "And thank you, Bruce, for clarifying that for all of us."

Then Harvey Albright proceeded to summarize the allegations against me, reading generously from his own chronology that he had in front of him. Each of the other attendees had the same thick packet, and a few leafed through it while he talked.

When he was finished, he laid the packet down on the table and concluded.

"And so, inasmuch as Mr. Hastings is not a tenured professor, the standard for suspension is much more discretionary. For all the reasons that I have just described, I recommend that Mr. Hastings be suspended immediately, and that it be done without pay to him. And that a date be set for a final hearing, and that at that time Mr. Hastings be terminated as a member of the full-time faculty of Essex College."

The vice chancellor asked me if I had any response.

I jumped right into the fray. I charged Dr. Harvey Albright with a "sinister lack of appreciation for my efforts at this institution," and suggested—without elaborating—that I had recently encountered some "complications of a business and personal nature" that had caused some "interruption in my normal teaching schedule." But I assured all of those present that life—and my academic responsibilities—would be right back on track.

The vice chancellor pursed his lips and made one additional comment.

"Yes," he said, "we encountered some of your 'complications of a business and personal nature' outside the Humanities building today," he said with a grimace.

That was as close as anyone got at that hearing to touching on the real nerve—the ultimate force behind the quick emergency meeting that had been hastily arranged against me. That I had caused a minor scandal in the press—and that Essex College's name had been tragically linked to it.

But I saved my best argument for last.

"And finally," I said, filling the room with my argument, "I had almost no time to review these extensive allegations against me. I received them a mere five minutes before this hearing. Can that be called fair? Can such a process be called 'due' process?"

My closing remarks were loud enough to be heard by Jankowski. And he surprised me with the vigor with which he then tore into my argument.

"What is it exactly, sir, that you expect?" the old lawyer said sharply. "What if one accused faculty member was a slower reader than another? Would that require that we adjust the amount of prior notice we give...depending on the rate of their reading ability? This is an *emergency meeting*, Mr. Hastings. That means that quick business is required by the exigencies of the occasion. You were given a copy of the charges against you. You were given the opportunity to be present. And be heard. That is all that the law requires before we get down to the business of suspending you..."

I was speechless. I looked around the long table. Faces, all of them, that I had known, and that I had thought had known me. Men and women that I had shared coffee with in the campus café, and exchanged greetings on the quad as we passed. And labored together on administrative committees. Would any of them put a stop to this travesty?

"Point of order?" Bruce Eddington said, quietly, raising his hand.

At last, I thought to myself, *good old Bruce to the rescue.* I remembered the get-well card I had sent his wife last year when she went into the hospital for surgery. *That sure didn't hurt. So, now, here it comes. The turning of the tide. The uprising of the dissenters. The uncovering of the conspiracy. Go, Bruce, go...*

"Your question, Bruce?" Albright said with a grin.

"Just this," Bruce said, pausing for a moment to collect his thoughts. And then he made his statement. Which would be his second-to-last statement of the day.

"Are we going to run over into the dinner hour with this? Because if we are, then I need to call my wife. I know she was planning a pot roast and—"

"Not to worry," Albright said magnanimously. "I think we are all ready. Shall we vote?"

"All in favor," Albright announced, "of suspension of Mr. Hastings without pay, pending a final hearing, raise your hands."

Everyone in the room except two people raised their hands.

One was Jankowski, who, of course, was merely legal counsel and had no right to vote.

And the other was Bruce Eddington.

He then explained he had to abstain. The reason, he said, was that he did not have enough time to read through the thick packet of materials in order "to make an informed vote."

Although Bruce was a certified genius, one small matter of logic had apparently slipped his attention. If *he* hadn't had enough time to study the charges against me, then what did that say about the fact that *I* had not had enough time to study the charges in order to make my own defense?

But Bruce was not troubled with that minor inconsistency. The vote was unanimous—with one abstention—in favor of my immediate suspension without a continuation of my salary in the interim. A date for the final hearing was set two weeks away.

Bruce would be able to get home to the savory scent of a freshly cooked pot roast.

And I was now worrying about how much money I had left in my wallet. And hoping that I still had some dresser change lying around back at my apartment.

Twenty

After the disastrous meeting, I put my problems with attorney Tony DeVoe and Mangiorno to the back burner for a while. As it turned out, that was a luxury I really couldn't afford. But with fire raining down on me from several other fronts, you can hardly blame me.

While I was busy pondering poverty and professional misery, Vito Mangiorno and his son Buddy were meeting at a large construction site overlooking the Chicago River. Amid scarred-up ground, dumpsters, and construction debris at the partially completed office building undertaken by VM Contractors, the boss was getting a status report on the money-laundering scheme and the problems with the parking-structure plan.

Vito glanced over the scene to make sure they were alone. He saw only two cars parked nearby—the black Lincoln Town Car with his chauffeur behind the wheel and his heavy-set assistant, "Big Tut"—and the red Mustang that belonged to his son, Buddy.

Vito lit a cigarette and smoked it for a while before he started talking. His son could see the irritation in his father's face. He knew the clues. The flexed jaw muscles. The bobbing head that seemed to be musing on who to strike, and when, but not giving out any clues until it was too late for the victim.

After a while Vito, as always, led off.

"I was not the top of my high school class," he started out. "But I wasn't at the bottom either. So tell me something…"

Then he motioned for Buddy to come a few steps closer. His son complied, cautiously, as his father continued.

"You see, I can't figure this out. You make a good living with the outfit. You drive a nice car. Always have cash in your pocket. Whatever you want to buy, you buy. You see something you want, you get it. You come and go as you please. A pretty good life. And then there's that Tony DeVoe. Okay, don't get me started on that money-grubbing slug with a law degree. I pay him a small fortune to take care of things. So, this is what I don't understand. Help with this, college boy…"

"Two years, I never graduated, remember?" Buddy retorted.

"Oh, now I'm supposed to feel sorry for you…that instead of finishing college and studying stuff that teaches you zero you come to work for me. And that's a bad thing? Is that what you're saying?"

"No, Pop. That's not what I'm saying…"

"Okay then, answer this—between you and DeVoe, why is it," and with that Vito started blowing a gasket, shouting so loud that Mickey and Big Tut could hear from inside the Lincoln, "why is it that this parking lot deal is not getting done? And now I hear about lawsuits and it's all over the newspapers. And then Lenny called me on my cell two hours ago and says that his wife was watching TV today, and there is something about some flaky broad and her radical flaky group, they're carryin' signs, and protesting, and it's going to be all over the evening news, and this thing is getting totally out of control!"

"No, Pop, just listen," Buddy said, trying to calm things down.

"I'm listening. But you'd better have some answers. Understand?"

So Buddy explained how I was bushwhacked at a stoplight, as a way of gently motivating me to wrap the real-estate deal up. How immediately after that I retained Horace Fin to get things back on the dime, and that proved that the idea of giving me a little bit of a physical shakeup was a good call. And so he explained that Fin filed a lawsuit to force the city to allow the church to get demolished. And according to Fin, who has been in contact with DeVoe, as soon as the permit is approved for demolition, then the property quietly gets transferred to VM Contractors and they would be off to the races.

"Who is this Horace Fin guy?" Vito asked suspiciously.

"Some guy. Some lawyer."

"What do we know about him?" Vito said, still pursuing it.

"I don't know anything about him," Buddy replied. "Except that Hastings hired him to get things wrapped up after he fired Gentry, or Gentry quit, or whatever."

"What does DeVoe say about him, this Fin guy?"

"That he knows him, I guess. Or knows about him. That the lawyers in Chicago all know about him."

"Know about him, how?"

"Pop, I don't know," the son replied. "Just that lawyers in Chicago know the guy, and DeVoe knows him. And they've worked out a deal where Fin was going to get everything done, and that we're even going to get a break on the price now because of all the hassle."

That last part—the part about Mangiorno getting a break on the purchase price of the Tornquist property—was something that Fin had not told me. But, like most things that happened between Fin and myself, it was covered by his encyclopedic retainer agreement. "Attorney has the right to initiate nonbinding negotiations for settlement for any matter for which client has retained him, subject to client's subsequent approval."

Fin had not yet sought my "subsequent approval." That is the first point. But the second thing is that—in the world of Vito Mangiorno—there was no such thing as a "nonbinding" negotiation. When promises made in negotiations were not honored, they became very binding in ways that make the imagination quiver.

"So what's this about Fin's lawsuit against this Gentry guy, his first lawyer?" Vito asked. "I read that in the newspapers too."

"Malpractice case. 'Cause Gentry didn't do anything to warn Hastings that the church property might have some restrictions against demolition under this landmarking law they got in the city. I think they're trying to scam him for some money. I don't think it's going to be a problem for us."

"You make sure it isn't," Vito snapped. "And make sure that

there's no more publicity about this stuff. No more TV cameras. Nothing. You got it?"

Buddy nodded his head.

"So far we've been lucky," Vito continued. "The company hasn't been named. Nobody in the outfit's been named in the papers. No mention that we're involved in buying the property. It's probably a good thing, you know, that this Hastings didn't go through with the sale to us right away, 'cause then it would have been in the public records in the deeds office, and some snoopy reporter would have picked up on it."

His son agreed.

"One more thing," Vito added. "Come by the house tonight. We need to talk about some of our competition for the territory."

"What, you mean the Russian group that's muscling in?"

"Yeah, them, but also the Chinese—we're losing our shirts to those creeps on the drug business…"

"Actually, they're Cambodians," Buddy clarified.

"Whatever. You come by at seven tonight. We have to have a talk about some things."

By the time Vito and Buddy parted ways, it was late afternoon, and there were long shadows over the city, and the sun was sending a crimson reflection down the surface of the Chicago River.

~

Oblivious back then to the Mangiorno "outfit" or any of their nefarious meetings, I was mired in my own mess. I was consumed with thoughts of unemployment and life on the street if I didn't get some income pretty soon. *At least I can file for unemployment benefits,* I thought to myself.

I headed back to my apartment unit. The only good thing that had happened to me that day was the call I made to my utility companies as I started driving home. They verified that according to their computer screen, the utility bills had been paid, and they "apologized for the inconvenience." I wondered whether I ought to demand that they repay me for the weekend bill from the Night

Light Motel for my stay there. I figured that was something I could decide on later. Because something else was occupying my mind.

As I went up in the elevator to my condo, I starting worrying about my check from Essex. I was on a direct deposit system. The preceding Friday was the beginning of the next pay period. I was hoping that the check for my next two weeks would have gone through anyway, because it was the last workday before they suspended me.

Thinking it through, I remembered that I had, the week before, paid the rent payment for the current month assuming that my paycheck would get deposited. I was in a hurry to do that because the last month's rent—amidst all of the confusion of my life since my venture into real-estate speculation—had slipped my mind and I was almost two weeks late on that.

I nodded and smiled to several of the other tenants as I walked down the hall to my unit. One of them, an accountant who was on the same floor, kind of raised his eyebrows a little when I said hello. That should have tipped me off.

When I got to my door I noticed something different about the doorknob. Then I realized what it was. Oscar, the rental manager, had placed a large "overlock" on the doorknob so I could not get in. I had seen it used on a few other units over the years when people failed to pay their rent.

There was an envelope on the floor in front of the door with my name on it. I opened it up, and there was a note from Oscar.

"Mr. Hastings. Your check for this month's rent bounced. Last month was two weeks late. This is not good. Please make this good immediately."

I crumpled the note up in my hands with fury. I shook my fists with a barely contained rage.

Storming down to Oscar's unit on the first floor, I arrived at his door and banged loudly. There was no answer. I glanced at my watch. Suppertime. I surmised that he may have gone out for dinner.

Running to my rental car I climbed in and shut the door. And then I screamed several profanities and pounded the steering wheel with my fists.

All I could do was yell "NO" over and over again in the car.

TWENTY-ONE

AFTER RECOVERING MY ABILITY TO THINK coherently, I called my twenty-four-hour banking telephone service. It reported that, indeed, the rent check had bounced. There was no indication that my paycheck had been deposited. And I was overdrawn.

I then tried to call Uncle Mort from my cell phone, but only got his answering machine. I was thinking I might have to stay with him in Rockville for a few days until I got the rent situation straightened out.

So I called Tom Taylor next. I got him at dinnertime. I could hear his wife, Liz, in the background. I asked him how life was going. But he immediately picked up the fact that something was going on.

When I explained that I had been suspended at Essex he was aghast. The best I could do, when he asked what happened, was to explain that they must have been embarrassed at all the publicity surrounding the Tornquist property flap. But that I was confident that I would win my job back at the final hearing in two weeks.

"Two weeks?" Tom said. "Wow. That's tough. So, what are you doing till then?"

"Well," I replied, "I'm actually looking for somewhere to crash for the night."

"What do you mean?"

"I got locked out of my apartment. Some mix-up about the rent. I think that Essex may have played some game with my last paycheck. Anyway, I need somewhere to sleep until I get this cleared up."

There was an uncomfortable silence, and I could hear the buzz of his cordless phone. I guessed that he was moving into another room. That was not a good sign.

"Look," he said in a hushed voice. "Bottom line. Liz heard from Peggy, a mutual friend of Charlotte and Liz. Remember Peggy?"

"I think so—"

"Well, Peggy shared something with Liz recently. Things she had never heard before that Charlotte had said about Liz…"

I was trying to calculate what this had to do with a request from a friend to sleep over at his house.

"Anyway, Charlotte had been dissing Liz all over the place for the last year, it turns out. Liz always had a problem with Charlotte, as you know, but it was just this feeling she had that Charlotte didn't like her. Well, it turns out that after we spend all of this money on Liz redecorating the condo here, Charlotte says to Peggy…something like…'Liz's decorating shows that she is a master at the "shabby chic" look—without the "chic."' Or something like that."

"Tom," I said interrupting. "That's Charlotte, I am sorry about that. But that's her, that's not me. I'm just wondering if you could put me up for a night or two that's all. We're friends, man…"

"You have no idea how upset Liz gets about Charlotte," Tom replied. "And frankly, and I'm not agreeing with her, but Liz associates you with Charlotte. And she probably wouldn't be too cool with you staying with us. Especially if you lost your job and everything. You understand what I'm saying, here? She'd think that you had visions of getting too comfortable here and turning our place into the 'No-Tell Motel'…"

I didn't respond.

"All I am saying is this," Tom continued. "You need to look around for another place to stay. Now if you really, *really* get desperate and you tell me you've been sleeping on a hot-air grate at night, and you're using a shopping cart for a clothes closet…then I'll just tell Liz you have to crash here, and that's the end of the story. But honestly, I'd really rather not go that route…"

"No, that's alright," I snapped. "Don't do your friend any favors. I'll take care of myself, thanks anyway."

I clicked my cell phone off.

If I hadn't been so depressed at the time, I would have felt betrayed.

But I was starting to shift into survival mode by then.

It's funny how, in a crisis, the sting of a friend's unfriendliness doesn't sink in right away. Not right at first. The brain processes it, but stores it up for another time to reflect and feel the pain. That's probably because the "fight or flight" survival instinct is busy taking over.

I was feeling like someone lost out in the blue cold of a snowy wilderness. And all around I could see the wolves circling and flitting in between the trees. Hovering off in the distance. Maybe that is what Napoleon's troops felt like after their commander led them into an unwinnable war in Russia in the dead of winter.

But only one difference, as I saw it. I was my own Napoleon, and my failed battle plan was ultimately my own colossal failure— and belonged to no one else, not even my persecutors.

I knew exactly how much credit I had left on my credit card. Enough for a night or two at the Night Light. But then I wouldn't have any food or gas money. I had twelve dollars in my wallet.

There was only about one hundred and fifty dollars left in my savings. I decided that the few dollars left on my credit card, and what was remaining in my savings, had to be protected at all costs.

I decided to drive by the rental manager's apartment again. After knocking on the door, but receiving no answer, and noticing that the lights were out and Oscar's car was still gone, I found myself wondering seriously about my lodging for the night.

That having been said, there was no rational reason why I decided to drive around at that point. But I did.

At first, I had thought about parking in Oscar's parking spot and then confronting him whenever he arrived home. But to what end? If Oscar made a demand for the rent, what could I do? There was no way I could guarantee that any additional check I gave him wouldn't bounce also. If he needed enough cash to cover the whole month's rent, I couldn't give it to him.

So instead, I got in my car and started driving, trying to figure things out. I went past the Tornquist church. I made a few turns and down a few blocks. I stopped at a stoplight. There on the corner was a drab concrete building with a sign that read, "Windy City Mission."

Mired in my own worries, I noticed the red light ahead of me only at the last moment. I screeched to a stop just short of a startled pedestrian in the crosswalk.

I watched the man circle around to my side of the car. The last thing I needed was another punch in the face.

As I rolled my window down a crack, I recognized him. Pastor Loveland. The same guy I'd met in front of the church the first time I'd seen it.

His serious expression changed as he recognized me.

"Hey, Kevin, good to see you," he said with a smile. "That was a pretty close one, though. You ought to be more careful—you could get into trouble."

I just wondered how he could have remembered my name.

"Say, could I ask you a favor?" he said.

"Sure," I responded, a little startled.

"Could you give me a ride a couple blocks down to the bus stop? I'm taking the bus home tonight."

I agreed and he hopped in the passenger side.

"I hope I'm not imposing on you," he said. "My car is in the shop today. The bus stop is just four blocks down. So how are you, my friend?"

"Hanging in there," I quipped.

"Sorry to hear about your troubles with the church property. I read the article in the paper. We never dreamed that somebody would want to tear the building down. Landmarking restrictions can be a real problem if you want to make some big change to it."

I agreed but kept my responses to a minimum. A cold rain started falling as we were driving.

"Naturally," he said with a laugh, "the day I don't bring an umbrella…"

As we pulled up to the bus stop on the corner, the rain was coming down in sheets.

"Well," Loveland said, "you were really kind to give me a ride. Thanks so much."

I looked out at the rain-drenched bus stop, and saw no sight of the bus.

"Is it coming soon?" I asked.

"No problem. It should be here before too long."

Loveland reached out to give me a handshake.

"May God bless you, even in the middle of everything else," he said with a smile that seemed to reflect that he knew more about me than he was letting on.

I shook hands with him. Then he turned to get out of the passenger seat.

Then I said something that had no real explanation, except that I enjoyed the company of another human being at the time, and felt like taking a chance.

"Look," I said, "how far do you live? Why don't I just give you a ride home?"

"Oh, you don't have to," Loveland said. "That's not necessary. I don't mind waiting for the bus." Then he gazed at me. And then he said, "But that's real nice of you...you sure it won't put you out?"

"No. It won't," I said. "I wasn't going anywhere anyway."

Loveland nodded when I said that.

"It's about a forty-minute drive...you sure you don't mind?"

"Nope."

"Well good then. I'd love to hear more about the church property," Loveland said. "It's too bad that this has all gotten so complicated for you. At least that's the impression I got from the newspaper article. And then the TV report...you know, it's really interesting that we bumped into each other like this. My wife called me at the mission, right before I left, to let me know it was just on the five-o'clock news. The protest rally that the group had at your college, I mean."

"News travels fast," I muttered.

"It seems to," Loveland said with a smile. "Amazing, isn't it?"

Twenty-Two

~

On the way to Loveland's house the rains were coming down hard and made the highway glimmer with wet reflections from our headlights. The windshield wipers monotonously thumped back and forth. Loveland got me talking about myself. But he asked very little about the Tornquist property, or my myriad of legal and professional problems.

Instead, Loveland seemed more interested in me and my family. I explained that I was an only child and my parents had passed away. He asked why I ended up pursuing history on the graduate level. I told him how I took an undergraduate course from professor Aubrey Sumner Tuttle at the University of Chicago. He made an impression on me—showed me how the study of history was something that could be objectively studied regarding the facts of the past, obviously relevant to the present, but also an index to the future. "He also showed me that history could just be plain fun...often amusing," I noted, "but always fascinating. So I applied for graduate work at the same university. And I was accepted."

"So—you agree with this professor, that you mentioned..." Loveland said.

"Professor Tuttle?"

"Yes, Professor Tuttle, that history is something that can be objectively studied?"

"Sure," I admitted. "I know there are some theorists who abstractly talk about historians never being able to leave our own subjective assumptions aside...but I couldn't buy into that."

"And that we can really look into things in the past," Loveland said, "and sometimes figure out what really happened? Who lived—who died—who really did what?"

"Sure. That's the stuff of history. That's what historians do."

"How about religious things?" he asked. "Have you taught on that from the standpoint of history?"

I figured it was just a matter of time before a pastor would get down to his favorite subject. So I was happy to oblige. I thought perhaps a sheltered clergyman ought to know that historians aren't afraid to venture onto ecclesiastical turf.

"It's impossible to study the broad sweep of history," I said confidently, "without talking about the role of religion."

"And revivals...the Great Awakening as an example...you've taught on that?"

"Well, early American history isn't one of my fortes...but yeah, I studied it...I mean as a social and cultural phenomenon."

"Do you think," Loveland said casually, "that spiritual revival...a miraculous regeneration of the hearts of men and women...do you think that kind of thing is real?"

"That's a religious question," I said with a dodge. "That's a little out of my line of work."

Loveland paused. The rain had slowed considerably, but there was still a mist in the air, and I still needed my windshield wipers, though I adjusted them by then to a slower setting. After a few quiet seconds, where we heard only the metronome of the wipers, Loveland then spoke up.

"The state of every man's soul is every man's business...don't you think?"

I didn't exactly know how to answer that one. It was a peculiar question—not bizarre or nonsensical necessarily—just peculiar.

"Unlike religion," I said, "I'm afraid that the study of history can't really show us much about the human soul," I finally quipped.

"What if it could?" he replied.

"Could what?"

"Show us something about the soul...the spirit. What if studying history could do that?"

I was surprised that I didn't feel more uncomfortable in that kind of dialogue with a storefront street preacher. But, considering how the human race had been treating me recently, I was enjoying the company. So I decided not to decimate the fellow with a lot of PhD terminology. I kept it civil—courteous.

"Then in that case," I said, "it would be pretty surprising. But I wouldn't take bets on it."

"Hmmm," is all that Loveland said in response.

Then he changed the subject dramatically.

"You said something, Kevin, when you picked me up tonight. You said you weren't heading anywhere in particular. So, why were you out driving tonight? If you don't mind my asking..."

"No," I replied, "I don't mind."

But I did. Considerably. I really didn't want to get into it. Any of it.

"I was just trying to figure out something..."

"Oh?"

"Yes," I said.

Loveland didn't go any further. Which I was glad about. But there was silence, as I noticed that my windshield was dry now and turned off my wipers.

Then there was more silence.

"I had this problem with my apartment," I said, "it's a long story."

"Kevin, are you looking for a place to stay?" he asked, with a surprising kind of directness.

Lucky hook shot, I thought to myself. Loveland had made a really lucky guess. Like when I used to horse around with my pals as a kid in the alley in back of my house—the neighbor kid had a basketball hoop. And we would take turns making wild, behind-the-back hook shots, with our backs turned away from the hoop. And sometimes we would actually make the shot—purely by chance. And we would really go nuts when that happened.

"That was part of the reason for my driving around," I said, trying not to be impressed by Loveland's intuitive sense.

No, that was not just part of it—it was all of it, but I didn't want to explain that to Loveland.

"Look," Loveland said, "I don't want to stick my nose in your business. But if you need a place to stay, we have an extra bedroom. You are more than welcome to stay the night tonight and tomorrow night too. And then, if you are still having a problem with accommodations, then we can talk about some other ideas. Okay?"

"Well, I wouldn't want to put you out..."

"Not at all. Lilly and I take in house guests all the time. It comes with the territory."

"You're sure?"

"Yes. Absolutely. We even have extra toiletries and such in the guest room. You can make yourself right at home."

My pragmatism was now kicking in. At least I had a place to stay. Tomorrow, I told myself, I would drive immediately over to the unemployment office and apply for unemployment compensation. From what I knew of the process, it wouldn't cover all of my prior salary—but it would give me most of it. At least that was a start. And then, after I got confirmation of some expected income, I could go visit Oscar the rental manager and get him to take the overlock off the door of my apartment.

Things were looking up.

"Right over there," Loveland said pointing to a little red brick bungalow, "that's the house."

The lights were on inside, and the windows were squares of yellowish illumination in the night, which by then had fallen.

TWENTY-THREE

"So, Mr....Hastings, is it?"

"Yes. Hastings. Kevin Hastings," I said.

The unemployment compensation examiner was leafing through my application.

After a good night's rest at Pastor Loveland's house, I had gone, bright and early, over to the unemployment office.

"Your paperwork looks like it's in order."

That was good.

"Now Essex College's legal counsel has already faxed over their response this morning," the examiner said. "Boy, they were really Johnny-on-the-spot with this. Anyway, Essex, your former employer, they are claiming a couple of things. Let me go through that with you. They are claiming that you committed misconduct on the job, and as a result, they are contesting your right to unemployment benefits."

That was bad.

"Okay. Could you explain that to me, because I certainly contest what they are contesting..." I said abruptly.

"I'm sure you do," he replied curtly. "Let's go through this..."

Then he pulled out the fax from Hubert Jankowski, Esq., counsel for Essex. After studying it for a minute or two, he started asking me some questions.

"Now, Mr....uh..."

"Hastings," I snapped.

"Right. Mr. Hastings. When you were first employed at Essex was there an employment handbook given to you to read?"

"I think so…"

"And did you sign a document that indicated that you had read, and understood, and agreed to all of the requirements in the handbook for a full-time faculty member at Essex?"

"Boy, that was a long time ago…"

The examiner detached a piece of paper from Jankowski's fax, and then showed it to me.

"I'm going to show you something called 'Acknowledgment Regarding Essex Faculty Handbook'—is that your signature at the bottom, Mr. Hastings?"

"I guess I did sign that…"

"And according to attorney Jankowski in section II of the handbook there are some requirements regarding the handling of your class load in the event of an absence…"

"Technically. Only technically…"

"And according to section II, if you are going to miss class then you need to a) secure a competent and skilled substitute at a PhD level, or master's degree with credits toward a PhD, to take the lecture for you…"

"Nobody did that at Essex, I can tell you that…"

"Or b), post a notice," the examiner continued, "at the departmental bulletin board, and post also on the Web site of the department, at least 24 hours in advance of the class, a notice to the students of your class indicating 1) the fact of the class being cancelled, and 2) any new assignments for the next class, or anticipated tests that may not appear on the syllabus—except for *pop quizzes,* and that phrase is defined elsewhere, let's see, back in section I under definitions…"

"None of the faculty—seriously," I said, interrupting him, "none of the other professors ever followed that. I can guarantee you that. Just canvass any other members of the faculty. Just call up any of the other professors in the history department for instance…"

The examiner put down his file and stared at me. I could hear the receptionist out in the lobby, and in the cubicle next to ours, another examiner was shuffling through his papers and opening and closing a filing cabinet.

"This is your application for unemployment compensation benefits, Mr. Hastings, not theirs," he finally retorted.

I recognized that look. It was similar to the expressions on the faces of the members of the Essex College disciplinary committee when they started my hearing in the big boardroom at Old Main.

"Your former employer," he continued, "has listed a number of absences from your classes over the last few months. But within the last few weeks you have had three…"

"I had some emergency events in my life, mostly dealing with legal issues…"

"And that you failed to follow the explicit requirements of the handbook in each of those instances…is that a correct statement Mr. Hastings?"

"Like I said, there were some very unusual matters, several crises…"

"Did you fail to follow the handbook procedure?" he asked flatly.

"Yes," I said loudly enough that the paper shuffling in the cubicle next to us stopped momentarily.

"Okay. I think that about does it," the examiner said.

"Did I mention," I interjected quickly, "that I got runner-up for the 'Teacher of the Year Award' two years in a row as voted on by the student body at Essex?"

"Congratulations," the examiner said, with the same degree of enthusiasm as you might expect from a 7-Eleven clerk when you tell him you have exact change.

"So," the examiner continued, "I am going to find, for purposes of this stage of your application, that you have committed *misconduct* and thus are disqualified from any unemployment benefits…"

"Runner-up for Teacher of the Year," I said forcefully, "does that sound like somebody who would be guilty of *misconduct?*"

"It's just a technical term, Mr. Hastings. I don't mean to impugn you personally. It just means that you're disqualified from unemployment benefits. Of course you can appeal my decision…"

"And I certainly am going to appeal…"

"And so here is the notice of appeal to fill out and drop it at the desk in the front where you came in," he said handing the form to me.

"So, that's it? Our government in action? Due process as envisioned by our Founding Fathers?" I said, barely containing my anger.

"Mr. Hastings," he said with a steely stare, "this concludes your interview. You need to leave now."

As I stood up, the examiner added one more thing.

"Life goes on, Mr. Hastings. Good luck on your appeal."

I went out to the lobby, quickly filled out the notice of appeal, dropped it on the secretary's desk, and left.

"Life goes on," I fumed to myself. *"Easy for you to say, buddy, while you're on the public dole with a guaranteed paycheck. There's always going to be people who are unemployed…so I guess that puts you in a real growth industry.*

As soon as I was in my car I called Horace Fin on my cell phone. When he answered, I first launched into the happenings at Essex College, and my suspension.

"Should have called me," Fin snapped back. "Should have never walked into that disciplinary hearing unrepresented."

"Yeah, but they dropped the notice of the hearing on me, like, five or ten minutes before the hearing," I complained. "I didn't have time to think, let alone call you…"

"You didn't need to think," Fin said. "That's what I get paid for. All you need to do is memorize something in the gray matter of your brain. Ready? Here it is. *Call Horace Fin.* When something bad is coming down, you just learn that mantra, chant it, memorize it, put it to music. *Call Horace Fin.*"

"But what I'm trying to tell you is that I didn't have the time to do that."

"Ever heard of cell phones? And even if you couldn't," Fin continued, "you should have made the demand to have your lawyer present. Demand it. That might have log-jammed things. Sometimes you just have to drop a bunch of logs in the river to slow down the current. Especially when the current is taking you over Niagara Falls." With that, Fin started chortling.

I then changed the subject to the issue of my unemployment compensation problems.

"Tough break," Fin said. "Misconduct is usually stealing from your employer, that kind of thing. But it also includes disobeying an express directive when it is deemed to be an important one. So, that's likely what he was basing it on."

Then I told him about being locked out of my apartment.

"Can't do that, unless he follows the proper procedure regarding eviction. Which it sounds like he hasn't," Fin said.

"Great," I said enthusiastically.

"Problem, though, is what I call 'the law between the cracks'…"

"What do you mean?"

"Well, there's the law. And then there's the law of what falls between the cracks. I'm sure your apartment manager knows he didn't follow the eviction procedure."

"Okay. So where does that lead us?"

"But he also knows that it will cost you more money than it will be worth for you to hire a lawyer and fight it. So, his little legal misstep ends up falling between the cracks. And meanwhile, he's got you all in a whirlygig over this—which was his intent I'm sure."

"So, where do I go from here?"

"Well, I am going to fax over to you some papers from a company in New Jersey. It does 'litigation financing.' Technically, this is a controversial thing—I can't intrude into this deal as your lawyer. But in some jurisdictions they allow companies to up-front the costs of civil litigation of a penniless litigant—like you—in return for a certain percentage of the recovery of your tort action—in this case against Gentry and his firm."

"But I need the rent money."

"Look, how you use the money is between you and them. And they are a finance company as well. Either way, they can probably get you a short-term loan. I can give you the number to call. They'll probably want to talk to me about the merits of the lawsuit against Gentry's firm because they will then want a lien on any proceeds if and when you win. *After my share for attorney's fees, of course,*" Fin added with a chuckle, "which always comes off the top."

I took down the number.

"Now," Fin said, "I've got some good news. We've got a hearing on our application for permit for demolition before the Landmark Commission day after tomorrow."

"Wow, that doesn't give us much time," I said.

"No problem. Come by here tomorrow at 2:00 sharp. We'll go over what to expect at the hearing."

After I hung up, I immediately called the number that Fin gave me for East Coast Litigation and Finance Partners, Inc., and got the paperwork started. Two hours later they called me back on my cell phone, after having talked with Fin about the case against Gentry, and said that they would extend some short-term financing to me. It would be enough to live on for about two months. At least it would be a start. They would fax the paperwork to me via the all-night copy store that same day, and I was to overnight the signed originals back to them. Then they would direct deposit the loan proceeds directly into my checking account.

Funny how—just like that—things can turn around. I called Oscar and told him that he could expect the rent check that week.

"By the way," I said boldly, "you broke the law, according to my lawyer, when you put the overlock on the door…"

"You guys," he growled, "you yuppies with your lawyers. Just make sure it's either cash or certified check or cashier's check."

As I hung up, I realized that I had just experienced Horace Fin's "law between the cracks."

TWENTY-FOUR
~

ACCORDING TO MY CALCULATIONS, the money from my short-term loan would be deposited directly into my checking account by the following day. After my telephone consultation with Horace Fin and my unpleasant exchange with Oscar the apartment manager, I had a little time left in the waning hours of the afternoon. There was something I wanted to check on the Internet. But I had been kicked out of Essex College, and therefore couldn't use my computer at work. And I was still locked out of my own apartment, which contained my personal computer.

So I stopped by a cybercafé, and paid a few dollars to log on.

Call me stupid, but I was still intrigued by the woman who loved Vermeer. In a way, even more so since seeing her with a bullhorn leading the protest at the college.

I was fairly confident that both she—and her group—had jumped on an architectural preservation issue with only half the facts. After all, I had no idea that some semifamous architect had designed the building when I agreed to sell it to Tony DeVoe's client. Did they know that? Probably not. Nor did I have the least inkling that by agreeing to guarantee the demolition of the Tornquist church I would be erasing some important aesthetic feature from the face of Chicago.

No indeed. I was just trying to get rich, and to do it quick. Women like Charlotte would applaud, even adulate that kind of personal initiative.

On the other hand, I had the general notion that women like—whatever her name was who was holding the bullhorn—cared more for beauty than base materialism.

And frankly, that was one of the things that intrigued me about her.

Together with the fact that she was delightfully pretty, had a quick wit, and wasn't afraid to engage me. Added to that was the undefined, yet powerful component of male-female relationships that we merely sum up with the too-biological term "chemistry."

There was definitely some kind of chemistry when we met in Dan's Diner. Or at least, there was the beginning of some positive chemistry, despite a little clumsiness on my part. Until we saw each other at Essex College, the day of the televised protest, when our eyes met. That was a category of human chemistry that was altogether different.

What it was, I didn't know. *But then, there are all kinds of chemistry*, I thought to myself as I sat at the computer, *so, was this the type that mixes volatile compounds—the kind that blows up the unsuspecting lab researcher?*

I typed in a Web search for *Society for Landscaping and Architectural Preservation*, and then added, "Chicago."

There were several listings, starting with their official Web site. I accessed that first.

It was a good looking site that had as a motto, "Aggressively Preserving the Architectural and Aesthetic Beauty of Chicago."

I blinked at the term "aggressively." But it didn't end there. Their site bragged about protests and lawsuits they had launched against "Gold Coast Money Barons Who Are Willing to Rape the Image of the City for a Quick Buck."

Hmmm. While I, personally, was certainly no "money baron," the rest of the shoe seemed to fit all too well.

I clicked onto the site button for "Staff." Listed as the executive director was someone named Tess Collins. There was a picture next to the bio. It was her—the woman who loved Vermeer. But the photo didn't do her justice. There was a dynamic kind of beauty to her, in person, that the on-screen image just didn't capture.

It said that she had a BA from Southern Methodist, majoring in art. After that she received a master's in urban planning from the University of Chicago. She had also "pursued postgraduate work at the Pioneer Institute of Art." And she had been the executive director for the last two years. Not a lot of information.

So I went back to the home page and clicked onto the category of "Projects."

They had not updated the site to include the Essex College protest. But there was a photo of her being dragged off by police, one on each arm, where, in the prior year she was protesting the destruction of a large stone art piece titled *Zeus Weeping*, which had been donated to a Chicago park; but it had to be broken apart when a water main directly underneath sprung a leak. Apparently the footings of this monument were dug too deep, right onto the water main. The stone art piece couldn't be removed without busting off the feet of Zeus.

According to the accompanying article she had proposed an expensive, impractical alternative route for the public works department—to dig a tunnel into the broken water main from the side. The city workers with the hard hats just laughed at that. So she, and several others from her group, chained themselves to Zeus. The police had to bring in welding equipment to cut the chains so they could remove them from the scene.

In the photo, she appeared to be going limp, dragged along by two burly Chicago policemen. Her face was contorted as she was screaming in protest.

So, that was Tess Collins. The woman who loved Vermeer.

It was then that I realized the depth of commitment she and her compatriots had for something as ethereal as the "architectural and aesthestic beauty of Chicago." I had studied the Tornquist church building. And while it was admittedly unique from a design standpoint, I can't say that it qualified for the label, "aesthetic beauty."

But then I was struck by something else. If Tess and her group were willing to raise a raucus on the front lawn of the Humanities building, they were certainly also willing to do whatever it took—

lawsuits, sit-ins, civil disobedience—to stop my plans to demolish the Tornquist structure and have Vito Mangiorno build an ugly cement parking garage in its place.

As I considered the matter, and logged off of the computer, I was struck by a thought, and it burst the bubble of temporary harmony I had been in since getting approval for my little loan.

It was like a vision. Resembling a TV wrestling match. A roped ring with screaming fans all around out there in the darkened, smoke-filled coliseum, and lights blazing down on the four-square canvas.

In one corner was Tess Collins and her organization of aesthetic radicals. In another corner was Tony DeVoe and Vito Mangiorno. And in yet another was the Landmarking Commission to whom we had appealed for demolition permission. And in the final corner there was Lloyd Gentry and his law firm, whom we had sued for "gross and reckless malpractice."

And there I was, in the middle of the ring.

Waiting to be rushed from all four sides.

TWENTY-FIVE

~

THAT NIGHT I ARRIVED at Pastor Loveland's house for dinner, as his wife had kindly invited me to eat with them. I figured that it would be my last night with them, as I was expecting to get the loan proceeds the next day, pay off Oscar, and then get back into my own apartment.

His wife, Lilly, was a willowy woman, soft-spoken, with glasses, but had her own way of putting her finger right on the heart of the matter. Case-in-point was our conversation near the end of her way-better-than-average meal of roast beef, parsleyed potatoes, and asparagus that she had prepared for us.

Pastor Loveland had been dominating the dinner conversation with me, mostly about current events in the news. He finally told me to simply call him "Jim," which I did.

"Jim," I said, "how long have you been over at the Windy City Mission?"

"Twelve years," he said between bites.

There was a break in the conversation. Then Lilly spoke up.

"Kevin," she said gently, "did you find your way to the address that you asked me about?"

"Yes, I sure did, and thanks for your help," I replied. Remembering that I had discreetly asked about the quickest way to get to the address of the unemployment office, without tipping her off to where I was going.

"You know, Kevin," Lilly continued, "I drive by there every day, on my way over to the Christian school where I work...remember, I told you that I'm the assistant to the principal?"

"Right, I remember."

"So, going by there every day," Lilly continued, "of course I notice the building at that address that you asked me about..."

I was chewing my last bite of asparagus when she said that, but my chewing got a bit slower as I tried to ponder her point.

"And so I just guessed that you were going to the unemployment office there..."

I smiled, and swallowed hard.

"Yes," I said, but did not elaborate.

"Well, I was just thinking," she said softly, then she turned to her husband. "Jim, if Kevin is looking for some temporary work... why not mention to him about the situation over at the mission, and Bob Moody?"

Jim Loveland perked up and apparently got the point.

"Say, that's a great idea," he said. "Bob Moody is the administrator of the mission. My role is pretty well limited to pastoral duties. Bob used to have an assistant, but she moved out of state. Anyway, Bob has an even more urgent need for help now. He's pretty well wheelchair bound with ALS..."

I was trying to remember what condition that was, when Lilly cleared it up for me.

"Lou Gehrig's disease," she said. "He's limited to an electric wheelchair. His mind is still very quick. But his muscle control is going quickly."

"You know," Jim Loveland continued, "with your educational background and training, you would be a natural to fill-in for a while, helping Bob out with mostly paperwork, reports, that kind of thing. At least until we can get a permanent replacement. What do you think?"

I was struggling for a way to back out of this gracefully.

"And I could make sure," Loveland added, "that they pay you the full $16 per hour for the position. I think it's thirty hours a week. How about it?"

I was never very good at higher math. But I did know that I

CRAIG PARSHALL

was getting an offer that was $16 an hour more than the zero I was getting from my denied unemployment benefits. So I hedged my bets a little.

"That might be…something I would be interested in," I said with some reserve. "Only as a temporary fix…till I get back into teaching…Let me get back to you on that. Can I?"

"Of course," Jim chimed in.

After dinner, I turned in early. I had a big day scheduled for the following day. I had to make sure the loan proceeds were deposited into my checking account, and then withdraw enough cash to pay Oscar the rent, plus a little left over for myself for food, gas money, and incidentals. Then I had a conference on the books with Horace Fin.

The next morning, after breakfast, I thanked them both for their kindness and generosity in putting me up, but I told them that I would be able to get into my own apartment that night. So I gathered my things and, with a small measure of regret that I would probably not see them again, and after shaking Jim Loveland's hand and letting Lilly hug me, I got into my car and drove off.

You see, by the time I was in my car I had figured something out. Horace Fin had sounded optimistic about getting city approval for the demolition of the Tornquist church. Once that was accomplished (and the hearing was coming up later in the week) I could then complete the sale to Mangiorno/VM Contractors through DeVoe. Which meant that I would, once again, be financially solvent. And in just a few days.

Which also meant that I wouldn't need to take the offer for the job at Windy City Mission, something that I was trying to avoid anyway. While I didn't consider myself religion-phobic, I nevertheless wasn't looking for an employment opportunity that would surround me with people whose idea of entertainment was hymn singing and memorizing the names of the more obscure Jewish kings of the Old Testament.

So, as I saw it, as soon as the Landmarking Commission gave us the go-ahead, I would phone in my regrets to Jim Loveland. And that would be that.

On the way to my bank I called my 24-hour banking service and, to my everlasting happiness, verified the loan money was now in my account. I went to the bank window, pulled out the money, and sped off to my apartment. I noticed that Oscar's car was there—an equally good sign. He answered the door right away, and I handed him the cash for the rent.

"How about the overlock?" I asked.

"Already took it off."

"Really?"

"Sure. You think I'm lyin'? Look for yourself," he grunted.

I had always wondered why a guy like Oscar would be chosen to be the apartment manager for units that catered to young professionals, bankers, college professors, accountants, and lawyers. But then again, upon further reflection, it did make sense. After all, why did well-dressed Mafia dons employ "go-to" guys who have big shoulders and thick necks? Oscar was a kind of rental "enforcer."

"I would like a receipt, please," I said to Oscar with a bit of attitude in my voice. The kind of tone of entitlement that you might use when you ask someone to move over as you climb into the lifeboat; when ironically, just moments before, you thought you might be left behind on the sinking *Titanic*. Funny how we uniformly expect the good things to come our way—as a matter of personal right—but we are ready to curse the fates, or heaven, or God, when bad things happen.

Oscar came back with a hand-scrawled receipt. Without thanking him, I snatched it up and then bolted up to my apartment. I unlocked the door, walked into my unit, and breathed a sigh of relief.

There were a few messages on my voice mail. One from Uncle Mort explained how he was leaving for California to be with his daughter, who'd been injured in a hiking accident. Another was from Tom Taylor, wondering how I'd fared in finding "alternate temporary housing." That was ironic, because he must have known I was locked out of the apartment where my answering machine was, and I didn't have the capacity to retrieve messages remotely.

And there was also a message from Alice, the secretary for the history department, reminding me of the "final hearing of the disciplinary committee" at Essex that was scheduled for the following week.

The apartment smelled a little musty. But it was good to be back. I drew back the curtains and opened a window. After strutting around my abode, I glanced at my watch and decided I had better get going.

I needed to get over to Horace Fin's office to prepare for the hearing before the Landmarks Commission. That hearing, and the demolition approval, I was convinced, would be my Rubicon.

History tells us that when Caesar decided to cross that particular river in northern Italy it would lead, inevitably, to his subsequent seizing of complete power to the Roman Empire. For me, my goals were considerably less lofty.

I just wanted to get my life back.

TWENTY-SIX

~

WHEN I ARRIVED AT HORACE FIN'S OFFICE, I nearly ran head-on into a young man wheeling a hand dolly out the front door, stacked with boxes. He then proceeded to roll them up a sidewalk that ended on the strange loading dock that fronted Fin's office. Parked down below the loading dock was a truck with big lettering on the side that said "UltraSlice," and then in smaller letters—"the new document-shredding technology!"

I entered the office and was greeted warmly by Karin in her thick Slavic accent. I was told to wait for a few minutes. Because there were no chairs I just stood and looked around. Things looked the same. The ugly linoleum floor. The metal desks full of women, all of them on the phone. The ring of mismatched filing cabinets along the outer perimeter of the large room. But then I noticed a desk way in the corner—one I had not noticed before. An Asian woman had a stack of magazines and newspapers and she was going through them and cutting out things with scissors.

The more time I spent in Horace Fin's office, the more mysteries I encountered.

I heard Fin bellow out from his office for me to come in.

When I sat down I couldn't help but ask my lawyer about the young man with the dolly and the truck advertising a new kind of document shredder.

"Is that all part of your law office?" I asked.

"Don't worry about that," he said with a smile. "That's what you might call my creative fee structure…"

He then launched into an explanation. It seemed he had once represented a businessman who had obtained a patent on a new kind of laser technology in document shredding. It was, Fin assured me, revolutionary. With that technology, he said, coupled with a newly invented high-speed document-feeding device, those portable shredders are no larger or heavier than an ultrathin lap-top computer, and could go anywhere—they ran on batteries that were recharged with sunlight so they would "operate in the middle of a jungle"—and could shred hundreds of documents per minute.

"Each unit has extra durable plastic garbage bags connected at the bottom to catch the shreds," Fin explained proudly.

Fin must have seen by my expression that I was not getting the point. So he expanded.

"Look, Kevin, my boy," he said with bravado, "what did the corporate scandals in Enron, WorldCom, and Tyco all have in common?"

I thought about it for a minute and then I shook my head.

"Here's the answer," Fin said. "Not enough good document shredders!"

After further reflection, I wanted to argue the point a little. I had read the newspaper accounts of the prosecutions involving those companies.

"Well, but how about the evidence of incriminating e-mails on a computer hard drive...this document shredder wouldn't eliminate that, would it?"

"No," Fin said, leaning his immense girth back in his executive chair, and rocking back and forth a few seconds. Then he added, "And it doesn't pick up your laundry, walk your dog, or do your taxes either." He smiled as if he had just crushed my argument with a wrecking ball.

"So, what does this paper shredder have to do—" I started to ask.

But before I could finish, Horace Fin jumped in.

"You mean, with my law office?" he said. "Well, you see the guy who owned the shredding business was my client who shall remain nameless, and he had gotten into some trouble. Allegations of bank fraud. The feds say that he lied on federal loan papers. Anyway, I got all the charges dismissed. Ultimately. But by the time I did, he was flat broke. My fees were enormous, and were still unpaid. The only thing he had left was this fledgling paper shredder business, so..."

Then Fin spread out his arms to encompass his office and said triumphantly, "Voilà! We got his whole business, the building, the goods, the truck, the whole bit."

However, I didn't share Fin's exuberance. In fact, hearing that story left me with a sour feeling down in my gut.

"But let's not reminisce on such matters," Fin said with an awkward attempt at elegance. "Instead, let us prepare for the Landmark Commission hearing."

I was glad he was finally getting down to brass tacks.

My lawyer gave me a quick description of the composition of the Landmark Commission, and the procedure. I was moderately impressed by his grasp of the process.

He also explained his line of argument.

"First is the fact," Fin continued, "that, according to what you told me, you had no idea that the Tornquist property was a protected site under the Chicago landmarks code."

"Absolutely," I chimed in. "Nobody told me."

"Next," Fin said, "refusal to permit the demolition will cause a huge economic hardship to befall you..."

"Right again," I seconded.

Then Fin made his last point.

"And third, there is the matter of the location of the Tornquist building on the zoning grid of the city. It is in a commercial area. Zoned for business. And everybody knows that parking is at a premium down there. A parking structure on that site will be good for the people of Chicago."

Horace Fin then reviewed the facts of my purchase of the property again. As well as the terms of the agreement with VM Contractors through attorney DeVoe.

"By the way, where are we on the Mangiorno side of all of this..." I started to ask.

"Hey, the hearing is tomorrow," Fin countered. "They know that.

DeVoe and Mangiorno know that your hands have been tied up until the commission gives you permission to start demolition."

I was a little queasy about Fin's using metaphors about my hands being tied up, especially in the same sentence with Mangiorno, but I let that pass. Then I asked him about when we were going to be suing the real estate broker and the Nuveau Art Foundation, as he had promised, for failure to disclose the landmarking status of the property.

"All good things come to those who wait," Fin said with a smile. Then he explained that he wanted to sue them only after Gentry and his law firm, in the legal malpractice case, formally pointed the finger of blame at them first.

"And that has now happened," Fin said. "When Gentry and his firm filed an answer to our malpractice complaint, they lodged a defense that the cause of all of your problems was the negligence and wrongdoing of the broker and the art foundation for failing to disclose the fact of the landmarking status."

Fin said that now he would be filing a suit against the broker and the foundation, and possibly joining that suit with his pending malpractice suit against Gentry and his firm.

It seemed to make sense to me.

That is, until his last comment, before excusing me from his office.

"By the way," Fin said tossing a photocopied stack of papers to me. "A little bad news for you...nothing I can't handle."

As I glanced down on the first page I saw that it was a lawsuit filing. Lloyd Gentry's name was at the top, next to "plaintiff." And my name was down lower, next to "defendant."

"Gentry has now sued you for defamation of character. For that comment of yours in the *Chicago Sun-Times*. You can read his lawsuit there at your leisure. And one other thing..."

I was still sitting there in stunned silence, already doubled over from that blow to the solar plexus. Now came the karate chop.

"Gentry and his lawyers have scheduled you to give your deposition in that case...day after tomorrow. But we'll talk more about that tomorrow. After the commission hearing."

"What?!" was all I could shout out, so loudly in fact that Fin winced a little.

Unruffled, he proceeded to hustle me out of his office, telling me he had places to go, people to see. I protested loudly and angrily that I needed more information about the latest bomb he just dropped on me, and I needed it now.

But all he would say, as he closed the door to his office in my face was, "Kevin, litigation is like the tide, it comes in, it goes out…for a while it looks good, then looks bad, then it turns good again…the point is to ride that surf, up on top, but don't ever try to swim into it. 'Cause then you get a gut full of salt water. And maybe worse."

I was still trying to figure that one out as I climbed into my car, dazed.

TWENTY-SEVEN

~

I DIDN'T SLEEP VERY WELL that night. At one point, in the middle of the night, after tossing and turning I got up, drank a glass of water, and then turned on the news on TV. After a while I meandered over to my computer. I logged on to the Web site for Tess Collins's radical architectural preservationist group. I studied her picture for a long time. Then I clicked over to the news photo on their site with her getting arrested.

Somehow, it struck me as odd that a political activist like her would have a passion for an artist like Vermeer. A painter whose work, according to my jaunts to the art museums with Charlotte, "subtly plumbed the depths of love, longing, and beauty in the ordinary settings of life" according to a brochure I had picked up when she and I had attended a show on the Dutch masters once.

I had discovered the brochure under a pile of papers in my apartment around the time I first ran into Tess Collins. After that encounter, I decided to pin it up on my bulletin board in the kitchen.

Perhaps, I thought, there was more to Ms. Collins than I had guessed.

I went back to the home page of the Web site. There was an e-mail box to use if the browser wanted to contact the Society for Landscape and Architectural Preservation. So I typed in my e-mail address. I was mindful of Horace Fin's early advice to me not to discuss any aspects of my legal cases—or anything having to do with the Tornquist property—with anyone else without going through him first. But my doubts about Mr. Fin were increasing exponentially.

Sometimes you just have to grab the tiger by the tail—and use your own two hands to do it.

So I typed in a short e-mail message. It read:

> Dear Ms. Collins:
>
> You will recall that we have met three times. The first two were at Dan's Diner. The third was at Essex College where I have been a professor. It's really too bad that all of this business over the Tornquist church building has become so complicated and controversial.
>
> I think it might help if the two of us were to talk directly. What do you think? Maybe we could come up with some solutions.
>
> Warmly,
> Kevin Hastings

At first, I wasn't going to bother to put my cell phone number down. What were the chances that she would call me directly? I was betting that if she were going to respond at all, it would be through e-mail—through the arm's length posture that electronic communication permits. A safe form of interaction...particularly for a woman who preferred a Dutch artist known for giving the illusion of personal intimacy but all from a safe distance. But in the end, impulsively, I decided to type my cell number into the e-mail anyway.

By then I was tired, and I collapsed into bed. The next thing I knew, my clock radio was blaring with a report about the early morning traffic conditions.

I was bleary-eyed and slammed my hand blindly down on top of the radio to turn it off. And as I swung my legs over the side of the bed and tried to pry my eyes open I had only a random series of thoughts, all having to do with one thing.

"This is it. This is the day. Make or break. The Rubicon."

If Horace Fin could just cajole, manipulate, or intimidate that Landmark Commission into granting me permission for demolition,

I would finally have the wind at my back. Then, a little obliquely, I thought about Pythagoras, the ancient Greek philosopher who said he could move the whole world if he just had a long enough lever.

Horace Fin was my lever. I was banking on that leverage to change my world. To turn back the hands of the clock, back to when my life was sane, and predictable, and normal.

My destination was North La Salle Street where the commission held its hearings. I struggled through the rush-hour traffic that morning, leaping forward a few feet in my car, then slamming on the brakes, and repeating that unnerving process a thousand times as I inched toward the downtown district. My car was swallowed up in the middle of a slow parade of vehicles inching and stuttering forward in small incremental fits.

Off in the distance were the skyscrapers of Chicago's Loop, and those just beyond, on the other side of the Chicago River. The sky was gray and foggy. Out of the mist I could see the skyscape of the great towers. The Hancock. The Sears. And the lesser, soaring rectangles of commerce that were crowded around them like Monopoly pieces stacked all the way up to the shores of Lake Michigan.

The poet Carl Sandburg wrote about Chicago. "Hog butcher for the world," he called it. And "city of big shoulders."

But as I made my way into the snarl of downtown, the city did not seem poetic. Not on that day. As I pondered what might happen if Horace Fin was unsuccessful I realized that Carl Sandburg could have added another very personal description of Chicago: "Destroyer of Kevin Hastings."

About a block away from the commission building I drove my car down into the spiral depths of one of those multilayered underground caverns of a parking lot. Then I grabbed my briefcase and scurried to the elevator, and then up into the daylight of the street level. I ran across traffic and into the building. When I arrived at the floor where the hearing was going to be held, I was shocked.

The entire floor outside the hearing room was crammed with people. I saw several cameramen from TV stations. And several reporters with tape recorders. One of them was already interviewing a woman in the crowd. Then the TV lights clicked on and flooded the woman with illumination as a TV reporter stepped in with a second interview with the woman.

As I walked closer, I saw that it was Tess Collins. She was smiling. Looking confident. Animated, and energetic, she was talking quickly to the reporter.

Then I felt someone grab my arm.

It was Horace Fin.

"This way," he shouted, and pulled me through the double doors and into the hearing room. The room was already filling up. There were two floor microphones planted in the aisles of the audience section. At the front was a counsel's table facing a semi-circular dais with nine leather chairs—one for each commissioner.

The commissioners were milling around close to their chairs. Horace pointed to a chair next to his at the table and told me to sit next to him.

Then the commissioners started taking their seats. I heard the doors swinging open in the back as people flooded into the hearing room and squeezed into the remaining seats.

As I sat down next to Fin, that was when I decided to turn slightly and look back over the room behind me.

In retrospect, I was sorry I did.

In the very back of the hearing room, against the wall, were two men standing, with their arms crossed.

One was the squat, broad-shouldered Troy Armstrong.

And standing next to him was Tony DeVoe, in a shiny dark suit, his eyes obscured behind his tinted glasses. But his head looked like it was jutted forward a little bit. I noticed it even from my position at the front of the room.

And DeVoe had that spring-loaded posture, tensed, and glaring. Like a wolf in the wilderness, motionless, eyeing the prey. Waiting.

Twenty-Eight

~

THE CHAIRMAN OF THE LANDMARK COMMISSION was a tall, stately black man in his thirties named Isaac Williston. His chair was in the dead center of the commissioners' table. He gaveled the meeting to order and quieted the commotion in the hearing room. Then he announced that the sole matter of business was a formal public hearing on the "application of Mr. Kevin Hastings for approval of a permit for demolition."

After shuffling through the papers, he leaned over to his right and conferred with a Korean female commissioner next to him. She pointed to a document in the file. Williston nodded and then leaned forward to the microphone and continued speaking.

"Mr. Horace Fin, you are here representing the applicant, Kevin Hastings?"

Fin jumped to his feet, answering "yes" that he was there as my counsel, and waved for me to stand up, and as I did he also introduced me.

"Very well," Williston said. "My fellow commissioner Mrs. Kim Schu was kind enough to help me locate your letter in the file Mr. Fin, wherein you indicate…yes, here it is…you agreed to waive a preliminary decision under sections 2-120-770 and 780, as well as the informal conference under 790 so we could proceed directly to a formal public hearing on this. Is that correct?"

"Yes, Mr. Chairman," Fin said confidently. "Because we feel that there are exigent circumstances that make it critical that there is a timely decision on our application…"

"Yes," Williston snapped back. "As you say in your letter. But you haven't told us what those are."

"Mr. Hastings," Fin continued, "has a buyer under contract for this property. He is under some pressure as you can imagine to honor that contract which had as its premise the demolition of the existing structure and a subsequent construction of a new structure in its place."

"A parking lot. A multilevel parking lot," Williston said with a cocked eyebrow. "That's what is envisioned to replace the landmarked Tornquist church building?"

With that there were a few groans from members of the audience and a general murmur of discontent.

"Am I correct?" Williston asked.

"Yes, Mr. Chairman. Something that we feel will serve the people of the city of Chicago well, I might add."

But Williston cut him off, indicating that Fin's arguments would be received only *after* the taking of public comments. And with that, Williston was handed a list from the clerk containing the names of citizens who had signed up to speak on the proposed permit for demolition. But after glancing at the list Williston shook his head and then said, "There are no names on the side of the list indicating that they are *in favor of the demolition—only names of persons who wish to oppose it*...is that right? Is there anyone here today who wishes to *support* the application of Mr. Hastings?"

There was a hush in the room. Several seconds elapsed. No one raised a hand. Not even Tony DeVoe, standing in the back.

As Mangiorno's attorney, why in the world isn't he signed up to voice support for my application? I wondered. Of course, under the circumstances, I hadn't been privy to the fact that Vito Mangiorno had given DeVoe orders to keep as low a profile as possible. I might have surmised it, though, by the "cloak and dagger" stuff that DeVoe and Armstrong pulled in the very beginning regarding their "undisclosed" client.

But sitting there, at the commission hearing, none of that came to mind. All I knew was that things were already looking bad.

The ride was about to get bumpier.

"Very well," Williston intoned dramatically. "The Commission for Landmarks calls the following citizens for public comments...

and please line up at the closer of the two microphones there on the floor, you've got two minutes apiece…and don't simply repeat the comments of someone else…if you have nothing new to add, give your place in line to somebody else…"

And with that Williston started calling the first batch of citizens who paraded up to the standing microphones.

The first to address the commission was an elderly Hispanic man who said he was concerned about the traffic congestion to his neighborhood if a multilevel parking structure went up.

"But the structure there now is a church building," Commissioner Kim Schu said, interrupting. "If that building goes back to being used as a church, then that would also bring a lot of cars back and forth. Right?"

"But just Sunday mornings," the man replied. "Or a few times during the week where there is a wedding or something. But a parking lot has cars coming and going all day long, every day, and weekends too! That's going to drive me crazy!"

I slumped back into my chair. I felt like I was in Wrigley Field. The other team had just brought their first batter to the plate, and the guy ends up hitting a home run on the second pitch.

That speaker was followed by a high school art teacher who complained that "G. Dudley Tornquist never got the credit he deserved. He was overshadowed by Frank Lloyd Wright. Now are we going to put the final nail in his coffin by ripping down his first major architectural project?"

After her there was a bus driver who asked why Chicago bothered to have a landmarking ordinance to protect unique buildings if the commission wasn't going to enforce it.

And then there was a self-styled "freelance writer" who gave a rambling narrative which mentioned, in no particular order, the author Nelson Algren, "mean streets," the "lapse of meaning in the Chicago skyline," and finally, after he exceeded his two-minute allotment, he ended with some poetic quote about "*the temples of beauty which are no more…*"

That is when Tess Collins's name was called and she stepped up to the microphone. She quietly described her organization, and her title as executive director. And then, concisely but forcefully she explained in the remaining ninety seconds why this particular edifice was the most significant example of Tornquist's short, but controversial, body of work. That it "contains the graceful flow of floor-to-ceiling panels of colored glass, in perfect harmony with inlaid wood separated by burnished ribbons of steel—a pagoda-like feeling reminiscent of Buddhism but topped with a Christian-type steeple that has an almost humorous skyscraper-like thrust, adorned with tiny window panes, a parody on the commercial buildings in the Loop."

Then she ended by saying, "What this landmark district, indeed what all of Chicago, will lose if the Tornquist is demolished, is irreplaceable. Because it was...and is...a unique expression...a memorial to G. Dudley Tornquist himself. If we lose it, then we shall have lost a part of his artisan's soul as well."

A whole block of the audience burst into applause, many of them jumping to their feet in a standing ovation.

I expected Williston to gavel them into submission. But he never did. He just kept the clock ticking while the applause exploded and reverberated in the hearing room.

As Tess walked back to her seat, Horace Fin leaned over to me and whispered, "That chick sounds a little flaky to me."

I bristled at that, but could not possibly hope to explain to Horace Fin my complicated feeling about Tess. So I just kept my silence, but threw Fin a dirty look.

After that, I lost track of the witnesses that paraded up to the microphone, each of them describing the ghastly and horrendous crimes against aesthetics that would accompany a demolition of the Tornquist church. Eventually, when the last of the complaining citizens had said their piece, Horace Fin was given the opportunity to address the Commission. He stood up, with no notes, and began his presentation.

Fin recounted with ease the history of my purchase of the property. How the site bore no marker or emblem of its landmarked status. How the real estate broker and the art foundation had fraudulently failed to disclose that to me during the negotiations. How my own lawyer had failed to warn me of the landmarking possibility. And how I had entered into a sale of the land to an "undisclosed third party" on the condition that the building could be demolished so a parking garage could be erected.

Ted O'Leary, a broad-faced Irishman on the commission, asked who the "undisclosed buyer" was. Fin handled it with ease, indicating that no adverse inference should be drawn from the fact that "a local businessman simply wants his identity protected until it is known whether his plans for a parking site can be realized."

But Williston followed up himself.

"Are you saying you won't divulge the name?"

I glanced at the back of the room. DeVoe was shifting back and forth a little where he stood.

"I am saying that I am required by the terms of our negotiation not to," he replied.

Then Fin listed each of the reasons why the permit for demolition should be granted, ending with the best argument of all. That the landmarks ordinance allowed for exceptions to strict enforcement of the preservation of landmarked buildings in cases of "economic hardship" to the owner. There it was. The silver bullet. To his credit, Fin fired it right into the heart of the matter. Bull's-eye. He contended that my financial investment would be ruined "in toto" unless I could convert the site to the most marketable commercial use—to wit: a multilevel parking structure. A few of the commissioners prodded him a little on the specifics of such a structure, but Fin adroitly made it sound more like the creation of the Sistine Chapel, rather than a series of concrete parking decks ugly in design and obnoxious to the eye.

By the time Fin sat down, I was already starting to calculate the net profit that I would yield after the site was finally turned over to Mangiorno.

But then a Vietnamese lawyer named Mr. Phou, who represented Tess's group, was allowed to make a rebuttal argument.

"Is this fair?" I whispered to Fin.

"Yeah," he grunted. "Last week the commission decided to allow their group to formally intervene in this hearing process."

Mr. Phou's argument was simple, but devastating. He listed

every example in the last two years where this same commission had denied permits for demolition under situations where the economic hardship to the owner was even worse than mine. One by one he listed the examples that undercut the extent of my financial hardship if the permit were to be denied.

Frantic, I whispered to Fin, "Can't you do something? We're getting killed."

"Observe," Fin said with controlled glee, "the master at work."

Then he jumped to his feet.

"Excuse me, Mr. Phou," he said loudly, "but who exactly is the owner of the Tornquist property. Do you even know who it is?"

My lawyer had picked up on the fact Phou had never mentioned me by name.

Phou seemed a little embarrassed and shuffled through his papers looking for my name. Fin's ploy of sidetracking him seemed to work.

"We all know who it is," Commissioner Williston said diplomatically.

"Yes," Phou said. Then he, unfortunately, added a comment—one that would shortly cause a legal core meltdown on the measure of Chernobyl. Particularly in the hands of Horace Fin, master destroyer.

"The owner is the white guy sitting next to you, Mr. Fin."

"Which white guy?" Fin asked innocently. "I'm not sure I know who you are referring to. There are a number of 'white guys' in this room, Mr. Phou. Which one?"

"*That* white guy!" Williston said loudly, losing patience with Fin's tactics, pointing to me.

"By *that white guy*," Fin countered, "does the chairman mean Kevin Hastings, *that* white guy?"

"Of course!" Williston bellowed. "Kevin Hastings is the white guy we're talking about!"

A stunned and disquieted pall fell over the room for a moment.

But Fin was smiling. He knew that the proceedings were being tape recorded. And he had managed to get a few statements out of

Isaac Williston that could conceivably, if taken sufficiently out of context, be used to tarnish his political ambitions.

What Fin knew, and I was soon to find out, was that a) Isaac Williston had plans for a bid for the next Chicago mayoral election, and b) Williston already had one past "reverse discrimination" claim filed by a fellow by the name of Monty Wingless, a white ex-employee of Williston's house-siding company who said he had been fired because he wasn't black. Fin knew that Wingless was let go because he came into work consistently drunk, but never mind that. The point was that Wingless's "reverse discrimination" case was still pending against Williston. That was one.

Now Fin was preparing to insinuate that our application hearing was case number two.

"It is truly regretful," Fin said in a voice loud enough to be heard all the way out in the hall outside, "that the color of a man's skin can be injected into a solemn proceeding like this...where I would have presumed that the motto should be equal justice under law. Commissioner Williston, I'm simply shocked that you would refer to my client as 'that white guy'..."

That is when pandemonium broke out in the room. All nine of the commissioners began hurling objections at Fin. The crowd, now on its feet, was yelling and booing, and pointing with teeth bared, at Fin and me.

For a moment, I had the urge to stand up and simply walk out of the room. But as I glanced back at the double doors, I saw Tony DeVoe and Troy Armstrong standing directly in front of the doors with their arms crossed, blocking any chance at exit.

In the middle of the verbal free-for-all, Commissioner Williston was now standing up and pointing to Fin and pronouncing some indecipherable curse on my lawyer.

And meanwhile, through it all, I, alone, was forced to sit there, in the vortex of this swirling catastrophe. I was like a swimmer without a life vest, being sucked down into the whirlpool, along with the groaning, collapsing remains of my legal case, which had now taken on too much water, and would sink down to the frigid regions of the bottom of the ocean.

Twenty-Nine

~

THE CHAOS IN THE HEARING ROOM did not quell. Finally one of the commissioners called for uniformed police officers to arrive and ensure that violence would not break out. During all of this time, the assembly of commissioners was standing up, milling around their table, and trying to calm Isaac Williston down.

After two officers arrived they talked with the commissioners for a while. Then the commissioners sat down, one by one, Williston being the last, but eyeing Horace Fin as he did. The two police officers posted themselves at either end of the commissioner's table. Which I found to be paradoxical. Why were they protecting Williston and his group? Fin and I were the ones who were at risk of being torn limb from limb.

When the room was finally quiet, Williston made a short statement "to clarify the record." He vehemently denied that his statement was in any way meant to be racially prejudicial. That he was only "reacting to attorney Fin's comments about attorney Phou's statement...and attorney Fin appears to have engaged in *race baiting* of the worst kind...however, I will not hold attorney Fin's misconduct against his client. I will judge, as I am sure my fellow commissioners will also judge, the merits of this matter with complete objectivity."

Then he called the commissioners into a short huddle in the front of the room for a few minutes.

Meanwhile, I was struggling to figure out Horace Fin's game plan. Why entice Williston to make the off-hand comment anyway?

All I could figure out was that perhaps Fin was engaging in a kind of tactical blackmail. If Williston voted against my application for demolition, Fin could then charge him with reverse racism.

At the end of the huddle, all the commissioners nodded. I don't know why, but I took that as the worst possible sign.

Williston announced the decision. It was short and concise. No frills.

"Eight of the commissioners have voted *against* the application of Mr. Kevin Hastings. Only Commissioner Kim Schu votes in favor. Therefore, the application of Kevin Hastings for a special permit for demolition of the Tornquist church is hereby denied."

He slammed his gavel down on the table, and the commissioners, flanked by the two officers, slipped out through a door situated just behind their table. Then it locked shut behind them.

A few of the audience members meandered over to Fin and myself with ugly looks on their faces. The rest of the crowd flooded toward the double doors. I could see DeVoe and Armstrong in the human tide, pushing their way through, trying to keep an eye on me.

"I need to leave immediately, with you walking right in front of me," I whispered to Fin urgently.

"What am I, your flying wedge?" he sniped sarcastically.

"Do it now!" I said in a hoarse, whispered scream. "You've sunk my case, almost got me killed here, just do this one thing for me!"

So Fin snapped his briefcase shut and started walking ahead of me in the crowd, with me right behind. People all around us were making remarks against him, like "slime bag," "ambulance chaser," that sort of thing. But Horace Fin just smiled as he waded through them, impervious to their insults—like a medieval executioner who, despite the revulsion of onlookers, just happened to take pride in his work.

By the time we pushed our way to the doors I could see DeVoe and Armstrong, who had been pushed to the side, still struggling to stay within the doorway amidst the flood of people. When Fin and I were almost to the door, I slipped around to Fin's side, farthest from Mangiorno's two minions, and then pushed my way out through the doors and into the hallway. At the far end there was an elevator, and an exit sign just a few feet past it marking a stairwell. I sprinted through the crowd, provoking a few humorous cat calls directed toward me, until I got to the stairwell.

I swung open the door and started down the concrete steps.

Then my heart sunk. I hit a long line of citizens who had decided to do the same thing, taking the stairs down instead of waiting for the elevator. They were slowly walking down in clusters, blocking my ability for a quick escape.

Then I reached a landing between floors. As I did, I felt a big hand on my shoulder. I turned around.

It was Troy Armstrong, with a sick grin on his face. He shoved me over against the wall. Then Tony DeVoe appeared, as people continued to file past down the stairs.

"You've been very disrespectful, Mr. Hastings," DeVoe said quietly, getting in my face. "That's not good."

"Not good," Armstrong grunted.

"Running away from us. Avoiding us," DeVoe continued.

"Fin was taking care of this for me. He said he's been talking to you," I countered.

"Horace Fin?" DeVoe said with a laugh. "He's a joke. Your lawyer's a joke. Look, I don't care what Fin's been telling you. We're upset. More important—my client is very upset. That is not a good thing. My client feels that you've welched on a written contract with him. That also is not good. My client's reputation is at stake here. If my client just sits back and takes this from you, what are people going to think?"

"You can see that I've been trying every way I can," I protested, "to get permission from the city to tear down the church so you can build your parking lot..."

"Yeah, sure. Cry me a river," DeVoe said. "Well, time's up, Professor Dingbat. You struck out. So here's what we're going to do. You're coming with my associate Mr. Armstrong and me. We're all going over to my office together. Right now. In my car. And when we get there, you're going to sign a written document. A conveyance. Transferring the Tornquist property to VM Contractors. And after you do that, you will be free to go. And then we'll leave you alone."

"But without city approval for demolition, what's your client going to do with the property?" I asked.

"None of your business," DeVoe snapped

"And you're going to pay me the agreed price for the property?" I asked.

DeVoe laughed loudly.

"I'm afraid not," he said with amusement. "No. You will be paid the entire sum of one hundred dollars. That's what the law calls good and sufficient consideration to bind the deal. And you ought to be thankful we're only asking you to sign a piece of paper. Be glad you're young. And healthy. And still have a good hand to sign a document with."

"A hundred dollars!" I yelled. "You have got to be joking."

"Do I look like a comedian?" DeVoe said. "Now let's get going."

But I didn't move.

Armstrong reached out to grab my arm.

I put my finger in his face.

"I'm not going anywhere with you," I said. "Anyway, I need to talk to my lawyer."

But I looked around and noticed that the number of people going down the stairs past us was now dwindling. Pretty soon there would be no one around. No audience.

DeVoe noticed that too. And when he did, he smiled.

"In a few minutes," DeVoe said, "it'll be just us in this stairwell. So, make up your mind, professor. You want to settle this easy? Or hard?"

Something caught my attention. I was aware of someone standing behind Armstrong and DeVoe. The person stepped out so I could see.

It was Tess Collins.

"I didn't want to interrupt."

You're not—" I started to say.

"Yes, you are," DeVoe snapped.

"Well. Some other time. I just was responding to your e-mail," she said.

"Yes," I blurted. "Were you willing to…to do what I suggested?"

"Well, I guess so," she started to explain.

"Excuse me," DeVoe said with great irritation. "But I was talking here. So lady, take your tea party somewhere else."

With that Armstrong turned to Tess and gave her shoulder a shove.

"Take a hike, little lady," he said.

"Hey, don't touch me!" she said loudly.

"Get your hands off her," I yelled, and grabbed Armstrong by the sport coat that was stretched over his wide back.

He whirled around to face me and was saying, in a kind of strange, singsong voice, "Big mistake. Biiiiiiig mistake.…"

There was a noise from up the stairs.

"Down here," someone was shouting.

Then some more voices.

A man with a television camera and several reporters were scrambling down the stairs toward us. In seconds, the floodlights from the camera were on my face, and on Tess, and also on DeVoe and Armstrong as well.

DeVoe turned away from the camera to face me.

"You'd better be at my office tomorrow morning to sign those papers," he muttered so low that only I could hear him. "This is your last chance."

Then he disappeared down the stairs with the burly Troy Armstrong following after him.

I was barraged by questions from the reporters. But I begged off, indicating that I couldn't make a statement without talking to my lawyer first. But it really wasn't a talk I wanted to have with Horace Fin. I wanted to have him publicly flogged. And then have him put in stocks in the village square.

Tess was queried by them, but she simply smiled and said she had nothing more to add, beyond what she had already said upstairs in the hallway after the hearing. But she did add, "Our organization will be sending out a press release tomorrow. You'll all get one."

When we were finally alone in the stairwell, she turned to me and said, "So. What is it you want to discuss?"

"Can we go somewhere else?" I suggested.

"Like where?"

"Anywhere. You name it, but you'll need to drive me there."

She gave me a startled look. I wasn't going to explain that I didn't want my vehicle tailed, as DeVoe, or some of his goons, might still be lurking around the building.

"Oh, I really don't feel comfortable with that," she said shaking her head.

"I understand. You don't know me. Although, by now, after tonight, you know one thing—I'm apparently the guy singly responsible for destroying the 'temples of beauty that are no more'..."

She struggled a little to keep from smiling. Then she clicked on her cell phone and called Mr. Phou, her lawyer.

"Dienh?" she said. "Tess here. Are you still in the parking lot? Okay. My car is parked right next to yours. Wait for me, will you? I want you to follow me over to Dan's Diner. Right. That's the place. Just follow me, okay?"

Then she clicked her phone off and put it in her pocket.

"Shall we go?" she said.

THIRTY

~

"WHAT'S YOUR RECOMMENDATION?"

"It depends," Tess said, then pausing to say "hi" to a waitress as she passed by our table at Dan's Diner, "on whether you are looking for dinner or not."

Suddenly remembering exactly how much money I did not have in my wallet, and the present state of my financial misery, I said, "Oh gosh, just desert."

"They have some killer pies here," Tess said. "Especially the pecan pie."

When the waitress came to our table, and after some small talk with Tess, she took our orders. Tess ordered the pecan pie.

So did I.

"Decaf coffee, right?" she said to Tess, who smiled and nodded.

"Same here," I said.

"À la mode, right, double scoop maple nut?" the waitress said to Tess.

"Oh Betsy, you know me too well," Tess said, laughing.

"And you, sir?" the waitress asked.

"No ice cream, just the pie," I said, trying to calculate the ice cream differential in coinage without looking at the menu and making myself look totally abject.

"So, what do you want to discuss?" Tess said.

"Well, obviously I thought we ought to talk about the Tornquist property. See if there is some common ground. Middle turf. Room for negotiation."

"I doubt it," Tess said bluntly. "We don't want the building demolished. You do. So, where do we go from there?"

The waitress came with our coffee. As she did, I caught myself looking at Tess a little too closely. I hadn't realized that she had deep, brown eyes. Big eyes. And she was leaning her chin on her hand, with her hand kind of folded under, demurely. There was a paradox here, I thought. Between the aggressive community activist who had torn the bottom out of my boat in the commission hearing, yet up close, seemed to have a kind of fragility.

"Well," I said, trying not to stare at her, "how about this. First, do you believe me when I say that I bought this property not knowing anything about this Tornquist guy, or that the site was under landmarking restrictions? I was just trying to make some money."

"I'm willing to believe you on the first part. That you were an innocent buyer. But the problem is this…that I also really believe you about the second part…that you were just out to make a fast buck. You see, I have a real problem with people who do that to the detriment of everybody else."

The waitress delivered my plain piece of pie. Then she came with Tess's, which was piled high with two huge scoops of ice cream.

I couldn't help but laugh a little.

Tess gave me this weird look when I did, and I felt bad about it. But there was no way I was going to explain to her why I really laughed.

"Why are you laughing?" she asked.

"Just, it's nice, that's all…"

"What?"

"That you like to eat. I like that…"

"Why?" she asked. "Why should you like that?"

What I really wanted to say was, *Look, Tess, you're this woman who is really cute…no, actually way more than cute…and you're little, and the idea of you mowing down on this huge dessert is, how should I put this—endearing. That's it. Which is pretty idiotic for me to say because I don't even know you. But somehow I get the feeling that I do. Does that make any sense?*

But I didn't. Instead, as my friend Tom Taylor might say, I gave her brand X instead.

"Oh, I just think it's…just, good…you're so little, but you still have a great appetite. And you like pecan pie with ice cream. Somehow that says something good about you…I guess…"

She stared at me. After a few seconds she said, "Little?"

"Well, yes."

She looked down on her plate, and then took a spoon and lopped off one of the large scoops of ice cream.

"Here," she said balancing the mound of ice cream on her spoon, "you take this. I can't eat it all."

But as she reached the spoon over toward my plate, the huge scoop of ice cream fell off her spoon and plopped down on the middle of the table.

She stared at it for only an instant, and then broke out into a hearty belly laugh.

That broke me up as we both laughed.

The waitress swooped down, cleaned off the table, and promised to bring another scoop, but we both told her not to worry about it.

"See, all my good intentions get me into trouble," she said with a smile.

"Don't lose that," I said.

"What?"

"Your good intentions. There are a lot of people out there who don't even know what those are."

"That sounds a bit downtrodden, Mr. Hastings."

"Call me Kevin."

"I'm not sure I should…"

"How about I call you Tess? And then you'll have to call me Kevin. See, that's a start. Détente. We're getting somewhere."

"I'm not so sure," she said taking big swallows of her pie and ice cream.

"Look, I'll admit that I was trying to get rich. Okay? I won't bore you with the details, but there is a story behind that. I didn't want to go to war with anybody. I was just trying to get control of my life. And now I'm at war with the whole world it seems."

"That sounds pretty desperate," she said, not looking up.

"I'm dealing with a real crisis here," I said. "That's the truth of it. Now I'd like to make things right. But sometimes that can be unbelievably difficult."

"In other words, dealing with a radical like me?" she said.

"Oh, I don't see you that way," I said. "Not at all."

There was a pause. Then I kept going.

"If you don't mind my saying, I think you're just the kind of person who's passionate about beauty...as a value I mean. But that doesn't make you a radical."

Tess stopped eating, and cocked her head a little. Then she said, "What makes you think that?"

"Well, for instance," I led off, "on the car ride over here, in your little yellow VW, you had a vase filled with water in the dashboard. And you had some real flowers, not fake ones, in the vase."

"That's a stretch," she said with a smile. "VW makes their new cars with the spot in the dash for flowers. It's a chick car. Everybody knows that."

"Well," I continued, "then there's your line of work. Preserving buildings which you think add something...an element of beauty...not necessarily prettiness. I think those are two different things. But beauty of design. Creativity in the middle of a city that can look dreary, and cold. And even ugly in places."

"So, anything else?" she asked.

"Yes. One other reason for my opinion."

"What's that?"

"Vermeer," I said. "You're a woman who loves Vermeer."

Tess was just looking at me, with a expression that didn't seem to say anything, except her eyes, which were looking into mine. So I kept talking.

"So, what I am saying is this—if this building is important to you, then maybe it should be important to me too, that's all. It's just that I am in some...well, significant trouble right now over this property. If you had some suggestions on what I can do, so we can both come out alright, I would love to hear them."

She finished eating. Then she changed the subject all of a

sudden and asked about my family. I told her about my parents both being gone. That I was an only child.

I asked about hers. She said both of her parents were killed in a car accident when she was young. She was raised by an uncle. Her voice changed when she talked about that. There was sadness in it, with a kind of anger, but suppressed.

Then she added something.

"And yes, there is ugliness out there. And not just ugly buildings either."

As I looked at her, I got the sense that her passion for beauty was, maybe in large part, a reaction to something. But ironically, at the same time, I was willing to bet that she couldn't accept that she was exquisitely beautiful herself.

"I know I haven't explained my situation in very much detail," I said. "But do you have any suggestions for how we can resolve this? I really want to try to do that."

Tess delicately wiped her mouth with the napkin and put it down on the table.

"I'll need to think about it," she said.

"Good. That's great," I said. "Think on it and give me a call on my cell phone." I quickly scribbled it down on a piece of paper and gave it to her. She reached for her purse, but I beat her to the punch.

"No, let me take care of the check," I said.

She got up from her chair. I walked her to the door.

"There's Dienh Phou," she said, pointing to his car. "He'll drive you back to your car at the parking lot."

But as she was leaving she turned and added, "Thanks, Kevin, for being a gentlemen when that goon in the stairwell shoved me."

I smiled and nodded.

Then we shook hands, and she stepped out into the night.

As I watched her go, I thought about the handshake. And how it seemed to have lingered on for a second or two longer than just pure business.

But, then, maybe that was just me.

THIRTY-ONE

W HEN I DROVE HOME, my mind was overflowing like a delta flood plain; a slow tide of thoughts and impressions about my meeting with Tess. Most of them were good.

But when I got back to my apartment that night, I was jolted back into reality. There was a message on my answering machine. It was the friendly Slavic voice of Karin, Horace Fin's secretary. She was reminding me of my appointment with Fin the following morning, the purpose of which was twofold. First, to prepare for my deposition in Gentry's defamation lawsuit against me. And second, to prepare for the formal termination hearing at Essex College, scheduled for the day after that, on Friday.

The way I saw it, Fin was getting nervous. I had let him know at the Landmark Commission hearing that I was getting pretty disgusted with his legal representation. Maybe he was going to try to placate me.

Boy, was I wrong.

"Look," Fin led off as I seated myself in his office the next morning, "I know you're tired of getting kicked in the teeth. But litigation is like that. You've got to eat nails for breakfast. Let them know they can't break you. That you'll just keep coming back. Keep getting up off the mat. Like those Rocky movies. You just wave them over to the center of the ring, and point to your face and say, 'Come on and hit me again, you can't hurt me. I can take anything'…"

"Stop!" I said with a raised voice.

Fin's eyes widened a little, but he kept chomping on his unlit cigar. At least he wasn't lighting them up now, out of deference to me.

"Look," I said, "I don't like the way things are looking. And you pulling out that reverse race discrimination card in the hearing last night...that was totally uncalled for."

"Oh, weeeeell," Fin said with a big gesture with both arms spread out wide, "you should have told me..."

"Told you what?"

"That you didn't have the stomach for this. I told you my philosophy of litigation when you came into my office all worried and distraught. Remember? You want to discharge me? Fine. You can do it right now. Before you do, just refresh your memory on the retainer agreement. Page twelve, paragraph seventeen. All your legal fees from my work heretofore will be accelerated...that means due and payable right now."

I was almost afraid to ask the next question.

"So...roughly...how much would I owe you to date?"

"You'll be getting a bill shortly. Just to let you know what kind of tab you're running. But if you want me to figure it out now, it'll take some time. And I'll have to use my advanced calculator. The one with the huge memory capacity."

Then he chuckled.

I was starting to see why he wasn't sweating. He was going to win either way.

Right then, I decided on two things. First, I needed to keep Fin on board, at least until my deposition that afternoon and the Essex College hearing the next day. And maybe longer. But unless things changed radically, I couldn't stick with this guy. He wasn't even a hired gun. He was more like a loose nuclear warhead, just like attorney Jack Thomas had warned me.

But before we continued, I told him about almost getting mugged by DeVoe and Armstrong in the stairwell. Fin didn't seem surprised at that.

"Yeah, they play rough all right," Fin said. "Especially now that we lost the first round in front of the commission. But now for round two. I'm filing a lawsuit appealing the commission's ruling over the noon hour. I cooked up the papers late last night. Williston is just about going to implode when he reads it!"

"And what do I do about DeVoe's threats?" I said.

"You'll have to watch your back until we get into Circuit Court to get the commission's ruling overturned," Fin said.

"That's it? Watch my back?"

"I could file an application for a restraining order against those guys. But, according to you, even though this Tess Collins was hanging around, the only person who actually heard DeVoe's threats against you was you, and DeVoe and Armstrong. Right?"

I nodded. I had asked Tess casually during our conversation at Dan's if she heard DeVoe say anything to me, but she said no. I didn't elaborate with her.

"Well..." Fin said with a smile. "Where do you think you're going with that?"

"So I just wait to get assaulted—or carjacked—or shot in the back of the head?"

"That's a little over the top," Fin said. "Look, they either want the property...or they want their pound of flesh. So we give them the property."

"What!"

"I'll draft up a deed—you'll sign it. I'll send it over to them. But it will expressly provide that title will pass to VM Contractors *only* if and when the Circuit Court overturns the commission and permits the demolition. I have the feeling that Mangiorno is leaning hard on DeVoe and he is leaning on you. We give them a piece of paper. It'll look good. It'll keep Mangiorno satisfied for a little while longer."

"What if that doesn't work?"

Fin took his cigar out of his mouth. It was crumbling into pieces at the end. He wiped his mouth, and then said something that I didn't want to hear.

"Well, in that event," he said tossing his chewed and unsmoked cigar into the wastepaper basket, "you may want to relocate yourself...to an undisclosed location."

THIRTY-TWO

THE REST OF MY CONFERENCE with Fin was spent in discussions about that afternoon's deposition. I tried to focus on that, but it was hard, given his ominous statements about DeVoe and Mangiorno and the possibility of my having to go into hiding. Too much water had gone under the bridge by then for me to question whether he was really serious. I knew he was.

I had also decided that Horace Fin's apparent callousness was probably not intentional. Maybe I was too easy on him, but the way I saw it he had probably spent his entire career up against vipers, piranhas, or thugs—men like DeVoe. The innately evil side of humanity had been his daily fare. So nothing surprised him.

Fin described what a deposition was—that I would give testimony under oath, with a court reporter present, and at Gentry's office with Gentry's lawyer asking the questions. I was to be truthful, but not any more helpful than I needed to be to answer the specific question. It was, Fin explained, Gentry's lawyer's job to ask the right question. If he didn't ask the right question, he was not entitled to get the right answers.

We went over the facts of the statement that was the subject of the lawsuit. Fin told me that he was going to stipulate on the record that I had authorized him to disclose the nasty comment about Gentry to the *Sun-Times* reporter. But he couldn't do that without my consent. I was tempted not to give it. Fin explained that without a stipulation, he would get pulled into the case as a witness himself. Which meant he would have to withdraw as my lawyer before the deposition started.

For a moment, that didn't sound too bad.

But then when Fin played the tape recording he had made of our conversation in his office, where he had cleverly positioned me into not only agreeing with his outrageous characterization of Gentry, but then authorizing him to give it out to the whole world, I knew I was boxed in.

"I guess we have to stipulate," I said.

But I did tell Fin to his face in that conference that I thought the whole affair, from his tape recording me, to his leveraging me into making a scathing cut at Gentry, was just plain rotten.

Fin, as always, was unperturbed.

"In the end," he said confidently, "you'll see that we're controlling the chess board. We're about to capture their knight, and after that, it's checkmate against the king. Have faith, my boy."

Somehow his chess analogy didn't fit. I felt like every one of my pieces on the board had been captured, except one. And that last one was me, stuck in the corner square, surrounded.

Fin repeatedly warned me not to allow Gentry's lawyer to question any of my conversations with him that ended up leading to his sharing my anti-Gentry vituperative with the media. That, Fin explained, was protected by the attorney–client privilege of confidentiality. And in his view, that legal protection was "like a kind of immunity against disease. If you open up the privilege in the smallest degree," he said, "it's a little bit like you lowered your immunity. And then whammy, the germs start pouring in, and next thing you know you're lying on a cold, stainless steel table in the morgue."

One thing about Horace Fin, he always used those nice word pictures.

We went together to the deposition. Fin was driving a relatively new Hummer.

When we entered the conference room in Gentry's office the court reporter was already set up with her stenographic machine. Lloyd Gentry was sitting at the table. Next to him were two other lawyers from his law firm. On his other side was Bob Bagley, the prominent insurance defense counsel who was defending him against my legal malpractice action. And next to him was attorney Roger Hammerset, Gentry's expensive plaintiff's counsel, who was prosecuting his defamation suit against me. And next to Hammerset was an associate from his office.

I looked around the table at the array of high-priced lawyers. There were so many expensive suits I felt like I was in Burberry's men's store.

Hammerset began the questioning by giving me about ten minutes of complicated, obtuse definitions and instructions. He leaned forward across the table, looking me straight in the eye as he did, not blinking.

Meanwhile, Fin seemed a little distracted. He had one of his hands thrust down in his suit coat pocket, and the other hand propping up his cheek, and he slumped in his chair.

Hammerset went on and on in his lengthy question about how I was to respond, and the rules of the deposition, and how I was to wait for the entire question before answering, and the difference between speculating and giving answers on matters from my own knowledge, and how I was to ignore the objections of the attorneys unless it was an instruction from my own lawyer to me not to answer a certain question, something which Hammerset said he doubted would "occur in this case, as I cannot conceive of my asking a question that will entitle you to refuse to answer." When he finally finished and wanted me to answer that I fully understood his instructions and would abide by them, Horace Fin belted out an objection.

"What is your objection exactly?" Hammerset said sarcastically.

"That you are assuming a fact that is not yet in evidence," Fin said.

"What fact?" Hammerset asked with bewilderment.

"That my client must be a genius."

"What are you talking about?" Hammerset barked. "My question assumes no such thing."

"Of course it does," Fin snapped back.

"It absolutely *does not!*"

"Sorry," Fin said calmly. "But you clearly must be assuming that Kevin Hastings, PhD, my client, is a certified genius. Because he'd have to be a genius with an IQ close to Einstein's to not only understand that convoluted set of instructions you gave him, but also remember each of them well enough to honestly answer 'yes' or 'no.'"

Hammerset's face was already turning colors. His eyes were squinted and his jaw was clenched.

"So that's how you're going to play this?" he said through his teeth. "I've heard about you, Fin. About your dirty tactics. How you try to drive everybody crazy. You're a blight on the legal profession."

"Oh my," Fin said, with a smile on his face, 'sticks and stones may break my bones, but'…well, I'm sure you know the rest."

"I'm going to call the presiding judge in this case, get him on the phone, and get you sanctioned right now, mister," Hammerset said.

"Sure, go ahead. And while you're at it," Fin said, "tell the judge that you asked a long, rambling, introductory, prefatory question that contained five-hundred-and-forty-two words in it, and then actually expected my client to comprehend it."

Hammerset paused for a moment, and stared at Fin.

"Don't play games with—"

"I'm not playing games," Fin shot back. "Have your court reporter read your question back. Right now. Five-hundred-and-forty-two words. Check it out."

Gentry shifted uncomfortably in his chair. Hammerset made a little grimace, and then instructed the court reporter to read the question back so everybody could count. And so she did.

When she was through, Fin said loudly, "Gentlemen, I owe you an apology. I was wrong. Five-hundred-and-forty-*three* words. I missed one."

That's when Hammerset's associate laughed out loud and shook his head in amazement. Until his boss glared at him.

So, that was only the first deposition question. Which will give you an indication how the rest of the deposition went.

Hammerset then waded into my background, my upbringing, my educational background, whether I had any criminal convictions, whether I was taking prescription drugs, every place I had lived during the last ten years. But when he went into the status of my employment with Essex College Fin jumped all over that and objected and instructed me not to answer.

When Hammerset demanded to know the objection, Fin cited some obscure sounding legal authorities about the confidentiality of employment disciplinary proceedings. With that, all of the lawyers, including Hammerset stood up and filed out of the conference room to go down to the law library at the end of the hall, presumably to check up on the cases mentioned by Fin.

About fifteen minutes later they all filed back in the room and sat down. Hammerset cleared his throat. Then, deciding not to pursue the last line of questions, Hammerset launched into a different area of inquiry.

He was slowly bringing me to the key questions about the allegedly defamatory statements I made against Gentry through my attorney. When Hammerset demanded to know the origination of the statement, Fin told me not to answer.

"We're stipulating," Fin announced, "on the record, that the statements alleged in the complaint in fact were the statements of my client, Kevin Hastings, and that he authorized me, as his agent and attorney, to publish, spread, and communicate said statements as broadly as possible."

Hammerset, Gentry, and all the rest smiled when Fin said that. So I took that as a bad sign.

"That's fine," Hammerset said. "That will simplify our defamation case against your client considerably. However, I am still entitled to know the circumstances of where and how and when that statement originated."

"Not if it involves attorney–client communications," Fin snapped back.

"By stipulating that your client informed you to publish those

scurrilous statements against attorney Gentry," Hammerset countered, "you've just waived that privilege. You have opened the barn
door wide open to all attorney–client communications, Mr. Fin,"
Hammerset said with glee. "Now we can ask your client about every
little nasty thing that he has ever discussed with you in your creepy
little law office down there on that industrial lane."

I was ready to panic. What if Hammerset could now ask me
any questions he wanted to about all the confidential discussions
I had with Fin? And what about all our conversations regarding
DeVoe and Mangiorno? If that got out, Mangiorno's name would
be dragged into the public record as the undisclosed buyer of
the Tornquist property. He would go ballistic. And I would be
a dead man.

"I am instructing my client not to answer any of those questions," Fin bellowed.

"That's it," Hammerset yelled. "I'm taking this to the judge."

"Go for it," Fin yelled back.

They dialed the judge's number on the speaker phone in the
conference room. They got the clerk. She said the judge was on the
bench. Hammerset gave her a short description of the problem.

"I would think Judge Janice Morley will want to deal with this
right away. As soon as she comes back into chambers," she said.

My heart sunk.

All of us sat in silence for close to twenty minutes. Then the
clerk called back, with the judge on the line. Hammerset made
his introductions, addressing the speaker phone, setting the background of the case, and the issues, Fin's on-the-record stipulation,
and how he contended that Fin had completely waived attorney–
client confidentiality with me by so doing. As a result, he argued,
he should be permitted to delve into every discussion I'd ever had
with Fin.

Then it was Horace Fin's turn. He said that formal stipula-
tions on legal issues cannot be deemed to be waivers of confidentiality, unless they divulge fact-specific, otherwise protected
communications between client and attorney. "Besides," Fin said,
"if you rule that my client and I have waived and given up the

privilege by stipulating to an issue we chose not to contest…then what attorney is ever going to want to stipulate to anything? And if that happens, cases get more complicated, take longer, more issues have to be litigated, the court dockets get more delayed, cases start getting stacked up, the public gets annoyed with all the delays, the politicians in the State House in Springfield jump into the fray…"

"I get the picture, Mr. Fin," Judge Morley said curtly, cutting him off. "Give me five minutes." The judge put us on hold. While we waited I was sweating through my shirt. Fin just sat there twiddling his thumbs.

When the judge returned her decision was concise and direct.

"Objection sustained," she said over the speaker phone. "Mr. Hammerset, I'm afraid that you won't be able to ask about Mr. Hastings' conversations with his attorney. I'm finding that the privilege has not been waived and is still intact."

That's when I started to breathe again.

Hammerset spent the next few hours quizzing me about what I meant, and what my intent was in calling Gentry "selfish" and "incompetent," and that his favorite color was "green"; he further interrogated me about what I meant by the comment that Gentry was guilty of "not caring whether he is crushing the little guy." I was having trouble answering—partly because of the tension— and partly because those words were not mine to begin with, but were simply ones that Fin had put into my mouth. Hammerset repeatedly tried in every way possible to get me to agree with him that my motivation in making the statements was to injure Gentry, to permanently destroy his considerable legal reputation. To cause him grievous damages.

By the time we finished it was early evening. I was exhausted. Fin seemed unperturbed.

I have to admit that I was impressed with Horace Fin's logistical strategy, and his arguments, and his clever legal game of dodge and weave.

But in the end, I felt that none of it made much of a difference to me. How was any of this going to dig me out of the quicksand

I was in? Fin's antics seemed superficially impressive, but irrelevant.

Like a guy who shows up in my hospital room and puts on an unbelievable demonstration of high-speed Ping-Pong. While what I really need is a doctor who can stop my hemorrhaging.

THIRTY-THREE

As we drove back to Fin's office where my car was parked, one question was driving me crazy. As I sat there in the passenger seat of Fin's Hummer, I just had to ask him a question about the trick he did with guessing the number of words in Hammerset's long question.

"What makes you think I guessed?" Fin said with a smirk.

"If you didn't, how'd you know the number of words?"

Then Fin fished down into his suit coat pocket and pulled out one of those little plastic inventory counting devices, the kind that fits in the palm of your hand. It had a number counter that rolled over with each silent click.

He displayed the last number on the counter. It read 5-4-2.

Fin must have been pushing down on the button every time Hammerset said a word. He only missed by one word.

"I called around," Fin said, "and got myself samples of some transcripts of depositions that Hammerset had done in other cases. And in every case, the guy gives these long introductory explanations and instructions. Like he's delivering the State of the Union address. So, I was ready for him."

I sighed. More of Horace Fin's carnival tricks.

When we got back to Fin's office I was really ready to pack it in for the night. But I knew he still wanted to talk with me about the final disciplinary hearing against me at Essex College set for the next morning.

"This will be short and sweet," Fin said. "I'm going to suggest that we not contest their firing of you tomorrow."

"That makes no sense!" I blurted out. "This is my livelihood."

"Then maybe you'll have to get another job."

"Horace, I'm really thinking it's time for me to get new legal representation."

Fin smiled.

"I can give you some references to other attorneys," he said nonchalantly.

I thought about it for a minute or two.

"And why should I not contest my firing?" I finally asked.

"Number one, I know these committees. These private boards. You think the Landmark Commission was a tough nut to crack? These folks at Essex want you out. Just read the signs, Kevin. It's like a bunch of Burma-Shave ads on the side of the road. And they all spell out the words, 'You're fired, Kevin, no matter what.' Sorry, but that's the fact, Jack. But that's not all."

"What else do you have for me?" I said, now contemplating the inevitable doom of my teaching career.

"*Anything you say*," Fin said, "anything that they say in that hearing—it's going to be recorded. I've read the faculty handbook you gave me. That's the procedure. And after they fire you—which they will—Hammerset is going to get a copy of that recording and use it to tar and feather you, make you look as bad as possible in his client's defamation case against you."

"But you objected to that kind of evidence at my deposition. And they seemed to buy into your reasons."

"Without getting too technical," Fin replied, "that was only a suspension hearing. Once you get formally terminated as a result of a final hearing, it will all be fair game in the defamation lawsuit—unless you let me have my way on this."

Giving Horace Fin his way was one of life's most dangerous gambles.

"What's *your* way?" I asked.

"I broker a deal," Fin explained. "They want you out. And we need to keep a lid on all of this. So...we offer, right at the beginning of the hearing tomorrow, not to contest the termination. On the other hand, they let you quit instead. A voluntary termination. Remember, there was no record kept of the preliminary hearing they held. I get them to put a statement in your permanent employment file that all of the allegations against you are totally withdrawn. The college sends a similar statement to the unemployment compensation office where you applied for benefits. You and the college both agree to keep the terms of the settlement confidential. So, you don't have any negative mark against your employment record—and at the same time, they can get rid of you."

It was sounding like the most reasonable solution. But Fin's comment triggered something in the back of my mind.

"Would that mean that I could apply for unemployment benefits, and get them this time?"

"No dice," Fin shot back, "sorry. You don't collect unemployment when you quit. Only when you're deemed to be fired."

After a few moments Fin asked if I would go along with his plan.

Reluctantly I did. Once again, it seemed like I had no other choice.

The next morning I met Horace at the college, and we walked into the boardroom together. Dr. Albright was there with the same cast and crew. Fin got Hubert Jankowski, their legal counsel, aside first thing and started working on him. He presented our deal. Then Jankowski asked us to leave the room while he discussed it with the faculty committee. They closed the door. After about half an hour, the door opened.

Jankowski was smiling, and he invited us back in.

"I think they took the bait," Fin whispered to me.

"Why do you think so?"

"Jankowski's smiling," Fin replied. "I know that look. He's thinking, now that the hearing is not going ahead, he can start his weekend early."

Fin was right. They agreed to the deal. It took another hour and a half while Jankowski and Fin hammered out the language and typed up a written agreement in the dean's office. When it was finished I signed, and Victor Bouring, the vice chancellor, signed on behalf of the college.

So, it was done. My life at Essex College had come to an end.

I had entertained that thought before, starting with when they suspended me pending the final hearing. But now it was official. When I had been ordered off the campus without pay several weeks before, I had been allowed to gather my personal belongings, pictures, personal papers, those kinds of things.

This time they let me wander up to my empty office and put my remaining books in some boxes. Essex furnished the empty boxes.

That was their parting gift to me for my years of service.

Part of me wanted to view that as a stepping stone—an island in the streams of my life. I tried every aphorism I could think of to ease the hurt and feeling of betrayal as I lugged my boxes down to my rental car.

But I also knew something else. That I was responsible, at least in some part, for the way things had turned out.

As I was driving out of the circle drive of the college, I stopped the car for a second. Then I turned around and gave one last glance at Old Main, the administration building, and the Humanities building, and at the students crossing the quad.

As I drove off there was one small positive. At least I felt some closure and finality to that chapter.

But there was still a whole sea of rough waters ahead of me.

There were the four separate lawsuits I was embroiled in—my malpractice suit against Gentry, his defamation case against me, my appeal from the Landmark Commission denial of my application for demolition, and the newest suit that Fin had filed against the bankrupt art foundation and its real-estate broker.

Worst of all, there was Tony DeVoe and Vito Mangiorno.

I knew they would not wait very much longer. I wondered if Fin's suggestion about giving them some kind of conditional deed to the property would mollify them for a little longer. And if it didn't? These were deadly serious guys. And I was running out of time.

Then, Tess Collins came to my mind as I drove back to my apartment. And our conversation at Dan's, and our laugh about the ice cream. I wondered where things would go from there. It was funny that I kept having these random ideas about trying to strike up a relationship with my opponent. I realized it was probably not a smart thing to do.

I was glad I had the weekend to crash, and try to sort things out.

And there was something else. Somewhere, in the mysterious inner recesses of my brain, I entertained the thought that maybe all of these things were happening to me for a reason. As incomprehensible as that might seem. That my various ordeals of late—both in the crucible of the courts and the lawyers' offices, and otherwise—that there was a latent meaning behind it all. If I could just discover what it was.

But my grand musings quickly came to a halt when I approached my apartment complex, and was ready to turn into the parking lot. It was dusk. Cars were starting to turn on their headlights.

That's when I saw a van slowly cruising around the building. It looked familiar. I had seen it once before. There were three big guys crammed into the front seat. A feeling of dread washed over me, as I recognized the van. It was the same one that had been involved in my carjacking.

Fin's idea to appease Mangiorno clearly had not worked. And now, something else was very clear.

That I would be running for my life.

Thirty-Four

~

I DIDN'T THINK THE GUYS in the van had seen me. I hadn't stopped, or even slowed my rental car very much. I hadn't done anything to draw attention to myself.

In fact, for all that I knew, they didn't even have a description of the rental car that I had been driving while my Jetta was in the body shop.

Speeding up a little past my apartment building, as the sun was setting, I glanced in my rearview mirror. Nothing. I looked at it again. Then I saw the snub nose of the van poke out of the opening of the driveway where it met the street, and then stop. Like a predator smelling the wind for the scent of blood—or listening for the sound of a wounded prey.

I kept driving, but while I was studying the van in my mirror I inadvertently touched the brake pedal. As I did, my car slowed slightly and my red brake lights lit up. My car was in the travel lane, with no stop sign nearby. That must have caught the attention of the thugs. Looking again into the rearview mirror I saw that the van turned quickly into the street and began pursuing me. It was accelerating rapidly. An instant later I could hear the van's engine racing as it was closing on me.

I stomped on my accelerator and sped up to the next intersection. When I got there I turned left.

Fifty yards later there was another stop sign that fronted a major boulevard. I skidded to a halt at the sign and then frantically turned left again, speeding up to merge into the flow of traffic in the far-left lane of travel in the double-lane avenue. As I did, I could hear the squealing tires of the van behind me as it was taking the corner on two wheels.

In the mirror I could see the van, which was three cars behind mine. The van was dodging in and out from its position in my lane, searching for a chance to close the gap.

Then the car directly in front of the van turned off into a hamburger joint. The van roared up to the next car, tailgating it. I wanted to turn off, but I was surrounded. There was a plumbing truck in the lane to my right, and in front of me was a plodding mini-van full of kids being driven by a mom. The car in front of the pursuing van, tiring of the aggressive tactics of the vehicle that was following it, shifted into an opening in the right-hand lane. The van filled the vacuum and raced up to the rear bumper of the next car, which was now the only thing separating the van from my car.

I knew I had to act, while I still had the chance.

Eyeing the right lane, I spotted an opening between two cars and I took it, slamming my car into the space between them. Behind me, in the other lane, the van started honking its horn. The thugs had spotted my maneuver. They were trying to get the remaining car in front of them to get out of the way. That car responded by speeding up in its lane, passing me on my left.

I threw a quick glance at my left sideview mirror. There was the van. The three big guys in the front bench seat appeared to be leaning forward, like the bulls behind the gates in a rodeo. Pawing the ground. Ready to explode.

There was a side street approaching to my right. I heard the sound of the engine of the van grinding full throttle and gaining on me. The front of the van was just entering my peripheral vision to the left. Now the side street was at my right. I swung my steering wheel to the right and jumped on the brake, skidding into the side street with squealing tires.

For the moment I hoped my dodge had worked. I was entering a quiet residential area with little bungalows and short streets and alleys. I turned down a street, then turned off onto another side street, working my way back toward the direction of my apartment.

As I raced home I planned on calling 9-1-1 on my cell phone. *But where was my cell phone?* Then I spotted it. It was resting on the floor mat in front of the passenger seat. The little plastic cover for the battery was gone. And so was the battery. In my frantic, jarring road rally it must have come loose and the battery was now somewhere under the passenger seat.

Something told me to look back in my mirror.

"No!" I yelled.

Two blocks back the van was roaring down the residential street toward me. I turned off onto another small lane and then into an alley. It was now getting dark. I turned my headlights off and coasted forward. I had to keep rolling forward but without tapping my brakes. I couldn't afford to light up my brake lights. There were wire fences and run-down garages lining the alley.

When I was about midway down the alley, I looked at my mirror again. The van was cruising past the opening to the alley behind me, and then it disappeared. Then it quickly backed into view, and swung into the alley behind me, turning on its high brights as it did.

But I never even got the chance to slam the accelerator down. Unbeknownst to me there was a second van. Without warning it swung into the alley at the other end, facing me, and blocking my path. Its high-beam headlights flicked on.

I was trapped. I saw two big guys leap out of the van blocking my path. They had baseball bats. As the bigger man ran past his own headlights, I caught a look at his face and recognized him from the carjacking.

I ducked down, as my car continued to roll forward, and crawled over to the passenger seat. I reached down and snatched my cell phone off the floor, grabbed the handle of the passenger door, and in one continuous motion opened the door and tumbled out. I hit the gravel at about twenty miles per hour. It felt like sixty.

"He's out of the car!" one of the guys in the van in the back was yelling.

My rental car continued to roll forward, until it slammed into the front of the van blocking the alley.

Each of the guys with bats jumped into the rental car and then quickly exited.

"I told you he jumped out!" the man in the other van yelled again, now screaming and swearing.

By then I was running, pell-mell, through a series of cluttered backyards, tripping over trailer hitches and garbage cans, and wooden crates, and finally, a discarded toilet and sink.

Then a huge, snarling dog bolted out of a doghouse and ran straight at me until it ran out of chain, just inches away. It was barking and frothing wildly.

I could hear the pounding feet of the men with the baseball bats about a hundred feet behind me, running hard.

Suddenly I wished that I hadn't missed all those basketball games with Tom Taylor. At least I should have taken up jogging. I felt out of shape and winded, and was panting like a dying man as I ran.

I had only one thought. *How long before they catch me?*

Then there was a gunshot. Back where the dog was still barking. And then some yelling from the guys with the bats.

And then some yelling and swearing from the homeowner. And another warning shot from the homeowner's revolver.

I couldn't hear the goons with the bats now. I stopped. Then I turned around, and peered into the gloom and darkness. A backyard light illuminated the men with bats, including the big one, walking backwards, their hands in the air, and then they turned and disappeared into the night.

The dog stopped barking. The chase had ended.

It was over. For a while, at least.

The only sound was from my own labored breathing and thudding heart, and from the rushing and pulsing of my blood through some tiny hidden canal near the eardrums.

THIRTY-FIVE

Q UITE UNEXPECTEDLY, as I was trudging through the back streets of Chicago that night, having narrowly escaped the wrath of Vito Mangiorno and his minions—men who clearly wanted to take batting practice on my skull—a memory of my graduate school days popped into my head. It was the image of Professor Aubrey Sumner Tuttle, pausing, during one of his lectures, to make one of his sly points.

He had been talking about the medieval practice of "outlawry." Back in the 1300s and 1400s, in England, if you had the misfortune to miss a court appearance, then the Crown would issue a "declaration of outlawry" against you. That meant, for all practical purposes, that the entire legal system had declared you to be a non-person. The law, having declared you an outlaw, no longer provided even the thinnest veneer of protection. You could be killed by anyone who encountered you on the road as you fled—for any reason, or for no reason at all. From a jurisprudential standpoint, you were a dead man.

After explaining that, Tuttle paused and pretended to shuffle his lecture notes a little. Then he looked out into the class, and delivered the punch line:

> As an "outlaw" you had no rights, no future, no legal protection, no place to rest your head without fear of being set-up from all sides. Much like a defenseless little fawn...like Bambi...fending off the jaws of marauding wolves. Or, more to the point, like being a Republican in local Chicago politics.

Kevin Hastings, the outlaw. That's what I was. I was slinking along in the shadows of night, avoiding streetlights, and eyeing street corners before I approached them. Admittedly, I had no clear proof that the men who had carjacked me, and were pursuing me still, were connected with the Mangiorno crime organization. But there was no doubt in my mind that they were. Still, what would I accomplish by scuffing my way over to the local police precinct and filling out a report? I did that once before, after they had played piñata with my Jetta. And where did that get me? I also remembered a casual remark that Horace Fin had made during one of our conferences, and after I described the involvement of Tony DeVoe and his client, Vito Mangiorno.

"I know a couple of beat cops are sort of involved with Mangiorno," Fin noted. "You know, as 'business associates.' If you get my drift."

I was racking my brain about my next move. My rental car was back with the thugs. I couldn't retrieve it. I would have to report to the car rental company that I had been attacked and had to leave the car behind...wherever it was. Horace Fin's ploy to keep Mangiorno appeased obviously wasn't working. And the bad guys knew where I lived. So, I couldn't go back to my apartment—at least for a while.

For a second and a half, I actually gave some thought to approaching Tom Taylor again. But a sample dialogue ran through my brain and convinced me not to waste my call. It went something like this:

Tom: So you're asking, again, to move in with me and my wife for a while?

Kevin: That's right.

Tom: But I thought that last time you called you said you were kicked out of your apartment, and you were losing your job and had all kinds of legal problems...your life was a nightmare, blah, blah, blah...that kind of stuff.

Kevin: Well, that was true back when I called you last time. But things have changed.

Tom: Yeah? Really? Glad to hear it. Things have all finally worked out for you, then?

Kevin: Well, not exactly. Things are just…different. That's all.

Tom: Oh? How so? You know, Liz is going to want to know… and this is going to be a hard sell with her…

Kevin: Well, just tell your wife that now my biggest problem is that a major mob boss has sent some guys the size of full-grown lowland gorillas to track me down and beat me to death with base-ball bats. So, anyway…when can I move my stuff in?

Obviously, Tom Taylor would not be a solution.

I had been walking more than an hour when I finally approached an all-night quickie mart on a street corner. I noticed that there was a pay phone on the side of the building. I didn't relish the idea of using it while standing there, bathed in the harsh fluorescent light from the gas station. But given that I had lost the batteries in my cell phone when I tumbled out of my car, I didn't have much choice. I needed to make a phone call.

And I had also arrived at another conclusion. It was about the place I was about to call at the pay phone. To place this all in context, I was desperate. With hindsight, I view that night as representing the very depths of my flight into full-fledged outlawry. I not only needed a "safe house" to shelter me; I also needed some means of supporting myself. I had no unemployment benefits and no salary, my savings were extinct, and I had gone through most of my short-term loan money.

Funny what you're willing to do, when your life has become like an undrivable used car—the kind they feed into the big, crushing, industrial jaws in one of those ugly junkyards.

So, I scurried over to the pay phone. I glanced around quickly. The ominous vans were not around.

Then I dug into my pocket for some change. I put it in the slot, and called information.

"What city, please?" the information lady asked.

"Chicago," I said.

"What listing?" she asked.

I gave it to her. And in a few seconds, the line was ringing.

THIRTY-SIX

~

My telephone conversation only lasted a few minutes. I wanted to verify the address. Happily, the place was only a mile or two from where I was standing at the Exxon station. When I asked the man whether they were open late, there was a pause. Then he said, "Sir, we are open all night long. Twenty-four hours a day. Seven days a week."

After I hung up, I realized that my question was a little naïve. Of course they were open all the time. When you're in that kind of business, it's around the clock. Business is always brisk, I figured, in that line of work.

And the best thing of all, is that my location would be literally untraceable to Mangiorno's group.

I walked down the streets, still feeling uneasy around streetlights and open intersections. I realized, then, where I was. I had passed by there before. The last time was when I had picked up Pastor Jim Loveland in my car, and then ended up staying over at his house for a while. After walking far enough where my feet started hurting, it finally came into sight.

I stopped in front of the unadorned, two-story concrete building. The windows on the first floor had protective bars over them. The sign was painted in large letters, over the one main entrance door, and a floodlight underneath it illuminated the words:

WINDY CITY MISSION

The front door was a heavy metal number, with no window.

I noticed a surveillance camera up above the door. There was a speakerphone attached to the side of the door frame. I pushed the button. When the voice answered, I identified myself. In a second there was a buzzing, and I could hear the door mechanism unlock. I opened the big metal door and looked back at the street, but saw no cars or pedestrians in the area. I was satisfied that no one saw me enter.

I walked down the hallway and was greeted by a fellow by the name of Lou. He was probably a forty-year-old man—though his face wore the kind of gaunt creases that made him look a lot older. He looked as if whatever road he had taken in life, most of the miles were still showing.

"Howdy!" he called out to me. "You must be Kevin. You called a little while ago."

"That's me," I replied.

"Well, praise the Lord," he said turning and leading me into a small office.

Following close behind him, I was now beginning to regret the decision that only an hour before seemed to have been so pragmatic and logical.

He sat me down in a metal folding chair, across from his desk, and went through some background information with me. Nearest relative, employment status, age, date of birth, physical health, any criminal record, any history of mental health issues, any past abuse of alcohol or drugs.

When he was through, Lou said, "Hope you don't mind all the questions."

I said that I didn't.

"I was a cocaine addict myself. Before I came to the Lord, of course," he added. "That was eight years ago. The Lord cleaned me right up. Along with the help of Brother Jim Loveland."

I nodded.

"You mentioned in the phone call that you knew brother Jim," Lou said. "So I called him up a little while ago. We're actually pretty close to capacity. But there is one more bed. Brother Jim says to give it to you. And he also says to say hello to you. He'll be seeing you tomorrow. So, any questions?"

"Just one," I said. "Do you keep the fact that I'm here private and confidential?"

"Yep," he said.

With that, Lou went into a closet and took out a folded blanket, a pillow, a clean white sheet, and a bar of soap in a plastic container and handed it to me.

"Here you go," he said. "Follow me."

We walked to a stairway and made our way up to the second floor.

"It's been lights out for more than an hour," Lou said. "Most of your roomies are pretty well asleep by now."

"Roomies?" I said with some hesitation.

"Sure. Four to a room. I think your bed's in the top bunk, left side as I remember."

The upper hallway was dimly lit. A tall man in bare feet and in his underwear was coming out of the community bathroom.

"Evening, George," Lou said quietly. "Everything OK?"

"Sure. Sure. Had to go. Feelin' shaky tonight. But I'm doing all right," George answered.

Then George disappeared into a doorway down the hall.

"Detox," Lou said matter-of-factly. "George's been living out of a bottle for a long time. Still trying to pull himself out."

Then Lou stopped in front of a door that had the number 12 on it.

"Here we are," he whispered. "Just slip in real quiet. We'll get you up at 8:00 sharp tomorrow morning. Have a good night's sleep."

I entered the room. I could see in the dim light from the hallway that there were four bunk beds. As Lou had said, there was an empty one in the upper bunk to the left. I could hear a chorus of loud snoring from three other men. I reached up to the bare mattress and tucked the sheet around it. Then I carefully lifted myself up and onto the bed, taking my blanket, pillow, and soap with me. I put the soap container under the pillow, and pulled the blanket over me. I laid back onto the pillow, and stared up into the darkness.

There was a convergence of sputtering, sneezing, snoring, and coughing from the sleeping strangers. *I am never going to get to sleep in this place*, I thought. I continued to gaze off into the void. Contemplating just how low I had sunk. And thinking that perhaps I should have picked a hundred other options of escaping the vengeance of a local crime boss rather than the humble bunk beds of the Windy City Mission. Anything. Like joining a traveling carnival. Or jumping on a tramp steamer to South America. Or hitchhiking to Canada.

I was still listing the endless possibilities when, at some point, I drifted off, and joined the snoring symphony.

THIRTY-SEVEN

I WAS THE LAST ONE TO WAKE UP in our dormitory-like bedroom at the Windy City Mission. One of my roommates had already risen and headed out of the room. I made a brief introduction to the other two men.

Miguel was a Hispanic man in his late thirties. He spoke broken English, but was a good-natured fellow with a generous grin, and a shock of black hair that curled over his forehead and dropped down over his left eye. He was sitting on the edge of his bunk, holding onto what appeared to be a Bible in Spanish. He displayed the black-covered Bible to me and spoke excitedly. I was unable to understand most of what he was saying, but I did hear him speak enthusiastically about "Jesus," and when he did, his smile broadened.

The other resident was Douglas, a lanky, older black man with a scruffy goatee beard. For some reason he decided, without prompting, to be a kind of interpreter.

"Miguel here," Douglas intoned, "is tellin' you that he got saved with Jesus. That's what he's sayin'."

"Oh," I remarked, nonplussed. "So...how did he end up here?"

"He's an illegal. After he got right with Jesus here at the mission, he decided to turn himself in to the INS."

"You're kidding," I replied.

"Yeah. Not exactly the route I would've taken either," Douglas said with a chuckle. "But, there you go. So apparently the INS tells the mission they can keep an eye on him here until they're ready to deport him back to Mexico. Or work out some kind of work visa or whatever."

"So, how about you?" Douglas asked. He was slowly slipping on a faded, frayed shirt that once had probably been the color blue, but had been rendered a kind of aqua-white with multiple washings over the years.

"Oh, things got complicated for me, you know," I said hedging. "It's a long story…"

Douglas threw back his head and just laughed out loud at that.

"Yeah. Sure," he said, not sounding like he was buying my sidestep routine. "Have it your way. But I'm tellin' you what…that ain't going to wash here. Not with Brother Jim Loveland."

"Well, I do know Jim personally," I replied, trying my best to let him know that somehow I was in a higher category than my other roommates.

But Douglas popped my bubble immediately by laughing even louder at that.

"Yeah, of course," he responded when his chuckles started to die down. "Everybody knows Brother Jim *personally*. What I'm tryin' to say is this…they feed you and house you alright…but they got one thing and one thing in mind all the time."

"What's that?"

"Bringin' you to Jesus," Douglas said. "Yes sir, bringin' you to Jesus."

I shrugged, not knowing how to respond.

"Don't get me wrong," Douglas said. "There's nothing wrong with that stuff…I was raised with it. My auntie, she dragged me to church every Wednesday night for prayer meetin', and twice on Sundays. I sort of went through the motions. But not in here," he said tapping his head. "Or here," and pointed an index finger to his chest.

"I'm what you call your basic procrastinator," Douglas concluded. "Always thought there's just too much sinnin' I still needed to do. So, I've been puttin' it off…"

I was amazed at his nonchalance on the subject. Douglas clearly was not stymied over complex questions about the existence of God. The questions with which the philosophers, poets, and skeptics had wrestled for millennia posed no problem for him. It was as if Douglas had no questions about the metaphysical reality of "coming to Jesus." To the contrary, for him, it seemed only to be a simple matter of delaying the inevitable reconciliation with his divine destiny.

Just then an announcement came over the loudspeaker.

"Breakfast in the cafeteria in five minutes," the voice said. "And this morning's gospel service at nine sharp!"

Douglas was fully dressed. I was still in my bunk. I rolled back over on my pillow.

"What do you think you're doin'?" Douglas asked.

"I think I'll skip breakfast this morning," I said.

"My oh my, professor, you do have a lot to learn."

I bolted up right in my bed. How did he know I was a college professor?

"Surprised that I know something about you?" he said in the doorway. "News travels fast here."

He turned to leave. But before exiting, he added one more thing.

"And just in case you're wondering…I used to be a master sergeant in the Army. Then one night in a bar, while I was pretty well lit up, I beat up a guy, nearly killed him. Spent some time in the brig. Got a dishonorable discharge. Couldn't adjust to civilian life. Went to prison for burglarizing shops at night to get cash to feed a drug habit. Got out of prison, hit the streets, and went on the skids again. I've lost my rank, my wife, and nearly my mind. That's my story…maybe you can tell me yours sometime. Meanwhile, I wouldn't get too relaxed if I were you."

Then he was gone. I laid in bed, staring at the ceiling, and thinking about what Douglas said.

But not for long.

Within minutes Lou poked his head in the doorway.

"Come on, Kevin. Breakfast time. Right now. Then gospel service. Day's a-wastin'!"

I jumped down from the bunk and threw on my shirt, and quickly tucked it in.

That would not be the last time that Douglas would be right.

THIRTY-EIGHT

~

THE SMALL CAFETERIA WAS PACKED with about forty men. They shuffled us down a food line with our plastic trays in our hands. The female food server piled scrambled eggs on our plates, along with toast. Coffee was served out of huge stainless steel percolators.

I grabbed a seat next to Douglas, who was seated next to Miguel. On the other side of Douglas was a younger white man with hair down to his shoulders and a vacant look on his face.

"This is Nolan," Douglas said, pointing to the young man sitting next to him.

"Hi," I said. But Nolan just stared at me, then looked back down at his plate as he ate.

"Nolan's the quiet type," Douglas said. "He's the other roommate you got in our room."

Then a few of the other residents at the table introduced themselves. Several of them had been on the streets for years. One man, with a long, grizzled beard, gave only a partially comprehensible story about himself, but it sounded as if he had been some kind of a musician at one time, and he tried to show me the calluses on his fingers from playing the guitar. Another was an unemployed electrician. A man sitting next to me, wearing a shirt with a Ralph Lauren logo but which was noticeably dingy, even said that at one time he had been a former commodities trader on the Chicago Board of Trade.

I artfully diverted questions about myself.

At 8:50 a bell rang, and the residents all collected their plates and trays and dutifully took them over to a place where they were stacked by the kitchen staff.

Then we all walked down to the "chapel." It was also a small room, with stained glass double doors, folding chairs, and a pulpit at the front, with a large cross just behind it.

We all sat down, and Jim Loveland appeared at the front, and sat down in the front room with a square faced, dark-haired man who looked to be in his forties, wearing a pressed denim shirt with a tie. As a woman sat herself down at an upright piano, Jim Loveland stood up quickly and greeted us warmly, and then led us in some hymn singing. We each had photocopied pages of songs on our chairs. He led us in a not particularly melodious rendition of an old hymn by Wesley:

> Weary souls, that wander wide
> From the central point of bliss,
> Turn to Jesus crucified,
> Fly to those dear wounds of His...

I hadn't realized people still sang that stuff.

Then Jim led us in a lengthy prayer, and when he finished he introduced us to the speaker for the morning's gospel service. As the speaker in the denim shirt and tie stood up, to be introduced, I squirmed a bit in my metal chair.

"Two-a-day's today," Douglas whispered to me from his seat next to mine.

I gave him a quizzical look.

"On Wednesdays," Douglas said quietly with a smirk, "gospel service in the morning, and one at night. Better pace yourself..."

Jim Loveland said that the speaker was Daniel Petranelli, who he described as someone who has "done some very important legal work for the Windy City Mission."

Then Loveland added, "Dan here is a Chicago lawyer."

I'm sorry to hear that, I muttered to myself.

With that sparse introduction, Petranelli, Bible in hand, smiled broadly at the crowd and then started speaking.

"I am sure every one of you gentlemen who are sitting here today probably feel, maybe even right now, that you're pretty low. That life's got you down. I'm not going to pretend that I can fully understand what any of you have gone through that brought you here."

He had one hand in his pants pocket, and the other was holding the Bible up, with its pages open.

"But I can guarantee you one thing," Petranelli continued. "Here it is—you are about to hear a story about a guy who was at a point in his life that was even lower than any of us in this room. And yet, at the same time, the same guy came into the greatest honor any human being could receive. This guy was a robber. A criminal. Now I know a few of you guys know something about that. You've spent some time in jail. You're asking yourself, *So he's a thief...a criminal...so, what's so special about that?* Well, let me tell you what was special about this guy..."

Petranelli was leaning up against the pulpit, in a relaxed but energetic pose. His eyes seemed to be fixed in my general direction.

Then the lawyer explained the story. He said that this robber lived at a time when the law came down hard on thieves. Real hard. The death penalty was meted out frequently for crimes like that. One day, he explained, the robber got caught. The long arm of the law had gotten ahold of him. The government put him in the slammer. And there he was, sitting in a jail cell waiting. And then, finally, the day for his execution came. And there was another robber who was also going to be executed at the same time.

And also, Petranelli said, there was one more man, a third person, who was being led off to this same group execution.

"And that man's name was Jesus," the lawyer said. "But unlike the other two men, he was no criminal. In fact, he was the only person who ever lived who never sinned. That's because he was the Son of God. The Savior."

I was getting the drift. Again, Douglas had been prescient. They were wasting no time hitting the salvation message.

Then Petranelli looked at his Bible and started reading out loud:

One of the criminals who were hanged there was

hurling abuse at Him, saying, "Are you not the Christ? Save Yourself and us!"

But the other answered, and rebuking him said, "Do you not even fear God, since you are under the same sentence of condemnation?

And we indeed are suffering justly, for we are receiving what we deserve for our deeds; but this man has done nothing wrong."

And he was saying, "Jesus, remember me when You come in Your Kingdom!"

Petranelli closed his Bible. "Here was this criminal, being executed for his crimes...you can't get any lower than that, can you? But this criminal does something smart...he recognizes that this Jesus is the sinless Son of God...but he also recognizes that he, himself, is a sinner...and so he reaches out in faith to Jesus, with his last breath. And says—'I believe you are the King of all creation, and you're going to be in your kingdom pretty soon. Just remember me, will you?'

"And what does Jesus say to this dying criminal?"

The lawyer smiled and answered his own question. "Jesus looks at him and says, 'Truly, I say to you, today you shall be with Me in Paradise.' And that guy, who couldn't get any lower in life, received forgiveness of his sins—and they were many—and he also received an honor that couldn't get any higher...eternal life."

I knew I had to endure some daily preaching as the price of hiding within the security and the anonymity of the mission. At least until I felt the risk from Mangiorno's men had cleared. I tried to mentally shrug off Petranelli's message by wondering what kind of lawyer this guy really was, anyway, if he got his kicks out of coming down to the Windy City Mission and preaching to the homeless and the downtrodden?

Jim Loveland stood back up and invited anyone who felt so motivated, to walk down to the front of the room, "and by doing that, to signal that they have decided to receive Jesus Christ into their heart as Savior and Lord."

One shabby-looking fellow stood up and ambled down to

the front. Jim and Petranelli spoke to him a few minutes, and the fellow nodded his head, and then they all bowed and it looked like they were praying together.

After that, we sang another hymn and then the group dispersed.

Lou hustled right over to me.

"Kevin, enjoy the message?" he asked.

"Interesting," I said with a half smile.

"Okay," Lou continued, "you've got a vocational meeting right now."

"What's that?"

"Everybody who stays here has a review of his job situation. Employment training. Things like that."

I was about to deal him a quick explanation that I was in a little bit different situation, but before I could, Lou cut me off.

"Everybody goes through this here. No exceptions. They're waiting for you down in the office next to mine. So hustle down there!"

Making my way down the stairs to the first floor, where the offices were, I was already calculating when I might be taking my leave from the Windy City Mission.

THIRTY-NINE

~

WHEN I STEPPED INTO THE OFFICE, I immediately recognized a face I knew. Jim Loveland was sitting behind a desk. Off to the side of the desk there was a middle-aged man in an electric wheelchair.

Loveland reached over the desk and shook my hand vigorously.

"Hey, Kevin, great to see you again," Loveland said. "I spotted you in chapel this morning. Wasn't Daniel Petranelli's message powerful? You know, I was hoping to introduce the two of you afterwards, but Dan had to scoot back to his office real quick. Maybe some other time."

"Sure," I replied.

"Kevin," Jim continued, gesturing over to the man in the wheelchair, "this is Bob Moody, our Executive Director of Operations."

The man in the electric wheel chair was thin, with a face that had a gaunt, angular look to it, but his eyes were piercing, and he had a radiant, effusive smile.

"Kevin...great to meet you," Bob Moody said, in a slow, labored voice that had a kind of faraway quality to it, as if he was on the other end of a distant, hollow telephone connection.

"Jim's said some...good things about you..." he continued.

Then he lifted his right hand off the arm of the wheelchair with some effort in order to shake mine, but was not able to raise his arm.

I reached over and shook his hand, which had only a meager grip.

"ALS," Bob said softly.

"Amyotrophic lateral sclerosis...Lou Gehrig's disease," Jim added.

Then I recalled what Jim had told me before, when I was staying at his house, regarding Bob Moody and his slow loss of muscle control.

"So, I know you're temporarily looking for housing again. Am I right?" Loveland asked.

I nodded. Loveland continued.

"Lou said that you arrived late in the night. Anything you want to share about that?"

"Well," I said, thinking of a way to avoid the nitty gritty of the recent chase by Mangiorno's men, "everything has fallen through for me. I'm back in the same boat as I was when you, Jim, were kind enough to put me up in your house..."

"That's a little general," Jim said with a smile. "Why don't you elaborate?"

I then explained the results of the debacle at the Landmark Commission hearing, and how it had dashed my hopes for a financial turnaround.

Loveland was listening intently, but there was a look in his eye that suggested he thought I was holding back...which, of course, I was. He said he had read the newspaper accounts of the commission hearing. Then he asked something very directly.

"Are you in any kind of trouble?" he asked. "I mean, outside of the legal litigation that you're embroiled in?"

I paused. I wanted to lay it all out, including the physical attacks by Mangiorno's thugs. But I just didn't think I could afford to be that open—or to be that honest, more accurately. So I hedged.

"No," I said. "Just everything connected with the property. You know, just those kinds of things..."

Loveland paused again. Then he asked if I remembered our discussion at his house about a temporary position, as an assistant to Bob Moody. That it was a paying job. I said that I remembered our conversation on that once before.

"This is a nonprofit Christian ministry here at the mission," Loveland said. "A lot of the folks, like Lou, our third-shift coordinator, are practically working for free. We have a number of volunteers. But the general rule, for all of our regular, full-time staff, is that they have to be able to say that they have personally received Jesus Christ as their Lord and Savior, and they can wholeheartedly agree with our doctrinal statement of faith."

"Sure," I said. "I guess I can understand that."

"On the other hand, some temporary positions…like the one we're talking about here, to assist Bob with administrative tasks—sometimes we make exceptions. On the other hand, if you are in a position right now to make a confession of faith…to receive Jesus Christ into your heart…"

"Well, not really…"

"No, I didn't think so," Loveland said, his eyes searching mine. "But quite apart from this job, it would be my hope and prayer that you would do so someday. Most important decision that you will ever make."

I nodded, but was careful not to make any commitments.

"Well," Jim said, "why don't you and Bob talk. And I'll be back later to talk to you." He slipped out of the room.

Bob Moody then asked me, in his slow, breathy cadence, about some of my educational and work experience at Essex. He asked me to elaborate on why I ended my work there. I told him the whole embarrassing affair, as best as I could.

He then slowly went through the kind of paperwork assignments I would handle for him. Grant application forms. Payroll. Reconciling some of the purchase ledgers for supplies, particularly for the kitchen. I told him I thought I could handle all of that.

"There's a spare office with a bed in it," Bob said with a smile. "No separate bathroom though…you'll have to use the common one on this floor…"

I told him that wouldn't be a problem. Suddenly, the thought of a private bedroom of my own seemed almost grandiose.

Bob gave me a big smile and added, "I think you'll do…fine…"

I rose and thanked him.

"One…more…thing," Bob said in his faint voice that was struggling for amplification. "You've got things on your mind…I think. When the time is right…would like to hear…about them."

Then Bob Moody gave me a little nod of his head. I could see the fatigue in his face, but it did not diminish his expansive smile. As I studied him, it seemed to me that my own problems were not as tragic as I had thought.

Bob reached for the control, and then put his electric wheelchair into a slow, quiet exit from the room.

FORTY

~

LATER THAT DAY, JIM LOVELAND TOLD ME that he and Bob Moody had talked together and decided to hire me as Bob's temporary assistant. Jim had me fill out some paperwork. I had mixed feelings. On one hand, I was elated to have some income, as well as a place to hide out from Mangiorno. And, while I was there, I would get three meals a day.

On the other hand, I was convinced there was no way that a Christian street mission was going to be part of my career ladder. Not to mention the fact that I had to sit through one gospel sermon a day—and two on Wednesdays. There was a time in my life when the mere thought of that would have sent me into a straight jacket. Yet, while I was not sure why, by the time I found myself at Windy City Mission, the idea of listening to Bible stories and contemplating God didn't seem so outrageous.

I asked Jim if I could use the office phone to make a call. He had me use the one on Lou's desk. I called the auto body repair shop. They were long overdue to have my Jetta back in shape. To my joy, they said they had called the day before and left a message on my answering machine saying the car was ready for pickup. When I put the order for the bodywork in originally, on a flight of fancy really, I told them I was tired of the red color and wanted to change it to dark blue. They had to repaint the whole thing anyway, and it wouldn't cost me any more money. Now I was glad I did. Maybe Mangiorno's guys wouldn't recognize the car so quickly.

The body shop manager said that my insurance company paid

up the whole thing, except for my deductible. I fished my check-book out of my pocket. According to my register, I had a balance of $136.28 left. I told him I would try to find a way down to their shop to pick it up.

"Speaking of that," the manager said, "about that rental car we gave you free of charge…"

"Yeah, I was meaning to speak to you about that…" I started out.

"The Chicago cops said they found it abandoned, with the keys in it in some alley. So the rental company had it picked up right away to avoid a towing charge."

I was stunned. Mangiorno's guys apparently left the car exactly where I abandoned it. They must have been scared off by the home-owner who fired the warning shots. More amazing still, the police came onto it before someone stole it.

"So you just left it there, Mr. Hastings…in an alley?" the man-ager said with irritation in his voice. "With the keys in it? What's up with that?"

"I know it sounds crazy," I replied sheepishly. "But it was an emergency situation. It's really…well, sort of a long story." That was rapidly becoming my pat answer for most of my recent life com-plications.

After the manager told me how lucky I was that something didn't happen to the rental car, there was a question I had to ask.

"Was it in good shape when they recovered it?" I was thinking back to the fact that my rental car rolled into the front of the van of my pursuers.

"Just a minor ding to the front bumper," the manager said. "It's covered by our collision coverage here at the body shop. Just…just don't ever ask for our free car rental deal, Mr. Hastings…if you ever have us do bodywork for you again."

I thanked him, and hung up just as Lou walked into the office. He was ready to check out for the day, because he started his usual shift at night. I asked him if he could drop me off at the body shop on his way home, which he said he'd be glad to do, now that he had been told I was classified as temporary staff with the mission and not just one of the residents.

I gave Jim the word where I was going, and said that I would be back by that evening's gospel service, as required. At the body shop, I paid off the deductible and drove off in my Jetta. Funny how good it can feel to have certain kinds of familiarity back in your life.

I then stopped at an electronics store to pick up a new battery for my cell phone, which left me now with less than thirty dollars to my name. But at least, with my cell working again, I felt connected to the outside world. I turned it on and saw the little envelope in the corner of the screen. I had a voice mail. I dialed in to retrieve it.

It was a woman's voice.

> Hi. Tess Collins here. Umm...nothing really new to report. Just wanted to let you know we're mulling things over here at our organization. But don't hold your breath, Kevin...I'm not sure there's any middle ground we can reach on the Tornquist property...or any real way we can help. Or change our position on that. Sorry. Oh...and thanks for the coffee and the pie. And the ice cream. Yes, the ice cream...(laughing)... and the conversation, too. So...thanks for everything Kevin. Really. Well...bye.

And then, right before hanging up, she suddenly added, "In case you need it, here is my cell phone number."

After I played her message, driving through the city, I just soaked it in. Then I played it back again, and listened.

And then played it back a third time. Just to make sure I caught it all. While I was stopped at a red light, I jotted her cell number down on a piece of paper.

What was that call really all about? I asked myself. As far as the Tornquist property issue, it was a non-call. A non-message. Basically she was calling to say that nothing was changed.

But then there was the other part. The personal stuff. That, I thought to myself, was significant. That meant something. Yes, there was something going on between Tess and myself. Some kind of a flicker. Not a forest fire. But a spark.

My day suddenly brightened up. For a little while, at least.

Until I decided to stop by my apartment to pick up my mail. I grabbed it out of my mailbox, and ran up into my apartment to check out things there quickly. I had surveyed the area and didn't see any suspicious vehicles. But I couldn't be too careful.

There were two messages on my answering machine of substance, and five from telemarketers. Mort had called to find out how I was doing. His daughter's recovery in the hospital was coming along well, he said. The other was from the body shop. Old news, there. I decided to rifle through my mail. Bad news.

There was a notice from the bank indicating that I was already late on my first mortgage payment on the Tornquist church property. Hopelessness washed over me.

But that was nothing. I was about to get hit with a tidal wave.

There was a thick packet from the law offices of Horace Fin. It included a copy of the lawsuit he filed for me, appealing the Landmark Commission ruling. Then I hit the gut-wrenching stuff. There were two bills. One showed a balance due of $3,067.44 for "costs and expenses to date" on my multiple lawsuits. He listed deposition transcripts, express charges, mailing, photocopies, copies of public records, and court filing fees. Then he also included a demand for $15,000 for "future costs and expenses," in those same cases. That money was needed for "expert witnesses, deposition transcripts, court reporter fees, anticipated photocopy and express delivery charges…"

"Where am I supposed to come up with all of that money?" I yelled out loud in my empty apartment. I grabbed the phone and punched in Horace Fin's number with fingers of fury. Karin put me right through.

"Kevin, my boy, you're still alive…that's good to know."

"No thanks to you!" I exclaimed.

"And what, exactly, is the source of your current indignation?"

"You!" I yelled. "You are the source of my indignation. You, and all the other lawyers. And the whole barbaric legal system. You are all conspiring to destroy me!"

"That's a bit paranoid, Kevin, don't you think?"

"Is it?" I yelled back. "Well first of all...you want over $3000 in past costs you've paid in my cases..."

"So?"

"'So'! 'So'!" I sputtered.

"Well, can you point to any expense charges in that bill that weren't necessary?"

I madly leafed through the list of charges.

My silence gave me away.

"Good. Glad to hear it. Now, let's move on," Horace said calmly. "I'm sure you don't like having to come up with that $15,000 for future costs. But let me tell you, that's going to get eaten up in the next sixty days. Maybe earlier. And, of course, the retainer contract requires you to provide advance costs for your cases. You know that."

"Expert witnesses," I countered. "You need expert witnesses? For what?"

"You've sued one of the best real-estate property lawyers in Chicago. Lloyd Gentry. For legal malpractice. You need a lawyer versed in real estate law to testify that he blew it..."

"Why can't you testify to that?"

"Because I'm your counsel. I can't be a witness too...remember? Not ethical."

"Since when are you so concerned about ethics?" I yelled.

"Oh, ouch," Fin said unperturbed. "*Et tu, Brute?*"

"Don't give me Shakespeare..."

"Oh, but I must," Fin said, who was just getting warmed up. "And here's another. And it's the story of your life, I'm afraid, Kevin. 'Trouble comes not in spies, but in battalions.' *Edward II.* Sorry about the bills. But while justice may be equal, it certainly doesn't come free."

I was silent on the phone. Then Fin added something curious.

"Don't feel alone in this, Kevin. You're not the only client who's had his back up against the wall, at the same time as the ceiling is falling."

Then he gave me his parting shot.

"I hope you can come up with the money. But I won't be

surprised if you don't. I do like you, Kevin. Despite anything else, that is true. However, if you can't pay the bills, let me know. I will have to file requests with the courts in each of your lawsuits, getting an order from the court permitting me to withdraw as your attorney. So let me know."

While I was driving back to the Windy City Mission, I found myself carefully checking every intersection, and eyeing every car suspiciously at each stoplight. Looking out for Mangiorno's men. I felt exhausted. Tired of the roller-coaster ride. I wanted it to end.

FORTY-ONE

Up to now, I have shared my story as best as I can recount it. And as a historian, I think I am a fairly accurate relater of facts. You've gotten the drift, I'm sure, that my life was in danger. And I certainly thought I had come to grips with that fact. But soon after I started working and sleeping over at the mission, something happened. Something dark and grisly. And it woke me from my inattentive slumber.

It was a small article in the *Chicago Tribune*. And after I finished reading it, and looking at the picture next to it, I felt jolted. The way I had been jolted only once before in my life.

When I was young, in grade school, there was a big kid, several years older than me, who was the neighborhood bully. One day I was walking by. He called me over, he said, to settle an argument he was having about something. I complied. He asked me whether I saw a jet plane up in the sky. I craned my head way back, and looked up in the sky. That's when he did it—he gave me a sweeping judo chop to my neck. I fell to the ground, gasping for air. Startled and jolted, I lay on the ground struggling to breathe again, while the bully was laughing coarsely to his friends. Later I realized how I had stupidly underestimated the cruelty of my enemy.

So, during my lunch break at the Windy City Mission, I noticed a headline in the Chicago newspaper that read, "Russian Hit Man Incinerated."

The article recounted how, in the early morning hours before dawn, a stolen car had caught the attention of passersby when it was seen bursting into flames at a remote park-and-ride lot in suburban Chicago. The fire and rescue people were called to the scene. After putting out the fire, they discovered that a chemical "accelerant" had been used to ignite the car, and quickly convert it into a broiling inferno. After the car fire was extinguished, the ranking officer with the fire department put a call to a detective at the homicide division. It seems that the car was not empty.

Inside, they had found the charred remains of a single occupant.

After DNA tests were done, and dental records were matched, the identity of the person inside the burning vehicle was discovered. His name was Boris Bittarushka.

Bittarushka, according to the article, had been suspected of being an "enforcer" for a small Russian syndicate operating in the Midwest. However, organized-crime experts were quoted as indicating that he had some kind of "falling out" with the Russians some two years before. They would not speculate on who he had been working for in the months preceding his death.

Boris had a nickname. He was known affectionately in the underground world of crime and corruption as "Boris the Bat"—apparently because his weapon of choice was a Louisville Slugger baseball bat he used to crush leg bones and kneecaps—and skulls.

That's when, as I read the article, I fixed my eyes on the picture adjacent to the article. I looked at it hard. And as I studied the photo I was convinced about one thing.

The man in the picture—this Boris "the Bat" Bittarushka—was the thug who was driving the van in my carjacking. He was also the big guy leading the baseball bat charge against me the night I abandoned my rental car.

I had no real proof about the reason for Boris's death. But I had a reasoned suspicion that it may have had something to do with me. And even more so, I believed it had something to do with Vito Mangiorno.

I had been jolted into taking action. I knew that I had decisions to make. *Should I go directly to the police? Or should I consult a new lawyer first? And if I did that, where in the world would I get the money to hire a new attorney?*

In my all-too-short career as an associate professor of history at Essex College, I had a quip from Dr. Aubrey Sumner Tuttle that I used to toss to my students. It went something like this:

> Those who study the catastrophes, defeats, and missteps of the past have the benefit of hindsight. But what is that benefit, really? It is simply this: to discover the blind spots of those who came before, and to appreciate them, in ourselves. To fully comprehend that what lays in the human heart—those deepest desires and the most dreaded fears—can either make us visionaries to the truth, or can blind us to the oncoming train, hurtling toward us.

Horace Fin's recent correspondence and money demands, coupled with his dreaded nuclear legal strategies, had finally convinced me that he had to go. Somehow, I had allowed my desires, or my fears, or both, to have blinded me to the mounting catastrophe, and to have caused me to cede to Fin too much of my case, and my life. I just hoped that it was not too late to jump off the tracks, and avoid getting smashed by the front end of a speeding bullet train.

FORTY-TWO

~

THERE WAS ONLY ONE TV in the Windy City Mission. It was in the "recreation room." Now that I was "on staff" I was privy to discussions about the possibility of buying another one. But funds didn't permit it. Nor could they see their way clear to expanding their space—something that both Jim Loveland and Bob Moody said was the highest priority. They wanted to eventually be able to house not only more men, but also women and their children, as well. But that didn't look like it was in the cards.

I was working with Bob Moody, in his office, the day that a report aired on the "news at noon" program on one of the local Chicago channels. It was a press conference in downtown Chicago. But I didn't catch it the first time it ran on TV.

I was preoccupied that day, still mulling over the face of Boris "the Bat" Bittarushka that had appeared in the newspaper the day before. When I finally took a break with Bob in the early afternoon and sauntered down to my room, I picked up my cell phone and noticed that I had one message. From Horace Fin.

"Kevin, my boy. There was a press conference down at City Hall this morning. Two channels covered it at noon. It's our case! Like I told you all along...we are shakin' 'em up! Well...thought you'd like to know. By the way...are you with me on this lawsuit or not? I need to hear from you, Kevin. *Ciao*..."

Except for the "are you with me on this lawsuit" part—a clear reference to Fin's demand for expense money on our cases with the promise of withdrawing if I couldn't pay—I couldn't make sense of the rest of his voice mail. So I made sure I was seated on one of the folding chairs in the recreation room when the local evening news aired. The room was empty, except for Douglas, who had spotted me glued in front of the television, so he plopped down in the chair in back of me.

The top story on the news was about a defective boiler in a grade school exploding. Happily, no children were injured. Then the press conference came on.

A reporter was announcing, with microphone in hand, in front of the City Hall building. I had driven past that huge, turn-of-the-century stone edifice with its towering columns a hundred times before. It was a massive block of historic architecture that dominated the intersecting block of Randolph, La Salle, Washington, and Clark streets. But, like so many other landmarks, I hadn't really noticed it.

But this time, I was looking at the building in the background differently. The television reporter standing in front of it was suddenly talking about "the lawsuit filed by former Essex College history professor Kevin Hastings."

Douglas was leaning forward out of his chair and grasping the back of the metal folding chair next to me.

The reporter related the "lawsuit filed in Cook County Circuit Court by Hastings' lawyer, appealing the ruling of the Commission on Landmarks, and charging its chairman, Isaac Williston, with reverse discrimination...

"Chairman Williston, an outspoken critic of the current city administration and a declared Independent candidate for mayor," the reporter continued, "spoke out today in a press conference in City Hall."

Then the camera cut away to the La Salle Street lobby of the building. Isaac Williston was standing in front of a podium that displayed the seal of Chicago, flanked notably by Jesse Jackson, as well as numerous advisors, lawyers, and community backers.

Poised in front of a bank of microphones, Williston's face displayed that calculated level of righteous indignation appropriate not only for a man who had been wrongly maligned in a lawsuit—but also for a man who was positioning himself as the heir-apparent to the political legacy of former Chicago mayor Harold Washington.

"These outrageous allegations," Williston said, jabbing his finger at a sheaf of lawsuit papers in his hands, "represent *lies*, desperate last-ditch legal *tries*, and a bigoted hatred in *disguise!*"

The crowd behind him exploded in support. When the wild applause died down, Williston then dropped his political bomb.

"As chairman of the Landmark Commission, I am authorized to announce that the commission voted unanimously today to launch a full-fledged investigation."

Suddenly, I had the sinking feeling that this was not going to be good.

I was right.

"An investigation," the commissioner explained, "into the secret and clandestine nature of Professor Hastings' non-disclosed business dealings with certain unidentified and confidential buyers of his interest in the historic Tornquist church property."

Then Williston wrapped it up by mentioning certain "as of yet unsubstantiated reports" the commission had received, "reports that a white-supremacy group, a neo-Nazi organization, may be bidding with Professor Hastings to buy out his interest in this landmark piece of irreplaceable architecture. I must emphasize these are only unproven reports as of now. But we plan to get to the bottom of this. And I call on the mayor of Chicago to join me in this effort to ferret out the truth!"

I turned to Douglas, whose face was now peering at the TV almost parallel to mine.

"Those allegations are a lie!" I said.

But he just smiled. "Yeah, and that's what *that fellow* just said too," Douglas said, nodding his head toward the TV. "He says the allegations in your lawsuit against him are a lie."

Then Douglas leaned back in his chair. "Well, well. So you *do* have a story, don't you, Kevin?"

Then he stood up, and started walking away. But he stopped for a second, turned and added, "Since you've been so busy lately working here on staff, I've sort of missed shooting the breeze with you..." Then he walked away.

"Me too," I said, calling after him. Douglas did not stop walking, but just held his hand up to acknowledge my parting remark, and then disappeared down the hallway.

I turned back to the television. The reporter was inside an office. Suddenly I recognized the face of Horace Fin, grinning like a Cheshire cat.

Fin was being asked to comment on Isaac Williston's announcement.

Please don't comment. Please don't comment, I was muttering to myself.

"What do *I* say?" Fin said with bravado to the TV reporter. "What does attorney Horace Fin have to say?"

Then he lifted his hands up in the air, on each side of his face, a little like he was framing a picture with his broad face as the subject.

"*Fiat justicia, ruat coelum,*" he said proudly. Then he added the translation.

"That's Latin for 'Let justice be done, though the heavens fall...'"

Then Fin looked right at the camera and winked.

He winked at the TV camera, I said to myself in disbelief. *He actually* winked.

I sat there in the empty recreation room alone for a while. Some of the residents finally wandered in. A few sat down and watched TV. Two of them played a game of Ping-Pong together.

What a disaster, I thought to myself, reflecting on Williston's comments, Fin's insipid quote, my legal quagmire, and a murdered Russian mobster who I believed must have had some connection to Mangiorno, who I presumed had ordered him to chase me down.

I had two telephone calls I knew I absolutely had to make.

The first would be to Horace Fin, to let him know he needed to withdraw as my attorney. Not only did I not have the necessary legal expense money—but even if I did, Horace Fin was the last lawyer I wanted.

Over the last few days I had made a few calls about getting a new lawyer. I called legal aid, but was told I did not qualify. Because my lawsuits were all—thus far at least—civil and not criminal, the public defender's office said they couldn't help.

The other phone call would have to be to Tess Collins. Some—how, I had to let her know that what she was undoubtedly hearing about me as a result of Williston's City Hall press conference was not true.

But that call was a delicate one.

I was sitting there, staring out in space, in the recreation room, when Jim Loveland walked by, with his coat over his arm, on the way out for the day.

"You look deep in thought," he said. "Can I help?"

"I doubt it," I said with a shrug.

"Well, why don't you try me?"

"Okay," I replied, struggling to sound matter-of-fact. "It's about all my legal issues…"

"And?" he added, still pursuing me.

"I need to find a new lawyer. Somehow. I'm obviously not in great financial shape to do that. And I've got some…well, pressures… bearing down on me. So I need to act soon."

Jim Loveland thought for a minute. Then he patted me on the shoulder.

"Why don't we talk about it tomorrow. I may have an idea on that."

Then he said good night to the handful of residents who were in the recreation room and left the building.

I made my way back to my little bedroom. I clicked on my cell phone. Pulling the piece of notepaper with Tess' number on it out of my pocket, I dialed her number.

It rang a few times, then her voice mail came on. I left a message.

> Hi, Tess. This is Kevin…Kevin Hastings. Thanks for the message you left at my apartment. I'm calling you on my cell phone because…well…I'm not at my apart- ment. That's a long story. But I wanted you to know something. Whatever you hear about the TV press

conference and about my lawsuit against the commission…the business about white-supremacy groups and
all that…it's simply not true. You really have to believe
me. I would like to talk. Is there any way you could
meet with me? Just call me on my cell phone.

After leaving my cell number, I hung up.

And I lay on my bed for a long while, listening to the sounds of
honking horns, and of sirens somewhere out there in the night.

FORTY-THREE

~

THE NEXT MORNING I WAS in Jim Loveland's office. He had caught the Williston press conference on the late news the night before. Needless to say, the expression on his face indicated that he had some concerns about me.

I strenuously pleaded with him not to believe the rumors about my alleged connection with some unnamed white-supremacy group. I told him I had no idea where those wild stories came from, but he had to know those allegations were totally false.

"I gather that you did have some dealings with a buyer for the Tornquist property though," Loveland said. "I learned that from the news report. And that you had decided not to divulge the identity of your buyer. Right?"

"Sure. That much is true." I replied. "But I had absolutely no dealings with neo-Nazis or anything like that…"

"Anything you want to share with me about the people that you *are* dealing with?" he asked.

I squirmed a little. Then I told him that at the present I couldn't disclose that.

"Maybe after I can talk to a lawyer—a new attorney—I could reconsider that. Maybe then I could tell you the whole sordid story, Jim."

He nodded. I realized he was taking a huge gamble even keeping me on the payroll after the scandalous statements that had smeared me over primetime Chicago TV the night before. But Jim Loveland, by that point in our conversation, seemed satisfied that I was leveling with him—at least at much as I could, given the circumstances.

Then Loveland talked to me about an idea he had.

"About your need for a new lawyer," Loveland said. "I have a suggestion."

"Oh?"

"Yes. Here it is. Why don't you contact Daniel Petranelli? You remember him, he's the fellow who gave the gospel message here the other day."

I wanted to be open to anything at that point, but I must have given Jim a dubious look.

"I know you may wonder why I would recommend him," Loveland said. "But the truth is, that he's an accomplished lawyer. He handled a difficult case for the Windy City Mission a number of years ago. It was a zoning issue. He defended us by arguing freedom of religion under the First Amendment. We ended up winning that. And he's done legal work for other organizations. Constitutional rights type stuff. And even some criminal cases, I think. Anyway, it's just a thought."

"I appreciate that," I said. "But first, I simply don't have the money."

"Sure," Jim replied. "But—you know—I think that Dan is the kind of guy who would meet with you at least initially, talk it over with you, and not charge for the first meeting. In fact, I happened to call him last night. I sort of felt him out about the idea. I hope it's okay that I did that…He said he'd meet with you, at no cost, no obligation. See if there was something he could do for you."

Then Jim tossed me one of Petranelli's business cards.

I smiled and thanked him, fingering the card. The concept of hiring a preacher to be my legal pit bull seemed incongruous, to say the least. But I knew I was running out of options. Besides, it was pretty obvious to me that I couldn't afford to cut Horace Fin loose until I had secured a new lawyer.

During my lunch break, I slipped back to my room and placed a call to Petranelli's office. After all, what did I have to lose?

A secretary answered the phone. I told her who I was, and that I wanted an appointment with Mr. Petranelli.

"Is he expecting you?" she asked.

"In a way, I guess," I answered. "Pastor Jim Loveland referred me. I think he has already talked to Mr. Petranelli about my case."

She asked if I could hold while she "checked her screen" for a message. Then she returned in a minute or two.

"Yes. I have a computer note from Mr. Petranelli indicating you might be calling. How about tomorrow at 10:00 AM?"

"Sounds okay. But one thing, about fees…"

"Mr. Petranelli is doing this first meeting with you pro bono, at least for the first hour. That's what his note says. Is that what you are wondering?"

"Exactly," I said brightly. "Great. I'll be there tomorrow."

I was hustling back to Bob Moody's office when my cell phone began ringing. It was Tess Collins.

"Hello, Tess," I said, answering. "Thanks so much for calling back."

"I'm not sure I should be doing this…" she said reluctantly.

"I can understand. But thanks anyway," I added. "Can we meet somewhere…and talk…"

"Like I said in my voice mail, a couple of days ago," she said, "I'm not sure we have much to talk about. Regarding the Tornquist property I mean. Not sure our organization can agree with you on that…"

"And I understand that," I replied. "But, aside from that, we do have one important thing to determine. Having to do with your sense of equilibrium and balance."

"And what would that be?" she said with a little bit of a giggle.

"Well," I continued. "We need to see whether you can balance a huge scoop of ice cream on the end of a spoon without dropping it on the middle of the table…"

Tess laughed. And so did I.

"Oh my," she said. "What would my board of directors say if they knew I was meeting with you?"

"Surely you're entitled to have a personal life, aren't you?" I said, searching for the right counter-argument. "Besides, I'm a fun guy to hang out with, right?"

"Fun? Sure," she said with a chuckle. "Judging by Isaac Williston's press conference last night...you're a regular barrel of monkeys! By the way, should I bring my own white sheet and hood when we meet?"

"Hey," I exclaimed. "I told you in my voice mail, those things were complete fabrications. Honest, Tess. I wouldn't lie to you about that..."

"I know," she said brightly, "I believe you. I'm not sure why... but I do..."

There was a pause in our conversation. I knew that I needed to step into it. If I trusted her, there was something I needed to say. A commitment of sorts. So I made the move.

"Tess," I said. "I want to promise you something..."

"Oh, hey," she said, "let's not get into promises..."

"No. This is one I need to make to you. If you meet with me tonight..." I said. Then I took a breath, and finished the sentence. "I am going to prove to you why you can trust me. And why you can believe me. So, how about it?"

After a few seconds of silence, she answered.

"All right. Should we meet at Dan's Diner again?"

"No," I said quickly. "That's too close to my old apartment. Somewhere else."

"Okay," she said with a little confusion in her voice. "Then let's go to the Pearl of China. Good Asian food."

"I know where it is," I replied. "How about seven tonight?"

"That will work," Tess said. "See you there."

After I hung up, I glanced at my watch. Now, I wanted the afternoon to fly by. Seven o'clock seemed a long way away.

FORTY-FOUR

~

THAT AFTERNOON I HELPED Bob Moody with some grant application forms for the Windy City Mission. After working with Bob for a number of days, I was beginning to form some impressions about him.

He was methodical, precise, and organized. It was clear he was a pretty good administrator, at least before ALS started cutting a wide swath in his life. Essex College could have used someone as efficient and insightful as Bob in their administrative staff. He also had a wry sense of humor that occasionally popped out.

Yet the thing that truly impressed me was less tangible than any of that. What happened that afternoon was a good example. Right in the middle of our reconciling some complicated forms, a call came into his office from the city building inspector's office. The mission had done some minor remodeling, but it required a sign-off from the city fathers. This guy had come by, unannounced, the day before, looking for Bob. But Bob was at the doctor's office at the time. So the inspector was mildly irate, and said he now had to make a second trip back to complete the inspection.

He was calling to set an appointment. Because I was now helping Bob with almost all his duties, Bob said he needed to have me listen in on the phone call. So he told the inspector he was putting him on the speakerphone.

"Fine, put me on speakerphone, I don't care," the inspector said gruffly. "But let's just get one thing straight. You got to be there

when I'm there. Got it? I'm not in the mood to make another use-
less trip to your rescue mission. You got it?"

"Sure," Bob said with a smile. "Sorry. If I knew you were going
to come yesterday, I would have canceled my medical appointment—"

"Yeah. Fine," the inspector snapped back. "Look, I really don't
care about your doctor troubles, Mr. Moody. We got a building
department to run. So…if I come by tomorrow at two in the afternoon, you gonna be around, or what?"

Bob looked over at me. I nodded, indicating that I could be
there with him.

"That…will work," he said.

I was flushed with anger. I wanted to grab the phone and yell
into it. Something like, *Listen, you City-Hall cretin, Bob Moody here
is slowly dying from ALS. You ought to be given a jail sentence for
treating him that way. I can't believe the respect he's showing you.
Because if it were up to me, I'd have you boiled in oil!*

Instead, I just looked at Bob Moody. He was smiling serenely.

After the phone call, I shared some of my feelings about the
way he was mistreated on the phone.

But Bob just smiled back, and then he got this twinkle in his
eye.

"But I did make…one mistake," Bob said. "Should have…told
him to come at ten tomorrow morning…instead of two…"

"Why's that?"

"Then," Bob said slyly, "could have…made him sit through…
our gospel service!"

We both laughed, and then Bob's humor got him coughing and
gagging a little. I jumped up in a panic, but he was able after a few
tense seconds to get his breath back and waved me off.

"Don't worry," Bob said. "When I start dying on you…I'll let
you know!"

So, that was the part about Bob that really got to me. I watched
him, and I began thinking that my personal "disasters" weren't so
bad. And that I might have something to learn from this fellow.
Particularly about his source of inner calm.

But his comment about the timing of the appointment made me think about my conference time with attorney Petranelli scheduled at ten.

I brought it up to Bob, but he said it wouldn't be a problem. I would also get a pass from the required morning chapel service.

I worked until five-thirty that day. Then I quickly showered in the men's locker room and dressed for dinner. On the way to dinner, I swung by my bank and made an after-hours deposit of my first paycheck from the Windy City Mission. It felt good to be earning money again.

Then I drove over to the Pearl of China.

It had become part of my pattern of living by then that I would remember the make and model of vehicles that were behind me on the road. If they followed me more than two blocks I would deviate from my planned path, and veer off course, to see if they were still following me. As I neared the restaurant I was suddenly struck with a thought of horror.

What if Tess, just by being seen with me, ended up being placed in danger?

I was seriously considering calling the whole thing off. But by then I was already at the Pearl of China. Tess was in the parking lot. She spotted me right off, and waved warmly to me.

Inside, we were seated immediately, in a quiet booth away from the windows. I ordering the shrimp lo mein, and she got the beef and vegetables. We both split an appetizer plate. Now that I had a little money in the bank, I wasn't worried about the bill.

There was a bit of nervous small talk at first, but then we quickly started to click. I asked questions about how she got into the business of architectural preservation. She wanted to know why I had been attracted to history.

Then, as our dinner plates were arriving at the table, she asked me a question.

"I know you're no longer at Essex College," she said. "And can I say something?...I hope...I really hope that our protest that day wasn't the cause of that..."

"Don't worry about that," I replied quickly. "I blame myself for a lot of what happened with the college."

"So, are you working somewhere now?" she asked innocently.

I think she could see the anguish on my face, because she quickly added, "if you feel comfortable telling me, I mean…"

"It's not that," I said. "It's something else. I told you if you came out with me I would show you how I could be trusted. And…how I believe I can trust you. I can't tell you where I'm working now. Or where I'm living. Not because I don't want to. But because I don't think it would be safe for you to know."

She stopped eating, and stared at me.

"I need to tell you some things," I said. "And when I do, I know I am taking the risk that I will never see you again like this. With us together, I mean. There's a chance that you will want nothing to do with me. And frankly, the thought of that happening really…is really tough for me. No kidding."

Tess was not moving.

"So," I continued. "Let me tell you a secret…"

FORTY-FIVE

~

TESS KEPT EATING, but her eyes were glued on me as I spoke. The "secret" I shared with her ended up being a fairly detailed chronology of my kaleidoscope of legal, personal, and professional crises of late. I hadn't planned on being that open with her, but something nudged me on.

I explained my ill-fated hiring of Lloyd Gentry and his failure to advise me of the possible landmarking of the Tornquist church, leading to my malpractice suit against him; how we were also suing the bankrupt art foundation because they concealed the fact of the landmarking status from us when they sold the property to me. (Tess, who seemed very connected in the art community, knew the foundation and had very little good to say about the former director.) I gave her a crash course on Gentry's vindictive counter-suit against me for defamation. I also explained my termination from Essex, and my denial of unemployment benefits. I also told her in no uncertain terms how repulsed I was at Horace Fin's ill-conceived "reverse discrimination" claims against Landmark Commissioner Isaac Williston, claims which he had filed purportedly to advance my "interests." One of the many reasons, I pointed out, why I was now looking for a new lawyer.

When I got to the part about Gentry's firm probably being behind the sabotaging of the electric power at my apartment, through their legal relationship with all the municipal utilities, Tess shook her head, and then asked a question.

"So," she inquired, "that's why you're staying away from your apartment?"

"No, that's not it," I replied. "It's worse than that."

"How worse?" she asked.

"Much, much worse."

That's when I went into my having unwittingly entered into a contract to sell the Tornquist property to a reputed mob boss.

I asked her if she knew who Vito Mangiorno was. Tess paused, and cocked her head a little, and then said she had read something in the papers at one time; and her impression was that there were questions being raised about his being involved with organized crime.

So I launched into the deep. About the contract I had signed with an undisclosed buyer, guaranteeing the leveling of the church and their ability to build a parking garage; how I was caught on the horns of a dilemma when it became clear that the landmarking of the church would prevent me from fulfilling my agreement with Mangiorno; and about the carjacking episode. And the chase by baseball bat-wielding thugs. And how I recognized the face of my pursuer in this week's *Tribune* article which detailed his recent gruesome murder.

Tess stopped eating altogether, and leaned back from the table.

She was fitting the pieces together in her head. Then she said, "So...those goons in the stairway...the night of the Landmark Commission hearing, when they looked like they were trying to rough you up. And rough me up too..."

"That was DeVoe," I said. "Mangiorno's lawyer. And the man with him was Troy Armstrong, a guy who hangs around with DeVoe."

Tess's eyes were wide and wondering at everything I had told her. I half-expected her to wipe her mouth with a napkin, smile courteously, thank me for the Chinese, and then run out of the restaurant. But she didn't.

Instead, she leaned forward and cupped her face in her hands, leaning her elbows on the red satin tablecloth with the oriental designs.

"Boy-oh-boy-oh-boy," she whispered. "Kevin, you have really been through it..."

When I saw tears welling up all of a sudden in her eyes, I had to turn away, for fear that I was going to lose control.

I cleared my throat and, trying to sound really together, I thanked her for being a friend and listening. I also shared my deepest fear that by consorting with me she might be putting herself at risk from Mangiorno's people.

"Didn't you say," Tess replied, "that Mangiorno apparently doesn't want any publicity on his involvement—on the fact that he is the undisclosed buyer of the Tornquist church?"

I nodded.

"Well," she said with a little laugh, and wiping her eyes, "I think I'm safe. After all, I'm like the world's biggest lightning rod for publicity in the city of Chicago—in case you haven't noticed..."

I laughed a bit at that, but I told her that I thought we ought to be very careful about being seen together publicly. That I couldn't stand the thought of anything happening to her because of me.

She looked down at the table, and then she said something.

She said, "Both my organization and I are firmly opposed to your legal position regarding the Tornquist building." Then she looked up, straight at me. "But on a personal basis, I like you, Kevin. Your life is a bit wacky"—we both chuckled at that—"but I like you...a lot," she said.

She took my hand, which was on the table, and took it in her two hands. And then she leaned down and touched my hand to her cheek, and then leaned back in her chair, still holding on.

"You said you were looking for a new lawyer?" she asked.

"I've got an appointment tomorrow morning," I said. "His name is Daniel Petranelli. He was referred to me by someone... someone I think I can trust."

"Name sounds familiar," Tess said mulling it over. "I think I may know of him. Wasn't Petranelli the lawyer who handled that zoning lawsuit in federal court a year or so ago? Our organization tries to keep up with those types of cases. I think the zoning department was trying to shut down some kind of Christian rescue mission...he won it on a constitutional argument of some kind."

"Yes," I noted, remembering Jim Loveland's comment. "First Amendment. Freedom of religion, I heard."

"Sure, he's the one," Tess said.

Then she added, "You know, he just may be okay. This new attorney may be able to help you. Who knows?"

As I walked her to the front door of the restaurant I told her I would watch her get into her car, from my position inside the lobby. I didn't want to be seen together in the parking lot. Then I insisted on following behind her car in my Jetta, to make sure she got home all right.

"I think you just want to find out where I live," she said with a smile.

"I want to know you're safe," I said.

But just as she was opening the front door to the Pearl of China to leave, she stopped and said, "By the way, we have contacts inside the Landmark Commission office."

"Oh?" I said.

"Yes. That business about neo-Nazis and all that," Tess said, "it was a single anonymous call to their voice mail, after hours. Nothing specific. Nobody downtown, or in my office either, believes that stuff. When something hits the newspapers, like your cases have, it brings out all the zanies."

I nodded.

"Now," Tess continued, "I wonder what Williston would say if he knew you were wheeling and dealing with a mob boss instead!"

I froze momentarily. But Tess laughed and said, "Don't worry. I have no reason...and no intention...of telling anyone what you shared with me."

Then she added, "Thanks, Kevin, for opening up with me." Then she walked through the door and out to her car. I watched her every move, until she was driving out of the parking lot. Then I walked to my car so I could follow her home. I was still ruminating on the possibility of a threat to Tess, though I tried to convince myself that she was probably not in danger.

If Mangiorno was involved in killing the Russian, I thought, *then maybe now he can't afford to come after me because he's got to have his guys lie low. Doesn't that make sense?*

But the thought came to me, as I pulled my Jetta out of the parking lot, that most of what was happening to me didn't seem to make much sense. Thugs with baseball bats who chase me through backyards—Russian mobsters who get set on fire inside cars—city-hall politicians who hold press conferences and label me as vermin—and lawyers like Horace Fin and Lloyd Gentry, who seem to delight in mutually assured legal destruction—none of that seemed to comport with reason...or logic either.

But one thing did make sense to me. As I followed Tess's car in mine, and thought back to her bright smile and big brown eyes, and the tenderness she showed me, I was convinced that whatever the questions were in my life, she certainly seemed to be one of the answers.

FORTY-SIX

~

AROUND THAT SAME TIME, Vito Mangiorno was holding a meeting in the inner office of his construction company. He was eating some grapes that were lying on his desk. Next to him was his heavy-set lieutenant, whose real name was Alfonso Tutti, but who everybody called "Big Tut." Across the desk, Tony DeVoe was peering through his tinted glasses and brushing the lint off his imported suit, trying to look relaxed. Troy Armstrong, DeVoe's constant shadow, had been told to wait outside in the car.

Of course, had things not resolved the way they did, had certain events—both diabolical and also, let's say, *divine*—occurred the way they did, no one in the outside world, including me, would ever have found out about that meeting.

DeVoe had just given Mangiorno an overview of all the legal developments to date that had anything to do with the Tornquist church property, which also meant having to do with me as well.

"This Kevin Hastings guy," DeVoe said, "he's got more lawsuits than a West Side slumlord. It's like a hobby with him, or something, to get served with new court papers."

Big Tut chuckled at that, but it didn't last long as he noticed that Mangiorno wasn't laughing.

"All the money we pay you," Mangiorno said to his lawyer, "all the high-priced legal fees. And all your bogus promises about putting this parking garage deal together. All of that...and it all ends," and with that, Mangiorno slammed his fist down on the grapes, smashing them into pulp on his desk. *"With a whole lot of nothing! Zero! You have given me zero!"*

Mangiorno looked down at the squashed grapes, brushed his fingers together, then gestured vaguely toward Big Tut. His lieutenant got the point, rose and fetched some paper towels, and then cleaned up the mess while Mangiorno raised his arms off the desk top.

"I can't exercise the kind of control over the legal system that you enjoy in your…various enterprises, Mr. Mangiorno," DeVoe said diplomatically.

"Why not?" Mangiorno shouted.

"Because the law has limits," DeVoe said, "unlike people. You can push the law, manipulate it, threaten it, you know, only so far…"

"The law! The law!" Mangiorno exclaimed. "What are you talkin'? The law is nothing but people who sit around courtrooms with suits and briefcases. It's still people. And I hired you to push the right people in the right way."

"I'm afraid," DeVoe said, "that unless Hastings' appeal to the circuit court ends up overturning the ruling of the Landmark Commission, we will never be able to tear down that church and build a parking garage. But, I've got another idea…"

"What?" Mangiorno asked.

"Well, certainly this is not the only site where we could build— or take over—a multilevel parking structure."

"My son looked into all that. He couldn't find anything—except this church property."

DeVoe and Big Tut looked at each other.

"What?" Mangiorno said, catching their side glance to each other.

"No disrespect, Boss, but your son's work on this," Big Tut said, "just didn't pan out. You know, he's been real busy with his night-club. And he's always taking out all of his lady friends—"

"Enough." Mangiorno replied, raising a single index finger, and closing that discussion. Then he added, "So how about the other thing? The business of my maybe being targeted in any investigations?"

"All of my sources," DeVoe said, "tell me your name hasn't come up in any Chicago grand juries."

"Federal too?"

"We're checking on that," DeVoe said.

"Something else I want you to find out," Mangiorno said. "I got to make sure the circuit court is going to rule the right way on this Commission appeal case of Hastings. There's a special judge over there. We got to make sure the case goes to him."

"Sure, I know who you're talkin' about," DeVoe said.

"You know, it's a matter of principle with me," Mangiorno continued. "I got a signed agreement with Hastings on this property. He said I could build a parking lot. Now everybody is saying, 'Sorry, Vito, your contract with the professor, it was all a big joke, this jerk doesn't have to honor his agreement with you.' You know how that makes me look? And I hold you to blame!" And with that he pointed his finger at DeVoe.

"It's not over till it's over," DeVoe said, struggling to keep the focus off himself.

"Alright," Mangiorno said to his lawyer, "get out. I'm done with you."

After he was gone and the door was closed, Mangiorno turned to Big Tut, and spoke in a low voice.

"You know, it's too bad about Boris the Bat. He was an okay guy. But something had to be done. You know?"

"Absolutely."

"When he broke from the Russians, I had my doubts. I wondered when he joined us whether he was some kind of spy. And frankly, I still think him and the Russians did your little brother, God rest his soul."

"Yeah," Big Tut said glumly. "Just last week someone asked me, 'Hey, where's Little Tut these days? Don't see him around anymore.' So I had to tell him. Boss, it makes me want to tear somebody's lungs out..."

"Sure. Sure. Me too. But anyway, when Boris botched it—couldn't put the muscle on this college professor—I mean, really.

Was he even trying? And then he starts bad-mouthing me. Trash-talking my operation."

"Boss," Big Tut said, "remember—I heard it with my own ears."

"So. There it is. That's our signal to Chicago. Just to remind people I don't tolerate disloyalty. Or total incompetence. That you don't mess around with me."

"Absolutely."

Then Mangiorno bobbed his head this way and that. And then he spoke.

"So—this parking garage thing. I'm no dummy. I realize it just might not happen. And if that's the way it ends up, then I think the college professor is gonna have to go."

"Really?" Big Tut said with surprise.

"Whatsa matter?" Mangiorno said. "You look like you just found a bug in your soup."

"No, it's just that…well, first it's Boris. Now the professor. We've been doin' good by keeping things quiet for a long time. But now—"

"Yeah. Doin' good. Thanks to me," Mangiorno snapped. "But sometimes measures have to be taken…"

"Why can't we just sue the pants off this professor for breakin' the deal he made with you?"

"Oh, that's a good one!"

"Just a suggestion, Boss. I guess I don't get it—"

"No, you don't!" Mangiorno yelled. "First, this professor is stone broke. The only thing we'd get out of him is maybe the property—maybe if we were lucky. And if it's landmarked and that can't be changed, then we can't touch the church building—and then who's going to buy it from us? What's it worth to us then?"

Big Tut was starting to get the picture.

"And furthermore," Mangiorno continued, "we got a bigger problem. You want the circuit court, and the court staff, and a bunch of lawyers and the whole city of Chicago to find out, when we file a lawsuit, that it was really me who wanted to buy the property to build an all-cash-run parking garage? Are you kiddin' me?"

His lieutenant was nodding by then.

"I can just see some nosy lawyer askin', 'Now, Mr. Mangiorno, exactly *why* did you want to build a parking lot anyway?' And I say, 'Oh, no reason…except we got a bunch of suitcases full of cash lyin' around. And we need to launder it somewhere.' Come on, put your brain on in your head! If we can't make this thing go, then the professor's got to go."

"Yeah," Big Tut said, "but what if we get the right judge and the professor wins this appeal—and the city lets the property get turned into a parking lot?"

"Well," Mangiorno said, leaning back in his chair, with the air of a judge considering the sentence of a defendant before him, "he's still probably got to go anyway. But just a little later, that's all. Hastings has too much information about me and the property. After the land gets transferred from him into the name of VM Contractors. Then there's got to be some action taken."

"So, that's it for the professor, huh?"

"In a manner of speakin', yeah. I can't risk having witnesses who can directly tie us to the parking-lot deal."

After thinking it over Mangiorno added, "But quietly. He's got to be made to disappear. No trace. And anyone else who knows he was dealing with us."

"His lawyer?"

"Maybe him too. That crackpot…what's his name…"

"Horace Fin."

"Yeah. Him too. And didn't DeVoe talk about some kooky chick—"

"The one who runs the organization?"

"Yeah."

"But boss," Big Tut said, "she is on the other side, I think. Wants to keep the church from being torn down."

"Yeah, but DeVoe said the two of them were talking together," Mangiorno said insistently, "right in front of him after the commission hearing. He said there was definitely something cooking between them. Anyway, we may have to disappear her too. We'll see. I'm still figuring this out."

"Sure," Big Tut said casually. "Whatever you say, Boss."

"See," Mangiorno continued, his voice taking on a new intensity, "the key to everything is to keep this under wraps. *No publicity*. Nothing tying me back to all this. Not tying me to the buying of the property. Or to the building of the parking garage. Or to what happens to the professor and his little circle of friends. You got it?"

Big Tut nodded and gave a reassuring grin.

"Sure, Boss," he said. "I got it."

PART 2

FORTY-SEVEN

~

AT THE BEGINNING OF ALL THIS, I described how I found myself standing at the door of a lawyer's office. Which is where we have come now. To that point. Me standing in front of the law office of Daniel Petranelli. Chinese laundry on the left. Pawnshop on the right. Wondering why I should believe that just one more lawyer was going to really fix anything for me. After all, didn't my problems start with lawyers in the first place? That—together with mobsters…and landmarking regulations…and my own naïveté…plus my mad dash in search of a slice of the good life.

I hesitated. But desperation, and necessity, pushed me through the door with peeling paint and into the lobby. A middle-aged woman was typing furiously at a computer. She turned and greeted me. "You must be Mr. Hastings. Mr. Petranelli will be with you shortly. Won't you have a seat? Care for some coffee? Soda? Water?"

I thanked her but declined. As I sat down my eyes swept over the office.

It looked like the space had originally been an old red-brick warehouse. They had done a respectable job of remodeling. The brick walls and high ceilings remained. But now they contained shelves with law books and some solid but not fancy furniture.

In a few minutes Petranelli, an energetic-looking dark-haired man who must have been in his forties, strolled out and greeted me. He was wearing a golfing shirt, khakis, and hiking shoes. Seemed to be in good shape.

He took me down a narrow brick-walled corridor to his office. He had me take a seat and, saying he would be right with me, ducked out.

Framed certificates from seven or eight different courts hung on the walls. I noticed he had a law degree from Yale. On the credenza behind his desk I saw a photo of him with his arms around a teenage boy and girl, and a woman next to him who I figured to be his wife.

Other pictures showed him with some golfing companions. There was one of him and his wife hiking—the background showed what looked like the Badlands of South Dakota. And another with them both, this time in front of a mountain range.

Petranelli strode back in with a file in his hand and a legal pad. He sat down, explaining he'd already received a little background on my dilemma from Jim Loveland. But now, he said, I needed to tell him everything I thought would be important for him to know about my legal problems.

"Everything?" I asked.

He nodded.

"You have all day?" I said sardonically.

"If need be," he replied.

I took a breath and dove in. I gave him the whole story. Chronologically. When I got to the part about learning—too late—who Vito Mangiorno was, and the fact that he was the guy who had bargained with me through DeVoe to purchase the Tornquist church, I told him I needed assurances that everything I was telling him would be kept strictly confidential.

"It will be," he said. "There's been a general movement to create more and more exceptions to the attorney–client privilege of confidentiality," Petranelli noted, "but none of them apply to our conversation as far as I can see."

He smiled. "The privilege is getting to be a little bit like Swiss cheese. It may have some holes in it...but there's still more cheese than holes."

Before I went on, he asked me something.

"Did Mangiorno's lawyer ever tell you why they wanted to build a parking garage?"

"They never did."

"Well," he continued, "I worked in the state attorney general's office for a while before going into private practice. That was a number of years ago. I did some stuff with the organized-crime unit. And I had regular contact back then with the Chicago Crime Commission. As a general rule, these criminal networks are always looking for a handy way to launder their illegal cash. They pass it through an otherwise legitimate business so the money looks legal. Parking garages do an almost all-cash business. So that might be why they may have wanted to build one. But that's just speculation on my part."

"Neither DeVoe nor anyone else told me anything about that—"

"Good."

"Why 'good'?"

"Because if you had such knowledge," the lawyer said, "or were complicit in the plan to set up money-laundering—and were still trying to effect that plan—then we'd be dealing with one of those exceptions to attorney–client privilege. If it was necessary for the prevention of a crime, I could disclose the information to the authorities even if you didn't want me to. But it doesn't look like that's the case."

I wasn't really worried about that point, because I was not helping Mangiorno in the least. All I knew was the guy wanted to build a parking garage and I had a contract with him that guaranteed he'd be getting some real estate that would permit him to do it.

When I got to the carjacking and the baseball-bat incident with Boris Bittarushka and the other thugs, Petranelli asked me for additional details. I felt the encounter was important because I considered myself lucky to still have my skull intact. But the attorney was thinking about something else.

"I would strongly recommend that you consider divulging that information—about recognizing Bittarushka at the carjacking and the incident with the bats—to the authorities."

But I saw the immediate downside.

"What if Mangiorno ordered the killing of Boris?" I said. "What if he finds out I identified Boris as the one chasing me? And what if that links Mangiorno to the murder of Boris?"

"That's just the point," Petranelli said. "That might be the missing link needed to put Mangiorno away."

"But what assurance do I have," I exclaimed, "that the police or the prosecutor I would talk to about all of this is absolutely, one-hundred-percent not on the take with Mangiorno's operation?"

"The odds are with you," he said. "Most folks in law enforcement—most prosecutors—are straight as an arrow."

"But what if I get the one rotten apple? And he tells Mangiorno? I'd be a dead man. Horace Fin tells me stories about some cops being in with organized crime."

"I understand your concern. Those are legitimate. All I'm asking is that you *consider* volunteering the information. That's all. How we would go about doing that is a whole different issue."

Frankly, I was now worried that this lawyer who was supposed to get me out of my legal wrangles was just getting me in deeper.

"Am I *required* to divulge this information to the police at this point?" I asked.

"No," Petranelli said. "I don't think so. The closest thing to that is a provision in the criminal code that says you can't leave the State of Illinois, or conceal yourself, if you have knowledge material to a criminal investigation."

The second I heard that my stomach knotted. I interrupted him.

"Yes, but I have knowledge about Mangiorno, and about Bittarushka, and about a possible connection between the two." I was getting a little cranked up. "And I've concealed myself, I guess in a way, by working and living over at the mission. Very few people know where I'm staying. So—am I in danger now of being prosecuted myself? I mean, you've got to be kidding! That's all I would need…"

"Hey, Kevin, take a deep breath. You're going to burn out your gears. You didn't let me finish. That criminal code provision wouldn't apply to you. Unless…"

"Unless?"

"*Unless*," he said slowly and deliberately, "you went into hiding *with the specific intent to prevent or obstruct the prosecution of Mangiorno.*"

"Oh."

"And from what you're telling me, that isn't the reason you've been in hiding."

"True," I said, feeling a little better. "No, the only specific intent I've had is to prevent myself from getting fitted with cement shoes."

I wanted to get finality on the point. "Alright," I said, "then I am not required to volunteer what I know to the police."

"Probably not," Petranelli said. "In other words, you are not required to act as a good Samaritan. The compulsion should be a moral one...but it's not a legal one."

"Oh, so you want me to be the good Samaritan? At the risk of my own neck? Is this the lawyer talking—or the preacher? Which one?" I snapped.

I was sorry instantly. But he seemed to take it in stride.

"I know you heard me at the mission," he said, "which is a good thing. Because you know where I stand in terms of my faith. To be honest, I integrate my faith into everything I do, including my practice of law. It's a little like my grandmother's vegetable soup. She'd leave it on the stove all day. By nighttime it was all pretty well stewed together. That's what you're getting with me. My relationship with Christ is pretty well stewed into everything."

I didn't know how to take that. Whether that was a good thing—or a bad thing. I was suspicious of his attempting to slip his religious opinions in. On the other hand, I was running out of places to hide in Chicago. And time was definitely not my friend.

"I'm going to have to think it over. About voluntarily talking to the authorities."

Then I changed direction. "Now about all the other snarls I've spent the last two hours talking about..."

"Yes?"

I ticked them off on my fingers. "My contract with Mangiorno, which I can't help but violate, it seems, because of the landmarking

restrictions. My lawsuits against Lloyd Gentry and the art foundation and its real-estate agent. Gentry's defamation case against me.
My appeal from the Landmark Commission's ruling. Commissioner
Williston's threats against me in his press conference. Can you do
anything to untangle this mess?"

Petranelli paused and doodled a little on his notepad, which he
had been filling up as I talked.

"I need some time. Let me look at this tonight. Whenever I'm
faced with complex litigation, what I like to do is draw it out on
paper...in a sort of diagram. With boxes and circles and arrows.
That's how I organize the information. And then I look at it."

"Look at it?"

"Yeah. Look at it."

I'd been hoping for some better assurances than that. The
lawyer must have seen that on my face. Because he added something else.

"Look—I'm not going to tell you something just because you
want to hear it and it will make you feel better. I need to mull this
over. That's how I problem-solve. To give you a snap answer right
now would be a lie. And I'm not going to lie to you, Kevin. Truth
is, you're in some deep trouble. All the way 'round. Give me until
tomorrow. Maybe I can figure something out."

As I shook hands and left, I knew that was the best I was going
to get for the time being. But somehow, hearing the "truth" didn't
seem to do anything for my downtrodden soul.

As I walked to my car I looked around diligently to see if I had
been watched. Then I looked under the car. I had heard plenty of
stories about car bombs. I popped the hood and looked in. After
satisfying myself I wasn't about to evaporate in a blast of frag-
mented metal and broken glass I started up and pulled out.

It was a little after one and the traffic was starting to pile up a
little. I looked at the other drivers around me as I slowly made my
way back to the mission, studying their faces. The tired. The bored.
The hurried. The angry.

I wonder what they see in my face? I asked myself as I sandwiched my car into a line of traffic.

FORTY-EIGHT

~

I MADE IT BACK to the Windy City Mission a few minutes after two, just as the city inspector was arriving. He strode in with his clipboard, and I led him to Bob Moody's office. Bob, as always, was gracious. The inspector was semi-obnoxious. As if he were just looking for some problem to complain about.

Happily, after Bob and I had shown him around and pointed out the alterations—a few walls moved, two closets added—he was satisfied we were up to code. So after writing down some notes, he was gone.

Bob guided his electric wheelchair back into his office. I could hear him calling his wife at the office where she worked and asking her to pick him up early.

He responded to something she'd said.

"Real weak."

As he finished the call, I heard him say, "Love you too."

Back in the office with him, I decided to venture into the question that had been plaguing me since my conversation with Daniel Petranelli.

"Bob," I asked, "did you ever have to make a really tough decision? Knowing it might put you at risk. But also knowing that it might do some good too. And you're trying to balance it all out in your head. Trying to decide what the guiding principle ought to be…to help you do the right thing."

"You mean…the right…ethical principle?"

"Yeah, exactly." I nodded. I still couldn't believe that as a college

professor I was turning to a Christian rescue-mission administrator for advice on a complicated moral quandary.

Bob looked right at me. "Confucius—" he began in his breathy
voice.

"Huh?" I asked, nonplussed. The name of a Chinese philosopher was the last thing I expected from the mouth of a fundamen-
talist Christian.

He nodded.

"Confucius said...thousand-mile journey...starts with the first
step."

I'd certainly heard that before. But I couldn't connect it to our
discussion.

"You have decisions to make..." Bob went on.

"True—some tough ones."

"Those are steps...along the way..."

"Alright," I said, trying to follow him. "But how does that relate
to my deciding *what* the right thing is to do?"

"But *moral* decisions start," Bob's face was now taking on a
vigor I hadn't seen before, "not with *what*...but with *Who*..."

I was starting to see where he was heading. I shouldn't have
been surprised.

"Moral decisions...start first in the *heart*...then they go to the
head."

"In the heart...so you mean my emotional response?"

"No," he said. "Your spiritual self...Bible says that all of us...are
fallen and sinful...inside...in the heart."

"Fine," I snapped, falling into my professorial role. "Which
would mean every moral decision would be flawed—and maybe
even meaningless—"

"Exactly." He smiled.

Wonderful, I mused. *Is this guy a nihilist?*

"*Unless,*" Bob said emphatically, fixing his eyes on me, "you first
find the One...Who fixes the heart. From the inside out."

"So that's it? The answer to all moral dilemmas?" I said incred-
ulously.

"Your dilemma," Bob said slowly with a look that I found hard to understand, "isn't just moral."

"Then what is it?"

"It's spiritual." Bob was now running out of breath. "Decide to get your heart right...with Jesus Christ...then your head can make the right decisions..."

I half expected some further sermonizing. But instead, Bob nodded toward a pile of paperwork he needed help with.

As we worked, I recalled his phone call to his wife and offered to take him home myself to save her the trip. But he just smiled and declined.

"Time with my wife...is precious," he said. "Even just...a ride in the car." Then he smiled.

FORTY-NINE

~

THE NEXT DAY I TOOK A CALL from Daniel Petranelli. After our conference, he said, he'd spent the rest of the day thinking through my cases.

"Let's start with a discussion about fees," he said.

Ah yes, of course, I thought to myself. *I'm about to get spitted and roasted by one more lawyer.*

"I thought I was pretty clear," I said very forthrightly, "that I'm pretty much penniless. That my only income is part-time, from my work here at the mission."

"I know that," the lawyer responded. "And I know how much you're making there...it's not very much. All I am suggesting is that out of your paychecks you send whatever you can to cover some of my out-of-pocket expenses. You look over your budget and propose something."

"Well," I replied suspiciously, "and what about your hourly fees for representing me?"

"Depending on one factor," he said, "I think we can work it out so you won't have to pay me anything up front."

"And what 'factor' would that be?" I asked skeptically.

"My getting your authorization to call Horace Fin right now and work something out with him."

"You actually think you can deal with that guy?" I was incredulous. "You don't know him. 'Working something out' with him is a self-refuting proposition. Can you reverse the fundamental laws of the universe? You have no idea—"

"I think I do," Petranelli interjected. "I know Horace Fin. Fairly well. Why don't you let me give it a try?"

I finally agreed, reluctantly, when Petranelli offered to conference me into the discussion with the other attorney.

I heard the phone ringing, and then Karin's thick Slavic voice answered. In a few minutes Horace Fin was on the line with us. Petranelli told him I was in on the call.

Immediately, and not surprisingly, he got defensive.

"Just send the substitution-of-attorney form over to me," Fin snapped. "We'll get it signed and filed in each of the cases. I'll withdraw, and you can hop on board Mr. Hastings' caravan of pain and misery."

However, Petranelli was unruffled. "Horace," he said brightly, "you make it sound like Kevin's cases are all losers—that they are all bound for the litigation scrap heap."

There was silence on Fin's end.

"Now, Horace," Petranelli continued, "I've read your fee agreement with Kevin here. You were banking everything on a recovery against Lloyd Gentry's firm and their errors-and-omissions insurance carrier. You obviously thought that lawsuit had merit."

"Perhaps I did," Fin said. Then he added acerbically, "But that was back when I knew that a competent, aggressive lawyer was in the driver's seat—"

"Meaning *you*," Petranelli supplied.

"Now that you mention it..."

"Oh, come on," Petranelli said with a chuckle. "Horace, you're still smarting because I beat you in that adverse-easement case two years ago."

"So, you would seek favor of me?" Fin said with almost Elizabethan formality. "Well, I take the advice of the brilliant Samuel Johnson, who said, and I quote, 'Treating your adversary with respect is giving him an advantage to which he is not entitled.'"

"Well, for my money," Petranelli said heartily, "I prefer Shakespeare: 'Do as adversaries do in law—strive mightily, but eat and drink as friends.' *Taming of the Shrew*."

"Hmmm, yes. Act I, scene 2. Glad to see you like the Bard too.

But the fact is, Daniel, even though you have a reputation for pulling rabbits out of hats...when it's all said and done...you may find nothing but skunks in Mr. Hastings' lawsuits."

"Not if you are in this with me. We'd make a good team."

What? I was screaming silently in my head. Suddenly my world had turned into one of those swirling nightmare landscapes by van Gogh. *Just when I thought I'd gotten rid of Horace Fin, now Petranelli is bringing him back in!*

"I don't approve of all your methods," the younger attorney went on. "But I always thought you were an extremely clever advocate. If you stay on, at least on paper, but agree to let me take the entire lead on this, to call the shots, it may work out for all of us."

In the pause that followed, I was tempted to call a time-out on the whole discussion. But before I could, Fin responded.

"What's in it for me?"

"I want you to see, from the inside, how the litigation is progressing—particularly against Gentry's firm."

"Why do you care about that?"

"Because you still have a lien on the entire lawsuit...for the recoupment of your legal fees. I want you to see how your investment is being handled. All I ask is that I get my basic hourly fees out of any recovery we make against Gentry's firm, and his insurance carrier, the real-estate agent's carrier, or both. My fees will reduce your lien dollar for dollar. Then what's left of your lien will belong to you. The balance after that would belong to Mr. Hastings."

"And how many hours will you end up putting into all of this?" the older lawyer asked with a tinge of suspicion to his voice. "How do I know your hourly fees won't be so enormous that they eat up all my fees as well?"

"Because," Petranelli replied calmly, "I'm willing to put a cap on my total fees. Forty hours' worth of work. That's all—"

"You're crazy!" Fin shouted. "You can't successfully wrap up all these lawsuits in just forty hours of work. Can't be done!"

"It has to be done."

"And why is that?"

"Considering," Petranelli said with a kind of iron resolve in his voice, "who is lurking out there in the background, prowling, waiting on the result of Kevin's cases—and I think we all know who I am talking about—considering that, I don't think I have any more time than that."

"Yeah…" There was a tone of understanding in Fin's voice.

"What do you mean, you don't have any more time?" I quickly interjected into the conversation.

"I think your new counsel," Fin put in, "is looking to pull some more rabbits out of hats. Before some really un-nice guys show up—and set fire to the hats and shoot all the rabbits."

FIFTY

~

AT THE END OF OUR CONFERENCE CALL, Horace Fin asked for a little time to think over the suggestion about settling the fee division between them, and about his staying on, subject to my new lawyer's absolute control as lead counsel.

The next day Petranelli called me and said Fin had agreed to the arrangement, on one requirement. He insisted on being copied on "all correspondence—e-mails or written communications" between Petranelli and me, or with counsel for the other parties. Considering his lien for attorney's fees was forty percent of anything I recovered—less Petranelli's hourly fees, which had been capped—he obviously wanted to protect his "investment" in me.

I, on the other hand, had more dire concerns than money. I was in fear for my life. And I also wanted to make sure that Tess, by virtue of her association with me, would not be at risk as well.

But all the huge financial issues still had to be resolved. My bank was going to commence foreclosure proceedings on the Tornquist property soon, now that I didn't have sufficient income to make the monthly mortgage. If I was to somehow salvage my investment in the church, it had to be done soon. Once the foreclosure began, the bank would begin running the clock on their attorney's fees, which, under the terms of the mortgage I signed, I would also be responsible for.

Petranelli reminded me of that when he called me to sign his fee agreement. Unlike Fin's book-length, instrument-of-torture contract, my new lawyer's was only a couple pages long. After I signed my name, I asked the ultimate question.

"Everything seems to be falling in on me at the same time. Are you sure you can untie all of these legal knots…before the ropes get tied to a cement block and I get relocated to the bottom of the Chicago River?"

In his characteristic understatement, Petranelli just nodded. "I can't make promises. No guarantees. But I took this on because I thought I could straighten things out for you. That's what I intend to do."

He paused and stared at the wall for a couple seconds.

"Have you decided about going to the authorities…about what you know about Mangiorno?"

"I'm still struggling with that," I replied.

He didn't press me. Instead he tried to explain to me he had located what he considered the very center of my massive legal knot.

"I think," he said, "once we unravel that knot, we'll start freeing you up from everything else."

"And where's the center of the knot?"

"Gentry's defamation case against you," he said confidently.

"Really?" I said with a measure of disbelief in my response. "I don't understand. Why don't you think the bottom line for all of my problems is my contract with Mangiorno to sell him the property with the guarantee? Or the bank's foreclosure? Or my appeal from the Landmark Commission? Or Williston's threat to launch some kind of investigation against me?"

"Look. Do you need money to pay the bank so they don't foreclose?"

"Well, sure…"

"You need a recovery from Gentry and his firm for their negligence—to reimburse you for the diminished value of the property you bought, that you now know has limited salability."

I nodded. But I didn't see how Gentry's lawsuit against me had anything to do with any of that.

"So," Petranelli said, "I plan on persuading Mr. Gentry, and his firm, and their insurance carrier, to help you solve those problems."

I stared blankly at him. Privately, I was thinking, *Is this the law you're talking about—or science fiction?*

As doubts chased around in my head, Petranelli got Horace Fin on the speakerphone.

"Horace," he said. "One quick question. I haven't seen the file yet on Kevin's cases—"

"I've got a courier bringing them over today," Fin said.

"Great. But I need to know something. The original defamation complaint by Gentry against Kevin—was it signed by Gentry's firm, or by their counsel, Roger Hammerset?"

"That's easy," Fin shot back confidently. "I recall very clearly... the complaint was signed by Gentry personally, acting as his own counsel. Then a few weeks later we received a notice of retainer indicating that Hammerset had taken over as Gentry's plaintiff lawyer in the defamation case against Kevin."

"Thanks," Petranelli said. "One more thing. Can you find out if Gentry has ever sued any other of his clients for defamation?"

"It's all public record," the other snapped. "Why don't you do a Lexis search?"

"I did. It turned up nothing."

"What makes you think I can find things computers can't?"

Petranelli chuckled.

"Come on, Horace—are you kidding? Your reputation precedes you. You've got stuff on every high-profile person in the city of Chicago."

"I'll see what I can do," Fin said primly. "In the spirit, of course, of truth and justice." And after a dramatic pause he added, "As well as protecting my attorney's fee lien..."

After Fin hung up, Petranelli turned to me.

"Fin filed a motion some time ago asking Judge Morley to dismiss Gentry's defamation lawsuit against you."

I told him I remembered that.

"The hearing is coming up in a few days. I am hoping everything will come together by then. My plan is to try to turn this around by the day of the hearing."

Then he told me about one more attack he was launching.

"I'm also going to be filing a motion for the court to sanction Gentry for bringing his defamation case against you," he said. "It's a form of punishment. Not easily proven. But attorney's fees can be assessed against a lawyer who brings a frivolous suit, especially if the case was filed in bad faith."

"Boy," I responded, unconvinced, "that sounds like putting a lighted match to a can of gasoline."

"Exactly," Petranelli replied. "But the key to using explosives is to control the blast. I heard that from an uncle of mine who was in construction. He used to demolish old buildings. Same principle applies here."

He could see doubt still written all over my face.

"Look, Kevin," he said earnestly, "what I've got planned has a chance to dig you out *only* if you do *your* part."

"And what's that?" Deep down, I knew what he would tell me. And I dreaded it.

"You have to be willing to go up against Vito Mangiorno," my lawyer said. "You have to help put him away."

FIFTY-ONE

As I drove back to the mission after meeting with Daniel Petranelli, I was consumed with his parting words. But I was quickly jolted out of the mental conversation I'd been having with myself. Life brusquely intruded into my preoccupations, as legitimate as they were.

There was an ambulance parked in the mission's tiny staff parking lot. As I was getting out of my car, two EMTs rolled a gurney out of the back door.

Lying on top was a large black zip bag. A body bag.

Pastor Jim Loveland was walking alongside the gurney. The EMTs carefully lifted the bag into the back of the ambulance and, as they put away the gurney, Loveland climbed in and they closed the doors after him.

The ambulance slowly pulled out of the parking lot, its flashing lights on but no siren. Down the street, its rotating lights cast a rapid staccato of illumination along the sides of buildings. And then it was gone.

I looked toward the door. Lou, the night manager, who had been called in to help while Loveland was gone, was standing in the doorway. Next to him was Douglas, a somber look on his face.

Lou put his arm around Douglas's shoulders, squeezed them, and walked away.

Douglas saw me and waited.

"Who was it?" I asked.

"George."

I nodded silently.

"He went early this morning," Douglas said. "Best as we could determine. Wouldn't get out of bed. I shook him. He was cold as quarry stone. I knew right away."

"What happened?"

"Don't know. But the EMT guys figure it was his liver. Alkies are like that, their livers balloon up, then all of a sudden…they just give out."

Douglas was one of the residents who would take the time to try to talk to George. Sometimes try to play a game of checkers with him. Or walk with him down the hall to the cafeteria.

"You were good to him," I said. "You were a friend to him."

"Was I?" he replied with a strange look on his face. "Who knows? But it didn't matter much in the end, did it?"

He turned and walked away.

That night in the cafeteria I spotted Douglas, Miguel, and several of the others eating together. I sat down with them. The conversation drifted to George's death. But Douglas didn't talk.

After dinner, at the gospel service, a guest pastor from a downtown Chicago church preached. He spoke on the story of Lazarus and the rich man. Jesus told it to His disciples, but in the perspective of the preacher, it was primarily aimed at the skeptical Pharisees, who were sitting back, watching Jesus, and sneering.

There was a rich man who had lived in luxury all of his life, but his heart was cold, hard, and unrepentant. There was also a poor beggar, miserable, with open sores and ragged clothes. He languished by the rich man's gate, hoping for a few crumbs to eat from the leftover garbage. Both men died at the same time.

"But the downtrodden Lazarus," the preacher said with a Bible draped open in his right hand, "who it's clear had a heart that repented and sought forgiveness from God, entered paradise. Where he was met by Abraham. But the rich man went into the fiery flames of hell. And between the two men was a great abyss separating them."

The tormented rich man pleaded for someone to return from the dead to his family and warn his five brothers of the horrors that awaited them if they did not turn to God, the preacher explained.

"But Abraham just shook his head. Why would they believe someone from the dead when they had Moses and all of the prophets who had warned them throughout the Scriptures, yet still they did not believe?"

As always, the service ended with an invitation for anyone who wished to "believe on the name of Jesus Christ, the Son of God, and in the blood He shed on the cross for your sins, and in the power of His resurrection from the grave" to stand up and step forward.

A few feet shuffled. Someone coughed. Then I noticed people turning around and looking toward the back.

And just as I turned, I saw Douglas slowly walking down the center aisle. When he passed me he gave a little nod.

"Today's the day, professor."

He walked up to the preacher, who smiled and shook his hand. They talked a bit and then prayed together.

Leaving the chapel, I glanced back and saw Douglas mingling with some people at the front of the room. For a split second our eyes met. And in that whisper of time, I thought that perhaps he wanted to talk with me. But I decided to hustle back to my room.

Something was stirring me up and troubling me. I could not sit still. I paced and looked around, resenting the ugly concrete walls of this place where I was confined. I was fed up—maybe even angry with the circumstances of my life that had put me in such financial and emotional despair.

My phone rang. Tess was calling. She and I had been talking almost every night since our dinner together at the Pearl of China.

As we talked, my spirits lifted a little. Slowly, with each conversation, she had been letting me into more and more of her life, which I found exhilarating. We both studiously avoided discussions about the Tornquist church property dispute. And although I couldn't tell her anything about my work or living situation at the mission, I did share with her that someone had died where I was working.

"Oh, that's pretty heavy," she said with a sweet sense of sympathy. "Are you okay?"

"Yeah. I really didn't know him very well. And maybe I'm feeling guilty about that…"

"Well, *should* you have known him better? Is that part of what you do?"

"Not really. But that's not the point. You know, it's a little like the scene out of the old black-and-white movie of *A Christmas Carol*. Someone, I can't remember who—maybe one of the ghosts—maybe the visitors who come to Scrooge's door—anyway, they tell Scrooge something. They say, 'Mankind is your business.'"

"So," Tess said quietly, "you're wondering whether this guy who died—whether he was part of your responsibility? Part of the business of your being a member of mankind?"

"Yes…I think that's part of what I'm thinking."

"You know something, Kevin?"

"What?"

"I like the way you think. And I like your heart."

I was stunned. Before I could think of a reply, she started telling me about her family struggle. Her uncle, after being out of her life for years, had resurfaced. He wanted to "make amends." Tess said she was struggling with that. While she'd never come right out and said it, I gathered that her uncle had been a source of some kind of abuse. He'd left a wake of destruction sweeping back to her childhood.

We both decided to call it a night after a full hour of conversation. But first I asked her something.

"Are you safe?"

"Of course," she said. "You know, you're the one who has to be careful. Not me. Besides, you've got me looking over my shoulder every couple of seconds now…"

"Good."

"You know, just last night—" She stopped abruptly.

"What?"

"Nothing."

"What is it?" I demanded.

"Oh…just that I saw a car with some guys in it. Driving behind me. I thought I recognized them from the night before. When I think they were also driving behind my car…"

"Do you remember their license plate number?"

"No. And I didn't need to. Because when I parked they just kept driving by. No big deal."

"It is," I insisted. "Tess—you are a big deal to me. Please start jotting down every time you see a suspicious car. Please?"

"Okay. I will," she said, trying to laugh it off. But I could sense anxiety under her casual banter.

After I said a lingering goodbye, I tried to get some sleep. But my mind was full on, clicking, processing, whirling. Worrying about Tess. Realizing there might be only one way, ultimately, to make sure she was safe. As frightening as that might be.

I was considering what Daniel Petranelli had been urging me to do.

I needed to decide. I had to go after Vito Mangiorno somehow.

FIFTY-TWO

"OKAY. YOU WIN."

"Are you sure?" Petranelli asked.

"Yeah," I replied. "I'm sure. So how do we do this?"

"Well, I've already started a preliminary step," my lawyer said. "I thought you might come around on this...on talking to prosecutors about Mangiorno. So I have already made some initial calls. I never mentioned your name. Or even that I had a client who knew anything. What I said is, 'I might have access to information concerning Vito Mangiorno.' And asked if they had any open investigations."

"Who did you call?"

"I started with the people I knew on the Crime Commission. People I could trust. Then the same thing when I called over to the state attorney general's office."

"And?"

"Unfortunately, I struck out."

"So where does that leave us?"

"Well," Petranelli said, "that only means there is no active investigation of Mangiorno right now on the *state* level."

"Alright..." I said, waiting to see where this was heading.

"So," he continued, "we could still have you meet with a state prosecutor here. Sort of a cold-call meeting."

"Is that good or bad?"

"It's not particularly useful. The information you have here regarding Mangiorno is bits and pieces. You only have DeVoe representing VM Contractors in the deal to buy the church property. Someone else would have to make the link between Mangiorno and the company. Then there are the threats and extortion-type activities of DeVoe against you. But again, you can't link him, based only on what you know, directly to Mangiorno. And of course, you have information about being carjacked, and about the other attempt against you by Boris Bittarushka, who's now dead. All of it timed *suspiciously* along with your negotiations with DeVoe."

I was waiting for the punch line.

"However," Petranelli said with a note of defeat in his voice, "those bits and pieces wouldn't be significant enough, I don't think, to interest a state prosecutor unless your information filled in some holes in an existing investigation against Mangiorno."

"And you said there isn't any such investigation."

"That's right."

"Well," I responded in exasperation, "where does that leave me now? *Where?*"

"Here is where we are. I wouldn't recommend a meeting with state prosecutors, based on what I now know. But I do have one other idea."

"And that would be?"

"Contact the feds," Petranelli said. "It's possible they may be spearheading an investigation against Mangiorno. If so, your information could be just what they have been waiting for."

"How can we find out?"

"I want to make a call to an assistant U.S. attorney I know well," he said. "He is expecting my call right now. I didn't tell him what it would be about. I want your okay to put the call through. With you in the room. Right now."

I took a breath, wondering if I had any choice. I knew I didn't.

"Do it."

Petranelli clicked on his speakerphone, and punched in a number. A receptionist answered, "United States Attorney's Office."

My lawyer asked to speak to one of the assistant attorneys, someone called David.

After several minutes of silence, the receptionist came back on.

"I'll transfer you," she said.

In a moment an assistant answered. Petranelli asked to speak to David. Again we were put on hold.

Then a man answered the phone.

"Daniel," the voice said in greeting. "I got your message that you wanted to talk."

"Good, David," Petranelli said. "Glad we've connected. I think I've got something for you."

"Okay, go ahead and—say, do you have me on a speakerphone?" David asked.

"I do. I hope that's not a problem."

"Well, Dan, that depends on what we're going to talk about."

"Let me just say"—Petranelli's hands were folded in front of him on his desk, but his fingers were tensing and flexing—"that I would rather not go into why I have to have you on speakerphone. At some point I would hope the reason for that will be made clear…"

"You're being vague and mysterious," David said, "which is not like you. You're usually really up front."

"I take that as a compliment. But I would like you to trust me on this…I need our conversation to be on speaker."

"Fine," David said with mild irritation in his voice. "Let's move on."

I figured Petranelli needed me to verify exactly what was going to be discussed with the other attorney. On the other hand, and commendably, he did not want to divulge he had a client with information of a possibly criminal nature.

"David," he continued, "I need to find something out. I need to know whether the U.S. attorney's office in Chicago is currently investigating Vito Mangiorno."

There was a pause.

"Well…first of all…as you know, I work in the Civil Division. You're talking criminal investigation, I gather."

"Right."

"Okay. So I can't address that myself, really. And secondly, even

if there was an investigation or, let's say, a grand jury convened…
as you know, they are secret. We couldn't divulge that anyway—"

"Not the case," Petranelli said, interrupting. "Witnesses who
have relevant information, and who work with the federal prosecutor's office in testifying before a grand jury, are privy to that
information."

"Of course that's true. So…you have a witness who has relevant
information?"

"I can only say this—that I may have access to certain information that could help any investigation being conducted against
Vito Mangiorno."

Another pause.

"Well, like I said, I'm in the Civil Division…"

"Then, could you walk down to the Criminal Division and
make some inquiries?"

David sighed.

"I could talk to some people…but it would help if you could
give me some names…who your witnesses are…"

I was tempted to wave my arms in my lawyer's direction and
telegraph a gigantic "no!" but it wasn't necessary.

"No way," Petranelli replied bluntly. "Can't tell you anything
beyond what I've already said. All I can say is that *I have access to
certain information*—that's it."

After some silence, my lawyer prodded again.

"So, David, you going to do this for me?"

Another pause.

"I'll talk to some people in Criminal. That's all I can tell you.
Can't make any promises."

"Understood," Petranelli replied.

A second later, David's phone clicked off.

After all the buildup, all the anticipation, I thought to myself,
*where is this getting us? We can't find a prosecutor who has any
interest whatsoever in Vito Mangiorno. Is Petranelli, with his Ein-
steinian master plan to save me, living in a fantasyland?*

I looked at him and shook my head. "I don't see any of this

getting me anywhere. Gotta be honest with you. Maybe this was all a huge mistake."

But Petranelli was unruffled.

"Give it some time," he said. "When my momma made bread, it always had to rise. So give this a little time to rise."

FIFTY-THREE

~

I SPENT THE NEXT DAY feeling generally lousy about life. Though I couldn't put my finger on exactly why.

Despite that, I tried to put a good face on as I helped Bob Moody in his office. Jim Loveland joined us for a few minutes. George had no next of kin, he said, so he had to make all the arrangements for him. Burial and so forth. He had done the same thing on a number of occasions.

I had come to understand Jim Loveland's particular, unique clientele a little. They were the homeless, the displaced, the helpless—the forgotten men. Men who wandered the streets of Chicago wearing clothes indelibly discolored with grime—men with faces that showed almost completely on the outside all the broken stuff on the inside. Some of them would wander into the mission. And a few of those might die within the rooms of that sanctuary. So when that happened, Loveland would be the one to bestow on them in death the dignity they been denied during their life on the street.

After the pastor left, I looked over at Bob Moody, who was leaning back in his wheelchair. He had been looking paler and weaker each day. I figured any day he would just stop coming to work.

"Can I get you anything?" I asked.

Bob smiled and shook his head. But then he replied in his effortful manner, "Soon…I'll be done here," he said, almost out of breath. "Time…running out…"

I wanted to say something encouraging. But there wasn't a single thing in my head. Though I struggled against it, I found my eyes starting to fill up with tears.

"Good man," Bob said, giving a labored nod in my direction. "But you're lost...need the Lord."

He added, "That's where...love starts..."

I reached over, grabbed his hand, and squeezed it. Then I went back to the paperwork on his desk.

Neither of us talked again until it was time for him to be picked up by his wife. At noon he said goodbye to me. He headed down the corridor toward the door where his wife would be waiting for him. But before he was out of sight he stopped and wheeled around. I walked up to him questioningly.

"Where I'm going," he whispered, "you can come too...at the end...plenty of room." He smiled and continued down the hallway.

It would be sometime later when I understood what he meant.

Back in the office, I checked my cell phone. Daniel Petranelli had left a voice mail for me. When I returned his call, he said he had been attempting negotiations with the attorneys for the Nuveau Art Foundation and the lawyer who represented their real-estate agent.

Early on, even back when Horace Fin was in charge, we all knew those lawsuits would not be much of a solution to my financial problem. Admittedly, my problem with the Tornquist property had started with them. Fin's discovery had showed that the Nuveau Art Foundation unquestionably knew of the landmarking status. Indeed, they had encouraged the city to landmark the odd-looking building in the first place. But that was back when they were a flourishing museum foundation operating out of that building. Then the scandal broke over their director, the money dried up, and they became insolvent.

Those in the foundation knew the landmarked status would make the building generally unmarketable. So the real-estate agent was never told, which would place a great amount of legal responsibility on the back of the foundation. But there was a problem. They were bankrupt. And their insurance policy specifically exempted coverage for acts of fraud by omission as well as commission.

On the other hand, the real-estate agent hadn't needed to be told anything by the foundation. Fin had also determined that the agent had actual knowledge that the Tornquist building was landmarked.

On the other hand, in her deposition she had taken the tack that she had "the general custom of always informing prospective buyers of that kind of information." She speculated that she "must have" told me the building was landmarked. Of course, she also had to admit she had no actual recollection of any such conversation.

And that is because no such conversation ever took place. Which would make her greatly responsible for the gaffe. Unfortunately, she had allowed her professional-liability insurance policy to lapse. There would be no financial pocket with her to make me whole.

So when Petranelli said he wanted to tell me about the status of his negotiations with the lawyers for the foundation and the real-estate agent, I didn't hold my breath.

And what my lawyer had to tell me didn't exactly leave me breathless either.

He'd managed to work out a settlement. Between them, the two defendants had scraped together $7500. It was chump change. But on the other hand, it would cost me more than that just in court expenses to continue the lawsuit against them. I told Petranelli to go ahead and finalize the settlement.

But there was a hitch. He told me they would not pay the settlement amount until *all* of the litigation surrounding the Tornquist property—especially my suit against Lloyd Gentry—was finally resolved.

I didn't see why they were insisting on that until Petranelli explained it. Because Gentry's lawyer had filed a cross-claim against those defendants, blaming *them* for my losses—rather than his malpractice—Gentry still had them embroiled. They would not pay out unless the whole litigation got resolved.

Once again, I thought as I clicked off my phone, it came down to our ability to settle things against Lloyd Gentry. It was looking more and more like Daniel Petranelli had been right all along. At the center of this tangled web was the celebrated La Salle Street real-estate lawyer, my case against him, and his vindictive countersuit against me.

Going back to my paperwork, I couldn't stop thinking about the court hearing on our motion to dismiss Gentry's defamation lawsuit, and our motion to assess attorney's fees against Gentry for bringing the case in the first place. It was only forty-eight hours away.

During one of our conferences in his office, Petranelli had once said my legal situation was "like momma making pasta—when the water starts boiling, you only have a certain amount of time to cook it. Too short, and it's tough and chewy. Too long, and it's overcooked and tasteless."

Then he'd looked at me. "Our court date—that's when the water is at full boil."

"Why is it," I'd asked him, "that all of your legal metaphors seem to deal with food?"

"Good question. I guess because in my household, growing up, food was more than just nourishment. It was family. And conversation. All the important things revolved around it. Weddings. Funerals. Before church. After church. When the uncles got together. Or when the cousins showed up. It was at the center of what was essential. Tables full of food. And all the time, family members laughing…arguing. The children playing under the table. Food was love, Kevin."

Whenever I asked a question of my new lawyer I usually got more than I bargained for. After Petranelli had said all that, he added something else.

"Sometime I'll walk you through the Bible and show you the spiritual significance of food. Did you know," he'd said, his eyes taking on an unusual energy, "that some of Jesus' most important conversations took place over food?"

~

I had been thinking back to that part of the conversation as I continued with Bob Moody's paperwork, sitting alone in his office.

Then my cell phone rang.

"Okay," Petranelli began. "We've got a meeting. Tomorrow morning. Nine-thirty. Downtown Chicago."

"Who?"

"You and I," he said, "and an assistant U.S. attorney, fairly high up in the Criminal Division."

"What are they going to offer?" I asked.

"David wouldn't tell me anything except what I just told you. The time and place of the meeting. And, of course, that we would be discussing Vito Mangiorno."

It was a short conversation, but it really shook me. I knew we were approaching something important—and very dangerous. Considering the fact I might be volunteering myself as a witness against Vito Mangiorno, I thought back again to Petranelli's food analogy and his religious mini-lesson. I knew very little about the Bible. But I did remember one thing. Psalm 23. Was it from somewhere in my youth—when I had first heard it? A phrase suddenly flashed into my mind.

> You prepare a table before me in the presence of my enemies.

FIFTY-FOUR

IN PLANNING HOW THE TWO OF US would rendezvous for the meeting at the U.S. attorney's office, Petranelli wanted me to take the train down to the downtown loop on the El. I was to get on the blue line, get off near Jackson Boulevard, and go over to the corner of Michigan and Jackson. He would be there in a cab waiting for me at 9:10.

I did as he told me. That morning I found myself sitting there on the El amid the business commuters with their laptops and cell phones as they sipped from their plastic-topped cups of Starbucks coffee and checked the financial and sports pages. I was with the fellows who had splashed on a little too much aftershave. And the guy who had overslept and was rubbing a chin that bore that morning's stubble. And the women in their business suits, tugging at a hem to keep it all neat and straight in the middle of a sweaty, shoulder-to-shoulder press of humanity.

I listened to the conversation around me. About the markets. The newest movies. And now that spring training had begun, speculations about what kind of season to expect for the Cubs.

I couldn't help but do a little reflecting on my life. How the past few months had taken me out of the safety and predictability of everything I had known. I had lost my job at Essex, and maybe my entire academic career. I had lost the woman I thought I loved. But, I met someone else. A woman who had endeared herself to me in a way I hadn't thought possible. I had been run out of my apartment, then forced to go into hiding. I hadn't talked to Tom and my other friends in weeks. My woes had been splashed over television and the pages of the Chicago papers. My entire life's savings were gone like water through a sieve—and all I had to show for it was a funny-looking church building.

And now I was on my way to meet with federal prosecutors, believing I might have some evidence against a major crime boss who, I was convinced, had been behind two separate attacks against me.

In a funny way I didn't know exactly what to think about it all. Though I felt it had to mean something. *What's the point of everything I've gone through?* I felt a little like you do when you're playing *Jeopardy* and the answer is right there on the tip of your tongue. But you can't quite name that president, or that famous singer, or the capital city of South Dakota. (Hint—it's not Bismarck.)

Somewhere in all this mess there's a meaning for me, I thought.

But when the El started shuddering to a halt at my exit, the cold reality of the reason for my visit to the Loop set in. In the crush of business passengers elbowing their way out with their cups of coffee, newspapers rolled under their arms, and briefcases smashed up against their chests, I shuffled my way out.

Once out in the open air, I glanced at my watch. It was 9:01. I scurried across the street, past the honking jam of traffic, and over to the corner of Michigan and Jackson. As promised, there was a cab at the curb. I saw an arm waving to me from the backseat. It was Daniel Petranelli. I jumped in next to him. He gave me a warm handshake and asked how I was feeling.

I told him the truth.

"Like the chicken crossing the road—just before it becomes roadkill."

Petranelli broke up laughing at that. He laughed so hard I couldn't stop from chuckling myself.

When the cab pulled up alongside the federal building, we both scooted out and went in immediately. At the security desk, we showed ID, and Petranelli explained who we had a meeting with. We both got numbered stick-on name tags that said "United States Attorney's Office—Visitor." I was glad my name wasn't visible.

We took a crowded elevator up to the Criminal Division, ID'd ourselves to another receptionist, and took a seat. About ten minutes later, a middle-aged man in a white shirt and conservative, striped tie, sleeves rolled up, came breezing into the lobby.

"Ken Jarvins," he announced, and shook hands with us.

He was the number-two guy in the Criminal Division, Petranelli had told me in the cab.

Jarvins used his security key to unlock an inner door, then walked us quickly through a labyrinth of corridors to his office. It was an expansive workspace, but it was cluttered with filing boxes, files, and law books piled on top of one another with yellow stick tabs marking the pages.

One of his assistants was already seated there, and he jumped up and shook hands with us.

After we were seated, Jarvins led off.

"David speaks highly of you. He tells me that you were in the state AG's office for a while."

"That's right," my lawyer said.

"Do any organized-crime stuff?"

"Some."

"Were you there when they had the pension-fund indictments?"

"I was one of the guys working on that."

"I remember that one," Jarvins said. Then he pulled a legal pad in front of him.

"So," he continued, "what can I do for you?"

Petranelli took the ball and ran with it, giving a concise summary of my litigation. But he omitted any mention of Vito Mangiorno.

"This VM Contractors," Jarvins said. "The company represented by this lawyer, DeVoe…the party that contracted with your client to buy the church property. Tell me more about that."

"I think it's pretty common knowledge that the company is a front for Vito Mangiorno," Petranelli said.

"Well," Jarvins replied with a tinge of sarcasm, "that kind of common knowledge plus about a buck-fifty will just about get you a coffee latte."

"I would like my client to make a verbal, off-the-record proffer to you," Petranelli shot back. "And when he's done, I would like to propose something I would like you to do for us."

Jarvins arched an eyebrow.

"And when Mr. Hastings here is finished," my lawyer added, "you can buy me that coffee latte. I take mine with sugar."

Jarvins smiled slightly and told us to proceed.

Petranelli then turned to me. In question-and-answer format, he led me into my dealings with DeVoe, including his threats in the stairwell after the commission hearing, the carjacking that suspiciously followed my refusal to give in to his demands, and my identification of Boris Bittarushka and his involvement in the later baseball-bat chase.

As I finished, I saw that Jarvins had still not written down a single note. I took that to be an utterly dismal signal. Apparently he had found nothing I'd said to be of sufficient interest to even write it down.

Jarvins shifted a little in his seat. Then he spoke.

"Is your client, Mr. Petranelli, willing to give us a sworn statement today to be transcribed by our court reporter—laying out again, word for word, exactly what he just told us?"

Petranelli looked over at me. I nodded.

"But we have some conditions..." Petranelli said.

"No discussion of conditions unless your client is also willing to testify to those same things he just told us—if need be."

"You mean before the federal grand jury currently investigating Vito Mangiorno?" my lawyer said.

"What makes you think we've got a grand jury looking at him?" Jarvins said tersely.

"Let's say it's just a wild, speculative, bald-faced guess on my part."

"What if I were to say you are absolutely wrong?"

"I'm banking you're not going to tell me that," my lawyer said. "Because I'm banking on the fact you are a man of honesty and integrity. And given that, you wouldn't lie to us."

Jarvins paused.

"Is your client willing to testify in a grand-jury proceeding to what he just told us?"

Petranelli looked at me again. I nodded again.

Jarvins tapped his pen a few times on the table.

"And what is this about some conditions?"

"Here's what I need you to do," Petranelli said without skipping a beat. "I need you to deliver a target letter—relating to the grand-jury proceedings."

"Whoa," Jarvins said, then threw a look over at his assistant. "Mr. Petranelli, you're forgetting you're not the prosecutor anymore. I'm the prosecutor. I make those decisions. You're just private counsel for a client who just might—or might not—be useful to us as a witness."

"No disrespect, Mr. Jarvins," my lawyer said calmly. "I don't mean to crowd into your prosecutorial discretion. But there's a very good reason why I am making that request. I think when we get into this further, you'll understand why."

Jarvins looked a little skeptical. He tossed his pen onto the desk and stretched a little, giving a little groan.

"Man, I think I'm getting out of shape. I used to run over the noon hour. But lately, just haven't had the time. Caseload is killing me. You look pretty fit, Petranelli—you work out?"

"I try to. I do a fair amount of outdoor sports."

After a few more moments of silence, Jarvins brought it to a head.

"I'm going to have to pass this all by my boss." He rose to leave.

Without thinking, I stood up to leave, assuming we were done for the day.

But Petranelli waved me back into my seat and gave me the faintest hint of a smile.

"So," Jarvins said, "I'll be back in about ten or fifteen. You guys want some lunch sent up?"

We both nodded.

"Sandwiches okay?"

We both nodded again.

"Assuming the U.S. Attorney gives me the green light," Jarvins continued, "particularly on your one condition, Mr. Petranelli, then we'll have your client give us his sworn statement. It'll be in the conference room right across the hall. You both can wait there. And you'd better plan on spending the rest of the afternoon here in our luxurious facilities." He gave us a parting smile and quickly stepped out of the room, and his assistant jumped up and scurried after him.

Jarvins was wrong about something. It wasn't ten or fifteen minutes. It was almost an hour. But when he came back he told us the deal had been accepted.

Petranelli and I spent the rest of the day in the government conference room, with a court reporter, Jarvins, his assistant, and two other assistant U.S. attorneys. They were the ones asking the questions this time.

When we had finished, it was close to five. We were told to wait a few minutes before leaving.

A few minutes later an assistant came into the room. She was carrying a large Styrofoam cup with a lid on it, and a paper napkin.

"Mr. Petranelli," she said, "this is for you. Your coffee latte."

"You didn't happen to—" he started to say with a smile.

"Make it with sugar? Yes," she said as she turned to leave. "Mr. Jarvins mentioned that specifically."

FIFTY-FIVE
~

WHEN I RETURNED TO THE MISSION at the end of the day, I was exhausted. At the same time, I was encouraged by our meeting with the U.S. attorney's office. On the eve of the court hearing against Gentry, it seemed to have accomplished at least one of Petranelli's critical components just in the nick of time.

Despite our apparent victory in garnering a working relationship with prosecutors who had an interest in going after Vito Mangiorno, I still had massive doubts. After all, my lawyer's scenario for overall victory seemed not only to be audacious, but also nearly impossible to achieve. It assumed nearly perfect timing of several complicated events—many of them outside of our control.

Petranelli had listed them for me:

1) We had to be successful in getting Judge Morley to dismiss Gentry's defamation lawsuit against me.

2) Then, using the "lever" of an attorney's-fee sanction because he had brought a bad faith, meritless lawsuit against me, we needed to pressure Gentry and his malpractice-insurance carrier to settle our claim against him for his negligence in not warning me of the possible landmarking of the Tornquist property before I purchased it. Further, the settlement would need to be a substantial one—big enough for me to pay Petranelli, Horace Fin, the bank that was threatening to foreclose within the next few days, and any other claims.

3) Commissioner Isaac Williston, who was still smarting from Fin's race-baiting scheme and had threatened to launch an

immediate investigation of me, needed to be cooled down. We needed to stop him from scuttling our settlement scenario by firing off the wrong kind of publicity volleys. Even beyond that, we needed to enlist his active assistance.

4) Then we came to Vito Mangiorno. Somehow Petranelli had to convince him, through his attorney Tony DeVoe, to give up all his legal rights to the Tornquist property—despite the fact that they seemed to have an ironclad contract with me to purchase it with the added guarantee they'd be able to demolish the existing building. Not only that, but the mob boss had to be convinced to give up any breach-of-contract claims against me. Further—and this was of particular interest to me—Mangiorno had to be sufficiently boxed into a corner so he would not retaliate with deadly force.

5) Oh, yes—and all of the above had to done within the next thirty-six hours or so. According to our calculations, that was how long we would have this window of opportunity to tie things up. After that, things would start unraveling—quick.

It all looked a little like BASE jumping off the Sears Tower…but with an untested parachute…and hoping against hope that your calculations of updraft, wind velocity, and wind direction were all perfectly correct.

The results are unforgiving if you are wrong.

~

But then there are other kinds of "leaps"—different, yet equally death-defying, acts of personal commitment.

When I returned to my room at the mission, I saw a printed memo:

> To: All Staff at WCM
> From: Jim Loveland
>
> Bob Moody did not come in today for work. His battle with ALS has reached a stage that prohibits his continued work with us.

Those of us who have worked with him know his dedication to the Lord and to the ministry of WCM. We will cherish the days we labored with him in bringing the gospel to the city of Chicago.

I am informed that soon he may begin needing hospice care. Please continue to keep Bob and Ginnie in your prayers as they enter this difficult time. If you would like to help provide some dinners or assistance to Ginnie as she cares for Bob, please let me know.

It was no surprise to me. But the memo struck a chord of sadness and hit me with a kind of in-the-gut finality.

I decided to pass on dinner and stayed in my room. As I lay on my bed and stared at the ceiling, I felt weighed down by forces I neither understood nor was capable of calculating.

The next day was to be the court hearing in Gentry's defamation case. It was scheduled for eleven. Before that, Petranelli was scheduled to meet with Isaac Williston and his personal attorney, plus the lawyer for the Landmark Commission. As usual, Petranelli had invited me to attend. But this time I begged off.

I had too much on my mind to attend the meeting with Williston. Mulling it all over, I felt a little like a soldier gearing up for battle. A number of weeks ago Loveland had asked if I had studied the "Great Awakening" and other significant religious revivals much. And now a story I'd read—an account of an event during the Civil War—came to mind.

According to a few obscure but well-documented reports, a phenomenon erupted in Fredericksburg, Virginia, just before the bloody battles of Second Fredericksburg and Chancellorsville. On the evening before the Northern troops crossed the river to attack the city, the churches of Fredericksburg suddenly jammed to overflowing and beyond. It was the capstone of a nearly continuous revival that had broken out in the city as it readied for the conflict. Reports were that some fifteen thousand of General Lee's soldiers ended up being converted by the around-the-clock gospel preaching.

Sociologists and historians have quick and easy explanations for that kind of thing. But their references to "foxhole conversions" tell us only the *circumstances* of these spiritual phenomena. They don't tell us anything about the *reality* of them.

Like the reality of Bob Moody's radiant faith in the face of impending death.

The buzzer went off, signaling chapel service in ten minutes. I slowly got up and walked down to the bathroom. As I stared into the mirror above the row of white porcelain sinks, I studied my own image. Then I felt a hand on my shoulder.

Douglas was standing there with a smile on his face. He didn't say anything. I wadded up my paper towel and tossed it into the basket about twenty feet away. It bounced off the wall tiles and went in.

"Bank shot," he said, grinning. "Guess you're the kind that needs to bounce it off the backboard…"

We walked to the chapel and sat down next to each other.

Jim Loveland was preaching that night. After we sang "What a Friend We Have in Jesus," Jim got up.

His text was the third chapter of the Gospel of John.

In the story, it was evening. Loveland figured it had taken place just outside the city walls of Jerusalem. A scholar by the name of Nicodemus wandered up to the little encampment where Jesus and His disciples were. He was burdened with many questions. His heart was troubled.

He began confiding in Jesus.

"Rabbi, we know you are a teacher who has come from God. For no one could perform the miraculous signs you are doing if God were not with him."

But what Jesus replied must have been shocking, Loveland pointed out. Especially for a learned professor like Nicodemus.

"I tell you the truth, no one can see the kingdom of God unless he is born again."

Nicodemus, an academic, an intellectual, could only translate that into mundanely physical terms.

"How can a man be born when he is old?...Surely he cannot enter a second time into his mother's womb?"

But Jesus was talking about something else, something that whispers to us, blows past us like a winsome breeze, from beyond the observable, Loveland pointed out. "Flesh gives birth to flesh," Jesus said, "but the Spirit gives birth to spirit."

The professor was having a hard time computing.

"How can this be?" Nicodemus asked.

Jesus minced no words with him.

"You are Israel's teacher...and do you not understand these things?"

And Jesus proceeded to summarize His entire mission. No complicated syllogisms. No obscure religious theorems. No arcane historical footnotes.

> God so loved the world that he gave his one and only Son, that whoever believes in him shall not perish but have eternal life. For God did not send his Son into the world to condemn the world, but to save the world through him. Whoever believes in him is not condemned, but whoever does not believe stands condemned already because he has not believed in the name of God's one and only Son.

Pastor Jim gave the same invitation I'd heard so many nights before. "You can receive Jesus into your heart, by faith believing on Him as Savior and as Lord. And you can signify that by stepping forward."

After a few moments, Loveland gave the woman at the piano a nod, and she began playing.

Up at the front of the room, he was smiling. But he broke into a bigger smile and gave me a slow nod when I had finished walking down the aisle.

He put his arm on my shoulder, and my knees buckled a little. And try as I might against it, my eyes filled up. I felt my shoulders shuddering.

I had come to realize something. Not surprisingly, I had been focusing almost entirely, and for as long as I could remember, on my avalanche of problems. On my epic ordeal against lawyers, lawsuits, and evil men possessed of cruel intentions.

But that was merely the background. If there was to be any meaning in any of it, it couldn't be *just* about that. The meaning had to be about me. Whether I would crumple up with the impact—or whether, as I had decided that night, I would bounce off and land on the very spot where I was supposed to be.

Douglas was right about that. I was the kind of guy who needed to bounce it off the backboard.

FIFTY-SIX

~

DRIVING UP TO THE COOK COUNTY Courthouse the next morning, I realized what a neophyte I really was in the legal system. I had never been in that building before. In fact, before my present troubles had begun, I'd had absolutely no experience with lawyers or lawsuits at all.

Once in the building I pushed my way through the crush of people congregating in the lobby, waiting for the elevators.

Here I mingled with the cast of characters. The players in the drama of the law. Lawyers with briefcases dangling from their hands, speaking to their anxious clients in hushed, confident tones; attorneys who bantered with their adversaries in pin-striped suits about this case or that judge. Tired court clerks holding stacks of files and glancing at the wall clock. People clutching their speeding tickets on the way to the traffic judge. Squabbling ex-spouses from fractured marriages on the way to what is euphemistically called "Family Court."

I made my way to Judge Morley's courtroom. Daniel Petranelli was just outside, waiting in the hallway. He whisked me aside to give me the scoop on his meeting with Isaac Williston and his two lawyers.

Petranelli had attempted to break the ice by going there without Horace Fin. But the commissioner didn't care who was there on my behalf. He was going to have his say. And the lawyers there knew him well enough to know they would not, and could not, prevent that. I got a complete blow-by-blow.

~

"Do you know anything about me, Mr. Petranelli?" Williston had demanded. "Do you?"

"I know a few things."

"Well, I would love to hear them. I certainly would," Williston barked.

"You are a decorated veteran of the Gulf War, where you served your country admirably. You have an MBA degree. Your wife is named Denice. You are a successful Chicago entrepreneur. You have been the chair of the Landmark Commission for seven years."

"My, my, my." Williston turned to his lawyers with mock astonishment. "Gentlemen, take note—isn't an Internet search an amazing thing?"

"You want me to continue?" Petranelli asked calmly.

"Oh, by all means!"

"You have been a popular city councilman. And now you have intentions to run for mayor of Chicago."

"Anything else?"

"The polls have you running behind by about fifteen points. But that doesn't particularly concern you. Your political strategy is to come from behind."

"Well," Williston said acidly, "I am afraid you've left out the most important thing of all, Counselor."

"I was just saving the best for last—"

"Oh?"

"That's right."

"And what might that be?"

Petranelli studied Williston.

"You are a man who cannot stand to be wrongly accused—when it comes to racism in particular."

"And how would you know that?"

"Just an educated guess."

"Indulge us."

"Well, your first wife, Helen, died nine years ago in a car accident."

Williston was glaring at Petranelli now.

"And she was white. Making the charges of antiwhite racism especially loathsome…"

Williston's expression changed slightly.

"Horace Fin, my client's prior legal counsel," Petranelli went on, "was wrong in putting the racism charges into his appeal—plain and simple. I offer you my apologies."

"Too late for that," Williston replied tersely. "Horse is already out of the barn."

"Maybe not."

"You're going to have to go a long, long way to convince me of that."

Petranelli reached into his briefcase, pulled out three copies of a document, and placed one in front of Williston, and one in front of each of the lawyers.

"This is a motion to amend our appeal to the circuit court from your Landmark Commission ruling. As you can see, we are withdrawing all allegations of race discrimination from our appeal. And withdrawing them *with prejudice*."

"That's a start, I suppose," Williston commented.

"Why not," the commission lawyer chimed in, "simply dismiss your entire appeal? You're not going to win it. The court is going to apply an abuse-of-discretion standard to the commission's decision. Their decisions almost always get affirmed by the court."

"No dispute there," my lawyer replied. "And we can probably dismiss this appeal entirely—assuming you work with us on a related matter…"

Williston's personal attorney jumped in.

"What makes you think, Counselor, that you or your client are in any position whatsoever to bargain with us?"

Petranelli was ready with an answer.

"*Kelo v. City of New London*, the eminent-domain case recently decided by the Supreme Court."

"Yeah, sure—I'm familiar with it," the commission attorney bulleted. "But that case went against the property owners—"

"True," Petranelli conceded. "But there was some interesting language in the decision. Particularly the concurring opinion regarding 'public benefits' that are merely 'pretextual.' Makes me think that maybe we have a situation here where Mr. Hastings' Fifth-Amendment rights as a property owner have been injured by a 'taking' by the City of Chicago without just compensation. Because of your unwillingess to permit demolition of the building. Without the permission for demolition, Mr. Hastings has an argument that he's lost much of the commercial value of his property."

Williston was losing patience.

"You lawyers can haggle till the cows come home. But I still don't know why we are here. What is it you are proposing, Mr. Petranelli?"

"You, Mr. Commissioner, publicly called for a formal investigation into the circumstances of Mr. Hastings' purchase of the Tornquist property and all transactions dealing with it…"

"You bet I did," Williston said with a smile. "And right now I've got the mayor's office scrambling…wondering how they are going to weigh in on my call."

"You know," Petranelli replied, "those rumors that a neo-Nazi group contracted to buy the Tornquist building from my client—I'm sure you realize those are completely unfounded."

Williston pursed his lips, smiled, and turned to his private lawyer.

"We are currently looking into that anonymous report…"

"Like I said," Petranelli continued, "you realize that such allegations have no merit whatsoever."

"I have made a public call for an investigation," Williston said. "I don't plan on backing down on that."

"No need to," Petranelli rejoined.

"Oh?" Williston had a quizzical look on his face.

"Yes. If you, Commissioner Williston, agree to help a little with our side of things, I think you can come out on top."

"Define '*on top*,' " Williston said, his interest piqued.

"Being the hero. And letting the whole city of Chicago know it."

~

As my lawyer wrapped up the account of his meeting with Commissioner Williston for me, he glanced at his watch.

"Better go," he said. "Pray for me in there, will you?"

I nodded and stumbled around for a response.

"Jim Loveland told me about your commitment to Christ during chapel last night," he added. "Great decision. Best one you'll ever make."

Petranelli made his way up to the front row of benches, which were reserved for the lawyers who had cases on the docket. I wedged myself into an open space farther back, among other clients and court-watchers.

After a few more minutes, the court reporter appeared, then the clerk. As Judge Morley stepped into the courtroom from the door behind the bench, her black robe flowing, the clerk announced her, and the entire courtroom jumped to its feet.

Here we go, I said to myself silently. I could feel my toes reaching just over the edge of the top of the Sears Tower.

FIFTY-SEVEN

JUDGE JANICE MORLEY WAS A SHORT, thin woman with salt-and-pepper hair. Reading glasses were perched on her nose. She talked quickly, in an almost machine-gun fashion. As I watched her interact with the attorneys arguing the cases before ours, she seemed fairly friendly. But more than once her even-keeled demeanor metamorphosized into curtness with almost no warning—when she decided a lawyer was not being forthright about some fact or point of law. Or when counsel before her were wandering down some path of argument she deemed irrelevant. Clearly she did not like her time to be wasted.

Then the clerk shouted out, *"Lloyd E. Gentry v. Kevin Hastings.* Defendant's motion to dismiss and motion for attorney's-fees sanction. Counsel approach."

I stepped past legs and knees and hastened up to the counsel table to the right, farthest away from the jury box, which was empty. I sat down next to Petranelli, who had announced his appearance as "counsel of record for the defendant."

Over at the other table, things were more crowded. Lloyd Gentry was seated in the middle chair. On his right was his plaintiff counsel, Roger Hammerset, who immediately shot up and introduced himself. Then the man to Gentry's left rose and said his name was "Bob Bagley. I am counsel on…a related matter, Your Honor."

The "related matter" was no secret to me. I'd met Bagley, the insurance carrier's defense counsel, at my deposition.

Behind them were seated two other men. One I recognized from the deposition—an associate lawyer from Hammerset's office. But I didn't know the other one, a man who looked to be in his early forties, more plainly dressed than the other members of Gentry's team. He had a scowl on his face.

"Who's that?" I whispered to Petranelli.

"I think he's probably the claims manager from Gentry's insurance company," he whispered back.

Judge Morley cranked things up.

"Proceed, Mr. Petranelli," she snapped. "It's your motion."

Daniel strode up to the lectern with his big black binder and set it down. He quickly summarized the history of Gentry's defamation lawsuit against me and then, reading the exact words from the *Sun-Times* article containing Horace Fin's carefully crafted diatribe against Gentry as communicated by and attributed to me, got them slowly into the record. I listened as he recited my statements out loud to the hushed courtroom—my statements that Gentry, one of Chicago's most prestigious and successful real-estate attorneys, was "a selfish, incompetent human being," and that "his favorite color is green" and that both Gentry and his law firm were "known for not caring whether he is crushing the little guy or not."

Suddenly I was wincing inside, feeling embarrassed and defeated. *With those kinds of accusations, how can the judge do anything but decide I defamed Lloyd Gentry?* I thought to myself. A tide of hopelessness washed over me. Petranelli had said we needed to get the court to dismiss Gentry's case against me—that was an absolute necessity if his plan was going to work. But what if that didn't happen?

As Petranelli was finishing his recitation of the facts, he made one final observation.

"Finally, regarding Mr. Gentry's defamation case, I note, Your Honor, with great interest, that the plaintiff, Lloyd Gentry, did *not* also join as a defendant in this action the *Chicago Sun-Times,* the paper that actually published the article. He sued only my client, Kevin Hastings."

Hammerset leaped to his feet.

"That's outrageous!" he exclaimed. "Your Honor, I would like the court to strike that last remark. Whether we sued just Mr. Hastings, or decided to sue Mr. Hastings plus the *Sun-Times* and its entire editorial staff, together with every carrier who delivers the paper—none of that has anything to do with the motion to dismiss that Mr. Petranelli is supposed to be arguing this morning."

There was a flicker of a smile on Judge Morley's face at Hammeset's remark about the paper carriers.

"This is highly improper, Judge," Petranelli shot back. "Opposing counsel will have an opportunity to respond in his argument if he wishes. But *after I'm done*. It's procedurally inappropriate for plaintiff's counsel to interrupt my argument—"

"Well, this is my courtroom, Mr. Petranelli," the judge said. "Which means *I am the one* who determines what is or isn't procedurally inappropriate during argument. Now, as to Mr. Hammerset's point—and Mr. Hammerset"—she turned to Gentry's lawyer—"I understand your desire to keep that kind of remark off the record, however, you do need to wait your turn, I don't want chaos in my courtroom—" then she turned back to Petranelli and concluded.

"But as for the main point, I have to agree with Mr. Gentry's counsel. What possible difference does it make whether Mr. Hastings was the *only* defendant sued?"

"It goes to intent," Petranelli said. "It goes to the bad-faith character of this defamation suit. Lawyers refer to these as 'SLAP' suits—counterlawsuits designed to intimidate people from exercising their rights to pursue lawful claims in court—"

"Mr. Petranelli," the judge said, cutting him off, "get back to the point. You talk about 'bad faith' here—but doesn't that really go to the attorney's fee motion you have brought against Lloyd Gentry?"

"It certainly relates to that, yes—"

"But," the judge said, chiding him, "you're not going to even be able to argue that attorney's fee motion *unless* you win your other motion *first*—your motion to dismiss—the one we are supposed to be arguing right now. Right?"

"That's correct, Your Honor." Petranelli conceded the point.

"So, I don't want to hear any more about bad faith—or your attorney's fee motion—unless and until you convince me that Mr. Gentry's defamation suit ought to be dismissed."

Petranelli nodded and prepared to continue, but Judge Morley interrupted once more.

"And by the way, am I reading your other motion correctly, Mr. Petranelli? You are asking that the attorney's fee sanction be levied against only Mr. Gentry personally—and not against his counsel, Mr. Hammerset?"

"That's correct," my lawyer replied.

"Well," the judge said as an aside, "this court doesn't grant very many attorney's-fee sanction motions. But then again, we are not addressing that motion…yet," she added.

Petranelli nodded again. He argued in closing that, based on the legal precedents he had cited, the court should conclude that the statements attributed to me in the *Sun-Times* article did not constitute "defamation" because they were "nonactionable personal opinion, rather than a statement that contained objectively verifiable and defamatory facts."

Then he cited the case of *Wilkow v. Forbes, Inc.*, a decision of the United States Court of Appeals for the Seventh Circuit, in support of his argument.

Before he could turn to leave the lectern, Judge Morley stopped him again.

"Counsel," she noted, "you rely on the *Wilkow* case quite a bit in your brief, don't you?"

"Yes."

"But that's a federal-court decision, right?"

"That's true."

"And this court, my court, is a state court. Right?"

"That also is correct."

"So *Wilkow* is not binding on me in this case. Correct?"

"Not binding as precedent," Petranelli admitted. "But it should be persuasive nevertheless."

"Why?" the judge shot back.

"Three key reasons," he answered. "First, it was an interpretation of Illinois state law on defamation. Therefore, directly on point. Second, Judge Easterbrook authored an insightful and well-reasoned explanation of the law of this state on subjective personal opinion versus actionable factual defamation. Third, all three judges of the panel agreed. No dissents. There are some additional reasons I could give you—"

"Not necessary," Judge Morley replied abruptly. "Thank you."

Daniel sat down, and Hammerset strode up to the podium with a supercilious look on his face. A little like a National League pitcher who was deigning to play a game of sandlot baseball.

Hammerset was devastating. He reiterated his argument that my lawyer should not have interjected the business about Gentry suing only me and not others. "The fact Mr. Petranelli made that argument," he said snidely, "points out the utter weakness of the motion to dismiss. They haven't got the necessary merits to their motion," he continued, "so they distract, avoid, and obfuscate. Hoping to confuse this court. But Your Honor," he added, "you're not confused. You can see, I am sure, that the statements Mr. Hastings made, as quoted in the *Sun-Times*—and by the way, they admit this—are accurate. They conceded earlier that Mr. Hastings' prior lawyer, Horace Fin, was authorized to release the statement. And the *Sun-Times* did *not* misquote him."

Judge Morley sat unmoving.

Hammerset then jabbed at the use of the *Wilkow* case. "The facts in that case are totally different from ours," he argued. "That case dealt with *Forbes* magazine writing that in bankruptcy cases, certain 'judges, ever more sympathetic to debtors, are allowing *unscrupulous business owners* to rob creditors,' and the article went on to name specific businesses that had allegedly 'stiffed' a bank by twisting the bankruptcy rules. But Your Honor, those statements aren't anywhere close to what we've got here—"

"And what do we have here?" the judge asked, interrupting.

"We've got one of the finest lawyers in this city, one of the most accomplished real-estate attorneys in this state, viciously maligned by Mr. Hastings in a large Chicago newspaper. His professional reputation decimated—"

"How specifically?" the judge asked.

"Well," Hammerset chuckled. "Where do I start? Hastings called Mr. Gentry 'incompetent.' Alleging professional incompetence is defamatory per se. Hastings called Mr. Gentry 'selfish' and said 'his favorite color is green'; that he conducts himself 'not caring whether he is crushing the little guy or not,' implying he is unethical as well. These are incendiary statements Mr. Hastings made against my client. Certainly sufficient to overcome dismissal at this early stage—on a motion to dismiss."

"Surely you are not suggesting," the judge asked "that after further discovery this court might end up agreeing with attorney Petranelli, are you?"

"Of course not," Hammerset said with a broad smile. "In fact, we have had some discovery already. We took Kevin Hastings' deposition. And if you will permit me, Your Honor, I must say that in all my experience as a trial lawyer, I have never seen such an *outrageous* display by opposing counsel. Mr. Hastings was represented by attorney Horace Fin at that deposition," he noted, "and Mr. Fin, in my opinion, conducted himself in a conniving, irascible, and generally obstreperous fashion.

"But that should not have been surprising," Hammerset argued in closing, "given their failure to have mounted a meritorious defense to this lawsuit; and given the failure of their new lawyer, Mr. Petranelli, to have made any kind of convincing argument in support of their motion to dismiss this morning."

Hammerset then thanked the judge and sauntered back to the crowded plaintiff's table and the smiling faces of the lawyers seated there.

My lawyer asked for a chance for rebuttal. Judge Morley nodded with an indifferent expression.

As Daniel walked up to the podium, I tried to summon some measure of optimism. I had somehow believed Daniel Petranelli might be able to pull this off. That each of the chess pieces could be played perfectly. That every single domino that had to cascade into the neighboring one with geometric precision would, in fact, do so.

But after hearing Hammerset's argument—and sitting in that courtroom, that place of judgment—I was beginning to doubt all of it. I wondered whether I'd been foolish to have placed faith in anything.

It now appeared to me to be very much a game. Cruel, expensive, and emotionally taxing—but a game nevertheless. With rules that were obscure and labyrinth-like. Where "champions" of justice were just people in expensive suits who made clever arguments, and the more clever argument would win. This game was controlling the outcome of my life and, as Petranelli glanced down at his notes and prepared to speak, I felt it was one we were now losing.

FIFTY-EIGHT

~

BEFORE PETRANELLI GOT A SINGLE WORD OUT, Judge Morley was firing questions at him.

"The plaintiff's counsel mentions Lloyd Gentry's stellar legal and professional reputation. Do you dispute that?"

"No, Your Honor, I don't," Daniel replied. "But even excellent attorneys like Mr. Gentry can occasionally make mistakes. And when their mistakes seriously injure the economic interests of their clients—as happened when Mr. Gentry handled Kevin Hastings' real-estate closing—they must then be responsible for that harm."

"Wait a minute—wait just a minute," Judge Morley bounced back. "Aren't you trying to switch gears on me again? Now you're talking about your client's underlying malpractice claim against Mr. Gentry. While that file is also assigned to this court, we're not here on that case. We're here on attorney Gentry's defamation suit. Will you agree with me on that?"

"Of course," Petranelli replied. "But frankly, I am convinced that Mr. Gentry's defamation suit is nothing but a knee-jerk reaction to my client's malpractice claim. And further, Mr. Gentry's reputation as an attorney is a smokescreen here—"

"A smokescreen?" the judge demanded with some degree of incredulity. "Reputation is irrelevant in a defamation case? You really believe that?"

"Absolutely, at least on a motion to dismiss like ours, Your Honor. The pedigree of Mr. Gentry's reputation only goes to the issue of damages. That's not what we are arguing today. Whether

291

he is a blue-blood aristocrat or a homeless person living on the street—either way—the issue of reputation doesn't have a bearing *if the allegedly defamatory statement isn't really defamation under the law in the first place.*"

"Then what is the crux here?" Judge Morley's eyes were fixed on Petranelli with a kind of high-beam penetration.

"Here it is—and I quote, selectively, from the *Wilkow v. Forbes, Inc.,* case":

> This article is not defamatory under Illinois law...If it is plain that the speaker is expressing a subjective view, an interpretation, a theory, conjecture, or surmise, rather than claiming to be in possession of objectively verifiable facts, the statement is not actionable.

"There it is," Daniel concluded. "The quotes in the *Sun-Times* article about Mr. Gentry, attributed to Kevin Hastings, are nothing but a 'subjective view' of Lloyd Gentry as a human being—not as an attorney. The quote said that Mr. Gentry was considered to be a 'selfish, incompetent *human being*,' not an incompetent attorney. Besides, just because Mr. Gentry was negligent regarding one specific real-estate closing doesn't mean he is generally incompetent. And Mr. Hastings' statement clearly was not intended to convey that. It was an expression of someone's subjective feelings about Lloyd Gentry. That's not defamation."

"What about the other part?" the judge asked.

"Oh, you mean," Petranelli said, "about 'his favorite color is green'...and how he behaves, 'not caring whether he is crushing the little guy or not'? That part?"

She nodded. My lawyer stepped back from the podium and gave a casual scratch to the back of his head.

"Yes. Well, I looked at that, Your Honor, and I have to say I thought it sounded to me more like a reference to the Jolly Green Giant in a bad mood than a factual statement about Mr. Gentry's lack of professionalism."

Someone in the audience laughed out loud. Judge Morley folded her hands over her mouth.

"The fact is," Petranelli noted, "that nothing in the quoted statement really conveys any *false facts* about Mr. Gentry. At worst, it might imply that he is greedy. But, to quote *Wilkow* again, 'an allegation of greed is not defamatory.' Or it might imply that Mr. Gentry is uncaring, or lacks moral principles in the way he conducts himself. But again, as the court in *Wilkow* states: 'an author's opinion about business ethics isn't defamatory...neither is an allegation of sharp dealing anything more than an uncharitable opinion. *Illinois does not attach damages to name-calling.*'" And with that Petranelli slowly gestured toward Roger Hammerset.

"Which is a good thing for opposing counsel," Daniel said with a smile, "considering the names he called my unfortunate co-counsel Horace Fin today."

Now several people in the back of the courtroom were laughing.

"I jotted those names down." Petranelli pointed to his notepad. "Names like...'conniving, irascible, obstreperous'...I commend Mr. Hammerset on his vocabulary, though. Personally, I try to avoid using those kinds of words—I'm afraid I might hurt myself..."

Now the courtroom and Judge Morley were all laughing.

"Now I know this is a serious case," Petranelli went on. "And I do not intend to make light of its legal import. But I make this point for a reason—Mr. Hammerset, if he goes out on the sidewalk after court today, calls a press conference, and repeats what he called poor Mr. Fin—well, that's his prerogative. *Illinois does not attach damages to name-calling.* Which simply means, Your Honor, that the legal system is not going to punish that kind of language. Nor the language attributed to my client in the *Sun-Times*. But that doesn't mean we are prevented from turning to other, *nonlegal* restraints against uncivil discourse. What it means, Judge, is that restraints like standards of decency and respect will have to be relied upon—rather than courts and judges and laws."

Judge Morley stared at Petranelli for a moment, then she glanced down at her notes.

"This business where you keep referring to Mr. Gentry's lawsuit as being nothing but retaliation against your client for having filed the malpractice claim..."

"Yes, Your Honor?"

"I hope for your sake that is not just loose hyperbole on your part."

"It isn't. We have evidence of a pattern."

"You do?"

"We do."

At the plaintiff's table, Hammerset sat straight up in his chair. Like a horse at the starting gate he was ready to spring forward. To lodge an explosive objection. But his eyes were fixed on some uncertain point. He was considering, perhaps, some facts of which he had knowledge—and which he knew would bring in an unreasonable risk if he proceeded.

So he relaxed and sat back.

Lloyd Gentry was staring at the judge, unthinkingly drumming his fingers on the counsel table.

"Thank you, Counsel," Judge Morley announced. "I'll need ten minutes." She rose and quickly disappeared into her chambers. There was some murmuring conversation in the courtroom. But no one at the plaintiff's table was talking.

I was too nervous to ask Petranelli anything. He was calmly packing his notebook back into his briefcase. But he kept his notepad out, flipped to a clean sheet, laid his pen down on it, and folded his hands.

In exactly ten minutes, the judge returned. There was only a momentary pause, like an opera singer taking a quick breath, before she delivered her decision.

"In the case of *Gentry vs. Hastings*, the court has considered the context of this motion, in that the case is still at the pleading stage. Which means that this court can dismiss the lawsuit of Mr. Gentry only if I am convinced there is simply *no possible way* in which the words uttered by Mr. Hastings, as reported in the *Sun-Times*, can be interpreted as constituting defamation."

She paused, then continued.

"If I accept the logic of the *Wilkow* decision," she said—and then added, "which I do—I therefore must find that the statements at issue are, in the words of that court, mere 'uncharitable opinion,' only 'name-calling'…but definitely *not* defamation. The motion of defense counsel for Kevin Hastings to dismiss the lawsuit of Lloyd Gentry is hereby granted. That case is dismissed."

Then she turned to my lawyer.

"Which brings us to your next motion—whether I should sanction Lloyd Gentry for having brought his defamation suit in the first place, by having him pay your attorney's fees. Counsel?"

Petranelli strode quickly to the podium.

"Your Honor, I am prepared to argue that motion. However, I believe it may be appropriate to move that matter to the foot of the docket for the day—to give counsel from both sides time to discuss possible settlement. If we are unsuccessful in our negotiations, then we can have our case recalled in an hour or so—"

To the amazement of his attorneys, Lloyd Gentry jumped up and addressed the judge.

"Your Honor, I have no intention of discussing settlement—"

But Roger Hammerset was up on his feet too. I could see him squeezing Gentry's arm from behind.

"Your Honor," Hammerset said with a submissive smile, "perhaps Mr. Petranelli's suggestion warrants some consideration. I'm not sure it will be fruitful—but on the other hand, I've never known a case where there shouldn't be at least an attempt to settle…"

"Idea worth pursuing," the judge noted. "We'll recall the case later today. Good luck, gentlemen."

Daniel and I rose and quickly headed toward the back. As I exited the courtroom, for the first time I realized Horace Fin had been there, sitting toward the rear of the audience section. He grabbed his briefcase and pushed past people on the benches to get over to me. He had a look of glee on his face as he joined us. In the hallway he struck up a little ditty.

> The law is the embodiment
> Of everything that's excellent.
> It has no kind of fault or flaw.
> And I, my Lords, embody the law.

Horace Fin then pulled me over and whispered in my ear.

"Gilbert and Sullivan, my boy."

FIFTY-NINE

The small conference room down the hallway from Judge Morley's courtroom was crammed.

I was there with Daniel Petranelli. So was Horace Fin, clutching a manila envelope in his hand.

Seated across the table from Petranelli were attorney Hammerset and his young associate. Standing off in the corner was Lloyd Gentry. In another corner was Bob Bagley, Gentry's defense counsel. Standing in the middle between the two, with his arms crossed, was the claims manager for Gentry's insurance company.

With hope suddenly revived, I was now looking into the somber faces of the men who were about to determine my fate. Petranelli had brought us all the way to the twenty-yard line. But the two-minute warning had just gone off. And we were two touchdowns behind. We had to score against Gentry and his insurance company in this meeting—somehow convince them to pay my claim against Gentry with a fairly big settlement. Petranelli and I had gone over the figures, down to the penny. I knew what he was going to ask. I just didn't know how he was going to ask it.

And then we still had one more touchdown to go—we had to persuade Mangiorno to go along with our plan with him. But I didn't even want to think about that one yet.

Petranelli started off. The tension in the tiny room was palpable. He explained we would be willing to withdraw our request for an attorney's fee sanction against Gentry personally if we could settle the malpractice case against him.

"Absolutely not!" Gentry exclaimed.

"Well, you're entitled to your position, Lloyd," my lawyer said. "But your defense doesn't just belong to you. It belongs to your insurance company. They are the ones who stand to pay out huge amounts of damages at trial in our malpractice case."

"If you win," Bob Bagley boomed.

"Of course," Petranelli replied. "So let's cut to the chase."

He pulled out copies of a letter and passed them out to everyone in the room.

"This is a report from our expert witness," he said. "Most of you may recognize the name. He's the former chair of the real-estate-law section of the American Bar Association. He's also a certified real-estate appraiser. We've retained him to evaluate this case. As you will read, he has concluded that Lloyd Gentry and his law firm were negligent in multiple respects in the handling of Mr. Hastings' real-estate matter."

The room was silent as Gentry and his team scanned the two-page document.

"Further," Petranelli noted, "he has evaluated the damages to Mr. Hastings as approximately $500,000—or half the current fair market value of the property—as a result of his not being advised that the property might be landmarked. And actually, our expert, as you will note, indicates he is being very conservative in that appraisal. He believes the property was worth more than $1 million, but he is sticking with the lower figure because Mr. Hastings agreed to sell it to a willing and able buyer for that price."

"No big deal," Bagley responded. "We'll get our own expert. He'll say the opposite. So we'll have a battle of the experts. Happens every day. May the best man win."

"Bob, that's okay for you to say," Daniel replied, "but you'll be paid—oh, I don't know—maybe around $100,000 or so to defend this case through a jury trial and an appeal. With maybe another $40,000 in court expenses. And I'm figuring on the low side. Meanwhile, who's paying all of this?"

With that, he looked over at the claims manager from the insurance company, and the two locked eyes.

"You are, sir," Daniel said. "Your company will. And I am confident we are going to win. Which means, in addition to that $140,000 in defense costs, you'll be paying out the $500,000 in damages I think the jury is going to award. Now your company is up to $640,000," he further noted.

"Mr. Petranelli," the claims manager said, finally breaking his silence, "I can add up the numbers. I don't need your help with that."

Gentry smiled.

The claims manager went on. "Like Mr. Bagley, our insurance defense counsel, says—this will be just one more battle of the experts. We might want to chance that. And as far as your motion for attorney's fees goes—"

"Yes, let's talk about that," Petranelli said. "You might be thinking this is just one more pie-in-the-sky notion of an overoptimistic lawyer. Except for this…"

Horace Fin then pulled out several documents and handed them to Daniel.

"Lloyd" —Daniel had an almost regretful tone— "I am sorry. But the truth hurts. Your frivolous defamation suit against Kevin here was not the first time you've tried to intimidate a client who has sued you for malpractice."

"I am not going to stand here and listen to this!" Gentry shouted. He turned to walk out. But Roger Hammerset reached out and restrained him.

"Those are pretty strong accusations," Hammerset said calmly. "Can you back them up?"

"This is a memo," Daniel reported to the alarmed lawyers as he passed out the papers, "that details the name, case number, and particulars of a civil action commenced two years ago by one of Mr. Gentry's former clients, accusing him of malpractice in a real-estate deal gone bad."

"So what?" Bob Bagley bellowed. "People get sued everyday. Including lawyers…people hate lawyers." But he was casting a quick glance over at Lloyd Gentry, evaluating his client's response to the revelation.

"True," my lawyer continued. "But at the bottom of the memo

you will also see the name, case number, and particulars of a second lawsuit—a defamation case brought by Lloyd Gentry against his former client. *Less than two weeks* after being sued."

Gentry now had Bagley and Hammerset huddled in the corner. He was whispering intensely.

When the huddle broke, Bagley asked, "Is this information you list in this memo public record? Is it listed on the public docket of the court?"

"No, it isn't," Daniel replied.

"Why not?" Bagley thought he was now going in for the kill.

"Because, as we learned, Mr. Gentry agreed to dismiss his defamation case in exchange for the former client's dismissing his malpractice case. Even further, Mr. Gentry insisted as part of the deal that the whole matter be kept confidential and that the parties ask the court to seal the record—which the judge apparently did."

Suddenly the opposing legal team was radiant with apparent victory—laughing, shaking their heads, and grinning. Lloyd Gentry led the pack with an attack against Daniel.

"Buddy, you're in big trouble! I'm gonna get you for contempt of court! I'm going after your law license…"

"Mr. Petranelli," Hammerset seconded, smiling and looking in complete control again, "this is a very serious matter. You obviously violated a court order sealing those court files from public view."

But Daniel Petranelli and Horace Fin both looked unperturbed.

After a few seconds of silence, the insurance claims manager asked a simple question.

"Just out of curiosity, how did you get that information?"

"Well, in a way," noted Petranelli, "we got it from Lloyd Gentry."

There was a total absence of sound or movement—as if all the air in the room had been sucked out.

Then Daniel gestured to Horace Fin, who pulled several copies of another document out of his large manila envelope.

"You see," Daniel continued, "Mr. Gentry voluntarily waived any privilege of secrecy he might have otherwise had by revealing the lawsuit to a third party who had nothing to do with those cases."

Every lawyer in the room was focused on Lloyd Gentry…who

was leaning back against the wall, trying to manage a brave smile while preparing for the horrors of the inevitable.

"Horace, why don't you explain?" And of course, Horace Fin was only too happy to give a rapid-fire description of his investigation into Mr. Gentry and his prior lawsuits. And how he'd been able to locate an attractive former model by the name of Candace Stinski who'd enjoyed a romantic relationship with Gentry in an expensive high-rise on Lake Shore Drive.

"But alas, all that came to an end," the older attorney explained with a touch of drama. "And not too pleasantly, I might add. So, Ms. Stinski was only too happy to tell me everything I wanted to know about Lloyd Gentry. Including their pillow talk about Mr. Gentry's retaliatory lawsuit against his former client and the malpractice case that prompted it."

Gentry's face was scarlet, disfigured with silent rage.

"Don't be so surprised," Fin added. "Ms. Stinski was extremely cooperative. Especially when I told her how much I loved her TV work in those Carpet World ads."

"You are subhuman, Fin!" Gentry shouted.

"Ah, the hot, searing pain of the truth," Fin commented with a smile.

"Here are copies of her affidavit," Daniel said, passing them out to the now forlorn group of attorneys.

But Roger Hammerset was still struggling to snatch victory out of the jaws that were closing down on his client.

"One thing you forgot," he said, narrowing his eyes, "the former client of Mr. Gentry still has *his* right of secrecy regarding that settlement and those cases. Therefore his rights were violated by your disclosures today. He never waived his privilege of secrecy—"

"That's where you are wrong," Daniel replied. And with that, Horace Fin pulled the final document out of his big envelope.

"Here are copies of a signed waiver executed by that client. Once he was told that the privilege of secrecy had been breached by Mr. Gentry, he said he would just as soon the whole thing be made public. In retrospect, he said he felt pressured into dismissing his case against Mr. Gentry anyway."

After a few minutes of silence, during which each of the lawyers in Gentry's group were tallying the casualties, the claims manager spoke.

"I assume you have some kind of settlement proposal?"

"I do," Daniel answered. "One-time offer. Has to be accepted this afternoon. If not, it will be irrevocably withdrawn."

"How much?" the insurance manager asked.

"Well, considering the fact that our provable damages could be as high as half-a-million dollars, I think you are getting quite a reasonable deal."

"How much?" the claims man asked again, this time more forcefully.

"Your insurance company, on behalf of Mr. Gentry, pays my client the sum of $125,000. In return, Mr. Hastings dismisses his malpractice suit. And we withdraw our demand for an attorney's-fee sanction against Mr. Gentry. And then we all go home."

Bob Bagley was still bothered by it all.

"Look," he said, turning to the claims manager, "I don't like us getting hustled. I suggest we take some time to talk this over."

"We can't give you that time," Daniel interjected. "I wish we could. But we can't—and for reasons we really cannot go into here."

For a moment, there was a faint look of resolve growing on the insurance manager's face.

That's when Daniel landed the coup de grace.

"Maybe this will hurry it up. We are all out of documents, so you'll have to believe me on this one. But there is a former municipal worker named"—and he turned to Horace Fin.

"Corey Ulstead," the older attorney chimed in.

"Yes," Daniel said with a nod. "Mr. Ulstead was recently released from his position. Apparently some dispute with the municipal workers' union. He was with the water utility. His union is repre-sented by Mr. Gentry's firm. Attorney Fin here has a taped state-ment from Mr. Ulstead, testifying that his foreman was laughing about turning the water off at the apartment of some guy named Kevin Hastings."

Lloyd Gentry had his head cocked to the side and was staring at the wall with a kind of wincing look—as if preparing for a blow to the face.

"And Ulstead swears up and down," Daniel continued, "that the foreman was saying the request to stop the water service had come from the union law firm—the Gentry law office, that is."

All eyes were now on Gentry—all but those of one man. The claims manager was looking at Daniel Petranelli.

"Bob," he said to his insurance defense counsel, "I respect you. You're a great defense advocate. But I'm making the call on this one."

Then he turned to Petranelli.

"When will you need the check?"

"By no later than tomorrow morning."

"Cashier's check okay?"

"That will be fine."

The claims manager excused himself, said his goodbyes and left the room. Gentry, flustered and flushed, was next. Then the rest of the team packed up.

When it was just the three of us in the little conference room, Horace Fin congratulated Daniel, wished me the "best of luck," and then turned to leave. "Just mail me the check for my share of the fees and expenses," he said over his shoulder.

Daniel smiled. At last, I could let out a sigh of relief and flash a grin.

The two of us shook hands as we parted ways in the crowded hallway amid the clients, court bailiffs, and attorneys scurrying past.

"Remember our meeting tomorrow at Tony DeVoe's office. Ten-forty-five."

Then my lawyer added, "And there's one other thing you need to know about."

"What's that?"

"I've demanded that Vito Mangiorno be there."

SIXTY

~

I BOUNCED DOWN THE STEPS of the courthouse building. The wind was at my back. At long last I saw a real possibility that my legal and financial ordeal might be soon ending. Even the meeting with DeVoe and Mangiorno the next day couldn't dampen my mood.

I had to believe Divine Providence had played a role in all of the recent magnificent reversals. I had gained an attorney I could completely trust—he had even managed to rein in Horace Fin and employ him productively. Lloyd Gentry's defamation suit against me was history. My legal claim against him and his insurance company had been settled for an amount which, if Daniel's calculations were correct, would be sufficient to fund the last act in our piece of legal theater.

Sure, the final part of this drama seemed impossible. We would have to convince Vito Mangiorno to abandon his violent bluster. Even harder, we had to persuade him to move to the position where we wanted him, even if it meant a potential loss of the kind of respect built by instilling a sense of raw fear in others. Further, he had to be in such a place that taking mob vengeance on me or those around me would be disastrous for him.

And I had begun to think about my place in the cosmos. Or, more accurately, about God's place. Perhaps, even if pain and chaos can be attributed to pervasive evil, there was a Governing Authority to contend with—One more powerful and yet more pervasive.

Surely He would not have brought me this far just to abandon me. I focused my newfound faith on the task for the next day. I even attempted a silent, clumsy prayer. Something like, *God, help me to get out of all this trouble. I believe in Your Son, Jesus. Amen.*

Daniel Petranelli had told me he still had two things to do that day. First, he needed to stop by the Windy City Mission and talk to Jim Loveland. What about, he didn't say. Then he had one more follow-up with Isaac Williston, his lawyers, and someone from the *Sun-Times.*

When I was in my car, I picked up my phone to call Tess and share with her the good news of the day. But the envelope icon in the corner of the screen indicated my voice mail.

It was a message from Tess. It had come in the morning. I could tell immediately she was agitated. Though her words were ambiguous, the bottom line was clear.

> Hi...um, Kevin. This is Tess. I'm supposed to give you a message. I, uh, was just minding my own business when—

It sounded like she'd been pulled away from the phone. There were voices. Then she came back.

> These...these guys want me to tell you. About the meeting you're supposed to have tomorrow. You have to come ready to sign off on the deed. "You need to play ball," they said, and if you do what you're supposed to, then "everything's good." If you don't, then "everything gets bad."

The message ended.

I immediately dialed her at her office. She hadn't come in all day and hadn't phoned in. They were a little worried.

Her cell phone number went straight to voice mail, and at her home number, I just got her answering machine. So I headed straight over to her apartment, banged on her door, and kept banging. No response.

I ran down to the parking area, and my heart stopped when I

saw her car still in its usual spot—with two flat tires. It was locked. No notes left behind, and no sign of where she might be.

After considerable pleading, I was able to get the manager to open Tess's apartment. Everything seemed to be in order—except that Tess wasn't there.

Driving back to the mission I felt fear taking my breath away, like I was being hit with the freezing February winds blasting off Lake Michigan. I knew something awful had happened.

I called Daniel and told him everything. He said he'd call some people and get back to me.

It was well after eight that night when I finally heard from him. "I talked to the assistant U.S. attorney. I told him exactly what Tess had said. There is no clear evidence of foul play, he said. But they're going to post an APB with the local authorities. If she gets picked up somewhere they'll let me know."

"Is that all?"

"I'm afraid that's all they can do."

I was speechless. Why didn't they understand what it meant when Tess was told that if I didn't "play ball," then "everything gets bad"?

"Look, I have to cancel this meeting tomorrow," I blurted out. "I need to know where Tess is. That she's alright."

"We can't," Daniel responded forcefully. "That meeting has to go ahead. If Mangiorno is somehow involved with Tess's disappearance—"

"Yes?" I said, trying to stay calm.

"Then we need to meet with the devil—and look him in the eye."

SIXTY-ONE

~

W HEN I FINALLY RETURNED to the mission that night, Jim Love-land said he had something to talk over with me. But when he glanced at my expression, he immediately asked what the matter was.

I spilled it all out. My relationship with Tess. My fears for her right now. I gave him a sketch about my snarl with Mangiorno and how I believed he was behind her disappearance. Told him I blamed myself for dragging her into all of this.

He suggested we pray together for Tess's safety. But pastor Jim did all the praying. I was unable to form any words.

I tried to sleep, but around three o'clock I got up and went to the front desk. I told Lou I had to go out. He gave me a concerned look, but nodded and buzzed me through the door.

I drove over to Tess's apartment, half expecting her to be there, with some amusing story about the whole thing. But after knocking on her door with no response, I left. The sinking, desperate feeling I had was sinking even lower.

I was up at six. Couldn't eat. I spent an hour or two in my room trying to pray, but I ended up mostly just staring at my feet. Then I left to fight the traffic on my way to the law office of Tony DeVoe.

In the car I couldn't focus on anything but Tess. I called her office. The receptionist said they hadn't heard from her—I could hear the fear in her voice. Every fifteen minutes or so I would call Tess's cell phone, and each time I would get voice mail. I called her apartment. She never picked up.

Part of me doubted that Mangiorno would show up at the meeting at all. If he had anything to do with Tess's situation, I wondered, would he even come? But I supposed that, as a stone-cold mobster type, he probably would. Just to enhance the appearance of innocence.

I was glad I didn't have a gun. I'd never considered myself the violent type. But if I'd had a handgun, I was convinced I'd put it to Mangiorno's forehead.

When I pulled up in front of DeVoe's office, Petranelli was already standing outside.

"Any word?" he asked quickly.

I just shook my head. I couldn't speak.

"Don't worry. We'll find her. Now let's go inside."

At the front door he looked at me.

"Remember what Jesus said—'In this world you will have trouble. But take heart! I have overcome the world.'"

All I knew was that I was a mere mortal. And I hadn't the faintest idea how I was going to overcome the kind of evil that would be sitting across the table from me.

After we were in the lobby a few minutes, a secretary with a harried and displeased look stepped out to us.

"This way, please," she barked. We followed her through a door to a rather plain conference room, where we were seated.

Ten minutes went by. Daniel glanced at his watch.

Finally DeVoe strode in. He hiked up his pinstripe pants, threw us a nasty look, and slapped a file folder down on the table.

"This shouldn't take too long," he said, sitting down. He pulled a paper out of the file and slid it over the table to Daniel.

"Quit-claim deed," he announced. "I want your client, Mr. Hastings, to sign it. Giving us all the rights and title to the Tornquist property. Oh, and here's our part, just like we promised..."

He pulled out a one-hundred-dollar bill and tossed it over. It fluttered down onto the table.

"Now, start signing."

Petranelli sat still, staring at DeVoe, who was staring back at him. The hundred-dollar-bill sat there along with the deed. But my lawyer didn't make a move. Then he addressed our opponent.

"I said that Vito Mangiorno had to be here. Where is he?"

DeVoe sighed impatiently. He looked past us as he spoke.

"Mr. Mangiorno is a very busy man. So let's get a move on…"

"No Vito Mangiorno, no meeting."

"You're playing games with me? Who do you think you are?"

"The lawyer who is going to walk out of here in about five minutes if your client doesn't show up."

"Hey, get one thing straight," DeVoe exclaimed. "VM Contractors is my client. I never said anything about Vito Mangiorno having anything to do with this piece of property."

"Who's playing games now?" Daniel rejoined.

DeVoe snorted and shook his head.

For several minutes no one spoke. Something occurred to me that I'm sure had occurred to Daniel way before that. The fact was, DeVoe had no guarantee Mangiorno would be showing up. In the final analysis, he existed to do Mangiorno's bidding. Whatever that entailed.

Daniel checked the time again. I did too. One minute left.

After glancing at his watch one more time, he threw me a look and began to stand up.

"Time to leave," he announced.

DeVoe's face was beginning to show some strain.

Outside I heard a car door slam. And then another.

In a moment, it seemed, Vito Mangiorno would be in the conference room, looking me in the eye.

SIXTY-TWO

"OKAY, SO WE'RE ALL HERE. Isn't that nice?" DeVoe proclaimed.

Mangiorno, decked out in a black velour jogging suit, was sitting back with his arms crossed. He had a diamond pinky ring on each little finger. And several more rings with various gems including one with a huge nugget of unshaped gold on top—kind of like a fit of precious-metal frenzy. Behind him was standing a broad-shouldered, tough-looking character I later found out was "Big Tut."

"Sign on the dotted line," DeVoe said, pointing to me and then pointing to the deed.

"Now that all the players are here," Petranelli said. "let's get a few things straight."

"Oh?" DeVoe laughed coarsely. "You're going to tell us—"

"Exactly," Daniel replied, leaning forward. He slid the hundred-dollar bill and the deed toward DeVoe.

"We're not taking your money, and Mr. Hastings is not signing your deed."

DeVoe looked like he'd been choking on a piece of meat and had gotten belted on the back between the shoulder blades.

Before he could respond, Daniel went on.

"We've got a different proposal. One that we are convinced you are going to find—impossible to turn down."

Mangiorno threw an emotionless glance over at his lawyer, who was starting to fidget.

But before Daniel could start in, I decided to jump in.

"This is not going anywhere," I said, looking at Mangiorno, "unless you have Tess Collins brought here—right here, right now."

DeVoe began laughing.

"What a big man you are—"

"I mean it. I'm walking if I don't see her."

"What is this idiot talking about?" Mangiorno said, finally breaking his silence. He looked at me and asked caustically, "Who is this person, some kind of lady friend of yours?"

"You know exactly who she is," I replied.

"Hey, Mr. Professor," Mangiorno said, his voice now rising mockingly, "you got a cell phone? Why don't you try calling her?"

I grabbed the phone out of my pocket and dialed her number. It connected.

"Hello," Tess said. Her voice was thin and strained.

"Tess, where are you?"

"I'm okay."

"Really? Where? Tell me…"

"I can't really. But…I think you need to sign the papers." The phone clicked off.

"Can't even keep track of where your girlfriends are, huh?" Mangiorno said with a laugh, in which DeVoe joined him.

Big Tut leaned down and whispered something in Mangiorno's ear.

"My associate here informs me," Mangiorno said, "that there is a vehicle outside of the office. And it appears there is a young lady in the backseat. Maybe you should check it out."

I jumped up, but Mangiorno's "associate" cut me off and headed out in front of me.

From the picture window of the office I could see a large black SUV with tinted windows parked across the street. Staring, I saw a back-door window begin to lower. Tess's face appeared.

"Tess!" I yelled, starting to move to the office door.

A hand fell on my shoulder. "You better get your business done here first," came the warning.

I turned and strode back to the conference room.

"I want her out of that car!" I shouted.

But inexplicably, Daniel, after glancing at his watch, locked eyes with me and waved me down into my seat. Then, calmly, he started to talk.

"Here is the deal, Mr. Mangiorno. You have a written contract with my client to buy the Tornquist property—"

"Great thinking, genius," DeVoe barked out.

"And my client cannot produce that property to you with a guarantee you can demolish the building on it and build a parking garage, as his contract with you provides. Ordinarily, you could sue him for breach of contract—"

"Enough talking!" DeVoe exclaimed.

But Daniel kept on talking.

"However, Kevin here has some defenses against that. I'm not going to bore you with them all. But one is a fancy Latin term. *Locus poenitentiae.* It means that if a party—like Kevin—discovers a contract is for the purpose of attaining some illegal end, that party can rescind the contract—"

"Hey, hey, hey," DeVoe broke in, "you're talking crazy here."

Mangiorno was laughing, holding his arms up mockingly.

"Illegal," my lawyer continued, "such as a money-laundering operation through an all-cash business—like a parking garage."

DeVoe was now standing up and shouting profanities. But Daniel didn't miss a beat.

"Which I am sure you wanted to keep fairly quiet. But that's going to be very difficult now." He reached inside his briefcase and pulled out the morning's *Sun-Times*, then flipped it open to page three, folded it back, and threw it down on the conference table.

There above the fold was a photo of Isaac Williston under a headline that read, "Commissioner Finds Vito Mangiorno Link To Tornquist Building."

DeVoe snatched it and scanned it quickly. Then, jumping up, he started yelling.

"You're quoted in this article! We're going to sue you until your own mother won't take you in!"

"Sorry, that won't wash," Daniel replied. "Horace Fin signed your agreement promising not to divulge the identity of the contracting party. But I never did. And you forgot to make it binding on any successor attorneys."

"You are making a very bad mistake," Mangiorno sputtered.

Daniel smoothly reached into his briefcase and pulled out two documents.

"Now, here is what we are willing to do. We are willing to settle your potential claim for breach of contract against my client for the sum of $25,000. Here is a check. It's made out to VM Contractors and Tony DeVoe, attorney. And here is a release form that provides that VM Contractors is giving up any and all claim, title, and interest whatsoever in the Tornquist property. Mr. DeVoe, I am willing to bet your client has given you power of attorney to sign documents for him—just to make sure his signature doesn't show up. I will need your signature on this release form. When you do that, our business here will be concluded."

Mangiorno leaped to his feet, pointed his finger at Daniel, and began to scream.

"What right do you have to talk to me like that, you rotten little punk? Why should I take your measly twenty-five grand—"

"Because you're going to need it," Daniel broke in, glancing again at his watch, "when you have to pay Mr. DeVoe here to defend you in the grand-jury—"

"You're smokin' dope!" Mangiorno yelled.

A loud knock on the door interrupted the tirade. The secretary swung it open and, after apologizing, started breathlessly explaining about some government official who wanted to deliver some papers. Behind her stood a man in a white shirt and badge, carrying a sidearm and holding an envelope. He stepped into the room and walked over to Mangiorno.

"Vito Mangiorno, I am a United States Marshal. This is a letter from the United States Attorney's Office."

As the official stepped back, he said to Petranelli, "Our officers will stand by outside until you and your client have cleared the building." Then the marshal left the room.

DeVoe looked over Mangiorno's shoulder as he ripped open the letter. In it, I was sure, the assistant U.S. attorney was affording

Mangiorno official notice that he was a target of a federal grand jury, as Daniel had requested.

Mangiorno stood up, tossed the letter and several profanities at DeVoe, and stormed out of the conference room, still cursing. After his lawyer followed him, we heard the reverberations of an explosive argument from down the hall. After almost half an hour, DeVoe stepped back into the conference room with a look of utter disgust.

"You're going to regret this," he muttered, as he grabbed the check and quickly scratched his signature on the release form. Daniel rose, put the form into his briefcase, and joined me. We walked out into the sunlight together.

Three U.S. marshal's vehicles were parked outside. Standing next to one was Tess Collins. She ran over and wrapped her arms around me.

I just kept saying, "I'm so sorry...I'm so sorry..."

We lingered there for a few minutes. I told her I would take her home, but I had to talk to my lawyer first. I ran over to Daniel's car.

"I am calling the federal prosecutor's office," he said. "I'm going to get a security detail for both of you."

I tried to thank him, but nothing seemed to adequately express what I was feeling.

"Just answer one thing for me," I said, putting a thought together at last. "How did you know your plan would work with these guys?"

"Something my dad used to tell me," he said with a smile. "That cockroaches hate the daylight."

WRAP-UP

SIXTY-THREE

THE VOLCANIC CONFRONTATION with Vito Mangiorno in Tony DeVoe's office would not be my last contact with the ruthless mob boss. I wanted, of course, to push the "delete" button in my memory and erase any recollection of the guy. But it was not to be. The choice to not have anything further to do with him was no longer mine to make.

In fact, I was about to get pulled even further into his world. Go figure. Our continued interaction would be played out in the artificial environment of courtrooms and judges and lawyers, to be sure, but that held no solace for me. I had already sized up most trial lawyers as hungry hyenas stalking the savanna. My experience in the legal system had given me pretty much the same "satisfaction" as someone who's the subject of a prank on a TV reality show. You know, the kind where the unsuspecting victim is given a fake "you're fired" note from the boss.

As the prosecution of Vito Mangiorno commenced and plodded forward, it seemed that by some sinister force he drew me in even deeper. I was subpoenaed to testify in the grand-jury proceedings, which, as I discovered, had to be conducted in relative secret. But I was not the only one to receive a subpoena. Tess got one too.

Your testimony before a grand jury is just in front of the jury panel, with no judge. The accused is not even there. Neither is his lawyer. The prosecutor asks you questions. Then the jury asks you a few questions directly. And that's it.

~

As the grand-jury proceedings dragged on and eventually resulted in Mangiorno's indictment, Tess and I continued to grow closer. We talked more and more about our lives, and we spent a lot of time together.

One day in late February—it was a Saturday, about two weeks after Mangiorno's federal trial had commenced, and I was expecting to be called to testify any time—I even shared with her about my conversion to Christ.

We were strolling in Grant Park at the time, over by the huge fountain. The snow was still everywhere. The bitter wind off the lake was chilling us to the bone as we hunched under our coats. Buckingham Fountain was dead still. Waiting for spring to strike up its waters.

Surprisingly, as I described that night at the rescue mission— with a little reluctance, I have to admit—Tess didn't give me that look. You know, the one where the person is inwardly thinking something like "Which solar system did you say you came from?"

Instead, she began to tell me about her own "spiritual journey" more openly than ever before. After years of wandering in Buddhism, Taoism, and several California-bred variations on mysticism, she confessed she wasn't any more fulfilled than when she'd started. Everything in her life seemed to be leading just to more and more questions.

In her inimitable style, she then looked me in the eye and surprised me with one of them.

"Did you become 'born again,' as you call it, just because you were trying to sort of mentally flee from the bad stuff happening to you? Trying to escape from the reality that the world can be ugly and unfair?"

I didn't know how to respond to her right then. I had to think about it. But eventually I would be able to figure out my answer to her question, though it wouldn't be until later. That having your life revolutionized by Jesus doesn't mean you are taken out of the reality of the bad stuff—taken out of the world. You're still in it. But you're not in it in the same way. Not by a long shot.

And while you're in it, you start finding yourself recognizing true beauty, even if it's in the middle of a lot of meanness and brutality. And hopelessness. Like the way I learned that the folks at the Windy City Mission could look at ruined people, in stained clothing and smelling of urine, and still see the image of God there. Marred by sin—but worthy of redemption.

And the other thing is, you start to detect real truth, although sometimes it's out there talking quietly. And if you're not listening carefully, it can be outshouted by the hucksters, liars, and con men.

But as I said, I didn't say all of that to Tess on that particular day. Nor did I anticipate where our next meeting would be.

~

The first thing Monday morning, way before nine, I received a call from the office of the U.S. attorney. I was about to have my scheduled collision with truth. And justice.

"Ken Jarvins here," the caller began.

"Yes," I replied. "How's the trial going?"

"Good," he bulleted back. Then he added something in a very matter-of-fact way.

"You're testifying tomorrow."

I gulped.

"Oh?"

"Yeah. So you and I will have to meet tonight to go over your testimony one more time. Seven-thirty this evening, in my office. Okay?"

"Sure," I replied.

But after I hung up the phone, the reality hit me.

I had one more eyeball-to-eyeball meeting with a Chicago mob boss. And this time there would be a courtroom full of jurors, lawyers, news reporters, and curious spectators to witness it.

SIXTY-FOUR

~

"MR. HASTINGS? DO YOU REMEMBER THE QUESTION? Or do you need me to repeat it?"

"If you could." I reached over to adjust the witness-stand microphone in front of me. It was attached to one of those metal snake kinds of arms. When I moved it a little, the sound system let out a terrible shriek. A few people in the courtroom groaned.

The judge, a middle-aged jurist with an even-keel approach to the trial of Chicago's most notorious-but-evasive crime boss, leaned over toward me.

"Mr. Hastings," he said quietly. "Let the bailiff do that if it needs adjusting. That's what the United States government is paying him for—among other things."

I nodded and glanced around the room. There were armed bailiffs and security guards in every corner.

There I was, in the dock of the courtroom of the Chicago federal building, seated underneath the massive seal of the United States of America, which took up a large part of the wall behind the judge's bench. And Vito Mangiorno's chief defense lawyer, Robert Kincannon, was concluding his cross-examination of me. Tony Devoe had long since disappeared from representing Mangiorno, and with good reason. He was under indictment himself. Kincannon, his replacement, was one of Chicago's really slick—and highly successful—criminal-defense attorneys.

The government was wrapping up its case. Ken Jarvins had already put on evidence attempting to tie Mangiorno to the killing of the hit man Boris Bittarushka. But what little I knew about the progress of the trial indicated that Kincannon had skillfully distanced his client from the Russian's death. The prosecution had also laboriously detailed the various webs and connections between Mangiorno's VM Contractors and various drug-dealing, gambling, and prostitution rings. A large chart on display, one of Jarvins's exhibits, showed it all. Mangiorno's criminal enterprise was nothing more than a massive, old-fashioned vice operation, updated a little with computer records and a layer of public relations.

The problem was, at the very center of the whole network of crime, Mangiorno had very effectively insulated himself from direct involvement. The prosecution knew that was the difficult part of the case. The defense team knew it too. And they were capitalizing on it.

So my personal meeting with Mangiorno at Tony DeVoe's office had suddenly taken on added significance. The government needed to show that Mangiorno *personally* wanted to buy the Tornquist property and then build a parking garage as a means to launder the profits from all his illegal operations. That would be, I guessed, a kind of "bow" tying all the other elements of the government's case together.

"Let me repeat the question then," Kincannon said smoothly. "You said that, at the beginning of your meeting with Mr. Mangiorno, he made some jokes about your 'lady friend,' I think that's how you put it?"

"Yes," I replied. "Tess Collins. I felt Mangiorno had something to do with Tess's not being accessible. So I demanded that he produce her before I continued with our meeting—"

"Move to strike as nonresponsive," Kincannon snapped out, turning to the judge.

"It goes to explain," Prosecutor Jarvins countered, "why Mr. Hastings wanted to discuss the matter of Tess Collins' disappearance with Mr. Mangiorno in the first place."

"Objection sustained," the judge said impassively. He ordered my reference to believing that "Mangiorno had something to do with Tess's not being accessible" be stricken.

The defense lawyer smiled and continued.

"Now besides that exchange about your girlfriend—according to your own testimony, Mr. Mangiorno made only *three short comments* in your presence during the entire meeting. Right?"

I thought about it for a second. Then I searched my recollection a little longer. Kincannon was getting restless. I finally said I wasn't sure I could agree with that.

"Well, let me refresh your memory." His tone had the tiniest hint of a sneer. "First, when your attorney, Daniel Petranelli, made a comment about Mr. Mangiorno being indicted, my client simply said, 'You're smokin' dope.' Right?"

"Yes."

"*Do* you smoke dope? Take illegal drugs?"

"No. Of course not."

"Then my client was obviously making a joke, correct?"

"I wasn't laughing."

"Regardless, my client's joke was *one* of the comments he made. True?"

"That's correct."

"Let's go to a *second statement* my client made. You testified on direct examination that my client was not happy with the so-called settlement your attorney offered. Is that correct?"

"After he called me a 'rotten little punk'—yes, then he said he didn't know why he should accept my offer of 'twenty-five grand' to release his claim and interest in the Tornquist church property. I think he called it "Your measly twenty-five grand.""

"But my client never mentioned that he wanted to *personally* retain a legal claim to the Tornquist land, isn't that right? No mention by him that he wanted to *personally assert* a claim to that property, correct?"

I paused.

"I guess you're right about that…"

"So, that is the *second* comment he made?"

"Not in that exact order…but yes."

"Okay," Kincannon went on. "Then you mentioned a *third*

statement by Mr. Mangiorno. "Something to the effect that he didn't like a newspaper article that mentioned him…"

"Actually, he said, 'You're making a very bad mistake' to me and my lawyer," I replied. "Because we had talked with the newspapers and publicized the fact that his company was the party negotiating to buy the Tornquist from me. He didn't like that."

"Well, the point is, the comment you just related is the *third and last thing* Mr. Mangiorno ever communicated, in any manner whatsoever, about any of the issues relating to the Tornquist property issue—or anything else for that matter. Isn't that right?"

"That was the third thing he said—correct."

"So—those three things—they were the *only* things having anything to do with the Tornquist property you ever heard my client communicate in any way?"

I looked at the defense lawyer. I glanced over at the jury. They were all staring directly at me. I knew the importance of the moment.

Kincannon's argument would be that nowhere in those three comments was there any indication by Mangiorno that he had *personally* wanted to buy the property. During the trial, Kincannon had artfully painted the picture of Tony DeVoe's having abused his power of attorney on behalf of Mangiorno; that his client did not agree to, much less even know about, his various negotiations regarding the purchase of the church; and that at our final meeting, Mangiorno was complaining to DeVoe behind the scenes that he had not known anything about the property deal his attorney had roped him into.

At least, that was their defense.

But I knew something else.

"Mr. Hastings," Kincannon repeated. "No other communications by my client on that subject, right?"

"No—not right."

"Oh?" The attorney's face showed mock incredulity. "Didn't we count those statements down—*one, two, three?*"

"Yes, we did."

"You have a PhD in history?"

"Yes."

"You can count?"

I smiled.

"Yes. But there was a fourth thing…"

Kincannon paused. He eyed me closely.

"No further questions," he barked.

"Let the witness respond," Ken Jarvins said, leaping to his feet. "The witness has not completed his response."

"Are you finished?" the judge asked.

"No."

"Then proceed," he ordered.

"There was a fourth thing. Not a statement—not exactly. But it's a matter of something Mr. Mangiorno did *not* say—"

"Objection!" Kincannon broke in.

"Overruled," the judge replied calmly, not waiting for any argument from the prosecution. So I kept on talking.

"When DeVoe, Mangiorno's lawyer, was arguing with Mr. Petranelli, my lawyer, and Petranelli said, 'Mr. Mangiorno—you have a written contract with my client to buy the Tornquist property,' well, attorney DeVoe actually agreed with that—and Mangiorno, who was sitting right there, never opened his mouth to dispute that fact. *Never.*"

Kincannon smiled tolerantly. "Mr. Hastings, you've been embroiled in a lot of lawsuits recently, haven't you?"

"Yes. Unfortunately."

"And you know that a client hires a lawyer, among other reasons, to do the talking for him. Right?"

"Generally speaking. But with Mangiorno, I think it was different, perhaps."

"You had never met him before that day—you knew nothing about him. Isn't that correct?"

"I didn't need to. I saw him in action. Now if you are trying to suggest he had to let Tony DeVoe do the talking for him—well, then maybe he's a wimp. Afraid to say what's on his mind. Afraid to contradict his own lawyer, even when his lawyer was saying something that wasn't true…"

I was staring right at Mangiorno. Remembering how he had

treated Tess—how he had terrified her and made her think she was going to be killed. As the mob boss stared back at me, he had fire in his eyes.

"So that would make Vito Mangiorno a kind of coward, I guess," I continued. "Or at least an overcautious, gutless weakling…"

Mangiorno's face was now quivering with rage.

"Afraid to speak up even to his own lawyer."

Kincannon was barking out objections by then. But as I kept my gaze fixed on Mangiorno, he was mouthing the words, *You punk…you're finished…finished…*

One of the other defense attorneys, who was sitting next to Mangiorno, reached over, grabbed his arm, and whispered intensely to him. Apparently it was some kind of rebuke. That was when the trigger finally got pulled.

The mob boss shoved his chair back, nearly knocking the lawyer, who was already off balance, off his seat. "Shut up," he barked. "Don't talk to me."

The judge said curtly, "Mr. Mangiorno, please—"

Mangiorno stood up, flailing his arms. "I want this guy out of this courtroom, Your Honor. Then he shouted at the wide-eyed lawyer next to him, "You! Get out of my sight!"

When the courtroom had finally quieted down and the associate defense lawyer had skulked out, Kincannon wrapped up his question, trying to put a good face on everything.

But I knew something. The jury had seen it all.

"On the other hand," I added a final comment with a smile, "maybe you're right, Mr. Kincannon. And maybe I'm wrong. Maybe your client really *isn't* afraid to speak up to his lawyers."

I think, as I stepped down from the witness box, that the smiles among the twelve jurors were close to unanimous.

SIXTY-FIVE

~

IT WOULD BE NICE IF I COULD take the credit for what ultimately happened. But truthfully, I really can't. The day after I testified, Ken Jarvins called his next witness. They practically had to sedate Mangiorno when he saw that witness stride into the courtroom, he was so upset. The whole place went crazy, in fact.

The man stepped up to the witness booth, raised his hand, swore to tell the truth, and then sat down.

Jarvins asked him his full name—the name on his birth certificate and baptismal certificate. Then the prosecutor asked, "Do you go by any nickname?"

"Yeah," the witness answered.

"What is that nickname?"

"Big Tut."

The government had approached Mangiorno's lieutenant and tried to get him to cooperate with the grand jury, but Big Tut had stuck to the usual "code of silence." Until they found and shared some additional information. The federal agents and prosecutors told him everything they had dug up about the untimely death of his younger brother, "Little Tut." It wasn't enough to indict Mangiorno for murdering Big Tut's little brother, they explained, but the evidence still cast some real suspicion on the mob boss. And when Big Tut put the evidence together with what he knew about his brother's death, it sure seemed the government's facts squared with that—and the story Mangiorno had told his lieutenant didn't.

So that was enough for him to break his silence. Big Tut cut a deal, including receiving the benefits of the witness-protection program. In return, he agreed to testify for the United States attorney's office. His testimony sewed up the case. He was able to put Mangiorno right in the middle of everything: the hiring of Boris Bittarushka to knock me off and then the ordering of Bittarushka's murder; all of the criminal enterprises; and specifically, the purchase of the Tornquist property for eventual use in a money-laundering scheme.

But I do think my final exchange with Mangiorno in court—and the mob boss's uncontrolled response—added some credibility to what Big Tut said the following day from the witness stand. And for that, I am grateful.

By the time Tess was called to testify, it was all over but the shouting. My lawyer, Daniel Petranelli, was never even called to the stand. When the jury finally returned their verdict, Vito Mangiorno had been convicted of so many federal crimes that I couldn't even keep track of them.

~

True to his promise, Daniel Petranelli had demanded and received long-term federal protection for both Tess and me. For my part, I promised Tess that, for as long as I knew her, I would pledge myself to the effort of returning her life to circumstances that were as normal as possible—that is, if you can call leading architectural protests and chaining yourself to sculptures "normal."

Though, to give the full picture, Tess has done some changing too. She finally decided to see a counselor about some of the bad stuff in her past. And it seems my new path with Christ has intersected with those deep questions she had been wrestling with also. So I finally did get to share my answer to the question she had posed to me on that wintry Saturday in Grant Park, and it was an answer she has come to accept.

For some time now we've been going to church together. On Wednesday nights she goes to a Bible study with other career-oriented women. Her newfound faith is like so much of my own personal ordeal—a journey that started from hard, mystifying experiences but that has ultimately led to a real sense of inner certainty.

~

While Daniel Petranelli had certainly performed superbly in extricating me from my legal difficulties, there was still one problem. What was I going to do with the Tornquist church property?

Like everything else, though, he had a good suggestion for that too. You remember how my whole ordeal began when Jim Loveland couldn't arrange financing to buy the church, and I ended up next in line? Well, the Windy City Mission offered to buy the property again—from me. Jim Loveland would finally realize his dream of expanding. The Tornquist would serve as a large chapel for weekly services open to the public—and a facility for displaced, homeless, and abused women and their children.

The mission had no cash to buy it outright, so they offered to take it on a several-year land contract. They would make the mortgage payments to the bank and pay the real-estate taxes. At the end they'd make a balloon payment to me and officially get the title.

I already knew what I wanted to do with that final payment. I wanted to buy a house.

The rest of my financial woes were pretty well taken care of with the settlements Daniel won for me. Out of the $125,000 from Gentry's insurance company plus the $7500 from the art foundation and the real-estate agent, I was able to pay off Horace Fin's legal fees and expenses, Daniel's much lower fees, and the two months' back payments to the bank that held the mortgage on the church, not to mention the short-term loan Fin had obtained for me.

After all of that—and the $25,000 we paid to settle the claim with DeVoe and Mangiorno—I was left with about $35,000. Not a fortune by any means, but enough for a new start.

Having been out of teaching for several months, I had the chance to reconsider what I was going to do with my life.

Now, after all I've been through, you may wonder if I've given up on the legal system.

That's an interesting question. Admittedly, there are the Lloyd Gentrys out there, highly skilled but fatally uncaring and indifferent. Even worse, the Tony DeVoes. But not many of them, at least.

And then there is Horace Fin. A few weeks after the settlement checks were all distributed I received a letter from him.

> Kevin:
>
> I received my check from Petranelli. Thanks. I'm all paid up. I hope there are no hard feelings. I do think I ended up earning every penny of it.
>
> By the way, if you ever think I was overpaid, just consider this: In representing the State of Massachusetts in the big tobacco litigation, the plaintiffs' attorneys got a whopping $775 million!
>
> Don't give up on the law. Perfect justice is left to the poets. The Bard himself described it in *King Lear:*
>
> > *When every case in law is right;*
> > *No squire in debt, nor no poor knight;*
> > *When slanders do not live in tongues;*
> > *Nor cutpurses come not to throngs.*
>
> So long. Adios. Good Luck.
>
> > Yours very truly,
> > Horace Fin, Esq.
>
> P.S.: I'm no longer practicing law. I'm now making my millions promoting my new portable document-shredding machine.

Now that Horace Fin is no longer stalking the courtrooms and deposition venues of Chicago, I must say it will be a far less interesting place—though the legal system is probably much safer for it.

~

Horace Fin was right about one thing.
Should I give up on the law?
Not on your life.

Looking back, I realize that Daniel Petranelli, by any definition under the ancient art of trial by ordeal, was proven to be my true "champion."

As for me, I'm just finishing up my first year at the University of Chicago School of Law. Daniel says he has a place in his firm when I graduate.

Now, one last point to add a little "updated personal interest" to my story.

Yesterday was May 1. I told Tess to meet me in Grant Park at exactly 9:55 AM in front of the huge Buckingham Fountain. Amazingly, for all the years she had lived in Chicago, she'd never seen the first immense burst of the waters for the season leap upward from that magnificent fountain—which is bigger than its inspiration at Versailles.

At exactly 10:00 AM, as the fountain burst into life to welcome the spring and the crowds burst into wild applause, I pulled a velvet-covered box out of my pocket, removed the ring, got down on my knees, and proposed. She said yes!

As we stood there arm in arm, watching the graceful arches of water, the Chicago skyline in the background, a fleeting but chilling thought came to mind. About water—and the cruel "ordeal by cold water" that would sometimes be used in medieval times to test the truthfulness of witnesses' stories or the sincerity of their testimony.

It was on the tip of my tongue—I was going to share it with my new fiancée.

But I didn't.

I didn't want the beginning of our new future to be tainted by the cruelties of the past. I think I had learned their lessons. Instead, I wanted to soak in the blessings that were unfolding around me. All of them. Both the mundane and the transcendent.

So I gazed over at Tess as I held her close—this woman who wore pigtails and loved Vermeer. As we watched the waters of the fountain dance in triumphant, gorgeously geometric streams, I simply murmured a single word to her.

Beautiful.

About the Author

Craig Parshall is a highly successful lawyer from the Washington, DC, area who specializes in cases involving civil liberties and constitutional rights. He is also the frequent spokesman for conservative values in mainstream and Christian media.

Besides *Trial by Ordeal*, he has also authored the popular Chambers of Justice series of legal suspense novels: the powerful *Resurrection File*, the harrowing *Custody of the State*, the gripping *The Accused*, the suspenseful *Missing Witness*, and the cataclysmic *Last Judgment*. With his wife, Janet, he has also authored the historical novel *Crown of Fire*, which takes place in the 1500s against the turbulent backdrop of the Scottish Reformation.

Also by Craig Parshall
THE CHAMBERS OF JUSTICE SERIES

The Resurrection File

When Reverend Angus MacCameron asks attorney Will Chambers to defend him against accusations that could discredit the Gospels, Will's unbelieving heart says "run." But conspiracy and intrigue—and the presence of Mac-Cameron's lovely and successful daughter, Fiona—draw him deep into the case…toward a destination he could never have imagined.

Custody of the State

Attorney Will Chambers reluctantly agrees to defend a young mother from Georgia and her farmer husband, suspected of committing the unthinkable against their own child. Encountering small-town secrets, big-time corruption, and a government system that's destroying the little family, Chambers himself is thrown into the custody of the state.

The Accused

Enjoying a Cancún honeymoon with his wife, Fiona, attorney Will Chambers is ambushed by two unexpected events: a terrorist kidnapping of a U.S. official…and the news that a link has been found to the previously unidentified murderer of Will's first wife. The kidnapping pulls him into the case of Marine colonel Caleb Marlowe. When treachery drags both Will and his client toward vengeance, they must ask—*Is forgiveness real?*

Missing Witness

A relaxing North Carolina vacation for attorney W[ill] Chambers? Not likely. When Will investigates a local inher[it]ance case, the long arm of the law reaches out of the di[s]tant past to cast a shadow over his client's life…and the li[fe] of his own family. As the attorney's legal battle uncove[rs] corruption, piracy, the deadly grip of greed, and th[e] haunting sins of a man's past, the true question must b[e] faced—*Can a person ever really run away from God?*

The Last Judgment

A mysterious religious cult plans to spark an "Arm[a]geddon" in the Middle East. Suddenly, a huge explosi[on] blasts the top of the Jerusalem Temple Mount into rubb[le] with hundreds of Muslim casualties. And attorney W[ill] Chambers' client, Gilead Amahn, a convert to Christiani[ty] from Islam, becomes the prime suspect. In his harrowi[ng] pursuit of the truth, Will must face the greatest threat y[et] to his marriage, his family, and his faith, while cataclysm[ic] events plunge the world closer to the Last Judgment.

Suspense on the Streets
from Harvest House Publishers

Forgiving Solomon Long
Chris Well

Crime boss Frank "Fat Cat" Catalano has dreams of building a legacy in Kansas City—but a coalition of local storeowners and clergy have banded together to try to break his stranglehold.

Detective Tom Griggs is determined to bring Fat Cat down, no matter what the cost. Even if that cost is neglecting—and losing—his own wife.

Hit man Solomon "Solo" Long is a "cleaner" flown in from the coast to make sure the locals get the message from Fat Cat.

It all adds up to a sizzling page-turner that crackles with wit and unexpected heart—and hits you in the gut with a powerful message of forgiveness.

> *"Fast-paced and thought-provoking."*
> SIGMUND BROUWER, bestselling author

Deliver Us from Evelyn
Chris Well

Kansas City, the heart of America—where the heartless Evelyn Blake lords it over the Blake media empire. The inconvenience she suffers when her billionaire husband, Warren, mysteriously disappears is multiplied when nearly everybody starts inquiring, "Where is Blake?"...

Detectives Tom Griggs and Charlie Pasch are feeling the heat from on high to get this thing solved.

Revenge-focused mobster Viktor Zhukov has figured out Blake was tied in with a rival gang's ambush.

Rev. Damascus Rhodes (his current alias) figures a man of the cloth can properly console the grieving Mrs. Blake.

By the end of this high-speed thriller, some characters find unexpected redemption…and more than a few are begging, *Deliver us from Evelyn…*

"Clever, snappy, and streetwise!"
CRESTON MAPES, author of *Dark Star* and *Full Tilt*

Original Sin
Brandt Dodson

What a life!

Colton Parker has just been fired from the FBI. He has a rebellious teenage daughter who blames him for her mother's death. And now he's hung out his shingle as a P.I., hoping to turn his detective skills into a way to support his family.

But his first paying client—Angie Howe—has enough money for only one day's worth of investigating. Wonderful.

Angie looks like she could use a friend, though. With her boyfriend in jail, suspected of murdering his aunt—an esteemed high-school guidance counselor—Angie's hopes depend on Colton unearthing the truth.

The investigator clashes with everyone from street thugs to highly respected public accountants—not to mention his own daughter. And when the case is finally resolved, Colton is resolved to improve his parenting skills. Even though father and daughter still struggle with their bereavement, *hope* finally gets a chance to grow.

To Original Sin, *author* BRANDT DODSON *brings the on-the-street realism of his family's multigeneration experience in law enforcement. A compelling debut in the Colton Parker Mystery series.*